F

"THE REIGNING Q

CE"*

MIND GAME

"Swift-moving and sexually charged . . . electrifying."

—**Publishers Weekly*

"[A] compelling and spectacular series. The amazingly prolific author's ability to create captivating and adrenaline-raising worlds is unsurpassed." —*Romantic Times*

"Explosive . . . An exciting, thrilling read . . . A phenomenal plot. Ms. Feehan has really outdone herself . . . The sexual chemistry is literally a scorcher . . . *Mind Game* is a definite page-turner." —*Fallen Angel Reviews*

WILD RAIN

"Feehan has a knack for bringing vampiric Carpathians to vivid, virile life . . . A romance that feels both destined and believable. Readers whose fantasies center on untamed wilderness and on untamed heroes who are as sensitive as they are strong will be seduced by this erotic adventure."

—*Publishers Weekly*

"Ms. Feehan is unsurpassed in romantic fantasy; her imagination knows no bounds in creating unique and fresh tales that abound in steamy sensuality, fantastical imagery, and lyrical prose." —*Rendezvous*

"A powerful tale that pumps up the adrenaline of the audience any time the lead couple talk or just stare at one another in loving disbelief . . . A fabulous jungle love story."

—*Midwest Book Review*

"A riotous adventure, chock full of beautiful imagery, edge-of-your-seat suspense, and passionate romance . . . The sex is spicy enough to singe your eyebrows."—*Romance Reviews Today*

"[A] terrific new series . . . Fascinating." —*Romantic Times*

continued . . .

SHADOW GAME

"Having fast made a name for herself in the vampire romance realm, Feehan now turns her attention to other supernatural powers in this swift, sensational offering . . . The sultry, spine-tingling kind of read that [Feehan's] fans will adore."

—*Publishers Weekly*

"One of the best current voices in the darker paranormal romance subgenre, Feehan has begun another series that, while lacking the fantasy feel of her Carpathian romances, is equally intense, sensual, and mesmerizing and might appeal especially to fans of futuristic romances. Known for her vampire tales, Feehan is a rising star in paranormal romance."

—*Library Journal*

"An exciting military science fiction romance suspense tale that never slows down until the final confrontation. The storyline is fast-paced and loaded with action."

—*Midwest Book Review*

"Sizzling sex scenes both physical and telepathic pave the road to true love . . . Action, suspense, and smart characters make this erotically charged romance an entertaining read."

—*Booklist*

"A very fast-paced action-packed thriller/love story all wrapped up into one . . . I highly recommend this book and will be adding it to my keeper's shelf." —*EscapeToRomance.com*

"Feehan packs such a punch with this story it will leave one gasping for breath. She conquers yet another genre of romance with ease, proving why she is a master . . . Ms. Feehan wields the suspense blade with ease, keeping readers enthralled and teetering on the edge . . . Guaranteed not to disappoint, and will leave one begging for more. A must-read book, only cementing Ms. Feehan's position as a genre favorite for yet another round." —*The Best Reviews*

...and the novels of Christine Feehan

"Just as I begin to think the romance genre has nowhere else to run, I get to read something that takes another giant leap down a totally unknown road. Romance, suspense and intrigue, and the paranormal . . . combined to make one of the most delicious journeys I have had the pleasure of taking in a long, long time . . . Definitely something for everyone."

—*Romance and Friends*

"Feehan's newest is a skillful blend of supernatural thrills and romance that is sure to entice readers." —*Publishers Weekly*

"If you are looking for something that is fun and different, pick up a copy of this book." —*All About Romance*

"This one is a keeper . . . I had a hard time putting [it] down . . . Don't miss this book!" —*New-Age Bookshelf*

"The characters and twists in this book held me on the edge of my seat the whole time I read it. If you've enjoyed Ms. Feehan's previous novels, you will surely be captivated by this step into the world of Gothic romance . . . Once again, Ms. Feehan does not disappoint." —*Under the Covers Book Reviews*

Titles by Christine Feehan

DANGEROUS TIDES
OCEANS OF FIRE
NIGHT GAME
MIND GAME
SHADOW GAME
WILD RAIN
DARK SECRET
DARK DESTINY
DARK MELODY
DARK SYMPHONY
DARK GUARDIAN
DARK LEGEND
DARK FIRE
DARK CHALLENGE
DARK MAGIC
DARK GOLD
DARK DESIRE
DARK PRINCE

Dangerous Tides

CHRISTINE FEEHAN

THE BERKLEY PUBLISHING GROUP
Published by the Penguin Group
Penguin Group (USA) Inc.
375 Hudson Street, New York, New York 10014, USA
Penguin Group (Canada), 90 Eglinton Avenue East, Suite 700, Toronto, Ontario M4P 2Y3, Canada (a division of Pearson Penguin Canada Inc.)
Penguin Books Ltd., 80 Strand, London WC2R 0RL, England
Penguin Group Ireland, 25 St. Stephen's Green, Dublin 2, Ireland (a division of Penguin Books Ltd.)
Penguin Group (Australia), 250 Camberwell Road, Camberwell, Victoria 3124, Australia (a division of Pearson Australia Group Pty. Ltd.)
Penguin Books India Pvt. Ltd., 11 Community Centre, Panchsheel Park, New Delhi—110 017, India
Penguin Group (NZ), Cnr. Airborne and Rosedale Roads, Albany, Auckland 1310, New Zealand (a division of Pearson New Zealand Ltd.)
Penguin Books (South Africa) (Pty.) Ltd., 24 Sturdee Avenue, Rosebank, Johannesburg 2196, South Africa

Penguin Books Ltd., Registered Offices: 80 Strand, London WC2R 0RL, England

DANGEROUS TIDES

A Jove Book / published by arrangement with the author

PRINTING HISTORY
Jove mass-market edition / July 2006

Cover design by George Long.
Cover illustration by Dan O'Leary.
Text design by Kristin del Rosario.

For information, address: The Berkley Publishing Group,
a division of Penguin Group (USA) Inc.,
375 Hudson Street, New York, New York 10014.

ISBN: 0-515-14154-2

JOVE®
Jove Books are published by The Berkley Publishing Group,
a division of Penguin Group (USA) Inc.,
375 Hudson Street, New York, New York 10014.
JOVE is a registered trademark of Penguin Group (USA) Inc.
The "J" design is a trademark belonging to Penguin Group (USA) Inc.

PRINTED IN THE UNITED STATES OF AMERICA

10 9 8 7 6 5 4 3 2 1

This book is special to me because it was written for my baby sister, Nanci Goodacre. At a time in my life when few people believed I could ever publish a book, not only did she give me encouragement, but she also gave me help, typing up my handwritten stories on an old word processor until all hours of the night. She's a wonderful mother, an excellent nurse, but most of all, she's what these books are really about—love of family, strength, the magic of sisters and absolute support when you need it the most!

FOR CHRISTINE'S READERS

Be sure to go to http://www.christinefeehan.com/members/ to sign up for her PRIVATE book announcement list and get a FREE EXCLUSIVE Christine Feehan animated screensaver. Please feel free to e-mail her at Christine@christinefeehan.com. She would love to hear from you.

ACKNOWLEDGMENTS

I was lucky enough to find Will Prater, the pilot of the Huey helicopter often used for over-water, short-haul rescue on the Northern California coast in thc very area where my mythical town of Sea Haven is located. He spent hours with me, showing me rescue equipment, videos of actual rescues and the helicopter itself. He patiently explained every phase of the rescue and answered so many questions. He and the men of the California Department of Forestry, especially those manning the Howard Forest Station, are extraordinary men performing a heroic service.

1

THE wind moaned, a soft pitch that rose slowly into an eerie wailing cry, almost as if a voice summoned him. Waves crashed on the jagged rocks, foamed white and sent spray high into the air. The sound was deafening, big thunderous booms echoing along the cliffs. Heavy rain had left the cliffs unstable, but Drew Madison ignored the warning signs and climbed over the fence to slip and slide his way through the soft, crumbling dirt close to the edge.

The water churned and boiled, a dark beckoning brew far below the jutting cliffs. The sight was mesmerizing. As hard as he tried, he could not pull his fascinated gaze away or stop listening to the voices murmuring in the thunder—calling—calling. He wiped his hand over his face to clear his head. His skin was wet, but he wasn't certain if it was the drizzling rain or his own tears. The waves boomed again, this time the sound hollow to his ears, a lost soul as haunted as he was. A summons.

He forced his hands over his ears to drown out the mournful howl, but the wind struck at him, demanding attention, insistent that he listen. He stumbled back, shaking his head, slipped, teetering for just a moment. *Let go. Let go.* The voices in the wind urged him. Freedom was a step or two away.

"No!" He shook his head and felt behind him for the security of the fence. His fingers gripped the wood so tight his knuckles turned white. He stared down at his hands, forcing his gaze from the roiling water below. He had to tell someone, make them understand what was going on. But who was there to tell? They'd lock him up if he told them the tides were dangerous. Something lived there, and it was hungry.

HANNAH Drake stood on the captain's walk facing the sea. The wind beat at her with unusual fury, sending her long hair whipping across her face. Waves pounded relentlessly, and somewhere in the distance she thought she heard a cry of alarm. Hannah stepped closer to the protective railing and turned in the direction she thought the elusive sound had come from. Three times now she'd felt uneasy—and three times she'd failed to find the source.

She glanced at her home. Her sisters waited for her, their warmth and happiness filling up the cold emptiness, but she couldn't go to them yet. She had to make one more try. She threw her head back and stared up at the sky. Clouds partially obscured the moon, casting dark shadows over the light. Her breath lodged in her throat as she caught sight of the double ring around the moon—dark red to black.

"Hannah!" Libby Drake called. "Come save me. I'm getting picked on!"

Hannah drew her sweater closer around her and hurried back into the safe haven of her home. Trouble was coming very soon, but she didn't know where—or at whom—it would strike. She needed the laughter and camaraderie of her sisters to dispel the fear growing inside of her. Sometimes her gifts were a curse.

Libby slipped her arm around Hannah as they went down the stairs together. "You okay? You're shivering with cold."

"I'm fine. I'm looking forward to our get-together tonight," Hannah replied, hugging Libby close. Just touching Libby could soothe away her fears. She forced a smile as she joined her sisters, throwing herself on the floor in the warm circle. "So tell me why you're all picking on Libby." She glanced one last time toward a window and then turned away. There was nothing she could do, so she turned her attention to her sisters and the enjoyment they always brought her.

"All I said was, I'm tired of being Goody Two-shoes. I'm changing my image completely and becoming a bad girl," Libby announced.

"Libby, you crack me up," Sarah Drake said to her younger sister. "You don't have a mean bone in your body. You couldn't be a bad girl if you tried."

Libby scowled at Sarah and then glared at the circle of faces surrounding her. "I am not the Goody Two-shoes you all think I am."

"Oh, really?" Joley Drake raised an eyebrow from where she was sprawled out on the floor. "Name one person in this world you'd like to see take a flight to Mars. Someone you utterly despise."

Laughter rang through the living room. "No way is that possible." Hannah leaned over to kiss Libby on her temple. "We all adore you, hon, but you really don't have it in you to be a bad girl. Not like me—or Joley." She looked at the youngest sister. "Or Elle."

The laughter increased and Elle shrugged. "It's the red hair. I take no responsibility for my . . . er . . . interesting personality."

"It's way more fun to be bad," Joley said, unrepentant. "No one expects you to do the right thing and you're never really in trouble. Mom and Dad never expected me to be polite and kind when we were growing up. They spent all their time telling me to censor myself." She reached for a cookie and sat up to drink her tea. "I tried to explain I *was* censoring, that five things came into my head and I picked the least offensive, but they still weren't thrilled."

Elle grinned at Joley over her teacup. "They got used to being called into the principal's office at school. I was really glad I came after you. You paved the way for me. I argued with the teachers over everything and the counselor said I had problems with authority figures."

"They could never actually catch me at anything," Hannah said, breathing on her fingernails and polishing them with a satisfied air. "One or two of the teachers suspected I had something to do with frogs pouring out of the desks of girls who weren't very nice to me, but no one could actually prove it."

Libby sighed. "I want to be like that. I detest being the good girl."

"But you are a good girl," Kate pointed out, patting Libby's knee. "You can't help it. Even as a kid you had causes. You couldn't get into trouble because you were too busy saving the world. That's not a bad thing."

"And you don't think mean things, Libby," Abigail added. "It isn't in you."

"You're responsible," Sarah said. "That's a good thing."

Libby, sitting cross-legged on the floor, covered her face with her hands, groaned aloud as she tipped over to land with her head in Hannah's lap. "No. It's so boring. I'm just plain boring. I want to be bad to the bone. Wild. Unpredictable. Anything but good old steady Libby."

"I'll dye your hair for you, Lib," Joley offered. "Hot pink tips and streaks of pink and purple."

Libby peeked out around her fingers. "I cannot possibly have hot pink tips and streaks of pink and purple and be taken seriously when I go to the hospital to work. Can you imagine the reaction of my patients?"

Joley frowned. "That's the point, Lib. You want a reaction. Throw caution and good sense to the wind. Changing your hair color isn't going to make you less of a doctor. You're as respected as any doctor could get."

Libby dropped her hands from her face and reached for an all important cookie. She needed comfort food. "I'm scheduled to go on a run with the Doctors Without Borders. I can't go to Africa with hot pink hair."

"Sure you can. The kids will love it," Joley insisted.

"It's different with you, Joley. You're a musician. People expect you to be wild and crazy. I have to look a certain way."

"Why?" The plate of cookics was empty and Joley waved toward the kitchen. On cue, the plate rose into the air and sailed toward the kitchen where the aroma of freshly baked cookies wafted out into the living room.

"Joley's showing off," Elle said. "It took her forever to learn that."

Joley swatted at Elle with a rolled-up newspaper. "It did not. I could do that before you were born. Get with the program, Hagatha, we're trying to teach Libby how to be a bad girl."

"Talk about Hagatha," Elle defended herself. "I tried to wake you up this morning and you made rude noises and threatened to toss me off the tower into a sea filled with sharks."

Joley poked Libby. "See, hon? That's how to be a bad girl. Did I get up and do the vacuuming like her majesty wanted me to do? No, I slept in and she did it for me."

"As if." Elle snorted. "I didn't do your job. Libby did it so you could catch up on your sleep which you wouldn't need if you weren't up at all hours of the night."

A collective groan went up. "Libby, you didn't." Joley tried to sound disappointed but she only managed to choke on laughter.

Libby ducked her head so that her black hair fell in a cloud around her face and shoulders. "I thought you might need a few extra hours. It wasn't a big deal."

Sarah hugged Libby. "You are incredible and don't even realize it."

"No, I'm not," Libby insisted. "I want to be a Hagatha. I just don't want to color my hair. Sorry, Joley, thanks for trying, but seriously, pink hair isn't for me."

Joley grinned at her. "There you go, trying not to hurt my feelings. We need a school for bad girls. It would be the only time in your life you got less than an A."

Libby lifted her chin and glared at her younger sister. "I could get an A in bad girl class. I *always* get A's."

Joley shrugged. "I tried not to get good grades. Once you start, the mom and pop want it to continue. Then you're stuck."

Hannah nudged Joley with her foot. "Good philosophy. Wish I'd thought of it." She waved her hand toward the kitchen. "And you never stay on task. We might all perish without cookies."

"Did you do the ones with that butter frosting you make, Hannah?" Kate asked. "I love those."

"For you." Hannah smiled at Kate but turned to give Sarah a hard look. "But *not* for you. You sided with Jonas Harrington over the movie the other night. You're in the doghouse so no frosting on your cookies."

"Hannah," Sarah protested. "You can't deprive me for liking a movie you didn't like."

"I'm not depriving you because you liked the movie, you treacherous wench, I'm depriving you because you admitted it in front of the caveman and inflated his ego."

"I'm sure Sarah didn't mean to side with Jonas," Libby said.

Another round of laughter went up. "You're hopeless, Lib," Hannah said. "I'm showing you how to be Hagatha and you just can't grasp the concept."

A gust of wind blew through the house as the living room door opened, admitting a tall man with broad shoulders. Jonas Harrington, the local sheriff, slammed the door behind him and strode in as if he owned the place.

Hannah's gaze jumped to the huge window overlooking the sea, her heart pounding in sudden alarm. The fury of the wind whipped the dark clouds around, but failed to hide the blood-red circle slowly seeping into the blackened ring around the moon. Her hand went to her throat—a purely defensive gesture—as her gaze met her youngest sister's. Elle had the same knowledge of impending danger in her eyes.

"Hannah?" Libby ran her hand down Hannah's arm to comfort her. "Is something wrong?"

To distract her sisters, Hannah gestured toward the sheriff and groaned. "Speak of the devil. I swear, it's like you whisper his name and it conjures him up, just like a demon from hell."

Joley nudged Libby. "See, that's censoring. She was thinking way worse than that, right, Hannah?"

Hannah nodded. "You'd better believe it." She felt the instant shift of power in the room, the subtle flow of her sisters automatically helping her, keeping her from the curse of stammering or worse, having one of her panic attacks simply because someone other than a family member was with them.

"Baby doll," Jonas greeted Hannah, deliberately provoking her with a hated nickname. "It's impossible for you to teach Libby how to be a Hagatha. You were born that way. She, however, is nothing but goodness." He grabbed a handful of cookies as the plate floated by and expertly tossed his jacket on the couch without looking.

"Why don't your obnoxious guard dogs bite him?" Hannah asked Sarah. "The next time either of them wants food I'm going to remind them they failed in their most important job."

Sarah shrugged. "They like Jonas."

"They have good taste," Jonas said, smirking. He sat on the floor, wedging himself between Hannah and Elle. "Move over cupcake." He pushed his leg hard against Hannah's thigh. "I'm joining the family powwow tonight."

Hannah opened her mouth, then closed it abruptly, studying the grim lines etched around Jonas's mouth, noting the smile didn't quite reach his eyes. She knew, as did all her sisters, that when something went terribly wrong at work, Jonas sought the comfort of the people and the one place he called family and home. Hannah waved her hands in a graceful, complicated pattern toward the kitchen and at once the tea kettle whistled.

"Libby wants to be a bad girl," Sarah announced.

Jonas's eyebrow shot up. A slow smile spread across his face. "Libby, hon, there is no way you can be corrupted by the rest of your sisters. You're just too sweet."

Libby glared at him, totally exasperated. "I am not. Come on! You could help out a little, Jonas. I have the ability to be just as wicked as the rest of my family."

"Hear, hear," Elle said. "Well said, sister."

Joley nodded her head in agreement. "Not true, but well said," she agreed.

Hannah lifted her hand palm out and a mug of steaming tea floated out of the kitchen toward the circle of sisters. She caught it carefully, blew on it until the bubbles quieted and handed it to Jonas.

"So why do you want to be a bad girl?" Jonas asked.

"My life is boring. Borrrr-iing," Libby said, drawing the word out. "I want to have fun. I don't want to be the responsible one anymore."

"Then you're dropping your Doctors Without Borders and your Save the Whales and Support Big Cat Rescue causes?" Jonas asked. He snapped his fingers. "And you definitely have to stop recycling and your save the environment thing you do every year."

"Wait," Joley added. "You can throw out the save the rain forest as well. That should give you plenty of time to be a bad girl."

Libby kicked her sister with remarkable gentleness. "You're not being nice and neither is Jonas. You're laughing at me."

"No, I'm not," Joley replied immediately. "I love you just the way you are. You just have to accept that you don't have a mean bone in your body. It's why you can't think of anyone you'd like to put in a rocket and send to Mars."

"Jonas," Hannah said. "Because he's so bossy."

"Hannah," Jonas said simultaneously, "because she craves so much attention she's always showing her bod to every Tom, Dick and Harry who wants to see it."

"I'm a model, you toad," Hannah said. "I don't show off my body, I show off the clothes."

"And brilliantly, too," Kate said, blowing her a kiss. "I'll second Jonas for being mean to Hannah."

"It isn't fair to gang up on me," Jonas protested. "She was mean to me first."

"You said it at the same time," Kate pointed out.

"Only because I knew what she was going to say."

"Jackson Deveau." Elle named a deputy sheriff. "Because he annoys me no end."

"Illya Prakenskii," Joley added a heartbeat behind. "Because he needs to be off planet and he's just plain spooky." She rubbed the palm of her hand as if she had an itch.

"Frank Warner for breaking Inez's heart," Sarah said.

"I can't very well say Sylvia Fredrickson because she's turned over a new leaf," Abigail said, "so I'll just have to say I'm going with Joley on this one."

Everyone looked at Libby. She sighed, feeling the weight of their stares. "Not Jonas. He's bossy but really has our best interests at heart."

Hannah rolled her eyes when Jonas poked her.

"Certainly not Jackson. Honestly, Elle, how can he be annoying? He never talks, poor man. Illya Prakenskii helped us, Joley, and Frank's in jail paying for his crimes. Inez is hurt, yes, but she's a strong woman and understands that people make mistakes."

"So who would you send on a rocket to Mars?" Joley prompted.

"I'm thinking." Libby sipped at her tea, frowning. "There was one nurse who always made fun of me. She said I was flat-chested and not in the least attractive."

Hannah sat up straight. "Who is she? I'll have a thing or two to say to her."

The room thickened with sudden tension. Tea boiled in the cups.

Libby shook her head. "No, poor thing, she had such a horrible life. She has so many problems, it's really no wonder she isn't very nice. I felt sorry for her."

The Drake sisters blew on their tea before exchanging looks, but Libby was frowning in concentration. "I'll think of someone."

"Face it, Lib, you can't think of anyone because you just aren't mean."

Libby ducked her head. "I can think of someone. He went to school with me on and off and was in all the accelerated programs. He even attended Harvard when I did." She looked up at her sisters. "His grades were better than mine."

Jonas grinned at her. "I'll bet that really set your teeth on edge."

"It wasn't just that, Jonas, he doesn't believe in magic. He thinks we lie about our gifts and that my family members are charlatans and con artists. He's very arrogant and opinionated."

"Well, put his name on the rocket to Mars, sister," Elle insisted.

Libby sighed. "It's just that he has an incredible brain. The world really needs him. He won a Nobel Prize in medicine already. He's very gifted. Not that he does it for the right reasons."

"He's a glory hound?" Kate asked.

"No, he could care less about publicity. He's totally a lab rat. All he cares about is the science. Well, science and adrenaline."

"You're talking about Tyson Derrick," Jonas guessed. "He's crazy. When he isn't working in the laboratory, he's working for the forestry. He's a total adrenaline junkie. Skydiving, racing, motorcycles, white-water rafting, whatever is available, he's the man."

"He has no right to risk his genius," Libby said.

"You haven't put him on the rocket," Joley pointed out.

Libby blushed. Color swept up her neck and into her face, turning her skin bright red. Scarlet. Crimson. It was the bane of her existence, that and being flat-chested.

"Uh, oh," Joley said. "I think your Tyson Derrick is a hottie. He is, isn't he, Jonas?"

"How the hell would I know?" Jonas objected. "I don't look at the man unless I'm stopping him for speeding and giving him a ticket."

"He speeds?" Libby asked, fanning herself and trying to be subtle about it.

"On his motorcycle or in his car. The man doesn't know the meaning of the words 'slow down.' "

"He looks good," Sarah admitted, "but he's a pain. Thc man can't do polite conversation. I've seen him get up abruptly in the middle of a double date with his cousin, and just walk out, no explanation at all, leaving Sam sitting there with two very angry women. He just doesn't care."

"If he didn't talk, he'd be hot," Libby admitted. She wasn't admitting anything else. She didn't seem to have a normal sex drive. The only time it kicked in was when Tyson Derrick was around and then her libido was stuck in overdrive. She'd never live that one down. So no way was she putting him on a rocket to Mars, not until she had the chance to sleep with him. And that would never happen because he was an obnoxious jerk who thought too much of himself. She would never *ever* admit to anyone she dreamt of him. It was humiliating to be attracted to a man who treated her so poorly. He was the complete opposite of everything she stood for and valued.

"So what happened tonight, Jonas?" Elle changed the subject abruptly. "You're upset about something."

The smile faded from the sheriff 's face. "You don't want me to talk about work."

"This is the best place for it."

He sighed and took a drink of tea. It always seemed to soothe him, or maybe it was just being around the seven sisters. "We went out on a call this evening. A neighbor said she heard screaming. A forty-year-old man was taking care of his mother, who obviously is ill. He's been collecting her checks as they come in, but he was starving her and he certainly was beating her if she bothered him. He had a complete home theater set up, top of the line, and his mother is in the back room with dirty shirts and no food or water. I wanted to . . ." He broke off, glancing around the room. "I'm sorry. I know you're all able to feel what I'm feeling and I try to keep it under wraps but . . ." He trailed off with a small shrug.

Hannah and Elle both put a hand on his knee. Libby leaned in and did the same. Sarah and Kate touched his shoulders while Abigail and Joley wrapped their fingers around his arm. At once he felt the flood of warmth, of family stealing into him.

"You don't have to do that," he insisted. "I didn't come here to have you expend energy on me. I just needed to be with you. I was hoping your parents and Aunt Carol were back."

"No, they decided to take a few days and tour the wine country. The Napa valley is so beautiful this time of year and they thought they'd take advantage and do a little sight-seeing," Kate explained.

"More likely they needed a break from us," Joley said. "Aunt Carol brought home a couple of magazines, you know the ones with the latest scoop on the wild singer, Joley Drake. I think I'm supposed to be in a rehab this week."

"That was last week," Elle corrected. "This week you were arrested for tearing up a hotel room."

"I did?" Joley looked pleased.

"I want to tear up a hotel room," Libby said. "Well. Maybe not. I don't really want to destroy someone's property."

"Am I still in jail?" Joley asked hopefully.

"No. Your latest lover bailed you out. In case you don't remember him, he's got longer hair than you do, a scruffy beard and he plays for some heavy metal band."

"I haven't actually met him," Joley said, "but we were in the same hotel for about five minutes. He must be quick on action with no foreplay."

"The mags are really after you lately, Joley," Sarah said.

Joley sighed. "I know. Hopefully it will blow over soon."

"I've never understood why you don't sue those writers when they make up so many lies about you, Joley," Jonas said. "It makes me angry."

"In the beginning I was angry and hurt, and worried about my family having to read really ugly lies, or maybe even get interviewed and be asked questions about me, but I've learned to live with it. There are so many crazies out there, Jonas, but I guess you already know that."

"Unfortunately. I talked to Douglas about your security with this last concert," Jonas added. "They let someone rush the stage. I couldn't believe it. If that had been someone out to hurt you, it would have been all over." His voice had gone grim again.

"It was an overzealous fan, Jonas." Joley tried to soothe him. "Security carried him off and I was just fine." It had shaken her, but she wasn't going to admit it to him. Singing in front of thirty thousand people was easy. Dealing with stalkers and crazed fans and the paparazzi could be nerve-wracking.

"Well . . ." Elle hesitated, biting at her lower lip. "There was more in that magazine." She looked at Libby. "Do you remember that incident a couple of months back when you healed that child and the parents told their miraculous story?"

Libby nodded. The magazine had run a full-page picture of her. Fortunately, the article was so theatrical, she was certain most people would dismiss it.

"Another reporter interviewed the parents and did a little digging. He turned up a few other former patients willing to sing your praises. One of them was Irene Madison."

"No way," Sarah said. "Irene would never betray Libby."

"She was very upset the last time we went to see her son, Sarah," Hannah pointed out. "She kept insisting that Libby cure Drew's leukemia. Libby bought him time, but Irene wants a cure."

"The magazine paid her," Elle said.

"How do you know that?" Jonas asked.

Elle simply looked at him.

Jonas put up his hands in surrender. "Sorry I asked."

Libby rubbed her suddenly pounding temples. "I should have known. At work today someone came to see me. He was well-dressed, a suit, definitely from out of town and he wanted to arrange a meeting between me and his boss."

The faint smile was gone from Jonas's face and he shifted closer. "Who was he?"

"That's just it. I don't know, but I recognized the name of his boss. Edward Martinelli. He's a big name in pharmaceuticals, but he has a certain reputation. There are always rumors flying about him and the people who back his company. I told his representative that I was too busy. The man didn't threaten me, but I *felt* threatened. He mentioned my family, specifically Hannah, that she was beautiful and high profile."

"Damn it, Libby, just when were you going to mention this little chat to me?" Jonas snapped. "You should have reported it immediately."

"I reported the incident to the hospital security—and to my sisters," Libby said. "It wasn't like he threatened me—or Hannah. What was I going to say to the police?"

"Not the police, me," Jonas corrected. "You tell me."

"It isn't like this doesn't happen all the time." Libby defended herself. "The gossip rags love to come out with the 'faith healer' and 'miracle worker' articles when they have a slow day." She pushed a hand through the cloud of dark hair falling around her face. "I just hoped it wouldn't happen again for a long while."

"Martinelli has ties to a crime family out of Chicago. He's been in San Francisco with his company for a few years and has been supposedly squeaky clean, but his family's been under investigation numerous times."

"Maybe he really is legit," Libby said. "If no one's been able to find anything on him, maybe he's just a businessman with unfortunate family ties. We all have skeletons in the closet."

"Then why would he send someone to threaten Hannah if you don't cooperate with him?"

"He didn't threaten her," Libby repeated. "I was tired, Jonas. I pulled an eighteen-hour shift and I wasn't happy having a stranger come up demanding a meeting with his boss. He wouldn't tell me what Martinelli wanted, but when I said I didn't conduct test trials, he did say it had nothing to do with his company. Maybe I was so tired I misunderstood."

"I'm going to be looking at Martinelli very closely. There was no reason for him to mention Hannah. Have you ever seen the list of wackjobs writing her threatening letters? She has as many or more crazies after her than Joley."

"Lucky me. And just how are you seeing these letters?" Hannah asked.

"Since I know you're too stubborn to turn them over to me, I have an agreement with your security and your agent."

"Great. Have you ever heard of privacy?"

"Get over it, doll face. I'm never going to be politically correct. When I think it's necessary to protect any of you, you're getting protection whether you like it or not."

The Drake sisters exchanged small smiles.

"You're so good at beating your manly chest," Joley said. "I swear, Jonas, I'm about to swoon."

"No one would blame you." Jonas closed his eyes, not in the least intimidated by the women around him.

Hannah waved her hand to turn off the lights and set the candles flickering. "You're so arrogant and bossy, Jonas, don't you ever get tired of it?"

"No. I'm stuck with the seven of you and someone has to be the brains."

Sarah hit him with a pillow. "You're lucky we love you, otherwise we'd let Hannah turn you into a toad."

"She tried that already, it didn't work. My mojo's too strong. Where are the doomed men tonight?" Jonas asked, lying back, hands linked behind his head. "Did they run for the hills?"

"We're having a girls' night," Sarah said with a small smirk. "No fiancés. Only sisters."

Jonas groaned, opening his eyes just enough to glare. "You could have told me. I won't live this one down for a while. They'll be merciless."

"And it will be so deserving," Hannah said. "You really only came tonight to harass us and eat cookies."

"Too true," he agreed. "It always makes me feel better.

But Kate nabbed the last cookie with frosting. When is this wedding? I'm beginning to think you aren't really going to have one, you just want to stay in Sea Haven to annoy me."

"It's my life's work," Hannah agreed.

"Aleksandr wants to elope," Abigail confessed. "He doesn't want to wait for the wedding of the century. He thinks it's crazy and we should just quietly marry."

"Quietly?" Jonas made a rude, derisive sound. "The wedding of the century is going to be a circus. Doesn't he realize the entire town has to be invited or there's going to be hurt feelings?"

"Hence the elopement."

"I think you want to elope," Sarah remarked. "You've never liked crowds, Abbey."

Abigail ducked her head. "Mom and Dad would be so disappointed. All the relatives are flying in and it's going to be such a huge event."

Kate placed a hand on Abigail's arm. "That doesn't matter. It's *your* wedding. If you want something very small, we can sneak in a minister and have it right here with only Mom, Dad, Aunt Carol and us."

Jonas raised his hand. "I'll kick Aleksandr's ass if you don't include me, Abbey, but I'm all for it. He is just as uncomfortable with a big wedding as you are."

Abigail let out her breath. "How upset do you think Mom and Dad will be?"

Elle turned on her stomach and stretched out beside Jonas. "Mom already knows you don't want a big wedding. I'm certain she's mentioned it to Dad. They want you happy, Abbey, not miserable on such an important day. You should know that."

"It's just that Mom seems so happy planning the weddings."

"I'm torturing Damon," Sarah said. "He's going to have to do this because I've always wanted a big wedding and he needs to realize the people in Sea Haven are important to me."

"You just like to torture him on principal," Jonas commented. "What about Matt, Kate? Is he fine with the big wedding?"

Kate flashed a small smile. "His mother is in seventh heaven. And she wants babies immediately. She told us to go out and multiply. Quickly. I've never seen anyone so eager for grandchildren. She's already had a play yard built at her house. I wouldn't want to take her moment away from her and neither would Matt. It's different with you, Abbey, you don't have anyone else to please. I say you should have a small private ceremony right here. We can keep it under wraps."

"I'll do the music for you," Joley offered.

"I can do all the baking, including a wedding cake," Hannah said. "That way no one outside the family will realize anything is going on."

"I'll do the decorations in the house," Kate said. "Matt will help."

Abigail's face brightened. "Are you sure Mom and Dad won't be upset?" She looked at Elle when she asked the question.

The youngest Drake sister shrugged. "They're expecting you to tell them you want a small private ceremony. Mom and Aunt Carol have gifts, too. You all need to remember that."

"Mom has *all* the gifts," Elle reminded them in a low voice.

Joley made a face. "I'll say. Mom always knew I was going to sneak out of the house before I tried it. Sarah, you're going to be so lucky when you have children. They'll never get away with anything. Mine will turn out to be like me, so no way am I reproducing. The world, and especially me, couldn't take it."

"You'll have children, Joley," Sarah said.

"How? I'm not about to let some idiot of a man tie me to him." Joley shook her head adamantly. "I can't take the bossiness. And if they're yes men I'm so bored I want to scream. There just isn't a middle ground for me. I'm doomed to be alone."

Jonas snorted derisively. "You don't sound very unhappy about it."

"Would you want to live with you?" Joley demanded.

"I'm perfect," Jonas declared.

"A manly man," Sarah teased.

"You got it babe."

"I am turning you into a toad," Hannah said. "No one could ever live with your arrogance or your bossiness. Your poor wife would be browbeaten and your kids would run away."

"My poor wife would keep her clothes on around other men and the world in general and only take them off for me," he said.

"Why do you insist I take my clothes off? I *wear* clothes, that's my job."

"Inez carries all the magazines if you're on the front cover, baby doll. I'm not sure I'd call what you're wearing most of the time, actual clothes. When are you getting a real job?"

Hannah turned her face away from Jonas. Elle and Libby instantly put a hand on her, warmth and energy flowing into her. Sarah kicked Jonas. "Go home. You're annoying all of us now. You know you don't want us all angry with you."

Jonas made it smoothly to his feet. "Protecting the Barbie Doll again. You aren't doing her any favors. She can't live off her looks forever."

Hannah winced visibly. Her hands trembled so that she curled her fingers into fists.

Elle stood up, her small, petite frame dwarfed by Jonas's much larger one. "You know, Jonas, if I didn't know the things I do about you, that your intentions are really the best, I'd kick your ass myself. Go away. And do it now." Her red hair crackled with electricity and in the darkened room, her body seemed to throw off light, as if all the energy inside of her was seeking a way to get out. The walls of the house expanded and contracted and the floor shifted slightly under their feet.

Jonas scowled at her, not in the least intimidated. "I don't care what you know, Elle. And don't threaten me."

"I'm not threatening you. If I did, you wouldn't be standing there, you'd be running for your life. In case you haven't figured it out yet, it isn't easy being me. You think I want to know what everyone is thinking or feeling at any given moment? You think it's easy to have a normal temper like the rest of the world, but be so dangerous I don't dare express anger?"

"You're expressing it right now."

"That's because I love you and I'd never accidentally hurt you. I don't love everyone else, you idiot. Go away before the house shakes apart and Mom and Dad are royally pissed at me."

"Can you do that? Shake the house apart?"

"Does it look like I can do that?" Elle countered, gesturing toward the walls.

Her sisters were up, surrounding her, Libby putting her hands on her younger sister's shoulders so that her healing warmth flowed into the mass of boiling energy. Elle sagged back against her so that Libby slipped her arms around her.

"It's getting harder for you, isn't it?" Libby whispered.

Elle nodded and turned to bury her face against Libby's shoulder. "I don't know what I'm going to do."

Jonas stepped closer and swept both sisters into his arms. "I'm sorry, Elle. I'd never make your life harder if I can help it. I can't stop being who I am, as much as I want to for you."

Elle shot him a small smile. "I know you would, Jonas. I feel very lucky to have you in my family."

Libby rubbed her sister's back as she watched Jonas slip out the door. The wind rushed in when he opened it so that the flames on the candles danced and flickered wildly, casting shadows along the walls. Libby didn't like the way the shadows leapt as if reaching for the Drakes, stretching clawed hands for them. She glanced uneasily at Sarah, the eldest, and saw the same recognition in her eyes. Hannah and Elle exchanged another long look of apprehension as Libby tightened her arms around Elle, holding her close to comfort them both.

2

SEVENTEEN-YEAR-OLD Pete Granger glanced toward the ocean and caught a glimpse through the drizzling rain of something—or *someone*—moving on the rising cliffs above Sea Lion Cove. His heart lurched in his chest as he slammed on the brakes to his old battered truck. Fortunately there wasn't anyone behind him and he peered at the sheer wall of rock rising above the churning ocean, swallowing the sudden lump of fear clogging his throat.

Instinctively, he reached for his cell phone, remembering, as he put it to his ear, that there was only limited service on the coastline and he wasn't on the one bluff that allowed him to make a call. The figure moved, and even at a distance Pete was certain he recognized his boyhood friend, Drew Madison. Frustrated, heart pumping, he set the truck in motion, racing through the series of hairpin turns before turning onto the dirt road leading to the cliffs. He nearly forgot to put on the brakes as he parked.

The wind hit him hard as he threw open the door and ran across the muddy ground to the top of the bluff. His cap blew off and the wind tugged at his shirt. Ignoring the small fence and the warning signs to keep away from the crumbling edge, he dropped to the ground, stretching his body out flat as he crawled to the edge and peered over.

"Drew!" The name was lost in the boom of the boiling sea. Pete cupped his hands together and tried again, putting everything he had into it. "Drew! Are you all right?" He doubted if his friend could hear the words, but then something alerted him, maybe the small trickling of dirt he'd displaced, because Drew turned his face upward toward Pete.

Drew Madison was several feet down the muddy cliff face. Nearly one hundred feet below him the waves crashed over large, jagged rocks, throwing white spray high into the air. The boom of the ocean was loud, reverberating off the sheer rock wall. The rain appeared a dank silver-gray, the steady drizzle making it much more difficult for Pete to catch a glimpse of Drew's stark white face.

Drew appeared small and helpless, his face streaked with mud. He shook his head and waved Pete off, hunching against a spray of ocean water as a wave dashed against the large rock formation directly below him. Pete could see skid marks in the mud, where Drew's body had gone over, sliding down the cliff face until he hit the small outcropping where he now clung.

Pete held up his cell phone and made the motion of throwing a rope. To his astonishment, Drew shook his head harder. The rain beat down steadily getting in Pete's eyes so that he had to use his knuckles to wipe the water away, for a moment cutting off his view of Drew's white, desperate face. When his vision returned, Pete's heart leapt to his throat. Drew was gone.

"Drew!" Pete screamed the name until he was hoarse. He inched forward until he actually slid in the mud and had to anchor his own body by hooking his boots into the fence. Frightened, he peered below to the raging water, the white caps of foam and the spray blasting over the rocks and churning up the cliff face, searching for a body. It seemed impossible for anyone to survive the fall. Even if Drew had avoided the rocks he would have fallen into the roiling sea.

Tears blurred his vision. He stared at the top of the rock formation so long it appeared as if something was moving in slow motion. He wiped at his eyes with his knuckles and looked again. There were several outcroppings making the angle more difficult so he slithered back and repositioned himself. At once he could see on the rocks rising to meet the cliff that Drew lay in a crumbled heap and he was moving! Excited, Pete cupped his hands around his mouth.

"Drew!"

There was no answer, but he knew Drew was alive. He looked to be wedged between two boulders jutting up out of the sea, a part of the formation of the caves below the waterline. It seemed impossible that he could still be alive, but he definitely moved.

"I'm getting help. They'll be coming for you, Drew!"

Pete scuttled backwards like a crab until he crawled under the fence to safety and rushed back to his truck. He needed to get out a little farther on the other side of the cove where the cell phone service actually worked. It was tricky; he had to stay in one place when his body was flooded with adrenaline and wanted to move, but he gave the details to the sheriff 's office.

He was almost back to the cliffs when he heard the wail of sirens and knew Jonas Harrington and Jackson Deveau, the sheriff and his deputy, were on the way. He sagged with relief and waited for the patrol car.

"TY'S tuning us out," Sam Chapman announced to the ring of firefighters sitting around the table playing cards. "This is his vacation, you know. He spends weeks, even months locked up in his lab at BioLab Industries. He doesn't eat or sleep and forgets everything but staring into a microscope. He doesn't talk to a soul, just stares at little wormy things dancing on a slide."

"He doesn't talk much here, either," Doug Higgens said.

"He manages to recertify for helicopter rescue every

ninety days," Sam said, "but that's because he likes the rush, not us."

"I don't like you all that much either, Sam," Jim Brannigan, the helicopter pilot, announced. "You took all my money the last card game."

Tyson Derrick barely registered the continuous ribbing of the other firefighters at the Helitack station. It was true, he often forgot to eat and went days without sleeping, so focused on his research he forgot the world around him. Working the fire season provided him with a small respite, an opportunity for interaction with others as well as the adrenaline rush he needed outside the lab. Yet even that no longer seemed to be working for him. Something was missing. He *had* to get a life.

"Wake up, Ty." Sam Chapman slapped him on the back. "You haven't heard a word I've said."

"I heard," Tyson replied. "It just didn't merit a response. And by the way, Sam, I keep telling you odds are always against you in cards. Right now you're looking at two-hundred-and-twenty-to-one odds. That's just not that good. Sean has a much better chance at forty-three-point-two to one."

"Thanks so much for that little lesson," Sam said, tossing his cards on the table. He grinned at the circle of faces surrounding them as he ribbed his cousin. "Ty told me last night he's ready to settle down with the perfect woman. He just needs to find himself a woman who doesn't mind him disappearing for weeks or months on end while he works in his lab, or goes skydiving or parasailing or mountain climbing. You know, a saint."

A roar of laughter went up at Ty's expense. He wasn't easygoing and comfortable like his cousin, Sam. Sam just fit in anywhere and he had a natural ability to make others laugh. Ty forced a faint grin. "That's what I should be thinking about," he agreed. "I can't seem to get my mind off one of the projects at BioLab."

Sam groaned. "I thought you completed all your projects and whatever you were working on . . ."

"Not exactly, I'm currently working on an ongoing project to identify a series of compounds that are potent in vitro inhibitors . . ."

"Stop, Ty." Sam shoved his hand through his hair. "You're going to give us all a headache. No wonder you're thinking of settling down. No one could live full-time worrying about things like that. I probably can't pronounce half the things you work on."

Ty shrugged, a frown settling over his face. "It isn't my Hepatitis C project I was thinking about. Some time ago the company began developing a new drug using the basic findings of the cellular regeneration study for external wounds I did a few years ago. They believe they have a potential internal drug to fight cancer, but I just have this hunch that something's not right with it. I've been doing a little moonlighting . . ."

"Ty . . ." Sam shook his head. "You're supposed to be putting all that behind you when you come here. You looked like hell when you showed up for training. You might as well be in prison the way you get so wrapped up in all that."

"It's just that this drug has the very real potential to help a lot of cancer patients if they get it right. Harry Jenkins is heading up the project and he isn't as thorough as he should be. He tends to take shortcuts because he wants recognition more than he wants to get it right." He was suddenly all too aware of the silence of the others around him. That was the way it was with him. He didn't fit in, no matter how hard he tried. Most conversations seemed trivial to him when his mind was always working on unlocking some key and preferred to keep working no matter how hard he tried to shut it off.

"This internal drug isn't even your department," Sam said. "I'll bet old Harry doesn't like you much, does he?"

"Well, no," Ty admitted reluctantly. Harry didn't like him at all. He doubted if many people did. He wished it mattered to him, but only Sam really counted. He didn't like letting Sam down. "But it isn't a popularity contest. This drug could save lives. And the new drug is based on my earlier work in cell regeneration. If they get it wrong, I'd feel responsible."

"Great. You're going to spend your off time in that makeshift lab in our basement, aren't you?" Sam asked. "I planned white-water rafting and a couple of rock climbing trips as well as parasailing. You'd better not back out on me again."

Ty sat back in his chair and studied his cousin's handsome face. Sam managed to look petulant at times. He was the only man Ty knew who could pull off the look and still appeal to women. He'd seen it a million times. Sam had charm. Ty often wished he had just a little of whatever it was that Sam had. Sam got along with people. He could bullshit with the best of them and everyone liked him.

Ty knew he had embarrassed Sam more than once through the years with his abrupt, abrasive manner. How many times had he missed some trip or outing Sam had planned because time got away from him and fun with the boys wasn't nearly as exciting as working in the lab, following the trail of an inhibitor that might work on T-cells? The bottom line was, it didn't matter that he had an enormous IQ; he felt awkward in the company of others—and he probably always would—but he just didn't care enough to make time to improve his social skills.

It was always an adjustment, living with Sam for three months out of the year. Ida Chapman had left her son, Sam, and her nephew, Tyson, her house when she'd passed away five years earlier. Ty always looked forward to visiting Sam, but that first month was difficult. Ty was used to being alone and not speaking to anyone, and Sam liked conversation. "I don't back out of our trips," Ty said. His frown deepened as Sam remained silent. "Do I?" He rubbed the bridge of his nose. He probably had, more than once. Disappointing Sam yet again.

Sam shrugged. "It doesn't matter, Ty. I'm just giving you a hard time. You're a biochemist. They're all crazy."

"And helicopter crews aren't?"

A roar of laughter went up. Sam held out his hands, palms up. "All right, you've got me there."

"I want to hear more about Ty's saint. Is she blond and built?" Rory Smith asked. He rubbed his hands together. "Let's get to the good stuff."

"That's your idea of the perfect woman, Rory," Doug Higgens observed, jabbing the firefighter in the arm. "And you definitely don't want a saint. What does she look like, Ty? You found her yet?"

Sam's mouth tightened. "He thinks he's found her."

An image flashed in his mind before Ty could suppress it. Her face. Pale. Midnight black hair. Large green eyes. A mouth to kill for. Ty shook his head. "She has to be intelligent. I can't spend more than a couple of minutes with someone who's an idiot." And that was the problem, would always be the problem. He wanted to talk about things he was enthusiastic about. He wanted to share problems at work with someone. Not even Sam had a clue what he was talking about and Sam actually tolerated him. Most women's eyes just glazed over when he started talking. And God help him if a date started talking about hair and nails and makeup.

"Geez, Ty. What the hell is wrong with you? Who gives a damn if they have brains? You're just doing the wrong things with her," Rory said. "Stop trying to talk and get on with the action. You need help, man."

Another round of laughter went up.

Three tones blasted through the air and the men went instantly silent. The three tones chimed again and they were on their feet. The radio crackled and command central announced an injured climber on the cliffs of Sea Lion Cove just south of Fort Bragg.

Ty and the others grabbed the rescue gear, loading it into the Huey as fast and as systematically as possible.

"Ben, go to the Fort Bragg command center first, but I'll want you to get as close as possible," Brannigan, the helicopter pilot, told the fire apparatus engineer. Ben would drive the heli-tender carrying the fuel for the helicopter as well as extra stokes—the baskets they put the victim in—and everything else needed in emergencies. He would have to take the large truck over the mountainous route to reach Fort Bragg and it would take him at least an hour or more. The helicopter would be there in fourteen minutes.

Ben nodded and ran for his vehicle. The helicopter devoured fuel and they never went anywhere without the helitender.

The familiar rush of adrenaline coursed through Ty's body, making him feel alive again after living in his cave of a laboratory for so long. He needed this—the wild slam of his pulse, the adventure, even the camaraderie of the other firefighters. He took his place in the back of the helicopter with the other four firefighters, the captain and pilot up front. His helmet was fitted with a radio and the familiar checklist settled everyone down.

"Commo check," Brannigan said into his mike.

The crew chief answered, followed by each member of the team.

"ICS isolation," Brannigan announced.

In the back, Ty, along with the others, checked their communication box and turned off all radios to isolate themselves from all unnecessary chatter. During the rescue operation it was necessary nothing distracted them.

Sean Fortune, the crew chief, answered. "Isolated."

"Pilot is isolated except for channel twenty. All loose items in cabin."

"Secured," Sean answered.

Ty felt the familiar tightness in his stomach. He loved the danger and he craved the excitement. In a few minutes they would be airborne.

"Doors."

Sean inspected the doors. "Right door open and pinned. Left door is closed and latched."

"Seat belts."

"Fastened," Sean confirmed.

"Rescue supervisor and crew chief safety harnesses."

Sam and Sean checked the harnesses very thoroughly. "Crew chief secured. Rescue supervisor secured."

"Rescuer rigging."

Sam stepped forward to inspect the rigging, giving Sean the thumbs-up. "Secured."

"PFDs." Brannigan continued with the checklist.

Tension rose in the helicopter perceptibly. They were going over water and the pilot and crew chief were required to wear personal floatation devices or PFDs, as the pilot was more apt to be trapped in the helicopter should it go down over water.

"Donned," came the response.

"H.E.E.D.S. and pressure. Pilot's H.E.E.D.S. is on and pressure is three thousand."

The H.E.E.D.S. was the Helicopter Emergency Evacuation Device, which was a mini–scuba tank with a two-stage regulator.

"Crew chief 's H.E.E.D.S. is on and pressure is good."

Sam answered as well. "Rescue supervisor's H.E.E.D.S. is turned on and pressure is good."

"Carabineers."

Ty gripped the edge of the seat. This was it. They were going up and he hadn't done a short haul over water other than in training in two years. He'd kept up the training and was confident he wouldn't let the others down, but the rescuer was determined by rotation and today he had the short straw. He was going out on the rope.

Sean responded to the pilot. "Unlocked." Over water they always flew with the carabineers unlocked as it would take too long to unlock them in the event the helicopter went down.

"Airborne," Brannigan announced calmly to command center as he took the Huey into the air.

The adrenaline poured into Ty's veins, a rush unlike any other. Nothing compared to it, not even the time when he unlocked the key to cellular regeneration and won a Nobel Prize in medicine. Nothing felt like this, soaring into the air inside a helicopter, surrounded by the other men as determined as he was to do whatever needed to be done.

Command responded with latitude and longitude, distance and asmith, the compass bearing. Brannigan loaded the information into the GPS and plotted a route directly to the victim.

Ty listened to the fire captain on scene giving details. There was a short conversation about the victim and whether the on-scene firefighters believed they'd have to do a short-haul rescue. A high-angle cliff rescue had already failed. Ty's heart jumped in his chest. Short-haul rescue was one of the most dangerous of maneuvers and they only performed the rescue if every single member of the team agreed it was necessary to save a life and they could perform it safely. He knew the flight crew would decide for themselves whether or not to perform the rescue, but Ty was already gearing up for it.

They could fly in the rain and even steady winds of up to sixty miles an hour, but not in gusts over twenty. It was raining on the coast, but the wind was steady with no sign of fog. This was exactly why he chose to join every year. It was why he went skydiving and parasailing. He needed something that required his full attention. The adrenaline rush was the only thing he found that cleared his mind of biochemistry and DNA strands and allowed his thoughts to be consumed completely by whatever was at hand.

He felt Sam's gaze and smiled at him in reassurance. With Aunt Ida gone, Sam was the only person he had left that gave a damn. He didn't want his cousin worrying he wasn't up to this. His nerves were already settling down and his hands were steady. Even his heart had resumed a rhythmic beat. Yeah. He was ready. The rigorous training had been well worth it to get him back in shape.

It was surprisingly fast flying over the mountains to the coast and Brannigan brought the helicopter in to hover over the victim to assess the chances of a safe rescue. As always they went over their short-haul analysis list to determine if the rescue was needed and justified the danger to the crew. They had the trained personnel available. Flight conditions were favorable. The load calculations were within limits. The firefighters had tried an alternative rescue plan and it had proved hazardous. The flight crew agreed trying a high-angle cliff rescue might jeopardize the safety of the victim.

Brannigan set the helicopter down after they had studied the victim's position from every angle. As always, they conserved fuel while they discussed the possibilities and came up with a viable plan to retrieve the victim.

Ty could feel his body humming now. Every cell alive, alert. Ready. They asked each member of the rescue team to confirm go or no-go. It was now or never. One dissenting vote and it was off. They would all go home and stay alive. No one was going to dissent, least of all, Ty. He gave the thumbs-up and Sean radioed his affirmation to the pilot. It was a go.

The coastal geography always determined which side of the helicopter the rescue was done out of. The coast ran southeast to northwest so typically they performed the rescues out of the right side, unless they had an unusual southern wind, which, thankfully, there wasn't. Helicopters liked to fly into the wind and they didn't like wind in the left door. The craft wasn't aerodynamically stable with wind through the left door.

Brannigan confirmed the medical helicopter was on its way and instructed them to set down in the clearing above the old mill on the far side away from the cliff. He took to the air again, wanting to do a power check. They needed to be able to hover with enough power margin to execute the rescue safely. They had the charts, but helicopter crews were notoriously skeptical and preferred to check everything for themselves.

"Power check complete, our power is good," Brannigan said.

Colors glittered with amazing vivid brightness. Ty watched the clouds and water sparkle, the rain looking like diamonds. He inhaled the scent of the coast, of the ocean. Beside him, Sam smelled of spicy aftershave and garlic. Doug needed a new deodorant and Sean was wearing cologne. Ty caught the faint whiff of chloroform and shook his head with a smile to clear his mind of his other life once and for all. He concentrated on the pilot's skill as he entered his flight pattern.

"Turning downwind. I'm abeam of the target. I'll let you know when I lose sight."

Ty had a great deal of respect for Brannigan. The man had been flying helicopters for over twenty years and he worked a kind of magic with them. He "felt" them. The closer he got to the cliffs, the more it brought out his skill. The Huey slowed significantly. Ty's gut knotted.

"Speed is back, you're cleared to the skid."

Sean unhooked his secondary securing strap as he replied, "Crew chief moving to skid." He stepped out onto the tank and then onto the skid, securing himself with careful precision. "O.K. crew chief is all secured and on the skid."

The traffic pattern was downwind, leg, base leg and final leg. Brannigan turned into base leg and cleared first rescuer to the skid.

Ty's heart leapt in his chest. He was hooked up to the rescue rope and the crew chief, with hand signals, told Ty to disconnect the seat belt.

"Rescuer one is moving to the skid." There would be a significant weight shift as Ty moved to the right side and the pilot had to compensate. Sam, as rescue supervisor, took a position where he could observe and double-check everything. Ty waited as the two men inspected everything a third time, from the ropes to his safety harness.

"Crew chief is performing a final rigging and safety inspection. Does the rescue supervisor concur?"

Sam's voice was hoarse. "Rescue supervisor concurs."

"Does the pilot concur with the mission?"

"Pilot concurs. Pilot has lost contact."

"Crew chief has the target, continue to move forward fifty, forty, thirty, twenty. Tail and main rotor are clear, you can come down ten." Move was horizontal and come was vertical. Sean directed the pilot as close to the target as possible while keeping them all safe.

Ty waited, his heart pounding in his ears nearly as loud

as the helicopter. It was moments now. The helicopter went stationary, hovering above the target.

"Rescuer will now be lowered out the door."

Sam began to feed the rope through to the breaker bar to lower Ty. Ty swung beneath the skid in a smooth, practiced move, the bottom of his boots snug against it to prevent oscillation.

"Rescuer one is going inverted," Sean reported to the pilot as Ty went upside down.

From that point the ball was in Ty's court. He signaled with exaggerated arm movements to the crew chief who relayed instructions to the pilot. Everything would depend on what he found when he reached the victim. Blood rushed through his body and his heart pounded almost as loudly as the violent waves below. Time seemed to slow, to tunnel, as he narrowed his focus to the waiting victim.

As he descended, he could see the waves breaking over the more jagged rocks farther below where the victim—a teenage boy—appeared to be conscious, but was writhing in pain. As Ty drew near, he could hear the boy screaming.

"Rescuer is four feet, three, two, one. Rescuer is on the ground. Come down five for slack."

Ty disconnected the moment he was stable on the huge rock formation.

"Rescuer is D.C.ing. Rescuer is moving left-front."

The rope began to retract as Ty made his way to the victim. The rocks were slippery and he had to use extreme caution.

"Rope is coming back into cabin. Rescue supervisor is into cabin. Crew chief coming into cabin. Crew chief in cabin. You are cleared for forward flight."

Ty took a deep breath as Brannigan took the helicopter back to the clearing and shut down to give him time to assess the patient without distraction. The boy's face was twisted with pain, but he tracked his rescuer with his gaze as Ty eased his way over the outcropping and around loose rock. To his astonishment, he recognized the kid.

Drew Madison was a leukemia patient. What in the world would he be doing climbing the cliffs of Sea Lion Cove?

"Drew. You've got yourself in a bit of a mess, but I'm here now. We'll get you out of this." He kept his voice soothing and calm. "Work with me. I know it hurts, but we're giving you a ride in the helicopter. How many people can say that?" As he talked, he quickly checked vitals and looked for places the blood was coming from. "Do you know where you are?"

Drew nodded, his eyes a little wild. "On the rocks."

"Good, good. And your name?"

"Drew Madison."

Ty grinned at him. "You appear to have fallen off the cliff, Drew, and you have a couple of broken bones. I want you to lie quietly and be very still for me. It's slippery up here."

Drew had a bump on his forehead. His legs had taken the brunt of the fall. He'd landed on his feet, gone to his knees and had fallen forward, facedown, which wasn't consistent with most falls. Most victims of a fall had massive head trauma from landing on their heads.

Drew had multiple fractures for certain on the left leg, and at least one clean break on the right. He had numerous scrapes and a couple of deep cuts, a possible broken rib where his elbow drove into his side on impact, but most importantly, his head had escaped with no more than a few bumps and bruises. He had signs of shock, his skin was cold and clammy, his pulse rapid.

"Copter one hundred and one, this is rescuer one hundred and one."

"Rescuer one hundred and one, this is copter one hundred and one, go ahead." Brannigan's voice came back very clear.

"I need second rescuer and stokes."

"Okay. We're about two minutes out, see you in two."

Drew grabbed at Ty's arm. "Don't leave me here. I shouldn't have done it. I'm sorry. I'm sorry. It hurts. It hurts so bad."

"I'm not leaving you, kid. We're taking a ride together." Ty's brain worked at rapid speed, assimilating data, and nothing about this fall was adding up. Drew Madison was a seventeen-year-old boy who had battled leukemia most of his life. He had no business climbing a cliff on any day, let alone one when it was pouring down rain and certainly not alone. Had there been some kind of dare? The boy that called it in, had he been a part of a stupid prank gone wrong?

Ty worked on Drew's wounds, stabilizing his legs for traveling in the stokes. The kid was in terrible pain, yet he fought back his need to scream and tried to cooperate with Ty. Shock was setting in and the boy shivered continually.

Ty kept talking to him. "It won't be long. You'll like the helicopter. And the medics are waiting and can give you something for pain right away."

"You won't leave me?" Drew kept a death grip on his shirt.

"No, we'll ride up together. Here's the helicopter now. They're sending down the stokes with another rescuer." The boy was shaking so hard Ty feared he might slide off the rock. He kept talking to distract him from the pain. "The stokes is a basket we put you in for the ride and then we'll hook both you and the basket to the collection ring and up we go. We'll be out of here in no time."

Doug Higgens was rescuer two and he dropped carefully to the rocks with the stokes in tow.

The pilot moved the helicopter. "Rescuer one, how long do you think?"

"About fifteen minutes," Ty answered.

"Okay, we're going back to the meadow and shutting down."

Doug and Ty worked quickly to package Drew in the stokes, doing their best to keep from jarring him as they immobilized his legs and double-checked his safety lines. They had done this before and, other than the rock being extremely slippery and the ocean pounding around them, the process was smooth. Ty kept up a running dialogue with the boy, his tone soothing and calm, noticing when he quit speaking the teenager became more agitated.

"We're ready," he announced to Brannigan.

"Okay, be there in five," Brannigan answered immediately.

"What if I fall out of the basket?" Drew asked.

Ty noted the boy's voice was beginning to get thready. He frowned at Doug over the kid's head. "You're connected to a collection ring separate from the stokes, Drew. Even if the stokes should fall, if something fails, you'd still be connected. Not to worry, I'll be riding with you all the way. It's like taking a ride in the clouds."

The helicopter was overhead, Brannigan maneuvering beneath the rim of the cliff with his usual precision. The rope dropped almost in Ty's lap. He connected his line to the collection ring first, then Drew's line and finally the stokes. He signaled to the crew chief to come up.

"Come up ten for slack," Sean instructed Brannigan. "Rope is taut. Stokes is coming off the ground, hold for rescuer adjustment."

Ty adjusted the prussic knots so that the stokes was in position with his body for the ride. The rescuer always rode with the stokes waist level so he could reassure the victim and keep them calm. He signaled ready.

Sean's voice in his ear relayed the signal to Brannigan and the helicopter began to continue to climb. Drew cried out, closing his eyes tightly.

"You're fine," Ty said. "You might want to take a look around you . . ."

Abruptly Ty's voice faded as terror gripped him. Utter shock. He was suddenly free-falling. No warning whatsoever, simply tumbling away from the stokes, away from Drew and down onto the jagged rocks below. Time slowed. He felt as if he were falling in slow motion. He heard the roar of the ocean and realized it was the sound of his own heart thundering in his ears. He saw the horror in Sean's face and then his vision blurred as his body tumbled and the rocks grew larger.

"Fuck! Oh, shit. Hold! Hold! Hold! Rescuer just fell," Sean blurted. "Damn it, rescuer just fell."

There was a moment of stunned, horrified silence. Of comprehension.

Brannigan came back all business in an attempt to stay calm, to keep everyone focused. "What about the vic?"

Sean stared down to the rocks below. At the blood seeping everywhere. At the still body crumpled practically at the feet of the second rescuer who stared back at him with horror on his face.

"Say again. What about the vic?"

Sean swallowed the fear in his throat and forced his gaze—and his mind—away from the broken body below. "Victim is still there. Stokes is swinging. Move left."

"Hang on. I'm stopping the swing."

Automatically the rescue crew gripped whatever was closest as Brannigan maneuvered quickly over the victim in mid-swing.

"Stokes is stable," Sean reported.

"Do I put the victim down?"

Sean took a deep breath. "No, let's just move him over to the clearing."

Doug broke radio silence. "Rescuer one is in bad shape. He's bad."

"Do what you can, rescue two," Brannigan said. "We'll be right back. Command, are you getting all this? We need a firefighter to disconnect our victim for us. We'll need another stokes and another med helicopter. Ben, how far out are you?"

"Ten minutes."

"Ground crew standing by. Will D.C. vic in clearing."

No one looked at Sam. He sat in silence, his face grim, shock and horror in his eyes. No one spoke as they waited for the victim to be disconnected so they could get back to their fallen crew member.

3

"THAT'S my last patient, Evelyn," Libby told the nurse with a faint smile. "It's home for me."

"Did you hear all the commotion in the ER, doctor?" Evelyn asked.

"I heard two helicopters arrive," Libby replied, "but I was too busy to check out what was going on." Two helicopters were unusual, so she'd guessed there was an accident on the highway.

"I've only managed to hear a word here and there, but it sounds like Drew Madison was climbing the cliffs out by Sea Lion Cove and fell. They called in the rescue helicopter and something went wrong."

Libby drew in her breath. "Drew? Are you certain? What on earth would he be doing out in this kind of weather? And what would he be doing on the cliffs? He knows how dangerous they are." The cliffs were extremely hazardous, fractured by huge cracks, weakened by the ever-eroding sea, rock crumbling away without warning. Even without the signs posted up and down the coastline, all the locals knew better than to risk their lives climbing the treacherous, unstable rock faces. "How bad is he hurt, do you know?"

"Orthopedic is with him now. You'll have to check with the ER docs, Libby. We've been so busy here in surgery today I haven't had a chance to really hear much."

"Thanks Evelyn. I'll go see him on my way out."

Libby tossed her gloves into a trash can and lifted a hand as she hurried down the hall toward the ER. She had known Drew his entire life. He wasn't a kid who did stupid things. He'd grown up in the small town of Sea Haven and he certainly knew the hazards of the crumbling cliffs due to the continual pounding of the sea and natural erosion. It made no sense to her that Drew would be out in the rain on a dangerous cliff when he had worked so hard to keep his leukemia in remission.

The ER was bustling with more than usual activity. The moment she set foot in the emergency room, she felt her body respond to the call for healing. Her stomach lurched and her temples began to throb. Somebody was in bad shape. Normally she didn't feel the call to heal so urgently, but this time every cell in her body began to crackle with energy. Her palms grew warm.

One of the ER nurses was Linda Bowers, a friend from high school. "What's going on?" Libby asked briskly.

"Helicopter rescue," Linda answered, "off the cliffs of Sea Lion Cove."

"The weather's horrible with the wind and rain. I heard it was Drew Madison. I can't imagine what he was thinking messing around out there. Everyone knows how dangerous it is."

"Jonas and Jackson have been in with Drew and from the small bits of conversation I'm hearing, they aren't so certain it was an accident. Pete Granger spotted him after Drew had apparently fallen or slid or maybe climbed halfway down the cliff. Then he fell the rest of the way onto the rocks."

"How bad is he injured?"

"No brain injuries, but surgery on his legs for certain. Ortho is looking at him. He's refusing to talk to his mother. He doesn't want to see her and she's totally hysterical. We even offered her a sedative." Linda frowned. "I think you should know, she's blaming you and your sisters."

"What? How could we be responsible for Drew going out onto the cliffs? Kate owns the property, but the cliffs are clearly marked unsafe and there's a fence surrounding the bluff with warning signs posted everywhere. She can't blame Kate—or us for that matter."

"Apparently she asked you to cure Drew."

Libby pressed her hand to her stomach. The need to act was becoming far more urgent. Someone was in dire straights and it wasn't Drew with his need for surgery. She felt the pull toward her left and even took a step in that direction before she could stop herself. "I can't cure Drew. I told her that. My sisters went with me and we worked on him to buy him more time in the hopes that research will be more aggressive."

Libby worked at staying focused on the conversation. It was important to her, but the continual draw toward the room to the left was strong. She could see through the glass partition someone hooked up to machines. Whoever the patient was, his life was ebbing away.

"Irene thinks Drew tried to commit suicide."

That caught Libby's attention. "That's just not possible. He's battled leukemia for years. He's always been determined to live."

"She put him in an experimental program with some new drug with the hopes of a complete cure. She blames the drug as well, says a side effect is depression."

That caught Libby's attention. "Not PDG-ibenregen?"

Linda nodded. "That's the drug. Why? What have you heard?"

"I warned Irene to be careful of that drug. Drew fell into the age group where preliminary reports showed problems with depression. I didn't think the drug was ready for human trials and I told her as much." Libby rubbed her pounding temples, trying to resist the pull toward the patient in the next room. "Why in the world didn't she listen to me? She asked me about it and I've done a lot of research on it. I was interested because the drug was based on the original work of someone I went to school with, but in the first phase of clinicals, there were two teens with problems and that raised a red flag to me. You might remember the original researcher, Tyson Derrick; he actually lives here on and off with his cousin, Sam Chapman. A few years ago he received a Nobel Prize in medicine for his studies in wound-healing cellular regeneration."

"Well, he won't be winning any more Nobel Prizes for anything. He was the rescuer that went down the rope. His safety harness failed and he fell. Major head trauma, internal injuries. The scans are bad. They're sending him to San Francisco, but I doubt he'll live through the night."

Libby sucked in her breath and pressed her hand to her suddenly churning stomach. "Tyson was the rescuer?" She turned her head toward the glass partition, trying to see the face of the patient. "Are you certain? He's a biochemist. A renowned researcher. He's brilliant. Absolutely *brilliant*. Jonas mentioned only last night that Ty worked for the forestry, but I didn't think . . ." Her voice drifted off.

"His parents died a couple of years ago and left him more money than everyone in Sea Haven has put together. Sam will most likely inherit everything. This must be awful for him. They're very close and Tyson's his only relative."

"That's why he worked with the forestry. Sam's a firefighter." Libby couldn't pull her gaze away from the glass. "I can't believe this happened. Who worked on Ty?"

"I'm sorry, Libby, I can see you're upset, but Dr. Shayner did a thorough workup on the patient. Tyson was intubated immediately and the doctor ordered a CT scan as well as a head and spinal scan. His pupils were blown and his corneal and gag reflexes as well as ocular movement were all unresponsive. He's comatose."

"I want to see the scans."

Linda led the way into the room without comment. "Dr. Shayner is arranging to fly him to San Francisco. He's consulting with neurological."

Libby's heart dropped as she studied the scan. "The mortality rate for diffuse anoxal injuries is high," she murmured aloud, her frown deepening. The brain had been jarred too hard with the fall, causing the anoxals to tear. "The only method for treating is stabilizing. He has both subdural and dural hematomas." Libby continued to talk to herself.

Tyson was bleeding both on the brain and underneath. The brain was swelling. Libby closed her eyes briefly. She couldn't look at him. She had to leave while she could. Walk out the door and not look back. Her legs felt rubbery. Her body swayed slightly and she steadied herself with one hand against the wall, leaning forward to take deep breaths.

"Libby, are you okay?" Linda put her hand on Libby's back to stabilize her. With a little cry she lifted her palm to her mouth. "You're burning up, Lib." Her fingers felt scalded and sore.

There was no getting around it. Libby couldn't leave Tyson, not with his brilliance, his incredible brain so capable of doing so much good. She *couldn't* walk out. She heard Linda as if at a great distance, words buzzing in her head, but she couldn't focus. Libby pushed off the wall and found her body moving automatically toward the room where Tyson Derrick lay close to death.

No! Libby, get out of there. It's too dangerous.

Elle, the youngest Drake, was a strong telepath. Libby heard the urgency in her voice, the fear building to terror, but she couldn't stop, even though she recognized the danger wasn't just to her—but to *all* of her sisters. They were locked together as their ancestors had been before them. The gifts might be individual, but they shared power and energy and somehow, in a way they didn't fully understand, they were bound, one to the other, in those gifts.

She heard her own sob of despair, her plea for understanding and apology to her sisters for her inability to stop. She caught the edge of the door hoping to give herself time to think, time to stop, but her feet moved of their own volition carrying her to the side of the gurney. Light spilled out of her body, burst from her fingertips as she approached Tyson.

Libby looked down at the pale, blood-streaked face. Her

heart lurched. It was definitely the Tyson Derrick she remembered, although his piercing blue eyes were closed, black lashes forming two thick crescents over dark circles. His jet black, wavy hair spilled over his forehead, strands sticking in the blood. His shoulders were even wider than she remembered; his arms defined with muscle. Her breath caught in her throat and for some strange reason her heart accelerated.

Tyson Derrick was the only man who ever managed to get under her skin. Libby was used to deference and respect working in her field. She was brilliant and knew it. Only one man had ever bested her grades. Only one man talked down to her, sometimes so rudely she cried herself to sleep at night. It was silly, but she could never quite get him out of her mind. She thought about him more than she cared to admit. It shouldn't matter that he didn't respect her as an equal—but it did. She hid the knowledge away deep where no one, not even her sisters, would ever find it, ashamed that she could be attracted to a man who treated her so carelessly, one she didn't even approve of.

"So much blood. So much pain," she whispered. He looked mangled, his face gray and stretched. It wasn't right. Tyson Derrick was a man needed in the world of medicine. He saw things others didn't and he was tenacious in looking for answers.

Libby touched her fingertips to either side of his head.

Libby! Stop! Elle and Hannah yelled the command in her mind, desperation in their voices. The cries of the others—Sarah, Kate, Abigail and Joley—echoed through her mind and faded away as the heat built in her body.

Energy crackled around her. She took a deep breath to focus. Most of the time she relied on standard medicine, but already that place inside of her, a well of energy, of light, was shifting and opening, the force coursing through her every cell, filling her up.

It was too late to pull back. A compulsion seemed to have gripped her, a need she couldn't fight, to save this one man even at the risk to her own life and sanity—even at the risk to those she loved. It was insane, but the necessity was as elemental as breathing. She let the light and energy pour from her body into Tyson's.

Pain burst over her, through her, stabbing at her head, her chest, her insides until she thought she might pass out. She forced air through her lungs, breathing deeply to ride above the pain. Heat moved through her body, down her arms to her hands and into his brain, carrying with it raw energy and light. Blood trickled from the corner of her mouth, streaked her face, her arms. Stones seemed to settle in her chest, crushing her lungs.

Libby began to lose focus. She stumbled back from Tyson just as he began to stir. The heart monitor leapt with activity as did the EEG. Tyson's eyelashes fluttered. He blinked rapidly, looking up at her.

Ty knew he had to be dreaming. Sometimes, when he felt completely and utterly alone, her face came to him. Libby Drake. Like now. Perfect. No one else had such perfect features. He let himself just soak her in, his gaze fastened on her oval face. Her skin glowed in exactly the way he remembered it. Alabaster pale, so soft he wanted to reach out and run the tips of his fingers over it in a caress. Her lips were full, almost pouting. Kissable lips that conjured up way too many erotic fantasies, even when she frowned at him in disapproval. He thought about her lips far too much, even during the most exciting times when he was on the trail of an elusive answer, forgetting to eat or sleep. He fixated on her, driving the pain away for a few precious minutes while he concentrated on her.

It was her he was dreaming about when he'd told Sam of his intention to date and then marry just the other night. He'd first seen Libby Drake as a woman a few years earlier across the campus and realized it was the same girl he'd known in passing as a child, all grown up. She had those eyes. Large, perfectly shaped, a brilliant, vivid green, fringed with long, heavy lashes. Every time she looked at him he wanted to haul her up against him and kiss her until neither of them could think straight. She just had those dreamy, come-take-me-to-bed eyes he couldn't seem to resist or get out of his head.

His gaze went to her hair. In his dreams it was always down in the sexy, windblown tousled style she wore so casually all through school, but today it was pulled back away from her face and twisted into some sort of intricate knot at the nape of her neck. It gleamed a deep, rich midnight black, silky soft like the rest of her. The style should have been severe, but it only enhanced her classic bone structure and showed off her flawless skin. When he dreamed, he managed to dream the right stuff. Even with his head pounding with the continual force of a jackhammer and his body pulsing with pain, he felt the familiar stirring of his body, the way it always did when he thought of her.

He wanted to lift his hand and touch her face. Just once, feel her skin, but when he tried to move his head, the jackhammers erupted in a frenzy, boring into his skull. He heard a groan escape from between his clenched teeth. He tasted blood in his mouth.

Ty allowed his gaze to drift once more over her face, noting the complete concentration, almost as if she were in a trance. Strangely the pain seemed to flow up his belly to his chest and shoulders, higher to his head until he wanted to scream with the pain. Libby's face suddenly contorted into a mask of agony.

The pain in Ty's head was gone and awareness of his surroundings crept in. His dreams had turned to a nightmare. He appeared to be hooked up to machines in a place he didn't recognize. His brain no longer felt in such a hazy fog and memory returned slowly. He had grabbed the Madison kid off the cliff and something went wrong. He remembered tumbling through the air, but that was impossible. It meant his safety harness failed. Their equipment didn't just fail. He remembered the sound of bones smashing, his skull crumbling like a rotten pumpkin shell. It had been agonizing and *he shouldn't be able to remember*.

A soft, pitiful sound caught his attention and he turned his head to see Libby Drake cowering away from him. He wasn't altogether certain she was real. Their gazes locked and they stared at one another while time seemed to slow down, until he was only aware of her, of every detail. Her face paled even more. A fine sheen of sweat beaded on her skin. Her hands trembled and she pressed into the wall to hold herself up. She looked completely ill.

Libby pressed a hand to her churning stomach, looking around her, very disoriented. Where was she? *Elle? Hannah? Help me*. She took another step back, away from the gurney and all the machines. Someone watched her, his eyes a piercing blue, stabbing at her, so that her breath came in ragged gasps.

Get to the door, Libby. The door. Elle's voice was very calm. *You're not alone, I'll be with you every step of the way.*

Libby heard her sisters talking to her, encouraging her, all from a great distance, their voices brushing around her mind. Strange, she couldn't sort them out, or hear what they were saying, other than Elle.

I'm so cold. Libby shivered as she pushed open the door and stumbled out into the hall. She looked around her, unable to recognize where she was. A hallway. There were people, some looking at her, others going about their business. A man dressed in a gray suit stood just outside the door she emerged from. He looked vaguely familiar, as if she should know him. He went to step in front of her, but she shrank back, holding up a trembling hand to ward him off. He appeared puzzled, shifting slightly. Libby blinked several times wondering if she were hallucinating.

Keep walking, Libby. Concentrate on me. Elle encouraged her. *I'm holding on to you. I've got you safe. Ignore him and keep coming to me. I'm on my way.*

Libby couldn't feel or hear her other sisters, except maybe Hannah. Was she weeping? If Hannah was crying then Libby had to get to her. She forced her body to move, one foot in front of the other. Two nurses were talking at the end of the hall and they turned to stare at her. Libby's vision blurred and she rubbed her eyes. Her hand came away red with blood. She blinked down at her fingers.

Keep coming to me, Libby. Hannah needs you. Can you hear her crying? Keep walking, don't stop. I'm almost there.

Libby only heard Elle's voice now and it was nearly drowned out by a strange roaring in her head. Her heartbeat thundered in her ears, but she couldn't understand where she was or even what she was doing. She obeyed her sister blindly, stumbling down the hall toward the doors.

Before Libby managed to make it more than a few feet, a woman rushed up to her, planting herself squarely in Libby's path.

"This is your fault, Libby. All your fault!" Irene Madison shrieked the accusation at the top of her lungs. Her face was twisted with fury and she clutched her handbag like a weapon. "*You're* responsible for this."

Libby wrapped her arms around herself, shivering. She could see people looking at her, but she didn't know where she was. The woman shouting wasn't making much sense. Frightened, she reached for her sister. *Elle? What's wrong with me?*

"Surely you don't think my son's fall was an accident." Irene's voice rose to a screech. "Why would Drew be out climbing the cliff? If you had just shown a little compassion, just a little, Libby, this would never have happened."

Libby shook her head, which sent small needles drilling through her skull. She cried out and pressed her palms to her temples, looking around wildly for a way to escape.

"You never cured him. The cancer was there, eating him alive and I couldn't just watch him die. I *had* to do something. You left me no choice. You refused to cure him and the experimental drug program was the only option left to me. You told me the drug could cause depression. You never said a single word about suicide." Irene's tone escalated to a high-pitched scream. "You could have healed him. Why didn't you?"

Elle burst through the double doors of the hospital, running up the corridor, just as Irene hit Libby hard with her purse, not once, but repeatedly, driving her backward. Libby put up one arm in an effort to defend herself, but she was too weak and went down hard, sprawling on the floor.

Even as she ran toward her sister, Elle lifted her arms, her face a mask of fury. Wind tore down the corridor ahead of her, strong and vicious, whirling like a minitornado, slamming into Irene with such force it nearly lifted the distraught woman off the ground.

Irene screamed and covered her face as the wind whipped around her faster and faster, holding her prisoner. Her carefully styled hair stood straight up and her clothes twisted on her body. Even her earrings pulled out of her ears and hit the partition hard enough to pit the glass.

"Elle." Jackson Deveau inserted his large, stocky frame between the youngest Drake and Irene. "Stop it." His voice was very low, but carried the hard whip of command. The wind seemed to wash over the hard angles and planes of his face, whipping his hair into a turbulent frenzy, but he stood rock solid in the face of her wrath.

Elle's eyes glittered with anger. "Tell her to stop it. She assaulted my sister and you just stood there. Arrest her for battery. You're supposed to be the law."

No one argued with the deputy, not even when they were drunk out of their minds. Jackson was just too dangerous. He was always quiet and rarely spoke, but when he told someone what to do, they did it. His eyes were bleak and cold, as cold as ice. Scars ran along his face and neck and disappeared into his shirt. His dark hair was thick and unruly, his features honed by violent times. Beside Jackson, Elle looked small and fragile, her body half the size of the deputy's, but she didn't back up a step. Neither did Jackson, not even when the wild wind began to tug at his clothes.

Jonas pushed past Elle and knelt beside Libby. "Knock it off, Elle," he interrupted curtly. He'd come in with Jackson and caught the tail end of Irene's attack on Libby. "You're not helping anything. Libby's going to kick your ass when she comes out of this." He switched his furious gaze to Irene. "Libby's hurt bad. She's unconscious. Irene, damn you, what the hell did you do?" he demanded. There was blood around Libby's mouth and nose.

Irene wept hysterically. "I don't know. I just went crazy. Did I kill her?" She remained huddled against the wall, her clothes askew and her hair a tangled mess. "I didn't mean to hurt her." Her sobs increased and she slid down the wall until she was sitting on the floor, legs outspread, clutching her purse to her as she cried.

Elle sank to her knees beside Jonas, her palm skimming just above Libby's body. She cried out and snatched her hand away, cradling her arm to her chest, turning slightly to glance at Tyson looking at them through the glass.

"She needs to go home to the others. I'll call them in and have them waiting for her. She's in bad shape. Can you carry her to the car, Jonas?"

"Maybe she should be seen by a doctor," Jonas ventured. "I've seen you all in various states of collapse, but not like this. This seems too real."

"She needs to be home. We can take care of her," Elle repeated and this time there was a definite order in her tone.

Jackson's gaze narrowed on Elle's face. "You're giving her your strength." He towered over her, reaching down to brush fiery red strands from her face. "You're already trembling, Elle."

Elle pushed his hand away. "She's my sister. Whatever she needs. She gives to everyone all the time." She glanced at Irene, censure plain on her face. "No one is more compassionate or caring than Libby. She gives and gives until she's exhausted."

"I'm sorry. I'm sorry." Irene made an effort to get herself under control, blowing her nose loudly.

"Not at the risk of your own life. She wouldn't want that." Jackson reached down, his fingers wrapping around Elle's wrist. "Back the hell off, Drake."

It was impossible for Elle to remove the deputy's hand and she allowed him to pull her up without a struggle, but she kept her gaze fixed on her sister as Jonas lifted Libby into his arms. Libby's dark hair spilled from the knot and cascaded down Jonas's arm. Her face was stark white, eyes closed, dark red blood dripping slowly down her face. Jonas exchanged a long look with Jackson.

"I don't have a choice, Jackson." Elle made it a statement. "I feel what she's feeling and I can't disconnect. She's not going to make it without my support. Hannah's already with us and the others will be here soon. Hannah shouldered the worst of it. Once we all share the pain and injuries, it will be easier."

Irene pushed herself up off the floor. "Elle. I really am sorry. I don't know what got into me. I think I went a little crazy. Libby's always been good to us. Did I hurt her? Please tell me I didn't hurt her."

Elle glanced up at Jackson's rough-edged features, the dark shadow of his jaw and his bleak, cold eyes. He was staring down at her without expression, but his fingers tightened around her arm. She sighed. "The worst harm was done before you hit her, Irene. You'd better go see Drew."

"He won't let me into the room."

Elle closed her eyes briefly, shadows playing across her face as she concentrated. She sighed again as she gazed at Irene, looking suddenly weary. "He needs comfort and he wants you there. He's very confused and scared. You need to go to him."

Irene nodded and, still clutching her purse, she hurried down the corridor toward the room where the orthopedic surgeon was preparing to take the boy to the operating room.

"That was nice of you, Elle," Jonas said as he began to walk down the hall toward the double doors, Libby in his arms.

"I'm not nice, Jonas." Elle looked at Jackson when she made the admission.

A faint smile briefly touched the deputy's mouth and was gone before it could reach his eyes or warm his expression.

Jonas glanced down at the youngest Drake sister. She was obviously in pain, Jackson supporting her as she walked. "Yeah, you are, Elle. Protecting Libby when someone is pummeling her wasn't such a bad thing. You didn't hurt Irene."

Tears shimmered and Elle ducked her head. "I wanted to hurt her."

"I know, baby," Jonas said gently, "but you didn't, and that's what matters."

Elle flashed a wan grin. "Thanks, Jonas. You aren't all bad either."

Jonas laid Libby in the back of his car, her head in Elle's lap. "Get Pete's statement, Jackson, see if you can get anything out of him while I take Libby home. I'll get back as soon as possible. They're taking Drew into surgery and it will be awhile before we can talk to him again. He didn't admit it, but he definitely went over that cliff on purpose. He would have gone into the ocean if he hadn't hit that outcropping. I want him seeing someone before he ever leaves the hospital."

Jackson nodded, brushed back Elle's hair again, the gesture casual, but his fingertips lingered on her skin. She scowled as she watched him stride away.

"Why do you deliberately try to provoke him?" Jonas slid behind the wheel, glancing back at her in the rearview mirror.

Elle picked up Libby's hand, wrapping her fingers tightly around her sister's palm as if she could hold her to them. "He's always so in control and he thinks everyone should do whatever he says. And everyone caters to him. Big bad Jackson. We're all supposed to be so scared." She bent and kissed her sister's brow. "No one orders me around, Jonas, least of all him. He thinks he can tell me what to do."

Jonas kept his eyes on the narrow, winding road. The highway was steep with several switchbacks. The mountain rose on one side and the ocean shimmered on the other. "You're the only one who gives that man guff."

"Someone has to do it." Elle leaned back and closed her eyes. "And I'm really good at it." Her head pounded and her chest felt broken into pieces. She could feel the presence of her sisters as they joined with her to hold Libby close. She had taken on the grave injuries of another and all they could do was shoulder part of the pain to give Libby's body a chance to try to heal.

"What is it between you and Jackson?" Jonas asked curiously.

"Absolutely nothing." Elle frowned. "Jonas? Who was the man that was treated just before Irene went crazy? Do you know how severe his injuries were?"

"Tyson Derrick. He pulled Drew off the cliff. They were being lifted up to the top of the cliffs when something went wrong with his safety harness; he fell about thirty feet into the rocks. Dr. Shayner said he was in bad shape, head trauma, internal injuries." He paused and glanced at her in the rearview mirror. "If he was that bad, how the hell was he watching everything through the glass? Damn it, she healed him, didn't she? Sometimes you girls set my teeth on edge."

"Why would Libby take such a chance? She's normally very careful. I mean she might have tried to take the edge off, but to take on the injuries, that's too risky, not just to her, but to all of us and she knows better."

"I don't understand any of you, so don't be asking me."

"You love us," Elle said with complete confidence.

He ignored that. It might be true but he wasn't admitting anything out loud. "How did you know Irene was going to attack Libby?" Before Elle could answer, he held up one hand. "Forget I asked. I don't want to know." He parked his car as close to the Drake home as possible.

The Drake house sat at the top of the cliffs, the rising tower and captain's walk giving a breathtaking view of the ocean below. Jonas carried Libby up the stairs and over the covered porch to the living room where her other sisters were waiting.

"Take her to her room, Jonas," Sarah, the eldest, advised. "We can make her more comfortable there. Hannah says this might take some time."

Jonas watched as Libby's sisters surrounded the bed. He could feel the surge of power as they joined hands. He had known them all of their lives and they still never failed to astound him with their combined power. Libby was the healer, the compassionate Drake. He couldn't imagine a world without Libby in it and right now he could barely detect her breathing. He stifled the urge to feel for her pulse and stepped out of the way.

He had watched over the Drake sisters for as long as he could remember. It wasn't always easy and more often than not, they were aggravated with him, accusing him of being a bully. But they always took risks in dangerous situations. He scowled down at Libby. Like now. He had the urge to shake her, shake all of them, for putting themselves continually in harm's way.

Sarah sighed. "Jonas. Go downstairs and make tea."

"Why? If you want tea, all Hannah has to do is wave her arms around and a cup will come floating." He sounded more sarcastic than he intended, but the feminine power in the house always threw him.

"We're trying to work here," she said, "and you're broadcasting your disapproval loud and clear."

"I don't broadcast. I'm the normal one," he insisted. "Is she going to be all right?"

Six pairs of eyes bored into him. He held up his hands in surrender. "I'm going to make tea. What kind? You have a tea shop down there. I wouldn't want to make the one with crushed lizard tongue in it."

"The canister is on the sink waiting for you," Sarah said. "And of course Libby will be all right. We wouldn't allow anything else."

4

LIBBY laid her head against the back of the chair and stared at the shimmering blue of the sea. There was something incredibly soothing about the ebb and flow of waves and the white foam capping the crests far out in the ocean. The continual cry of gulls and the fresh smell of the coast always lightened the sadness she couldn't quite shake. The weather was cool but there was little wind and it felt good to sit in the sun and listen to the surf.

She pulled the thin wrap around her legs and kept her eyes on the sparkling water. She had been so careless of her life, and worse, of her sisters' lives. Healing Tyson Derrick's head injuries had been criminally stupid. She couldn't remember the events leading up to touching him. She couldn't remember most of what happened afterward. For nearly two weeks she'd lain dangerously ill. Without the help of her sisters, she probably would have died, or worse, been left in a vegetative state. As it was, her head still throbbed if she moved around too much and she was often sick to her stomach.

Sarah had tried to talk to her about why she had risked

her life, but Libby honestly didn't know. It was frightening. She'd lost ten days of her life. Gone. No memories. She'd never experienced such a blackout before. Elle had simply told her sisters and Libby that the compulsion to heal Tyson had been beyond Libby's ability to resist.

A shadow fell across her and she looked up. Her heart began to race and her mouth went dry. The book she'd been holding slipped from her fingers to the sand. "Ty." His name came out a croak. He was the last person she expected to see.

Libby was grateful for her dark glasses and instantly switched her gaze to the ocean. Where were her sisters? Why had she told them she wanted to be left alone for a while? She didn't feel up to facing him, she felt fragile and near tears and guilty as sin.

Tyson stared down at her for a long time. He had no idea why she affected him the way she did, but just the sight of her always changed something lonely inside of him and made him feel strangely alive. He had tried to see her numerous times over the last week and a half. No one had ever captured his interest the way Libby Drake had managed to do. Everything about her intrigued him.

One time, on the university campus, he'd seen her rush to the side of a young woman who had been hit by a car. He had watched as the woman went from writhing in pain, to a few bloody scratches, while Libby had been hospitalized for two days. Everyone thought Libby had been the one hit by the car. The real victim had been shielded by the car, so he couldn't really tell if she'd been hurt bad, but Libby had believed it.

That was the day he had begun to suspect Libby Drake needed help. Her family had brainwashed her into thinking she could heal people. The memory of the victim had faded until he could only remember the agony on Libby's face. Someone had to save her, to convince her that magic didn't exist. She was smart and intriguing and yet so caught up in the legacy of her con artist family she actually took on the symptoms of a reputed victim much like a false pregnancy.

He drew up the wooden chair beside her. Close. Allowing

the armrests to touch. "Do you mind if I sit down and visit with you for a few minutes?"

Libby twisted her fingers in the thin wrap. "How did you get down here? The beach is private."

He didn't wait for her to give him permission, seating himself beside her so that his arm brushed hers. Libby shifted a little away from him in her chair and pulled up her legs to make herself smaller.

"I spotted you from up above. Did your sisters tell you I came by to see you a few days ago? They said you were ill."

"It's nothing serious." Could she sound any more stilted? Wasn't Elle supposed to have telepathy? And where was Sarah? Sarah knew things, didn't she? Didn't she know Libby was in trouble? What was the point of having sisters if they didn't rush to her aid? "How are you?"

"I've got a few broken ribs and sternum. Ripped cartilage, torn muscle, that sort of thing, but my head is in one piece."

"You got Drew off the rocks and saved his life," Libby said. Her sisters had been forced to repeat the events leading up to her injury numerous times before she could retain the knowledge. She didn't remember the events firsthand and felt vulnerable discussing anything to do with that day at the hospital.

"Do you realize the tide isn't as low or as high as it normally is?"

A small frown appeared. Libby had absolutely no idea where he was going with the conversation. The jump between the accident and the tide sent a small pulse of frustration ricocheting through her. She was trying to appear normal even though her brain was still recovering from last week's trauma. "It's a neap tide," she replied.

"Exactly." He sounded like a pleased professor. "When the moon is in the first or last quarter, the sun's gravitational pull is in a perpendicular direction of that of the moon. The sun pulls water away from areas of high to areas of low tide, resulting in lower high tides and higher low tides. That's how we get neap tides."

Up close he was even better-looking than at a distance—and up close he flustered her, but if he wanted to play science geek and start spouting little science facts, she could match him fact for fact. "Absolutely fascinating. Did you know that when oceans tides are at their highest they're called spring tides?"

A slow smile softened the hard edges of his face. "I do believe that was Libby Drake, her royal highness, putting me in my place." He liked it, too. He liked that she could match him fact for fact. His mind just threw random things out and most people stared at him as if he'd grown two heads. Libby stuck her chin out and threw facts back in his face. She had the same data stored at her fingertips as he did. Somehow that made him feel less of a freak.

He held out his hand. "Come on, let's go for a walk."

Libby stared at his hand, horrified. "I'm still a little weak." He was continually throwing her off balance.

He caught her wrist and exerted enough pressure to bring her to her feet. "I think I can manage to keep you upright." He looked down at her from his superior height. "You need to gain a little weight, Drake. You aren't anorexic, are you?"

She sucked in her breath, feeling her blood pressure rising alarmingly. She hated the fact that she was small. She would have loved to use the word petite, but she was just plain small. She was a stick, a miniature Hannah without the breasts. And all her life, never had that fact bothered her more than when she was around Ty, the quietly handsome-in-a-nerdy-genius-way boy she'd had a crush on since the first day he'd entered her seventh-grade classroom. She hadn't even seen him in several years and here she was, self-conscious all over again.

"I'm virtually overwhelmed by your extraordinary compliments, Derrick," Libby said, her voice dripping with sarcasm. She would not—*would not*—let him see how his casual dismissal of her feminine qualities still had the power to hurt her. "A woman always loves to hear she looks starved and unhealthy, thank you."

She made the mistake of looking up at him, her gaze locking with his.

He was watching her with a look she'd never seen in a man's eyes before, at least not when those eyes were directed at her. He looked hungry, like a predatory wolf. She swallowed hard and turned her face back toward the ocean. She just couldn't look at him and be rational. Everything he said annoyed her. He was the *only* person in the world who could get her riled, yet for some logic-defying masochistic reason she craved him. She always had.

"I never said you looked bad, Drake. It was merely an observation and genuine concern over your health. I hadn't realized you were so sensitive." He slid his fingers over her wrist to capture her hand, tugging until she came with him. "I noticed the paint on your house. It's very unusual."

She blinked up at him, more flustered than ever, trying desperately to follow the conversation. Her head was beginning to hurt. "The paint? Oh. The paint. What is it with men and paint?"

"Pardon me?"

"Damon, Sarah's fiancé, was quite interested in the paint as well. He never got around to examining it."

"Really? The first thing I did was take a sample of it."

"You chipped the paint off of our house?" Libby nearly stopped in her tracks, but he kept walking as if it were the sanest thing in the world to peel paint off other people's houses.

"Of course. Don't you want to know if an ancestor of yours found a preservative that would benefit the entire world? Even if he chose to keep it to himself to defraud the townspeople into believing it was magic, you would have the chance to set the record straight."

Libby felt a powerful rush of emotion so uncommon to her that it actually took a second or two to identify. Anger. Genuine, riled-up, I'm-so-not-a-good-girl anger. She yanked her hand away from him. "First of all, *Derrick,* most of my ancestors who lived in Sea Haven were women, so it's far more likely one of them found the preservative, if there is one, not a man. Women actually are quite capable of mastering science you know."

He didn't look at all impressed by her outburst. He reached

out to tuck a strand of dark hair behind her ear, fingers lingering on her face. "As I recall, for the most part, you were nearly as good as me in the sciences."

"*For the most part*?" she repeated through clenched teeth. "I totally kicked your butt the second semester at Harvard."

"I don't think so, Drake, you never even came close. That aside, the preservative is important. Paint in the salt air never lasts long. Did you know that the ancient Egyptians used varnishes and enamels based on beeswax, gelatin and clay at least as early as 3000 B.C.?"

"Fascinating," Libby said through her clenched teeth. "Did you know the druids of ancient times also knew how to produce durable protective coatings using ox blood and lime?"

He smiled down at her, not noticing her tone. "I remember when I was a kid and Sam first pointed you and your sisters out to me. You all awed me. The Drake sisters, the royalty of Sea Haven. You were all so beautiful. I wondered how you got your hair to be so shiny and why you were always laughing. It was a long time ago and your hair is still shiny and you still always laugh when you're with your sisters."

For a moment Libby thought the ground had shifted, she was suddenly so unsteady on her feet. She was ready to put him on a rocket to Mars and then he had to go and say something like that. "You thought of us as royalty?"

"Everyone thinks of you as royalty."

"Oh, right. That's just what Irene was thinking when she bashed me over the head with her purse. Elle told me she had a picnic smacking me around." Amusement crept into her voice.

The small note of laughter, of shared fun, startled him. There had always been awkwardness between them. His mouth softened, began to curve into a smile, but her choice of words hit him. Once again he brought her to a halt, pulling off her dark glasses and looking her straight in the eye. "You don't remember her hitting you with her purse? Your sister had to tell you about it? Did she give you a concussion? Is that what's been wrong with you? Damn, Libby, you should have said so. You should be sitting down."

"I'm perfectly fine. And I don't want to talk about that." She took the sunglasses back and pushed them onto her nose, frowning at him.

Ty had a very odd and disturbing compulsion to lean down and kiss the frown right off her face. He hesitated, not wanting to further annoy her, but weighing whether he should try insisting she return to her chair.

"You either have a little bite of disapproval in your voice when you talk to me or you get that frown," he said instead. He rubbed the pad of his thumb over her lips as if he could erase her expression. Her breath was warm on his skin, her lips soft. His stomach tightened and his groin hardened in instant reaction.

"I do not," Libby denied, but even she heard the note of disapproval. "What do you expect when you do things like that?" She had to pull away from him. That light touch, oddly intimate, set her pulse racing. She was just too darned old to act like a ninny just because he was really gorgeous. Libby pressed her lips together to keep from blurting out something ridiculous, like "shut up and just let me stare."

"Like what?"

Now he sounded amused and she clenched her teeth together. "Did you come here just to make me crazy?" She suppressed a groan and the need to cover her face. He always managed to reduce her to an idiot within five minutes of conversation. She was just too aware of him as a man. She could feel his body heat, or maybe it was her own body heat. Her temperature was definitely rising. He was definite bad boy material and try as she might, Libby was not bad girl material.

"Do I make you crazy?" He sounded pleased.

This time she took off her glasses to glare at him. "You're doing it deliberately, aren't you?"

His smile fascinated her. She hadn't realized he could smile. Most of the time he looked focused and brainy, oblivious or arrogant and too superior for words. Now that she'd seen his smile she was really gone. Libby shoved her glasses back on and tried not to be affected by his looks. It was so shallow. She wasn't a shallow person, was she? Because he just wasn't all that nice.

He took her hand and continued walking down the beach to the tide pools without answering her. He kept her off balance and instead of taking charge and ending things, Libby found herself content to walk with him. His stocky body made her feel ridiculously feminine, something else she wasn't going to admit to her sisters. She didn't hold hands. She couldn't remember holding a man's hand, but she liked walking with him, the feel of his fingers wrapped tightly around hers. He stopped to examine a crab and tucked her hand against his chest.

"Hermit crabs are fascinating. The right claw is larger and a different shape than the left. They use it for protection and holding food while the left is used for eating." A mischievous grin crossed his face and lit his brilliant blue eyes. "The male drags the female around with him using the smaller claw, much like a caveman." He twisted his fingers in Libby's silky hair. "All the while he fights off other males with his large claw, holding on to his mate until she's ready to molt and becomes receptive and fertile." He tugged experimentally on Libby's hair.

"Fortunately, I'm not a female crab," she said.

"You're crabby," he pointed out. He allowed the strands of silky hair to slip through his fingers.

Her heart jumped. "I actually had two hermit crabs as pets and they must have both been males because they didn't drag each other around. They were named Toothbrush and Toothpaste. They escaped and went on a suicide mission right off the deck. I cried for a week."

His eyebrow shot up. "You cried over a crab?"

"Well, of course, they were my pets."

"You aren't normal, Libby," he said with a faint smile, his tone affectionate.

"I suppose not. Everyone teased me." She pointed to the tide pool. "I've moved on to starfish, but I leave them in their own environment."

"Starfish?" He gave a little sigh. "That isn't saying much

for your taste. Starfish are carnivorous. They eat whatever they get their feet on. They flip their stomachs outside their mouth and digest prey from the inside out. Only after the animal is completely digested do they pull their stomachs back inside."

"Ew. You sound like Abigail. Leave me *some* illusions."

Tyson laughed aloud and it startled him. He didn't laugh. He pretended to laugh at appropriate times for the sake of his cousin, one of his small concessions to social niceties, but it was never genuine. Libby actually made him laugh for real. She fascinated him. She was a woman born into a family of con artists. Just knowing that should be reason enough to stay away from her, but he never could. She was just so . . . so nice. So real. Over the years he'd come to believe she wasn't part of her family's con, but was, instead, a victim of the very people who should have loved her, just as he was to some extent. Without the influence of his aunt, he doubted if he could even function in society at all.

"You're getting sunburned. I think we need to get you into the shade."

"I used sunscreen."

"Well, your nose is getting red."

"Great." Of course her nose had to be burned. She had such fair skin that every time she removed her sunglasses she looked like a raccoon. Her glasses were staying firmly in place. "I'm not certain there's much shade on this part of the beach." For some silly reason she wanted to stay in his company just a little while longer, even though she knew she should get out of the sun.

He took her hand and gently tugged until she followed him back to the chairs. "Where's your sunscreen?" He picked both chairs up as if they weighed nothing and moved them against the wall of the cliff in the shade. "Sit down here. You really need sunscreen but maybe this will do."

She was *not* going to have her nose be white, covered in zinc while she sat there talking to him. "I left it up at the house."

He folded his arms across his chest. He had great arms, all rippling muscle. He was a biochemist. How did he get arms like that? Libby bit her lip to keep from sighing. She needed darker glasses so she could just get away with staring. If he kept his mouth shut, she could fantasize and then life would be great again. If only he wouldn't talk.

"I saw the brain scans of my head after the accident."

Libby stiffened. All at once she was totally tense, leery of the real reason he must have sought her out. There was belligerence in his voice. She remained silent and pinned her gaze on the foaming surf.

"Shayner tells me I had major head trauma. Fractures, swelling of the brain, blood clots, that sort of thing. Basically, I had scrambled eggs for a cerebellum."

"Interesting."

"He said I should be a vegetable. Instead, I'm walking around with a smashed chest and a few broken ribs."

"I see."

"What do you see?" Tyson leaned close to her, his piercing eyes boring into her. "What the hell did you do? And don't give me any of your magic crap. I don't believe in it and I want the real explanation. You did something. You had to have. Shayner said before you were in that room with me, I was a vegetable. After, other than a few cracked ribs and other minor injuries, I was perfectly fine. What the hell did you do?"

"Crap?" Libby repeated. "Our magic crap?" Fury shimmered through her body, gripped her hard so that she actually looked around for something to throw at him. She'd endangered her sisters as well as her own life and he called what she did *crap*. "Is that what you call what I do?"

He ran a hand through his hair. "You know, I'm not saying what you do doesn't have some small validity, I'm just saying it isn't done with magic. You really don't believe in witches and voodoo and casting spells, do you? You're a doctor. There's a reasonable scientific explanation for what you do."

"Is there?"

"Well, of course. And I want to know what it is."

"Why?"

He shrugged. "Why? Are you serious? Libby, if what everyone says is the truth, you restored by what all accounts was an irreparably damaged brain—my brain. The possibilities, the benefits alone for medicine and science are beyond staggering, if you really could do it. Who the hell *wouldn't* want to know how you did what you did?"

She regarded him for a long time while the gulls cried overhead and the waves pounded the shore. If her blood pressure went up any more at the utter disbelief in his voice, she was going to stroke out. "You figure it out and come tell me how my sisters and I do that magic crap. It will give us all a good laugh."

He glared at her. He was getting angry. He'd come with the best of intentions, but he didn't want to hear her defend herself or her family. "I don't care to be the butt of your jokes. You've got this entire town fooled, but I don't buy it. Just tell me."

"Why don't you start with examining the tests? Maybe they were falsified."

"I already did that. They appear authentic. And you were busy in another part of the hospital when I was brought in so I don't see how you would have had time to tamper with the records."

"You *checked* to see if I falsified records?" Libby was appalled. She drew in a deep breath. "Go away."

"I *had* to rule falsifying documents out. That's the oldest scam in the world," Ty said dismissively. "Just tell me how you did it."

"You think I gave you some new drug I don't share with other brain-damaged patients?" Libby was furious. "I didn't do a thing. The scan must have been wrong. Maybe there was a glitch in the system. I'm tired and you're annoying me. Go away."

Tyson let a few moments of silence go by, hoping she'd calm down. "You're tossing me out because you know I'm going to fixate on this. That's just mean, Drake." He shaded his eyes and looked up at the cliff. "While you're at it, explain why you don't have erosion by your house when every other cliff around here is slowly crumbling. And yes, I took samples of the soil as well."

"I'm intrigued by your scintillating conversation, really I am, but erosion and paint don't do it for me. I'm reading. I'm resting. Or I was until you came along. If you're quite done insulting my family, Tyson, why don't you go back to your lab? I'm sure sleeping on the floor and eating Cracker Jacks while you discover the cure to the world's most deadly diseases is much more fulfilling than hanging around Sea Haven harassing the locals."

A slow grin replaced the stubborn set to his mouth. "You've been checking up on me. I sleep on the couch, not on the floor, but I do eat Cracker Jacks. Princess Libby Drake is interested enough to check up on me. Who have you been talking to?"

Libby felt the color sweeping up her neck into her face. She ducked her head so her hair fell in a cloud around her as she pretended to study her fingernails. "I run into Sam once in a while and he must have mentioned it."

"Oh, no, he didn't. Sam doesn't know anything about my eating habits in the lab and he isn't interested enough to ask." He sounded triumphant. "You actually asked about me. And when I was brought into the hospital after the fall you came to see me."

She shrugged. "I may have. Why wouldn't I? We went to school together. I checked in on you and left. You were Shayner's patient and I was on my way home."

"And I'm supposed to believe you check on all of Shayner's patients? Sorry, princess, that just doesn't fly. You had the righteous inflection and that little bite to your tone that usually throws people, but you aren't throwing me. Not this time. Admit it. You're interested in me . . ."

Libby gasped. "I'm *so* not interested in you. You're an arrogant—" She broke off abruptly as a shadow passed over them, momentarily blocking out the bright sun. Distracted, she looked around. "Something's wrong."

"Why do you think that?"

"The shadow." She was more than distracted, standing to peer around her.

"It was a bird, Libby, a seagull."

"It wasn't a bird."

Her alarm was catching and it annoyed him. There was nothing wrong. "C'mon, Drake. Do you really think I'm going to fall for that? You just don't want to admit, you're interested in me."

Libby ignored him, lifting her arms straight into the air. At once the wind answered, rushing past them in a small gust away from the sea towards the house on the cliff.

"What are you doing?" Ty asked suspiciously.

"That magic crap you don't believe in. Be quiet for a minute and let me concentrate. Something is really wrong. I can feel it." She frowned, facing the ocean, her eyes restless, quartering the beach around them.

Ty took a long look around, first at the ocean. It was fairly calm and he saw no signs of a coming sleeper wave, let alone a tsunami. What else could be wrong? He glanced up at the sky.

"A seagull might dive-bomb us," he reported, "but I don't see a plane going down."

She shot him a look that was meant to silence him.

He started to grin at her, amused by her certainty, but his gut reacted, an instinct that told him to move fast. Ty stood up abruptly, circled her waist and dragged her away from the chairs toward the steps. She was slight, but his ribs and smashed sternum protested, feeling like his chest was being ripped apart. He kept moving. He didn't believe in magic, but he trusted instincts and his own alarm bells were shrieking. A good scientist needed gut feelings and his had been honed by his firefighting training.

They'd taken several running steps toward the path leading up the cliff when he heard a sound from above them. As a rock climber the sound was one he'd heard before. Covering Libby's head with both his arms, he ran the last couple of steps to shove her against the cliff wall, his body crouching over hers protectively as rocks, dirt and mud rained down on them. He made himself as small as possible, wincing when debris pounded on his shoulders and arms. Dirt poured over them and Libby coughed.

He put his mouth next to her ear. "Try not to breathe."

She didn't reply but her hand slipped into his. He pressed her head into his chest. She felt small and fragile in his arms, unlike the Libby who seemed so self assured to him. He tightened his arms and tucked his chin over her head. It seemed an eternity before the rock slide stopped.

He remained holding her. "You think it's safe to move?"

"Thank you." She straightened, pulling her hand out of his, putting a small space between them.

He could still feel her body against his, an illusion, but all the same, she felt like she belonged there. "For what?"

Libby stepped cautiously over the rubble and pointed toward the chairs where they'd been sitting minutes earlier. The wooden chairs had been smashed to splinters by several large boulders. "You just had to mention the cliffs eroding, didn't you?"

The teasing note in her voice robbed him of breath. She looked on the verge of laughter. That was enough to stop his heart. He put his hand over his aching chest. "I had no idea the power of my suggestion was so strong. Next time, I'll be more careful."

"Jonas mentioned there'd been several slides after the last big rain we had. Sea Lion Cove took a major hit. The cliff is really unstable, but I guess we didn't pay attention like we should have."

Ty studied the rock face towering above them. "It didn't look that unstable. There wasn't even an earthquake. Did you notice the boulders looking as if they might fall as you were walking down to the beach?"

"I wasn't paying attention to it, Ty," Libby admitted. "I can't remember the last time any of us looked. Jonas is going to give us one of his many, many lectures."

"Where, exactly, does Jonas fit into your family?" Ty asked. "I remember that he was always around all of you, but he isn't related, is he?" He reached out to brush dirt from her hair.

Libby raised a hand to try to tidy the mass of blue-black silk tumbling around her face. Ty caught her wrist, preventing her from fussing. "You look beautiful, even all messed up."

Libby took a breath. Ten minutes earlier she wanted to push the man into the ocean, now all she could think about was kissing him. "That's a nice thing to say, Ty. I'm not feeling particularly beautiful, so it means a lot that you'd say it."

He shrugged. "I was just stating the obvious. You were telling me where Jonas fits into your family," he reminded. He'd had several bad nights lying awake, remembering the look on Jonas Harrington's face when he'd seen Libby crushed and bleeding on the hospital floor. Ty still hadn't been able to erase the image of Jonas carrying Libby down the hospital hallway.

Libby shrugged. "Jonas is family whether he's related by blood or not. He'll always be family. I think he'd like to disown us, but he can't. He's stuck with us and we drive him crazy."

He could imagine. Jonas was in law enforcement. With the family being outright charlatans, the man was bound to be in a difficult position trying to protect them. Ty didn't want to think about Libby's family, only that intriguing smile she'd flashed at him. He took her hand. As silly as it sounded, he liked holding her hand. "Let's get you back to the house. Do you think you can make the climb?"

"I'm fine," Libby said. She'd had a headache for days, but she wasn't going to admit it to Ty. She didn't pull her hand away, acutely aware of the way the pad of his thumb rubbed over her skin causing a small fluttering in her stomach. No one had ever made her stomach flutter before. "I can certainly make it back up the stairs."

Ty tucked her hand against his chest and began the long climb. The stairs had been dug out a hundred years earlier and each generation had helped to make it easier to climb. Somewhere along the way a railing had been constructed on one side. Tyson kept Libby pressed close to the railing for safety. "It's a good thing you're feeling fine, I don't want you using this little mishap as an excuse to avoid our date." He smirked at her.

"Date?" Her voice squeaked. "We don't have a date."

"Yes, we do."

Libby shook her head decisively. "I don't go out on dates."

"Well, you're going on a date with me. I asked. You said yes. Are you backing out?" He challenged. "I know you're attracted to me."

Libby looked horrified. It was all he could do to keep from laughing. "I am not. What gave you that idea?"

"You did. You said so, when I asked you to go out with me." He tilted his head, studying her face, looking her straight in the eye. "Come on, Drake, in the hospital. You're not going to pretend you didn't say you wanted to go out with me."

"What else did I say?" Pure suspicion was in her voice.

"That I'm brilliant. Which I am."

"This isn't funny, Ty. We never had the conversation. I don't date."

"Yes, you do. You dated that idiot doctor from the C.D.C. You remember him. He had a toupee."

"He did not. That's his own hair. And he wasn't an idiot." She narrowed her eyes, pinning him with her gaze. "How would you know I dated him?"

"Sam. He's a fountain of information. Remember, he told you I eat Cracker Jacks? And the C.D.C doc was too an idiot. I had one conversation with him and that was enough to tell me he got his position through family connections or politics."

Libby sighed. "Well, I don't really go out on dates so it isn't possible I said yes. And I only went to dinner with him once."

"Because he was an idiot," Ty insisted. "Come on, Drake, tell the truth. He was boring, he only talked about himself and he didn't have a brain."

"Whatever. You know darned well we didn't have a conversation in the hospital."

He put a hand over his heart. "I can't believe you'd pretend otherwise. You came into my room and told me to hang on, I had to live because I was so valuable."

Her eyebrow shot up.

"Okay, so you said my brain was valuable, same thing, Drake, whether you want to admit it or not."

"And I said you were brilliant." Sarcasm dripped from her voice.

"Well," he hedged, "not in so many words."

"I'll just bet not in so many words." Libby spun around and started back up the stairs. She couldn't remember anything about that day at the hospital. Elle had told her about her conversation with Irene. Irene's purse hadn't done the damage. Libby had collapsed all on her own. Elle had known she was in trouble, but no one would be able to tell her if she'd really had a conversation with Tyson Derrick. "You were unconscious."

"No, I wasn't."

"You were in a vegetative state."

"It was a miracle, according to Dr. Shayner. Maybe just you whispering all those compliments turned me around."

"You're so full of it." There was laughter in her voice again. "You're making all this up."

There was something about her laughter that affected him more than he cared to admit. It wasn't just that she made his body tighten and every cell come alive, it went deeper than that. He analyzed data, and she was messing with more than his hormones. When she laughed, his insides churned and his heart felt lighter. It didn't make sense, but she was nearly a drug in his system. Just being around her gave him that same rush of adrenaline he was so addicted to.

"Do I look like a man who makes things up?" he countered.

She paused again on the stair above him, turning to look up at his face. Her bottom brushed across his groin as she turned and the dull ache turned into a full-blown pain. He caught her by the arms and held her in front of him.

The smile faded from her face. Ty didn't realize he was so

close, his head bending down towards hers. Her mouth was sinfully tempting, her lips full and soft and parted just that little bit. He saw her eyes widen in shock and then his mouth took possession of hers. He wasn't thinking. If there hadn't been an earthquake before, there sure as hell was one now.

The earth moved. Maybe it spun. He didn't know. He didn't care. He kissed her again, his tongue teasing and dancing until she opened for him. Her mouth clung to his. The kiss deepened. He couldn't let go, gathering her closer, turning the kiss into something not so gentle. Blood heated, rushed and pounded as if he'd been injected with a potent testosterone-laced drug. He pulled her closer still, needing to touch her soft skin, to feel her heat, to feast on her addicting taste.

Her body moved against his and he forgot all about his ribs and his smashed chest. He forgot all about the new drug and wondering why his safety harness had failed. He simply felt, his body totally alive, every nerve ending sizzled as if he were dangling fifty feet off a rope over a blazing forest fire, intense heat all but melting him. He ravenously devoured her neck, her throat and back up again to her unbelievable mouth. He'd fantasized forever about her mouth, but not a single erotic fantasy had prepared him for the frenzied need to kiss her again and again.

Libby's arms crept up to circle his neck as she responded with complete abandon to Tyson Derrick's kisses. She wanted more. Always more. To be closer, to touch his bare skin, to feel his hard muscles, to warm her body against his heat. She needed to feel his hunger matching the sudden flare of her own. It came out of nowhere, a need so deep, so primitive, she didn't recognize herself. His kisses swept her away from the anchor of responsibility always weighing her down. She floated. She sizzled. She felt sexually desirable.

She was different. In his arms, she was different. No one had ever kissed her like that—as if he were on fire. As if he needed her, had to have her. As if she were everything to him. She ran her hand up his chest and he winced. Sanity returned in a little rush. Libby tried to pull back. His hand wrapped around the nape of her neck to hold her still and his mouth continued to command hers.

Libby's brain simply shorted out. She lost all ability to think, to reason, tumbling into a well of pure sexual feeling. It was impossible to breathe. They were exchanging air, but it wasn't enough. Her body burned for his, her fingers tangling in his dark hair.

"Libby." He whispered her name against her lips.

"I can't breathe."

"Neither can I. I can't move either. We're going to have to stand here forever unless you're willing to go find a nice quiet hidden spot on the beach."

Libby forced herself to pull back. "This isn't real, you know. I'm drugged. Totally drugged." She pressed a hand to her swollen lips, knowing she looked thoroughly kissed. The shadow on his jaw had rubbed her sensitive skin red and she was suddenly aware of her neck throbbing. She pressed her hand over her skin. "You didn't dare give me a hickey, did you?"

"Here, let me look." He pulled her hand down. "To be honest, I don't know what the hell I did." He lifted her hair and stared for a long time at her neck, finally leaning forward to press his lips against the offending spot. "I'd say you have a hickey, unless you have a strawberry birthmark."

Libby stared up at him, unable to believe he had managed to take her over like that. She was always in control. *Always.* She didn't lose her mind over men. She wasn't seduced by them and she certainly didn't have such powerful sexual reactions—not over an arrogant man who had absolutely no social skills, especially one who insulted her entire family. What was the matter with her? She wasn't all the way better. That was the only explanation for her madness.

"What drug?"

She blinked. "What are you talking about? I'm smart, Ty, but why is it I never know what you're talking about?" She let her hand glide over his sternum, rest there for just a moment before sliding it around to his ribs.

He tangled his fingers in her hair, rubbing the strands

between his fingers and thumb. "You said you were drugged, that this isn't real. I want to know what drug you're taking."

"Aspirin. I had a headache."

"And aspirin causes you to become sexually excited? Kissable? Totally alluring?"

"Obviously."

He nodded. "Make certain you take one before our dinner date."

A slow smile brought his attention back to her mouth. "Ty, we don't have a date. I'd remember."

"Not necessarily. I'm not so memorable unless I'm kissing you and I didn't kiss you in the hospital. I realize now that that was a big mistake."

Libby shook her head and took a tentative step up the stairs. She felt shaky without his arms around her. "What time is our date?"

He glanced at his watch. "In about a half hour."

"I can't get ready in half an hour. My hair's a mess and I need makeup to go out." She took a firm grip on the railing and pulled herself up the next stair. She was crazy to go out with him. He was arrogant and antisocial, didn't believe in magic and he thought all her sisters were con artists. He'd drive her crazy. Libby touched her fingers to her lips. But the man could kiss and that counted for something.

"You don't need makeup, Libby. I like the natural look."

She laughed. "You like artfully done makeup that makes women *look* natural. If I went like this you'd tell me my nose was sunburned."

"It is."

"Go away, Ty, before I come to my senses and change my mind."

"An hour, Libby. I'll be back and you'd better not be hiding in your house."

"At least you know my first name. If you'd kept calling me Drake I was going to shove you over the cliff."

"I kissed you. I can't call you Drake after I've kissed you."

"You have to forget you kissed me. There's no more kissing."

He touched the red mark on her neck. "There's proof. I won't be forgetting—and neither will you. Take the aspirin, Libby."

5

"YOU have dirt all over your face and a hickey on your neck." Hannah greeted her sister with a cup of tea. "I don't suppose you want to tell me what you've been up to while I've been grocery shopping."

Libby blew on the steaming cup. "I have dirt on my face?" She was mortified. Of course she had dirt on her face. Dirt, a hickey and a bright red sunburned nose. She was about as elegant as it got. Standing next to Hannah didn't help. Tall, blond, a runway supermodel with unbelievable exotic looks, Hannah had appeared on nearly every magazine cover there was. Hannah was thin, but she couldn't look bad if she tried.

"Yep. Your face is streaked with dirt, like a commando or something. What have you been doing? And I'm particularly interested in the hickey."

"It's a birthmark. A strawberry birthmark." Libby tried to look innocent as she sipped the hot tea.

Hannah nodded her head. "Mom will be interested in that birthmark. I'll bet she's never seen it before. She should be home in a week or two. She called and said Aunt Carol and

Dad were exploring the Napa valley, make that wineries, and she was busy hitting all the wedding shops to get ideas. I think they're having a great time."

"They always have a great time when they're together," Libby observed. "After I scared them to death, it's good for them to take a little time off." She paused before dropping the bombshell. "I'm going on a date tonight and I thought I'd wear something classy. You know, jeans and a T-shirt."

Hannah nearly tipped over her teacup. "You? A date?"

"Hey, now," Libby cautioned with a small frown of reprimand, "that's not very nice. I do get asked out on dates."

"Sorry. I know you get asked out, you just never go. Are you planning on washing your face or is your date the wild type?"

Libby sank into a chair. "I have no idea how I got myself into this."

"I'm guessing the brand new birthmark may have had something to do with it," Hannah ventured with a small grin. "You weren't rolling in the dirt with him, were you? And who is this man who managed to make you forget you're *Doctor* Libby Drake, always prim and proper?"

"I'm still prim and proper."

"Well, the dirt doesn't go with that image and neither does the hickey."

"Birthmark," Libby corrected.

"Neither does that very large and outstanding birthmark on your neck. *Were* you rolling in the dirt with him? Inquiring minds want to know."

"Of course not." Libby couldn't control the blush that stole up her neck and flushed her cheeks a bright rose to match her nose. "Of *course* not," she repeated.

Hannah shook her head, the platinum spiral curls swirling around her shoulders and down her back. "Oh, Libby. You're in real trouble with this one, aren't you? Who is he?"

"I'm not saying." Libby kicked off her shoes and put her feet up on the small ottoman. "I don't even like him."

"Oh dear, that's worse. He must kiss like a fiend. He's hot, isn't he?"

"He's an arrogant, antisocial adrenaline junkie. With an extraordinary body." Libby scowled at her sister. "I meant brain."

"Body, huh?"

"*Brain.* I meant brain. He has a brain, although he doesn't use it half the time. And he lacks social skills like you wouldn't believe. If he'd just stay quiet we could have a wonderful relationship, but he insists on talking."

"Bummer," Hannah said. "You still haven't told me his name."

Libby rolled her eyes. "Tyson Derrick."

Hannah choked on her tea. "Oh my God. You've lost your mind, Libby. You know that, don't you? You can't go out with him. He's as socially inept as Jonas."

"I know, I know." Libby covered her face with her hand and peeked out through her fingers. "I think my brain is still recovering from injuries."

A shadow fell across them and they looked up to see Jonas Harrington filling the doorway with his broad shoulders. Hannah made a face and Libby put a hand over her neck to cover all evidence. "Jonas, how good of you to sneak in."

"If I don't sneak, Hannah sends the dogs after me. I'm not socially inept, by the way. Many women find me appealing."

Hannah managed to make a snort sound elegant. The sheriff glared at her. She smiled sweetly and took a sip of tea.

"Is something wrong?" Libby asked.

"I got a call from Elle. She was worried about you. Something about a mudslide. She asked me to check on you."

"How strange that Elle felt it, too," Hannah said. "That's why I came home, Libby. For just a few moments, I felt something malevolent and then it was gone."

"Elle used that word, too," Jonas said, "but mudslides aren't malevolent. Don't turn this into one of those weird things that seem to happen when you're all together. I don't want things coming out of the fog or shadows reaching for people behind their backs. Let's keep this simple."

"I was alarmed, but I couldn't tell by what," Libby agreed.

Jonas crossed the room to crouch down in front of her. "You're covered in dirt. Something did happen, didn't it?" The teasing note disappeared from his voice.

"No big deal. Elle is so connected to all of us that she can't help but worry. It was a minor accident. Remember the conversation about erosion on nearly all the cliff faces after that heavy rain? I was sitting near the cliff wall and there was a slide. A couple of big boulders must have dislodged and started it. The rocks smashed the chairs, but I'm fine, a little dirty, but no scratches."

"But she has a new strawberry birthmark on her neck," Hannah contributed helpfully.

Libby glared at her. "Treacherous woman! And I'm helping you talk without stammering, too. What's gotten into you?"

"Why would Hannah be stammering?" Jonas asked.

"Focus on the important things, mighty sheriff man," Hannah urged. "Strawberries. Necks. Rolling in the dirt. What kind of a detective are you?"

Jonas reached over and pulled Libby's palm from her neck. He studied the mark for a long moment, finally whistling. "I'm impressed. Who managed to leave his brand on you?"

"Brand?" Libby croaked, outraged. "It isn't a brand. It's a *teeny* mark, a scrape, probably from a rock."

Jonas exchanged a long look with Hannah and they both burst out laughing. "Good try, Libby," he said. "Give me a name."

"Don't you have work to do, Jonas?" Libby asked. "I'm busy."

"You don't look busy to me," Jonas pointed out.

"Oh, she is. She has to get ready for a date tonight," Hannah pointed out. "With Tyson Derrick."

Jonas whistled again. "Tyson Derrick, the multimillionaire? You're moving up in the world, Libby. He's a hell of a lot better than the toupee guy. That man had ice water in his veins. Ty goes for excitement."

"He's a *biochemist,*" Libby said. "Not a millionaire. And he's matured over the years. I'm sure he's stopped all the crazy things he liked to do."

"Well, he climbed a mountain in the Himalayas last year. And he's gone rafting down the Colorado numerous times. He rock climbs and goes parasailing off cliffs. He fights forest fires and participates in helicopter rescues, but you're probably right. Other than driving race cars and getting speeding tickets on his motorcycle . . ."

"Don't tell me anything else." Libby covered her face again. "I can't take it. Why did I say I'd go out with him? I'm not even sure I did. I think he tricked me."

"How could he trick you?" Jonas asked. "You're pretty sharp, Libby."

"Most of the time," Libby conceded. "But I don't remember anything that happened at the hospital and he claims we had a conversation and he asked me out. I don't believe him. Dr. Shayner said he was severely brain damaged at the time which would preclude any conversation. I'm sure he made it up."

"You're sure?" Jonas teased.

"I'm almost certain." Libby sighed. "I'm confused. I don't even like him. For a man with a brilliant mind, which, by the way, I'm *positive* I wouldn't have said to him, he says the stupidest things."

"You may have told him he's brilliant?" Jonas asked.

"He's a good kisser," Hannah said helpfully.

Jonas glared at her. "You'd better not have firsthand knowledge on how that man kisses, baby doll. Having two of you getting silly over him is too much."

Hannah slammed her teacup into the saucer. "I'll kiss anyone I feel like kissing, Harrington. You're so bossy you think you can tell anyone what to do."

"You're forgetting I have a gun," he said complacently.

"I do believe you're threatening to shoot me," Hannah insisted, sparks beginning to form in the depths of her eyes.

"Not you. What the hell would I do without you to entertain me? I'd shoot *him.* Get it straight. Avoid locking lips with anyone if you know what's good for them." He stood up. "I'm going to check the cliff to make certain it's safe. I might have to rope part of it off and get some signs up."

"Thanks, Jonas," Libby said. "I didn't look at it. Ty was with me and I was distracted by his scintillating conversation."

"You mean his kisses." Hannah corrected her.

Jonas narrowed his gaze. "You seem obsessed with his kisses, Hannah."

She shrugged. "It's been a while. I'm looking for a little action."

His eyebrow shot up. "Oh, really?" Jonas leaned down, his hand twisting in her hair, holding her head perfectly still as his mouth took possession of hers.

Libby gasped in shock. The kiss seemed to go on and on forever. And there was definitely tongue. Hannah not only wasn't struggling, she seemed to be kissing him back.

Jonas pulled away just as abruptly, shoving his hat on his head and turning toward the living room. "That should hold you for a while. Next time you're feeling a little hard up, give me a call." He strode out of the room.

Hannah appeared dazed for a moment, her expression shocked, her eyes glazed and her lips slightly swollen. She opened her mouth twice before she succeeded in getting anything to emerge.

"*Eww.*" Hannah looked outraged. "He's gone crazy, Libby. Did you see that? I should have kicked him. Or kneed him. Or at the very least turned him into a toad. He *kissed* me. I've been totally violated." She glared at the empty doorway.

"You kissed him back, Hannah."

"I most certainly did *not*," she denied vehemently.

Jonas whistled as he walked out of the house, slamming the living room door as he left.

"Why didn't you kick him?" Libby asked. There was definite kissing on Hannah's part, but Libby thought it best not to pursue it.

"I couldn't think." Hannah defended herself. "He took me by surprise. He's never done anything like that before. Ugg. I can still feel him." She touched her lips with her fingertips, almost a caress, rather than rubbing the kiss off. "He's such a rat. I'm going to have nightmares. And I'm going to retaliate."

"You're going to waylay him and kiss him?" Libby asked helpfully.

"That's not funny. I'm going to find a spell that will turn his lips numb."

Libby burst out laughing. "You might want to be careful. Jonas would know and his retaliation might be much worse."

"It's always bugged me that the house lets him in, like he's family or something."

"He is family, you dope," Libby said affectionately. "Jonas is the only brother we have."

Hannah made a face. "Not to me. I'm working on finding a way to make all the doors slam in his face when he tries to get in. I tried the gate, but the lock just falls off if he approaches and I can't do anything about that."

"You spend entirely too much time thinking of ways to annoy Jonas."

"Well, that's because he annoys me. He called me scrawny the other day. *And* he said I'd lost weight again and if I lost any more he was going to put my skeleton to rest."

"When did he say that?" Libby heard the hurt in her sister's voice.

"Oh, he came by yesterday to check on you. You were asleep so he bugged me. I have to stay thin or I lose my job."

Libby studied Hannah for a moment. She was so beautiful it was easy to just dismiss everything else beyond the surface, but Jonas was right, she *was* thinner. A lot thinner. "You *are* losing weight, Hannah," she said as gently as possible. "You need to eat more."

"I can't. I have a big show coming up in New York and I was told to make certain I didn't have an ounce of weight on me. Greg Simpson implied I was gaining." Hannah looked down at her hands. "I had the phone on speaker and Jonas came in and went berserk when he heard Greg tell me to keep the weight off. Jonas said it was stupid to be so vain and I was killing myself in order to be famous and it was only my need for constant adoration." Hannah paused, pushing back her hair in an unconscious, sexy gesture. "Jonas even said he could put his hand around my thigh. He was horrible and my agent heard every word."

"Hannah. You didn't say anything to any of us. Jonas can be such an ass, but I'm sure he was thinking he was protecting you. You're beautiful and you're already very thin. I can't imagine that you've been gaining weight."

"No, but I'm getting older. You can't be on top forever."

Libby held her hand out to her sister. "You aren't old and you know it."

"This business is a young woman's game. Few careers last past late twenties and early thirties, not on the runway."

"You've banked nearly every cent you've earned. How long do you want to keep going at it?"

"What else do I have, Libby? I can't talk to people, you know that. Without you and the others to help me, I stammer and have panic attacks. I have no other skills."

"You speak several languages, Hannah."

Hannah laughed. "Libby, it doesn't do much good if I can't actually utter a word around people. Once my career is over, I'm done. I don't know who I am or what I'd do."

"I had no idea you felt that way." Libby leaned closer. "Hannah, you are eating, aren't you?"

Hannah hesitated briefly then shrugged. "I don't know how to eat anymore. I haven't eaten for the last seven years."

Libby was silent trying to remember just what Hannah did do at mealtimes. She was often in the kitchen. She cooked. She baked. She made tea. Did she actually eat? Libby couldn't remember one way or the other. Hannah did look too thin. Beautiful, but far too thin. Jonas probably *could* put his fingers around her thigh—and that was *way* too thin. Why hadn't Libby noticed? She was a doctor. "I'm sorry, baby, I should have seen you were in trouble. I'm so caught up in helping total strangers, I didn't see what was right in front of my nose."

"I'm not in trouble," Hannah denied. "Other than despising Jonas Harrington."

"If you aren't able to eat, you're in trouble, Hannah, and you know it," Libby said. "We have to get you some help."

"Not until after New York. It's a very important show. I'll concentrate on gaining a little weight after that." Hannah dismissed the subject with a wave. Her tone had a small warning note in it as she forced a smirk. "Meanwhile, I'm concentrating on working out a spell to keep Jonas out of the house and off the property. Which reminds me, your Tyson must have gone through the gate to get to the beach access."

Libby let out her breath. Hannah wasn't going to discuss her eating habits or her job anymore and was finding a way to change the subject. Libby didn't want to let it go, but she couldn't risk upsetting her sister. She needed to talk to Sarah and find the best way to handle the situation. It was highly probable that Hannah had an eating disorder. "He isn't my Tyson and the gate wasn't locked. I left it open in case Inez stopped by to see me. She said she might come for a short visit if she could get away from the grocery store." She glanced at her watch. "I'd better take a shower before Ty gets here."

"Are you wearing red panties tonight?" Hannah asked mischievously.

Libby wadded up a napkin and threw it at her sister. "Hannah, you and the rest of my sisters better not have been messing around with my underwear. Abigail's in enough trouble after that red panty ceremony . . ."

"Which you took part in," Hannah pointed out.

"For *Abbey,* not for me. I don't want to find a man. And wipe that smile off your face. If I fall, you're next."

"It's never going to happen. I can't talk to a man without all of you bolstering me. All I do is stammer or have an anxiety attack, so the possibility of me finding a man is just about nil." Hannah sounded very satisfied. "So I can cast spells, make up love potions and participate in the red panty ceremony with the rest of you to my heart's content."

"You're in so much trouble, Hannah," Libby said.

Hannah's laughter followed her up the stairs. Libby stood in front of the mirror and stared at herself. Her face was completely streaked with dirt and there was dirt in her hair. Her nose was bright red and because she'd been wearing sunglasses, she had a white raccoon mask around her eyes, just as she'd predicted.

She groaned and made a face. "Hannah! Get up here! I can't go out looking like this. Why didn't you tell me I looked awful?"

Hannah hurried into Libby's bedroom. "Just don't get under the lights and you'll be fine. We'll use a little makeup and no one will know."

"*I'll* know. I'm nervous enough around him without looking like a clown," Libby wailed.

"I hate to point this out," Hannah said, "but he's already seen you looking like this and he kissed you anyway. That's a pretty good sign he likes you. And he asked you out to dinner. How's your head? Mom and Dad aren't going to be too happy with you running around. It took all six of us girls plus Mom and Aunt Carol to save your life, Libby. If you're at all not feeling well, you shouldn't go."

Libby began to toss her clothes aside. "I still have a bit of a headache and I'm a little weak, but nothing serious. Believe me, Hannah, I'm well aware of how stupid I was risking everyone. Elle and you bore the brunt of it." Impulsively she hugged her sister. "I don't know what I would have done without you."

"Well, I happen to feel the same," Hannah said. "Why are you throwing all your clothes around?"

"I hate them all. Nothing I own makes me look"—Libby searched for the right description—"well, like you. I need perky breasts. Although at this point, *any* breasts will do, perky or otherwise."

Hannah shook her head. "You've got it bad. I've never heard you talk about your looks. I don't think you've ever even thought about how you look."

"You'll have to meet him at the door and tell him I can't go out with him. I'm serious, Hannah. I just can't do this." Libby sank down onto the bed in the middle of clothes strewn everywhere.

Hannah sat next to her. "You really like him, Libby. He wouldn't have asked you out if he didn't want to go out with you. You're beautiful and smart and funny and he obviously thinks so."

"He calls our magic 'crap.' He's abrasive and he rides a motorcycle and he's a multimillionaire. I don't want to go out with a multimillionaire. Do you remember his parents at all? Because I don't."

Hannah shook her head. "Only that they used to travel all the time and I don't think they wanted to be with him much because they were always shoving him off on his aunt. He lived with her on and off over the years. Sam told me Tyson's parents didn't understand him and were embarrassed because he was such a geek. They were jet-setters and very trendy. He wanted to stare into a microscope and talk about things—such as hot viruses—that they didn't want to think about. They died a couple of years ago and left him a fortune. I don't think he's done anything with it, but rumor has it Sam was living very well, so Tyson must have shared."

"How strange that I didn't know that," Libby said. "I know all about his education and the work he does, but I never really thought much about why he lived with Ida Chapman. It was obvious she loved him, so it seemed natural to me." She shook her head. "I just can't go out with him."

"Libby, go take a shower. You deserve to have some fun."

Libby made a face. "I'm not certain going out with him actually would be fun."

"You're stalling. I'll find you something to wear. It's just dinner, right?"

"He'd better not come to get me on his motorcycle."

"Libby!" Hannah gave her a little push. "He'll be here soon and then you'll really panic. What do I do if he comes while you're in the shower?"

"Well, don't send him up here for heaven's sake. Occupy him."

"With kisses?" Hannah teased.

"Jonas will shoot him. You'd better not do that." Libby pressed a hand to her stomach at the thought of Tyson with Hannah. "*Why* do you have to be so beautiful?"

Hannah stiffened. "I'm not really, you know," she said. "You don't see men knocking down the door to take me out."

Libby turned quickly enough to see the hurt on Hannah's face. "Baby, I'm sorry. I didn't mean to make you feel bad."

Hannah flashed a small smile, but it didn't light her eyes. "I'm just feeling sensitive. Greg asked me if it was possible to get a breast reduction. I'm down to a size two but apparently someone complained that my breasts are too big."

"Hannah, you're five foot eleven. You're intelligent enough to know that Greg is an idiot if he wants you any smaller. You're lucky you have breasts without any weight on you."

"I know. Like I said, I'm feeling a little sensitive. It isn't a big deal."

"It is to me, if you're feeling bad about yourself."

"I'd better go man the door just in case your date arrives," Hannah said.

Libby turned on the water as hot as she could stand it and stood under the pulsing shower contemplating what she should do about her younger sister. Hannah always seemed happy. She was loving and giving and generous with her time to her sisters. She didn't make friends easily and kept to herself, seemingly content in between her modeling assignments to stay at their home in Sea Haven. Hannah was the last person Libby would have thought might be unhappy. Why hadn't she noticed? Was she so wrapped up in her own life that she hadn't noticed her sister losing weight? Looking sad? She should have felt her unhappiness. Jonas Harrington had seen Hannah was in trouble before Libby had.

She shampooed her hair while she considered how best to help Hannah. Did she pretend to be happy because she already felt a bother to her sisters? They lent their support to her on a regular basis, so much so that it was automatic. None of them thought anything about it, but maybe Hannah did. Was she upset because she felt she needed her sisters to go out into the public and do her job? That was likely, now that Libby thought about her personality. They had all hoped she'd grow out of her anxiety in public, but it had worsened, rather than getting better.

Libby wrapped a bath sheet around her and covered her hair with a towel, turban style, as she stepped out of the shower. She nearly ran straight into Jonas and let out a little shriek when he grabbed her shoulders to steady her. "What are you doing? You're getting weirder every day, Jonas. This is the *bathroom.*"

"How the hell was I supposed to know what room it was? I don't exactly come up here that often. I have some questions."

"How did you get past Hannah?"

"She's busy making up some spell against me," Jonas said. "She looks kind of cute all serious like that, muttering to herself."

"Her spells really work, Jonas," Libby cautioned.

"Not on me. Not so far. And it gives her something to do besides get in trouble. Where's all your psychic intuition? You should have known I was in the house. So should Hannah, for that matter."

Libby shrugged. "We rely on the house to warn us. It knows you. You're no threat to us."

"I am to Hannah. If she doesn't start taking care of herself I'm going to do something drastic."

Libby looked up at the hard edge to his voice. His jaw was set in the stubborn line she knew so well. "I'll make sure she does. What did you want?"

"Well, I've been thinking about how odd it was for you to mess with someone injured so severely when you knew how dangerous it was. It's not like you. You're always careful that no harm can come to your sisters. And then there was Irene. It was completely out of character for her to start beating on you with her purse. And I've looked at the erosion on the cliff. That landslide didn't just start on its own. Have you done something to some . . ." He trailed off and cleared his throat. "You know. Sorcerer? Voodoo queen? Maybe one of you conjured up a spirit and it's royally pissed that you brought it here."

Libby burst out laughing. "Jonas. You're such an idiot. You know very well what we do and don't do. And we don't conjure up spirits, bad ones or good ones."

"Well, something isn't right, Libby. One of the boulders was pried out of the ground and it set off the landslide. I found two slide marks in the mud, but no real shoe print. I went down to the beach and examined the boulders. Most of the rocks are still intact and I could see scratches from some tool. How would someone have gotten on your property to do that kind of damage?"

"I left the gates open for Inez. I told her I was going to be on the beach. Maybe someone saw something suspicious."

"You can't see up there from the beach and the way the terrain dips down, no one from the road would have seen either. Was Hannah home at the time?"

"No, she just returned a few minutes before I came up from the beach."

"Do you have enemies?"

"Well, of course I do. People think I can raise the dead. Just like Irene, they think I'm *choosing* to allow their child to die. If someone believes I can heal their dying child, but I refuse, don't you think they're going to be really angry with me, especially if that child does die?"

"Have you had any recent threats besides Edward Martinelli?"

"Take your pick. I get them all the time." She didn't want to admit to him she didn't remember who Edward Martinelli was, but she must have looked confused because Jonas gave her a brief hug, towel and all.

"He sent someone to see you and requested a meeting, Libby. They weren't very nice about it and you said you felt threatened. They mentioned Hannah's name. I'm looking into it."

She pressed a hand to her throat. "I hate not remembering an entire block of time out of my life. I do know I have a file of threats, Jonas. I can give it to you if you think it's necessary."

"Absolutely I want it as soon as possible. I'm taking this very seriously and I want you to do so as well."

"It's a little impossible to be serious about anything when I'm standing here in a towel, Jonas," Libby pointed out.

"Harrington!" Tyson Derrick yanked open the door to the bathroom. "What the hell are you doing in the shower with Libby?"

"He's in the shower with her?" Hannah squeezed past Tyson to glare at Jonas, hands on her hips. "You're such a skunk."

"How did you get in here?" Libby demanded of Tyson, gripping the towel to make certain it wasn't slipping. "This is the *bathroom,* not a convention hall. Has everyone lost their mind?"

"Hannah let me in," Ty said. "And it's a good thing she did."

"Why is that?" Libby asked before she could stop herself.

"I'm going to throw Harrington out on his ass."

"Oh, good," Hannah said. "Finally someone with the right idea."

"I wasn't *in* the shower with her, Derrick," Jonas hissed between his teeth. "Whatever Hannah may have implied. I happen to be investigating what may have been an attempt on Libby's life, so back off." His eyes flashed sparks at Hannah.

Hannah wrapped her arm around Libby, the laughter fading from her eyes. "What do you mean, Jonas? Do you think someone's trying to hurt Libby?"

"I don't know, that's what I'm trying to find out. There are a couple of things that just aren't adding up for me."

Sarah, eldest of the Drake sisters, pushed her way into the bathroom. "What are we doing in here, entertaining?" Behind her, Kate and Abigail hovered in the doorway trying to see around Tyson.

Libby hid her face on Hannah's arm. "This is turning into a circus."

"Is it always like this?" Ty asked, one black brow raised in inquiry.

"Pretty much, yes," Jonas answered.

"Libby, what is that on your neck?" Sarah demanded.

Kate and Abigail crowded into the room to examine Libby's exposed neck. Libby turned bright red and clapped a hand over the offending mark.

"It's a brand new birthmark," Hannah explained.

The three Drake sisters turned as one to look at Jonas. He held his hands up. "It wasn't me. Why do you always blame me for everything? I'm not about to be biting on Libby's neck."

"It was Tyson Derrick." Hannah gave the name up without a qualm.

Ty held up his hand as all eyes turned to him. "That would be me. I don't believe I've met everyone. Sarah and Kate, yes."

"I'm Abigail."

"Nice to meet you. Libby and I have a date tonight. She's late."

"I wouldn't be late if everyone would stop coming into the bathroom. Get out. All of you. This dating business isn't as easy as it looks."

"She's cranky," Hannah said to her sisters. "Let's let her get dressed. Jonas can tell us why he thinks someone tried to hurt Libby."

"Good idea," Tyson said. "If there was an attempt on her life, I'd like to know about it."

"Libby!" Sarah said. "Why wouldn't you tell me?"

"I'm getting a headache," Libby wailed, pressing the heel of her hand against her forehead. "And if I don't dry my hair it's going to frizz."

"Libby," Sarah insisted.

"Jonas doesn't know for certain. The cliff sort of crumbled and it just happened."

"I've seen you with your hair frizzy," Ty said. "It wasn't that bad. More like frothy fuzz than if you stuck your finger in a light socket. Just throw on some clothes so we can go. And I was with Libby when the cliff crumbled. Erosion, pure and simple."

"When did my hair look like frothy fuzz?" Libby demanded.

Hannah signaled frantically, but Ty frowned at the ceiling, missing her gestures completely. "Several times. The most memorable was when you arrived ten minutes late to Dr. Chang's class and slammed the door, interrupting his lecture. He would have thrown anyone else out, but not the royal princess, Libby Drake. Your hair was wild and you were wearing jeans with a frayed hem and a hole in the right back pocket. Your shirt was two sizes too big and you had it knotted around your waist."

Libby pointed to the door. "Get out. Get out right now."

"I'm rather impressed he remembered every detail of what you were wearing when it was several years ago," Sarah said.

"You get out, too," Libby said. "My hair is not wild."

She glared at everyone until they filed out. As soon as the door closed, she pulled the towel from her hair and stared at her image in the mirror. Her hair was wild, but it wasn't her fault. She needed to tame it the moment she was out of the shower. And she still had those jeans. They were her all-time favorite. She'd even thought about wearing them to dinner, but now she'd have to find something else. The water had washed away the dirt, but she still had a raccoon mask from her sunglasses and her nose was bright red. Libby sighed and gave up. There was no miraculously saving the evening. Ty had already seen her as she really was.

6

"THE Chinese ideogram for trouble symbolizes two women living under one roof. What do you suppose the ideogram for seven women under one roof is?" Tyson asked as he broke off a piece of freshly baked bread.

"Joy," Libby answered immediately. "I like this place. I come here sometimes with my sisters. The food is excellent." She tried to relax, to just breathe and not blurt out that she didn't date much and was terribly uncomfortable. He'd probably laugh at her. She flew all over the world and exuded complete confidence in every area of her life except her personal one. The truth was, she had no idea why she was sitting across the table from Tyson Derrick.

"I knew you liked the restaurant."

She sat back in her chair and regarded him over the flickering candle. The shadows on his face emphasized his good looks, the stubborn set to his jaw and the sensual shape of his mouth. He wore a dark jacket over a blue shirt and faded blue jeans rather than slacks. Libby thought he looked incredible. "You seem to know a lot about me."

"People have a tendency to talk about your family."

Libby set her glass down and looked him directly in the eye. There was something about the way he said it, his tone, a curl of his lip, maybe even contempt in his gaze. "What does that mean?"

He shrugged. "Your family likes publicity. I think that's common knowledge."

She stiffened. "I am not going to sit with you and have dinner while you make disparaging remarks about my family. I can leave right now if you'd like."

"Don't be silly, Libby. You're too sensitive when it comes to your family. Of course people talk about them. Hannah is a supermodel. Her face is everywhere. Joley sells out every concert. If she makes a CD, it sells over a million copies immediately and hits number one on the charts. She wins every music award possible. Kate's books are bestsellers and stay on the *Times* list for weeks."

"That's only three of us, Ty. I'm a doctor, Sarah does security and Abigail is a marine biologist."

"And Elle? She does seem to manage to fly under the radar."

Libby's gaze shifted away from his. "Elle programs computers."

Tyson smiled at her. "Don't ever try to play poker, Libby. The point is, all of you are well known, whether you like it or not. Doesn't going into the music industry or modeling or even writing books demonstrate a need for attention?"

"No." She glared at him. "Joley plays music because it's who she is. She happened to get lucky and make it big, but that's beside the point. She was born to make music and Kate *has* to write. She'd be writing whether she was published or not. Abigail loves the ocean and sea life. I needed to help people." She leaned her chin into her palm. "What about you? Why do you work in a laboratory and fly rescues in helicopters?"

His eyebrow shot up. "You don't think it's for humanitarian reasons?"

"No. I think you're very removed from the human race

most of the time, Ty. That's part of the reason you don't understand my family."

The waiter placed the plates in front of them and Tyson waited for him to leave before he sat back in his chair and regarded her through half closed eyes. "I suppose I am. I wish I could tell you I find cures for various diseases because I want to help mankind, but I'm just not that nice."

He wanted to lie to her, to give her an answer that would make her admire him, but he wasn't about to deceive her. Her entire life was built around a deception and those closest to her continued to perpetuate it. He loved looking at her, sitting across from her watching the shadows play across her face, and it suddenly occurred to him that he should exercise a little diplomacy—an art he'd never bothered to learn.

Libby studied his face. There was an expression in his eyes, hunger, desire, longing, she couldn't describe it exactly but she knew he hadn't wanted to tell her the truth. "You aren't as bad as you think you are. You've done a lot of good, Ty."

"For selfish reasons."

She shook her head. "Is it selfish of Joley to need to play music? Or Kate to write books? You do what you do because your nature demands it. You *have* to find answers. You were driven in college and you still are as an adult."

Deep inside his gut twisted and a vise seemed to squeeze his heart. She was so nonjudgmental, accepting his need, the furious compulsions that drove him, that kept him in his laboratory for weeks and months. The need was so strong and he was so focused at times he had complete tunnel vision, uncaring of his own health or the needs of the people around him. No one, not even Sam, had ever understood his relentless pursuit of science let alone simply accepted it as being integral to his nature.

He was all too aware of her sitting across from him. Desire spread like fire, leaping through his body, igniting every nerve ending until he was acutely aware of every breath she took. His mind captured and stored every detail, the way she turned her head, the way her hair fell like tousled silk around her shoulders so that he needed to feel it against his skin. Everything about her intrigued him—and it always had.

He took a sip of wine and allowed his gaze to drift over her with infinite slowness. He could look at her forever. It was silly, really, how much he loved looking at her. He'd discovered the pastime in college when he was bored with his classes. She was so transparent, expressions chasing across her face, her eyes lighting up when she laughed—and there was her mouth. He loved her mouth, the way her lips were full and turned up at the corners. The way she could look sexy with her hair a mess, no makeup and in jeans, like now. Who else could do that? He had a sudden impulse to lean over and kiss her. The taste of her still lingered in his mouth—and mind, making him edgy with need.

"You're staring at me, Ty." Embarrassed, Libby lifted a hand to cover her sunburned nose. She couldn't wear dark glasses at night and not be conspicuous so he was probably staring at the white raccoon mask around her eyes.

"Am I?" He had fantasized about her a million times, but he'd never once thought she would be sitting across the table from him looking shy and confused, a soft rose color creeping up her neck to draw attention to her soft skin. "I like looking at you."

"That's a nice thing to say. Thank you."

"You're welcome. How much do you know about voodoo?"

"Voodoo?" Suddenly wary, Libby retreated, pulling back away from him. "I know a little bit. Why?"

"I just find things interesting and voodoo is a practice with thousands of believers even today. It's total bunk, of course, but the people who practice it are so fanatical they can actually present genuine physical symptoms or even die when they believe they're cursed. It goes to show how powerful our minds are."

She nodded her head in agreement. "I've seen women who want to be pregnant so badly that they manifest all the signs. The brain is extraordinary."

"The witch doctor holds tremendous power over his

believers and yet in the end, instead of benefiting his followers, he dupes them. When you get right down to it, he's nothing but a con artist."

"Not all of them, Ty. Many of the witch doctors I've met actually do practice natural medicine and have an extensive knowledge of herbs."

"I'll bet they do. Herbs and poisons. That's how voodoo priestesses gained the reputation for raising the dead and creating zombies to use as slaves. The truth is, they gave their victims a potent cocktail consisting of neurotoxins such as the poison of an adder fish, which is one of the strongest nerve poisons known to man."

Libby nodded. "The clinical drug Norcuron has similar effects and is used in surgery to relax the patient's muscles. The poison from the pufferfish would cause severe neurological damage primarily affecting the left side of the brain which controls the speech, memory and motor skills. The victim becomes lethargic and then seems to die. By the way, he's still awake to witness his own funeral and burial."

"You haven't by chance performed this ceremony have you?" Ty asked.

She smirked at him. "Along with the pufferfish poison, the potion contains gland sections from the bouga toad, which basically are the drugs bufogenin and bufotoxin. The compounds are fifty to one hundred times more potent than digitalis and are essential ingredients for making a zombie. The secretions also contain bufotenine, which is a hallucinogen."

"So not only do you know your drugs, but you know how to make a zombie."

Libby smiled at him. "Like you, I find quite a few subjects fascinating."

Tyson let his breath out slowly. She wasn't getting the correlation between the witch doctor and her family. She was extremely intelligent, but like the practitioners of voodoo, she had grown up completely brainwashed.

"Don't you find it the least bit embarrassing as a doctor to have to explain your family to other people?"

He asked so casually at first she barely registered what he'd said. When the words sunk in, Libby had to resist the urge to throw her ice water over him. "You think my family is *embarrassing*? Have you considered that maybe for all your brains you are the stupidest, most socially inept person in the world when it comes to understanding people? I am *not* in the least embarrassed about my family or what *all* of us do."

"You're angry, aren't you? There's no need to get upset, Libby. We're just having a casual conversation. Why do women always take things personally?"

"Calling my family embarrassing *is* personal."

Tyson moved food around on his plate before forking a piece of chicken while he contemplated the situation. He chewed slowly, a faint frown on his face. If he was going to get her to use her brain and see her family for what it was, he was going to have to go a lot slower. She was intensely loyal, a great trait, but one that would be a severe impairment to his plan. "I never said I found your family embarrassing. I simply asked if you did. You were the one getting personal saying I was socially inept. As for being stupid, the charge is ludicrous and I won't even address it." He took a sip of wine and regarded her over the glass.

"In answer to your question, I'm well aware I lack social skills. And for your information, my parents were embarrassed by me all the time, so much so that they foisted me off on poor Sam and my Aunt Ida. Can you imagine what it was like for Sam to have me in school in the same classes with him? I was several years younger, a total geek and a nerd. I completely embarrassed him more than once and I still do."

Libby couldn't break away from his piercing gaze. There was no self-pity in his voice, he stated only fact. She was an empath, and whether he knew it or not—and she doubted he did—there was an underlying sadness in Tyson when he spoke of his parents. He was talking about his past and what had been painful, and still was, yet there was such longing in his eyes.

"You're right." She was ashamed of herself for jumping down his throat. Had anyone else said what Tyson had just said, she'd have known they meant to be insulting, but Tyson didn't think that way. In his mind, she was certain he thought he was being logical, separating the issues and comparing them to his own life. "I jumped to conclusions. I'm sure your parents weren't embarrassed by you, Ty. As children we often draw incorrect conclusions about why our parents do things."

His eyebrow shot up. She had a thing for his eyebrow, black as a raven's wing, drawing attention to the intensity of his blue eyes.

"You sound like one of the twenty-seven psychiatrists my parents sent me to. They wanted to find out what was wrong with me, why I wasn't normal."

She sat up straighter. She could feel his pain, buried so deep he truly wasn't aware of it. "Ty, they didn't really send you to twenty-seven psychiatrists, did they?" She ached for him, for that never understood little boy.

"Absolutely they did. They wanted me to be normal. I think it was great to *talk* about having a genius for a son, but it was something altogether different living with one. I talked about things they had no interest in or understanding of. They told me many times I was a great embarrassment to them for my antisocial behavior."

She pressed her lips together to keep from expressing sympathy, knowing he wouldn't want it. She had wonderful parents who doted on her all the time. Her sisters were loving and supportive and her aunts and uncles and cousins were the same. She couldn't imagine parents not wanting a child around or saying mean, hurtful things to their only son. Tears clogged her throat, shimmered in her eyes.

"Don't look so sad, Libby," Ty said. He reached out to run a finger down her cheek, tracing the path of a tear. "I didn't even notice after a while. I had other things to occupy my mind. I think I obsessed over their opinion of me when I was around seven or eight, but then I just accepted the fact that I was different and they weren't going to change and neither was I. Once I realized it, I moved on to the things I was really interested in. And I had Aunt Ida. She may not have really understood me, but she loved me and she always wanted me. She gave me the entire basement for a laboratory. I was in heaven. My parents didn't want me messing with chemicals or anything that could possibly blow anything up. Aunt Ida encouraged me. After a while I wanted to stay here in Sea Haven with her. It was just easier."

"But you didn't," Libby said.

"No, my parents would drag me back every now and then so we'd look good for some write-up in a magazine. They tried, don't get me wrong, they wanted to be great parents, but they just didn't understand how to parent me."

"I didn't hear about their death until recently. What happened?"

"A plane crash. It was a couple of years ago. I still haven't sorted everything out. The estate was overwhelming. I hide in the laboratory and try to forget about it most of the time. I know I've got to deal with it, but it's just not a priority for me. Sam and I had a talk about it a couple of weeks ago. He took care of most of the details for me and has been overseeing a lot of things, but I can't keep expecting him to do it. He has a life, too, and sorting out the estate is a full-time job."

"You're very close to your cousin, aren't you?"

"He's more of a brother than a cousin. He tries to understand me just the way my aunt did." A small grin spread across his face, softening the hard lines that were etched in his face, making him appear almost boyish. "*Tries* being the operative word. He's given up trying to double-date with me. He says I'm abrasive."

"Imagine that."

He shrugged. "I get bored easily with inane conversation. I try to keep my mouth shut and just listen but after a while I can't take it and I have to leave. I see it as the lesser of two evils, but unfortunately, my dates don't agree."

"You don't sound like that bothers you very much."

He ducked his head. "Not especially. I wish it did. I want

it to. I just can't seem to dredge up the effort to care what people think of me."

"Not even for Sam?"

He sat back in his chair, fiddling with the stem of the wineglass, frowning a little as he thought about it. "No. Sam doesn't need me to be charming. We don't move in the same circles most of the time. He has his life and I have mine. Even when we're sharing the house, I'm mostly in the basement."

"You bring your work home," she guessed. "You take the time off, but you're still working."

"I can't let it go for long. I start thinking about things and then I have to experiment. Sam's used to me disappearing. He's the one that always looks after things, pays the bills, keeps the refrigerator stocked, but recently I realized what a burden I was putting on him and decided to get a full-time accountant. I'm trying to take some of the pressure off of him, to assume more of the responsibility."

"Sam? He's always so—" Libby paused, searching for the right word. Did Sam ever appear anything but charming? Certainly not pressured. "Laid back? Easygoing? I heard you shared your inheritance with him. That was generous of you."

He laughed. "Generous of me? The money doesn't mean anything at all to me. Half the time I forget it's there. Sam shared his mother and his house with me. The money is nothing compared to that, Libby."

She heard the complete honesty in his voice. Maybe it had to do with the fact that the money had belonged to his parents, or that he was quite capable of making his own very good living, or maybe it was just his character, but she believed him—and she admired him. There was a lot more to Tyson than she'd ever thought.

"Why do you go parasailing and fight fires and find the wildest river to raft down? What drives you to do that?"

"I want to feel alive."

"Doesn't it bother you that you risk your bril—" She bit off what she was going to say. "That you risk your mind?"

His smile touched his eyes, warmed them to a deep blue. And there was too much heat in his smile. It was sensual and set the blood pounding in her veins.

"You were going to say brilliant, Libby. See? You *did* call me brilliant, didn't you? In the hospital."

His smile was so sexy. Everything about him was sexy, especially when he was teasing her. "I'm sure I didn't. You made the entire conversation up. I didn't say yes to a date at all."

"You really don't remember anything?"

"Bits and pieces. What about you?" She was curious as to what he did remember of that day.

"The rescue. Falling. It's all a little hazy. I don't remember much until I was in the hospital. I swear I saw Joe Fields there. He was standing in the corridor, but if he was really there, why didn't he come in and talk to me?"

"Who's Joe Fields?"

"He works in the corporate offices of BioLab and he's a good friend of one of the biochemists working on the PDG."

"Really? He must have heard about your accident and came to see you. I'm sure you're very important to your company."

"He couldn't have made it to Sea Haven that fast. Even by plane. He didn't have time. He had to have been here before the accident." Ty shook his head. "Or maybe I was so out of it I just imagined him. On the other hand, I remember that I dreamt about you when I was unconscious." A faint, slightly self-derisive smile curled his mouth. "I do that a lot so it isn't surprising. Then I opened my eyes and saw your face and thought I was dreaming. God, you're beautiful." His voice roughened and his eyes darkened even more.

Libby felt the rasp of his voice tripping little arcs of electricity through her body. Why was she so susceptible to him? She'd never felt such an overwhelming pull towards one man in her life. Not so all-consuming. Her throat was dry, as were her lips. She wanted to touch him. Her fingers *itched* to touch him. Libby Drake, always in control, was fast sweeping out of control by the slow burn spreading through her body with every heated look he gave her.

"I'm not, you know," she said, "beautiful." It took a while to find her voice. No man had ever called her beautiful before, but Tyson couldn't seem to take his eyes off of her. His desire was so stark and raw she couldn't help but believe his sincerity.

"You are to me. I really do dream about you."

He took another drink of wine and she watched him swallow. Even that was erotic. She had it bad. "You dream about me?"

His faint smile failed to reach his eyes. "You don't want to know what I dream, you'd slap my face."

A slow flush spread over her entire body. His voice was such a turn-on to her. God help her, all she wanted to know in that moment was *exactly* what he dreamt about her. All she could think about was tasting his skin. She closed her eyes and took a drink of the ice water, hoping it would help. It didn't. She touched her tongue to the beads melting on the outside of the glass, wishing it was his chest.

"Damn it, Libby. You're killing me. I don't have as much discipline as you think I do. Maybe we should find a bed and get it over with."

His abrupt tone, almost a snarl, brought her up short. What was she thinking? Libby knew her nature inside and out. She wasn't a one-night-stand woman. She didn't have flings. And she had always, *always* been far too aware of Tyson Derrick to think she'd walk away unscathed. He wanted sex. Plain and simple and who could blame him with the way she'd been acting? She'd been mentally undressing him most of the evening. She pressed the glass against her burning face.

"Libby?"

She cleared her voice. "While I really appreciate the invitation, especially the utter finesse with which you delivered it, I still think I'll have to pass."

"Why?"

The challenge in his voice dug under her skin, raising prickles until she felt her temper beginning to stir. Or maybe it wasn't his challenge, maybe she just wanted him so bad she was edgy and restless and wanting to pick a fight with him. Need clawed in the pit of her stomach, raging at her so she had to look away.

Libby's gaze collided with a man at the table to her left, only feet away. Recognition jolted through her. Her breath left her body in a rush and she sat up straighter, her eyes suddenly wide with fear as she turned back toward Ty.

His reaction astonished him. One moment Tyson could feel the lust of a lifetime raking his gut, hardening his body, hammers driving through his skull until his head thundered and his blood thickened and poured into his lower region with such ferocious heat he feared he might spontaneously combust, and then she looked at him with fear instead of passion. She looked vulnerable and fragile instead of sultry and seductive.

Everything in him responded on the most primitive, protective level, just as it had on a sexual level. He had *never* felt protective in his life, yet he wanted to stand up and smash something—or someone. He wanted to sweep her into his arms and shelter her against his stronger body. Cracked ribs and torn muscles aside, he suddenly was a caveman, adrenaline rushing and the need to protect her swamping him, even dampening the intensity of his physical attraction.

He reached out to take her hand, wrapping his fingers securely through hers to let her know she wasn't alone. He heard several chairs scrape and turned his head as three men surrounded the table, pulling out chairs and seating themselves without an invitation.

"I don't suppose you noticed you're interrupting a private dinner." Tyson greeted them sarcastically. He raised his hand to summon the waiter.

One of the men moved his jacket casually to reveal a gun in a shoulder harness. Instead of sobering him, Tyson felt fury sweep through his body. He nearly came across the table to strangle the man. He was well aware of Libby's pale face and her fingers tightening around his as if to restrain him. "Is that supposed to intimidate me?"

"I want a few words with the young lady," the tallest of the three men said in a low tone. "I'm John Sandoval and these are my colleagues. I'm here on behalf of my boss, Edward Martinelli. I only need a few minutes of her time to avoid a lot of unpleasantness. I'm certain she doesn't wish to make these photographs public." He tossed several eight-by-ten's on the table in front of Ty.

Tyson glanced down at the pictures. They were of him in his hospital room, obviously taken through the glass partition. He appeared to be in bad shape, unconscious, tubes and lines running from his body to machines. Libby stood over his unconscious body. It must have been the reflection of the flash in the window because she seemed to glow, as if her body gave off a strange light, the aura surrounding her white hot. Her hands were on his head and her eyes were closed.

His heart jolted hard in his chest and then began to pound. There was pain on her face. Not just pain, but gut-wrenching agony. And in each succeeding photograph, the pain appeared to grow worse until blood flecked the corner of her mouth and tears tracked down her face. The last picture showed him alert and wholly conscious and Libby huddling against the wall looking lost and vulnerable.

"You see now." John leaned forward, flicking the pictures with his finger. "It would not be good for the tabloids to get these photos along with a copy of your brain scan after your accident."

"And just how would you have gotten his confidential records?" Libby demanded. Her fingers tightened on Tyson's until her knuckles turned white, but she kept her voice even.

John shrugged. "These hospitals are so careless leaving patient files everywhere. My boss simply is asking for a few minutes of your time. He's a generous man, but not a patient or forgiving one. You do not want to be his enemy."

"And he does not want to threaten me," Libby said and her green eyes began to smolder with quiet fury. The wine in Tyson's glass bubbled and frothed blood red. She tried not to let them see they'd kicked her in the gut. If those pictures were printed in a tabloid, she and her sisters would become the next media freak show.

"Edward Martinelli is a friend of mine," Ty said. "We go

rafting and climbing together. I intend to give him a call and let him know you're harassing and threatening Miss Drake." Tyson pushed the photographs back across the table, contempt showing in every line of his face. "Anyone can doctor photographs. All they need is a software program and they can produce any effect they want. I'm not impressed with your so-called evidence."

Libby didn't dare look at Tyson. She was catching some of his thoughts. He didn't believe in the Drake sisters' gifts and felt if they hadn't been so eager to get the world to believe they could perform magic, these kinds of threats wouldn't happen. He hadn't noticed the wine in the glasses or the coffee in the mugs bubbling. She took a breath and let it out slowly to calm herself down. Very casually she laid her palm over the nearest wineglass to still the bubbles.

Tyson ran a finger down Libby's arm to get her attention, giving her a brief smile. "The sheriff will be here any minute. He's rather fond of Libby and trying to blackmail her isn't going to go over big."

"You misunderstand," John said, reaching for the pictures.

A hand reached over his shoulder and scooped up the pictures. "Libby, I'm sorry we're late for dessert. Have you ordered yet?" Elle Drake handed the photographs to the man standing behind her.

Jackson Deveau towered over Elle, but only because she was short. He was a stocky man with broad shoulders and obvious power, unlike Jonas Harrington's much more subtle strength. Jackson's features were set in hard lines, his eyes glittering with menace. "Gentlemen, I believe you're in our seats."

The same man who had moved his jacket to show his gun, did so a second time, a casual gesture meant to intimidate. Instantly Jackson's hand circled the nape of the man's neck and slammed his head violently to the tabletop. The muzzle of the gun in the deputy's other hand pressed deep against his skull. "Libby, Ty, move back from the table now."

Tyson had already risen, pulling Libby out of her chair and behind him. Ty glanced around the room. The other occupants were silent, watching the drama unfold. Mason Fredrickson, one of Sea Haven's residents, and an older man Ty didn't recognize flanked Jackson. Both men were reserve law enforcement, willing to back up local authorities when there was no one else available.

John didn't move but the other man reached inside his coat and Mason pinned his hand. "I wouldn't. You don't know Jackson. He'd shoot all three of you and then we'd have to clean up this place before we could have dinner. Just keep your hands on the table."

Jackson cuffed the first man and put the second one in flex cuffs. All the while John Sandoval merely stared at Libby. "They have permits to carry the guns." His gaze remained on her face. "This is all so unnecessary. He only wants to speak with you, a few minutes of your time. To anger him would be foolish." He lifted Libby's water glass in a casual gesture and took a drink, no expression on his face.

Sandoval choked. He dropped the tumbler of water so that glass shattered across the table and the liquid soaked into the cloth. Both hands went to his collar. He tore desperately at it, his coloring mottled. Libby pushed Tyson out of her way and rushed to Sandoval's side as Jackson and the other two men pulled their prisoners away from the table. Sandoval went down to his knees, Libby's arm preventing him from falling. She took one look at his face, the gasping for air and turned her head, her gaze locking with her younger sister's. They stared at one another for a long moment.

Libby lowered Sandoval to the floor and loosened his collar. His lips turned blue and he made terrible gasping sounds. Using her body to cut off the view of the others in the room as best she could, Libby traced symbols in the air over his head. The lines glowed silver and sparkled, revealing another darker set of symbols. Libby hissed and glanced back at Elle.

The silver sparkles leapt over the darker ones, extinguishing them. Libby bent over the man, her lips against his ear as she seemed to be aiding him. "It would be *very* foolish of you to threaten anyone in my family," she whispered.

Libby stood up and moved back behind Tyson to Elle. She caught her younger sister by the arm. They stood, nearly nose to nose, staring at one another. Elle reached out and jerked Libby to her, holding her close. *I feel and see danger all around you, around your aura, and I can't find the source. I'm so afraid for you.*

Elle rarely used telepathic communication, so Libby often forgot she was a strong telepath, but her sister's voice was clear in her mind, the fear echoing loudly. Libby laced her fingers through her sister's, connecting them together so they could feel power leaping back and forth. On some level Libby was aware of Jackson removing the three men from the restaurant and the waiters hastily cleaning the table off, but it all seemed far away.

Is it Edward Martinelli?

I can't tell. I don't want to be away from you and Hannah is uneasy as well. I need to talk to Sarah to see if she's picked up anything evil lurking in the shadows around you.

When I was in the hospital, before I began to heal Ty, did you feel it then?

Elle looked confused, close to tears. *I don't know. I'm sorry. I don't know.*

For just one moment, Elle's mind was open to Libby and she caught a glimpse of the terrible burden her youngest sister had to bear. The continual bombardment of thoughts, of emotions, the awareness of people around her, especially her sisters and their private hopes and fears. Elle knew their secrets and she fought to keep their privacy. Libby felt the oppressive burden of all those secrets and the tremendous power always running through Elle's body, the feeling that she must keep everyone safe.

She hugged Elle close to her, deliberately allowed her hands to run up and down her sister's arms, the warmth opening deep inside her so that Libby could ease Elle's suffering. *I'm safe tonight, baby. Thank you for loving me so much.*

Elle blinked back tears and looked around her, startled to see Mason Fredrickson and a waiter and Tyson so close.

They were forming a wall with their bodies, blocking off the Drake sisters from prying eyes.

"You okay?" Tyson asked, reaching for Libby's hand. "You look pale." He drew her hand to his shoulder.

"Yes, I'm fine. I'm sorry to put you in that position. Martinelli must be desperate to send men with guns to intimidate me into talking with him. Do you really know him?"

"Yes. I know him and this just doesn't sound at all like him. Whoever this John Sandoval is, he isn't associated with Ed. I'll call Ed and let him know what's going on," Ty said.

"I hope you're right," Libby replied. She turned her attention to Mason Fredrickson, a man her older sisters had gone through school with. "Thank you, Mason. It was courageous of you to back Jackson."

"I was having dinner with Sylvia and she realized you were in trouble. She could tell by your expression. I'm reserve with the sheriff and so is Mike Dangerfield, so we just kept an eye on things. I'll catch you all later." He sauntered across the room back to the small intimate table in a darker corner of the restaurant.

Elle and Libby exchanged a quick glance. *Are they getting back together?* Elle sent the question to her sister.

Libby shrugged. She hoped so. Mason had been good for Sylvia and in spite of the fact that she'd had an affair, Sylvia obviously loved him and had helped save her ex-husband's life when someone had tried to kill him. Deliberately Libby peeked around Tyson's larger frame and waved to Sylvia, mouthing a thank-you.

Sylvia beamed, waving back. Elle added her small smile to Libby's larger one and lifted a tentative hand in response. "I guess I'd better be going."

Libby caught her sister by the arm and held on. "Have dessert with us." She didn't want to face Tyson's questions, or his judgment on the things her family could do. He'd seen the brief argument between the sisters and their magic. Elle had backed off, but she had resisted at first, her fear for

Libby overcoming her inhibitions of using their talents in public.

Elle shook her head. She was trembling. "I think I need to go home and lie down." She rubbed her temples. "I've been getting those headaches again, Libby."

"I'll come with you," Libby said instantly. She smiled up at Tyson. "Thank you for such a wonderful evening. I had fun right up until Sandoval and his henchmen joined us."

"I don't know, that was kind of fun, too," Ty said with a faint grin. "Didn't you come with the sheriff? I'm Tyson Derrick, by the way. You're Elle?"

"The *deputy,*" Elle corrected. "And yes, I was running here and he picked me up. Nice to meet you. I'm sorry for horning in on your date."

"I was getting myself into trouble anyway," Ty admitted. "I annoy Libby on so many levels."

"Not all of them, obviously," Elle said, brushing back Libby's hair from her neck.

Libby made a face at Elle. "Don't start, Elle. Hannah and Sarah and Kate were relentless. Elle's the baby of the family," she added for Tyson's sake.

"Come on. I'll take you both home." His hand went to Libby's back, his palm blazing hot through her thin blouse.

Suddenly she was very nervous. His tone was back, that sensual, husky voice, deep enough to vibrate right through her body and wreak havoc on her brain. Elle would know. Libby blushed, unable to prevent the color sweeping up her body.

Elle nudged her. *Jackson does that to me. I hate it.*

He does? That was a shocking revelation. And it had to cost Elle dearly to admit it, but she was fair. If she knew Libby's private secrets, she'd reveal her own in turn.

Sadly, yes. I stay away from him.

I should be staying away from Ty. If he'd keep his mouth closed and just let me look, everything would be wonderful, Libby admitted.

"What are you two doing?" Ty asked, as he escorted them from the restaurant.

Libby winked at Elle. "Elle's telepathic. We were talking about you."

He halted just outside the door, frowning, but regarding the two of them as if they were alien specimens under a microscope. "You're not serious, are you?"

"Absolutely. Would you like Elle to talk to you?"

Tyson bit back his first reaction. Libby was pretty shaken up. There was no point in talking to her about living in the real world—not yet. "No." He let the door close behind them and made his way to the car. "I'll pass."

He opened the door for Elle to climb into the backseat and stepped in front of Libby, preventing her from entering his car. His thighs pressed close and his body heat enveloped her. "On the other hand, at least you were discussing me. If you're talking telepathically about me, it has to be something really good." His voice had dropped another octave, sending a shiver of awareness down her spine.

How did he do that? She wasn't a sexual creature, she'd always known it and accepted it. Joley oozed sex. Hannah took men's breath away. Elle could stop traffic. Her other sisters could step into a bar and every head would turn—but not Libby. She just wasn't like that. She didn't think or feel sexually. Men were colleagues and she was busy, too busy to try to tame her wild hair and put on makeup and pretend she had breasts. But every single time she looked at Tyson Derrick she melted, grew hot and had extraordinary erotic fantasies. She *felt* sexy even with her raccoon mask eyes, her burnt nose and wild hairdo. He could make a goat feel sexy.

For heaven's sake, Libby, I can't keep a straight face. A goat?

Libby burst out laughing. *Stop reading my mind!*

You're broadcasting loud enough for the entire town to hear you. Elle definitely snickered.

Tyson wrapped his arms around Libby and drew her against him, distracting her. He looked down at her with his blue eyes and his sexy sinful lips and she was fixating before she could stop herself, staring at his mouth, imagining the feel, the taste.

"You shouldn't look at me like that, Libby," he cautioned, bending his head to hers until they were a breath apart.

She grew weak-kneed staring into his eyes but she couldn't look away. She couldn't remember why she was so determined to keep a distance from him. She felt him wince when he drew her close and almost of its own volition, her hand came up and with slow deliberation pressed against his sternum, and once again slid down to his cracked ribs. Heat spread between them.

His lips brushed over hers, feather-light, taking the oxygen from the air. Her heart leapt and began to pound.

Libby! Elle leaned into the front seat and hit the horn hard. The sound blasted Libby and Tyson apart. Elle glared at them through the window. "You're fogging up the windows."

Ty rubbed the bridge of his nose. "We're not in the car. Technically, that's impossible."

"Not really," Libby muttered and pulled open the door. "Sorry, Elle."

7

"LIBBY Katherine Drake, you little hussy." Sarah Drake regarded her younger sister with a stern eye. "You stood out on the porch kissing that man for half an hour. You have whisker burn to go with the Rudolph nose."

"Elle left me alone with him," Libby said. "It's her fault. She knew I had a weakness for him and she just went into the house and left me there. I deny all responsibility."

Elle made a rude noise and took a cookie as the platter floated past her. "She's so bad she was practically tearing his clothes off on the sidewalk outside the restaurant in front of the world."

Hannah flung herself onto the floor, stretching out her long legs and smirking. "Libby has fallen."

"I have not," Libby insisted. "I don't like him. It's pure sexual attraction and nothing else. He's just so hot and I can't resist. I'm using him for sex and throwing him away afterward."

Laughter filled the room. "Right, Libby," Kate agreed. "You do that. It's so your personality."

"It *is* my personality. I'm the love-them-and-leave-them type."

Another round of laughter went up. "You go girl," Abigail encouraged her. "We're all behind you one hundred percent."

"Well, I'm not going to see him again," Libby said, the smile fading from her face. "It was great, you know, while it lasted, but . . ." she trailed off with a small shrug.

"Why?" Sarah asked abruptly. "It's obvious you do like him."

"Is it?" Libby blew on her tea, frowning. She couldn't very easily tell her sisters Tyson didn't like her family. "He confuses me. I don't trust such a strong attraction. I'm not like that. It actually bothers me that I can't seem to think straight when he's around. And I feel silly. He held my hand and my heart started pounding like I was a teenager or something. It's all too bizarre for me."

"Before we deal with you being chicken of the century," Sarah broke in, "I think we need to address the fact that someone is threatening you."

Libby looked around at her sisters. They were all in the room, even Joley, although she'd just performed in a show the night before in front of thirty thousand people. Joley lay sprawled out on the floor as she often did, her fingertips tapping a rhythm on the throw rug and her head bobbing to some internal song, but her mind was clearly on Sarah's words.

"It doesn't make sense that this Ed Martinelli would want to hurt Libby when he needs her to help his sick child. Maybe he's trying to scare her?" Joley guessed.

Sarah nodded. "I was wondering the same thing. If it's so important that he speak with Libby about his child, what good will it do him if she's dead? Which is probably why Martinelli's henchmen threw out Hannah's name."

"Unless he's a complete moron," Abigail agreed. "Which is certainly within the realm of possibility."

"It doesn't feel like a threat to me," Hannah said. Her hands moved in a complicated, graceful pattern over Libby.

Small symbols leapt in the air and vanished as if they'd never been there. She shook her head. "I definitely think Libby's in danger, but I can't understand why I can't get any direction." She glanced at her youngest sister. "Elle, what do you think?"

"I'm running into the same problem as you've had. I *feel* a menace surrounding her, but I can't pinpoint it. I can't see it at all."

The sisters all looked to Sarah. She shook her head slowly. "I can't get anything either. One moment I feel the danger to Libby and then it's gone."

"We can ask Mom and Aunt Carol," Elle pointed out. "Maybe one of them can pick up on it."

"If they haven't already," Joley said. "Mom's called twice to make certain everything's all right. I told her Libby was turning into a hussy and she'd be horrified to learn I am now the 'good' Drake sister." She winked at Elle and Hannah. "The two of you can never be the good one because you both have such bad tempers."

A collective groan went up. "As if you don't." Elle sniffed. "If it's possible, you're worse than I am. And Hannah is, too. She just looks angelic."

"So true," Hannah agreed.

"Mom will never believe you're the good one, Joley. She reads the magazines. I even cut out articles and send them to her just to make certain she sees them," Sarah said.

"Thanks a lot." Joley grinned at her sisters, completely happy with her wild reputation. "I told Mom to relax, we could handle it, but now I'm not so sure. Has anyone tried looking in the mosaic?"

They all looked down at the beautiful masterpiece on the floor of the entryway into their home. It had been made a couple of generations earlier by seven sisters in the Drake family. In addition to being a work of art, the mosaic was an invaluable tool to them for scrying.

"Let's try then," Sarah said.

"Why haven't we heard from Jonas?" Hannah asked as they all sat on the floor surrounding the large mosaic.

"Shouldn't he be telling us about this man who threatened Libby tonight? He's had plenty of time to intimidate the guy. He does intimidation so well." She glanced up at the clock, uneasiness in her eyes.

"He's had plenty of practice on us," Abbey pointed out.

"Jonas isn't working tonight," Elle said. "Jackson said he went to see his friend Brannigan in Willits."

JONAS Harrington pulled his Jeep Wrangler up to the stop sign at the junction of Highway One. The drive from Willits had gone much faster than usual with so little traffic late at night. He'd put his favorite Joley Drake CD into the player and cranked up the volume, although he'd never admit to singing while he drove. Jim Brannigan had called him earlier in the evening and asked him to drop by the forestry heliport. Jonas stayed longer than he intended before heading for Sea Haven and home.

Brannigan admitted he was worried about the harness Tyson Derrick had worn on the day of the cliff rescue. The safety harness had been cut off of Tyson and taken back to the fire station for examination. Brannigan didn't like the look of it and wanted Jonas to have the laboratory check it out. The harness was in an evidence bag in the front seat beside him. Brannigan had convinced him there was no way the harness could have torn, but the material looked as if it had been eaten through. If it was defective, the helicopter crew needed to know as soon as possible. Jonas promised to overnight the harness to the lab.

Jonas frowned as he turned onto the coastal highway, his mind replaying everything Brannigan had said. If the harness hadn't been defective, why had it failed? He accelerated on the straight away, the only car on the deserted highway. Without warning a bottle flew out of the trees and landed in the middle of Jonas's lane, exploding on impact and hurling flames into the air.

Jonas slammed on the brakes, and the Jeep skidded across

the road. Bullets burst through the windshield. He yanked on the wheel in an attempt to use the passenger side of the Jeep as a shield. Tires screamed as he slid sideways, fighting for control of his Wrangler. More bullets tore through the door of the Jeep and slammed into his body, driving him against the driver side door.

It wasn't the first time he'd been shot, but he'd forgotten the intensity of pain, the feel of a bullet tearing through his flesh and cutting a path deep inside his organs. It took his breath, made him sick, so that he had to fight off waves of dizziness. He wasn't dying this way, not from a coward's bullet. There were too many things left unsaid and undone.

The Jeep hit the slight ditch on the shoulder of the road, ran up the embankment and flipped, rolling several times, throwing him around like a rag doll. The seat belt tightened as the airbag deployed and for a moment he was blind and deaf and disoriented.

Jonas tasted blood in his mouth and his chest throbbed as if a truck had smashed into him. He felt for his knife, stabbed the airbag and cut himself loose, his hand finding the familiar butt of his gun. Heart pounding, not sure where the enemy was, he kicked until the driver's door opened enough for him to drop to the ground. He fell hard, his legs rubbery, unable to support him. Using his elbows to drag himself forward, he crawled for the cover of the shrubs and grass of the embankment.

Shots sprayed the grass, thunked into a tree and slammed into his body. Jonas felt the impact tearing through his insides. He rolled the last few feet to make it behind a large rock, his only chance. He was off-duty and not wearing a vest. How many times had he been hit? There was movement by the Jeep but he couldn't see anyone. His arm felt numb. He couldn't feel the gun in his hand, but he had to stay alert. The Drake sisters would come and he would have to protect them.

Jonas stared at the night sky, listened to the pounding surf. The wheel of the Jeep was still spinning, but everything around him seemed to go still and silent. After a moment all he could hear was the sound of his own heartbeat and the steady dripping of his blood onto the ground.

"Hannah." He whispered her name to the night.

THE Drake sisters joined hands and stared down at the complex picture, the midnight blue sky, the stars and moon, the shadows forming, beginning to whirl around the edges and creep with long trails inside toward the very heart of the mosaic. The shadow spread, darkening the sky and blotting out the star that seemed to shine much brighter than the others.

Hannah gasped and pulled back with a startled cry, her hands going to her throat as it seemed to swell in panic. She looked at her sisters in desperation. "Jonas." She whispered the name around her raw, hurting throat.

Elle leapt up and ran for the phone, her face still and set, mirroring the same fright as her sisters.

"It's too late. It's too late," Hannah chanted, rocking back and forth. "Why didn't we see this? Why didn't we feel this?"

"We did. We just didn't recognize it," Sarah said, wrapping her arm around her sister to comfort her.

Elle turned back from the phone. "I've called Jackson and he'll get an ambulance started, but we have to go now if we're going to have any chance to save him. All of us." She looked at Libby. "We'll need you again, Lib. It's going to be bad."

Hannah ran for the car. "Hurry. He's not going to die. I'm not going to let him die. Reach for him Elle. I know you can hold him to us."

"I've got him, hon, but he's weak. Very weak. We have to find him fast."

Sarah nabbed the driver's seat and the other sisters quickly joined her in the car. "Where, Elle?"

Elle closed her eyes, her face pale as she sought outside herself for information. "He was coming back from Willits and had just made the turn onto Highway One. Someone shot up the car. He was hit multiple times. He's in pain, thinking of Hannah, counting on her to bring us to him."

"Hurry, Sarah," Hannah urged her.

"Why would anyone want to kill Jonas?" Abbey asked.

Kate held Hannah's hand tightly. "We're not going to let him die."

"Libby, are you up to this?" Sarah asked, glancing in the rearview mirror.

Libby lifted her chin. "Jonas is family. No way is anyone going to take him away from us. Drive faster, Sarah."

They all felt the same sense of urgency, of impending doom. They'd been feeling the darkness creeping in, holding them in its thrall, but it was an insidious feeling with no direction, no seeming strength until it struck without warning.

Sarah raced along the highway, the cliff on one side, the mountain rising on the other, speeding through the hairpin turns to get to Jonas before the ambulance. They saw his Jeep, so familiar to all of them, upside down, crumpled and ruined. Jonas lay a few feet from the wreckage up on the embankment, sprawled out behind a large rock.

Hearing a car coming, Jonas attempted to roll over. He was still exposed. He had fallen over, unable to keep upright even in a sitting position. He had hoped the killer would come in close, to finish him off, but only the wind surrounded him, rifling his hair and touching his face with gentle fingers. He heard Hannah's voice calling to him to hold on and he felt Elle touching him, gripping his arm as if she could physically hold him to the world.

Now as the Drake sisters' voices grew louder, more anxious, he tried to roll over again, out of the sniper's line of sight. He always told the Drakes he wasn't psychic, but he had a hell of an instinct for danger and he knew the killer was still close by.

Hannah's face swam into focus. There were tears in her eyes, running down her face. Sinking onto the ground, she lifted his head gently and propped him in her lap. "We're here, now, Jonas, you're going to be fine."

He tried to warn her, but he started choking on blood and turned his head so she wouldn't see. He could feel the sisters surrounding him with heat and energy. Overhead thunderclouds blew up fast and furious, leaping straight up like a tower.

A bullet plowed into the ground close to Libby. Jonas brought up his gun and tried to shove Hannah towards the relative safety of the nearby ditch. Elle spun around facing the direction of the killer, throwing her hands into the air. Above them, the sky crackled with electricity and on the other side of the road, below the cliffs, water smashed into rocks with a terrible fury.

Jonas coughed and fought to breathe. His lungs were filling with blood and he was drowning. Without Elle holding him to her, he knew he was slipping away, fast reaching the point where even the Drakes would be helpless to pull him back. The gun fell out of his hands, his fingers too weak to hold the grip. Desperate, he looked up at Hannah.

"Elle! Elle, we're losing him," Hannah cried, hunching her body protectively over Jonas. "Help us."

Elle hesitated a moment, fearing for her sisters' lives, but the call to save Jonas was too strong. She turned back to Jonas.

A sheriff 's car skidded to a halt, shielding the circle of Drakes from the road. Jackson emerged, gun drawn, face set, eyes as cold as ice. "Backup's coming, Elle. Take care of Jonas."

Two more police vehicles arrived, one from the city of Fort Bragg and one highway patrol. They used their cars as a barricade to help protect Jonas from the gunman. Obviously the shooter determined he was outmatched because there was no more gunfire. Other officers arrived and spread out to do a search.

The residents of the small towns up and down the coast nearly all had scanners and they would come immediately to see if they could help. Many were reserve for the sheriff or fire departments, helping one another when most aid was far away. Jonas was popular and the instant word got out that he was shot, they would come fast and there would be many of them.

Jackson pushed into the circle, kneeling beside Jonas. Blood was everywhere, soaking into Hannah's clothing, seeping into the ground beneath the sheriff and sprayed across the boulders behind them.

"Can you save him?" Jackson asked without preamble, his face set in hard lines.

Libby held her hands an inch away over his body and closed her eyes, feeling for his injuries, mapping them out, seeing them even more clearly than if she were reading an X ray. She swallowed hard. Four bullets had torn through his body, damaging organs and ripping through veins and one artery. She had to fix that fast or he was gone for certain. One lung had collapsed.

The internal damage was severe. This was going to be very bad. The worst damage and the most dangerous was to the pulmonary artery, the main supplier of oxygen to the lungs. Blood was already filling Jonas's lungs and beginning to suffocate him. If Libby waited for the ambulance to take him to the hospital, it would be too late. There was no way they could repair the artery fast enough to save Jonas—the damage was too severe.

"Hannah and Elle, you'll have to help me with this fast." Hannah and Elle both could heal to some extent, not with Libby's power, but she needed them. "Jackson, keep everyone else away but tell the paramedics he'll need blood when we're finished. Lots and lots of blood."

"It could get ugly," Elle cautioned. "We aren't in Sea Haven and people from all these towns know Jonas and don't know us."

"Just get it done. No one will bother you," Jackson promised.

Libby could feel the desperation in her sisters—in the gathering crowd as they arrived from nearby towns, some already weeping. The mob was growing larger and she caught a glimpse of the ferocity on Tyson's face as he arrived, striding toward them with determination. She closed her eyes, took a deep cleansing breath and focused everything she was—everything in her—on Jonas.

The pain hit with the force of a hurricane, a terrible intensity that took her breath and robbed her of her ability to think. She heard the collective gasp from her sisters and forced herself to rise above the agony, to take them with her. She needed their strength and focus, the tremendous circle of energy they could generate together. She called up the light and energy that was always there, always waiting, from somewhere deep inside her. It welled up and poured through her to Jonas. Her sisters connected; Hannah, nearly as strong even in healing as Libby; Elle, equal to Hannah, a force to be reckoned with. Sarah, Kate, Abigail and Joley sent their energy, their strength surging into the three sisters as they healed Jonas.

Libby focused on the worst of the injuries, the artery in desperate need of repair. She'd been right, Jonas would have died if they'd waited to transport him. He might die now, his wounds were so severe. She breathed away the fear and concentrated on the mess in his chest and abdomen, the two worst wounds. She felt Hannah and Elle with her and it was a comfort that she wasn't alone trying to fix such a massive destruction of a human being.

As if in the distance she could hear the wail of the ambulance as it arrived, as the people around them divided into two camps. Matt Granite, Damon Wilder and Aleksandr Volstov stood shoulder to shoulder with Jackson, preventing anyone from getting to the mortally wounded sheriff and interfering with the Drake sisters and their work. Inez from the grocery store joined them, followed by Donna from the gift shop and Gene Dockins and two of his sons. Matt's brothers joined the growing circle around Jonas, followed by Mason and Sylvia Fredrickson.

Tyson couldn't believe his eyes. The sheriff, lying wounded, covered in blood, desperately needed immediate medical attention, but he was surrounded instead by the Drake sisters. Even though Libby was a doctor, reputed to be a damned good one, the belief that she could heal the sick and injured was so ingrained in her, they were delaying getting Jonas real help. He was furious to think that besides Libby, several of the officers and many of the townspeople of Sea Haven appeared to be completely brainwashed. The atmosphere reeked of mass hysteria and a good man was going to die because of it.

Sam came up to him, pushing his way through the crowd of people. "What's going on, Ty? The scanner went off, but I didn't get all the particulars."

"Someone shot Jonas," Tyson answered in a low tone, "and I don't know why they aren't getting him to a hospital."

"It just adds to our growing legend of the infamous Drake sisters," Sam said. "Regardless they get the glory. If he lives, they saved him, if he dies, well, they tried."

Ty glanced at him sharply. "I thought you believed in them."

"Come on, Ty! Magic? You really think Libby can heal a man shot full of holes? If she could, she'd be a national treasure. Drew Madison would have been healed of cancer when he was a kid."

"Keep your voice down, Sam, this crowd could turn ugly," Ty cautioned.

"You know it's wrong, they're just looking for more attention. Sea Haven loves the idea of the magical Drake sisters, but this is real life and they're going to kill Jonas."

Tyson frowned warningly at his cousin as he tried to push past a deputy, but the officer wouldn't budge.

Sam shoved at Tyson, forcing him almost nose to nose with the man as tempers around them rose. "What the hell are you thinking, Jackson?" Sam demanded. "That's Jonas there. Do you think he'd allow you to die for a theatrical performance? Get the hell out of the way and let the paramedics see to him. Have you all gone crazy? Matt? Mason?"

Tyson put his hand on Sam's shoulder to calm him. "Getting upset isn't going to help anything. You have to allow the paramedics to transport Jonas." He turned toward the deputy, his voice very quiet. "Jonas could die without proper medical attention. He needs it now."

"Not could die," Sam snarled, his voice carrying in the night air, "*will* die. Whatever these con artists are doing, it isn't worth Jonas's life."

Several others from the surrounding towns added their own loud dissent to Sam's and the paramedics tried to push their way through the line.

Libby heard the sounds as if from a great distance, but she continued to concentrate her attention on holding Jonas to her. Power and strength flowed through her sisters into her. The air snapped with electricity so that their hair rose like haloes around their heads and stood up along their arms. Jonas had so many wounds, and the artery required all of Libby's attention.

Libby kept Jonas's heart beating, kept oxygen flowing to his brain. Time passed and she pushed panic aside, working her way through the massive destruction in his chest. Once she heard Hannah sob and felt Elle's internal weeping, but they never faltered and neither did she. Jonas would not die this night. The Drakes would never allow it. Sarah, Kate, Abigail and Joley sent every ounce of strength and energy they possessed to their sisters, giving freely to save Jonas, holding nothing in reserve, even knowing Libby would soon need their help as desperately as Jonas did now.

At a signal from Libby, Jackson waved the team of paramedics through the protective line. They rushed with their equipment to Jonas's side. As the officers parted, Tyson caught a glimpse of Libby covered in blood, her face stark white, eyes closed. Pain etched her face and sudden anger swept through him at the sight of it. He wanted to pound Jackson into the ground, even went so far as to take two aggressive steps toward him.

"Don't mess with me tonight." Jackson warned him.

"You're killing both of them trying to keep up this stupid myth of the Drake sisters and their magic. If she could wave her arms around and say an incantation or two, don't you think Jonas would already be up and walking around?" He couldn't stand the sight of Libby's white face, so pale she looked translucent—not of this world—a witch. "You people are sucking the life out of her, perpetuating this myth."

Jackson didn't reply, merely stared at him with flat, cold eyes. Obviously nothing was going to sway him, any more than it would sway the fanatics who believed the Drake sisters were real modern-day witches. Still, Tyson had to try. Keeping his voice low so no one could hear, he pleaded with the man. "Think, Jackson. This isn't logical. This is the kind of thing that brings the crazies after Libby. They believe all the hocus-pocus because they *need* to believe in it." He threw his arms into the air when Jackson didn't change his expression. "You're going to get her killed," Tyson hissed between his teeth.

"This is a crime scene," one of the other sheriffs said. "Move back."

"This is murder," Sam shouted and the crowd behind him buzzed louder. "You damn well had better not let Jonas die. Give him proper medical attention."

Tyson gripped Sam's shoulder hard to restrain him. Crowds grew ugly fast. Jonas Harrington was a popular man up and down the coast and only the people of Sea Haven believed in the Drake family magic. He didn't want things to get out of hand. He signaled Sam to stop stirring things up, feeling guilty since Sam was merely backing him up. As a firefighter, Sam wielded a lot of influence. He was well-known, popular and very persuasive. He most likely wouldn't have entered into the debate if he hadn't had Tyson's back.

Sam shook his head. "This isn't right," he said in a low tone. "The Drakes are going to kill him. They'll claim he was dying anyway, with four bullets in him, but the longer the delay the less his chances. Why the hell won't they allow the medics in?"

"They did let paramedics through," Tyson reminded him. "They're working on Jonas now. He doesn't look good and he hasn't moved."

The crowd pushed closer.

Movement caught Tyson's eye and he saw Libby topple over. She lay as if dead on the ground, blood covering her clothes, staining her skin, her face as white as a sheet. His heart nearly stopped, then began to pound hard.

Hannah swayed, was caught by Matt Granite. He lifted the supermodel and placed her in a squad car. Jackson carried

Elle and then Sarah as Matt helped Abigail, Joley and Kate get to the cars. The paramedics worked fast to bundle Jonas onto the gurney to transport him to the nearest hospital. Tyson pushed his way through the crowd toward Libby. A burly officer bumped chests with him.

"You can't go past this point. This is a crime scene."

"Like hell. Libby is my . . ." What the hell did one say to get past the law? "She's my . . ." Words failed him again. "We're dating."

"We have people looking after her. As soon as they move her, you'll be able to see her." The officer did not appear to be in the least impressed with Ty's declaration.

"Like hell I'm waiting," Tyson snapped. "Half the people running around your precious crime scene are not law enforcement personnel, so don't give me excuses." Behind him, the crowd pushed closer and Sam bumped Tyson hard, driving him into the officer's chest.

Immediately the officer shoved Ty away from him, sending Tyson staggering backward into Sam, who stumbled and fell into the angry mob. Chaos exploded. People began swinging wildly at the deputy and each other. Tyson helped his cousin up, ducked a flying fist and then took a hit far too close to his broken rib so that he was forced to protect that side of him, the pain taking his breath as he hunched over.

"I'm going to arrest every one of you." Jackson had come over and was speaking in a low, menacing tone that sobered the crowd instantly. "Go home and let us do our job. You're blocking the way of the ambulance."

Officers formed a barrier, shielding Jonas from the sight of the crowd as he was placed inside the vehicle. The deputies, joined by several highway patrol officers, drove the mob back to allow the ambulance to get onto the road.

Ty found himself staggering over to the edge of the road, holding his side and craning his neck in an attempt to spot Libby. She had several people surrounding her, mostly the men associated with the Drakes.

"You okay?" Sam asked, anxiety plain in his voice.

"No, I'm not okay," Tyson bit out between his teeth. "I don't know if she's dead or alive. She isn't moving."

Sam glanced at Libby's body, partially blocked by two burly men. "What really happened here, Ty? I heard 'officer down' and came running. What the hell happened to him? Who would do this?"

"I told you. Someone shot him. It looked like multiple wounds. No one knows why, or if they do, they aren't saying." Tyson pushed a hand through his hair. To his astonishment he was trembling. "I don't get this, Sam. I *know* she can't heal people. It isn't possible, we know that. Libby's smart. Damned smart, but she really believes she can heal people like some faith healer in a tent. I didn't realize how seriously she believes it until just now. She'd never have risked Jonas this way otherwise."

Sam shrugged. "The Drakes have always been different. Everyone in Sea Haven knows that. Maybe the answer is just as simple as they crave attention any way they can get it. God knows, they don't live low-profile lives."

Tyson's gut knotted. He had had this same conversation with his cousin before, back when he'd first mentioned he was interested in Libby. Sam had protested with surprisingly well-thought-out reasons why it would never work. Tyson had quoted part of the conversation to Libby at dinner, wanting to guide her gently toward thinking with logic. Libby didn't strike him as a woman who craved attention. In fact he'd never seen her intentionally draw attention to herself. He shook his head. "The motivation doesn't fit her, Sam. She's brilliant and skilled and maybe that makes her vulnerable to believing she can heal others."

"Whatever, Ty. If we don't get out of here pretty soon, we're going to get arrested. That cop is staring at you and he doesn't look happy."

"Go, Sam. This isn't your mess. I want to make certain Libby's okay. If I get arrested, sooner or later BioLab will bail me out."

"I'm sure they will. You're their big star," Sam said.

"I'm trying not to notice that there was sarcasm in your tone," Tyson said. He regarded his cousin through narrowed eyes, his attention on the cops, waiting for them to lose interest in him. "I'm sorry about the phone calls at all hours of the night. It's just that I've been concerned about that project . . ."

"It's not your project, Ty. You've got all of BioLab in an uproar. They're calling the house and sending couriers and showing up on my doorstep when I'm trying to entertain a beautiful woman. I was this close"—Sam measured the distance off with his fingers—"to getting her to stay with me. I've been after her for months."

Tyson's attention shifted back to the sheriff deputies. They'd lost interest in him now that the crowd had dispersed and he seemed to be obeying orders.

"I'm sorry," Ty mumbled. It was a habit from childhood and easily done and never all that genuine. He was always cramping Sam's style when he was home, although he spent so much time in his basement laboratory that Sam often referred to Tyson as "the mole." Sam was never serious about any one woman and if he messed up his chances to sleep with one woman, he simply moved on to the next. He was charming and easygoing and not overly ambitious. He loved being a firefighter for the forestry but didn't particularly want the responsibility of moving up the ladder whereas Tyson was driven to always move forward.

Sam shrugged it off with his small grin like he always did. "Don't sweat it, Ty, easy come, easy go. She'll come back when she gets over her snit." He followed Tyson's gaze to Libby. "The only reason you're interested in Libby Drake is because she's a puzzle and you have to solve it. She's too bizarre for you to really want to be with her."

Tyson flinched inwardly at Sam's matter-of-fact assessment of his interest in Libby. The worst of it was, he knew it wasn't true. She'd intrigued him from the first moment he'd laid eyes on her. There was something different about Libby and he wanted to figure her out, but he also loved being with her. He glanced at her again. She hadn't moved, but in the cars, three of her sisters were exhibiting signs of coming around. "They had to have put themselves in a trance," he muttered aloud.

"What?" Sam asked. He followed Tyson's gaze. "Mass hysteria at work."

Tyson might have used the phrase himself, but now that Sam had, it annoyed him. Libby didn't get hysterical and neither did her sisters, but it was entirely possible they did put themselves in a trance. That was a logical explanation. He frowned at Sam. "I thought you were friends with the Drakes."

Sam shrugged. "Of course I am, but that doesn't mean I'm not aware they're crazy. Come on, Ty, do you think all that heebie-jeebie stuff is for real?"

"Of course not."

"Then it's either all about sex or you having to figure her out or both."

Tyson waved him off, angry but not knowing why. He didn't like Sam's assessment no matter how true it might be. The officers were no longer even looking his way and he took advantage of the fact, moving swiftly over to where Libby lay on the ground just feet from the smashed car.

Matt Granite nodded at him. "We've got to get them back to the house."

"I'll get Libby." Tyson didn't want anyone else picking her up, holding her close. She looked dead, still unconscious, her skin like wax.

"No." Sarah made the protest, calling from the car.

Damon Wilder, her fiancé, immediately wrapped his arm around her. "We're taking you all home, Sarah. Libby will be fine once we're in your house."

"Have Jackson put Libby in the car." Sarah's gaze touched on Tyson.

He felt her instant rejection of him. There was none of her teasing laughter, no acceptance at all. She looked at him the way he might a virus under a microscope. Deep inside, everything he was welled up in protest. Stubbornly he pushed past Jackson to reach for Libby.

"No!" Sarah was sharper this time, steel in her voice. "You aren't what she needs right now."

Ty glared at her. "I'm *exactly* what she needs right now. Someone with logic."

Matt put a hand on his shoulder. "You don't understand any of this and you'll do more harm than good. We'll handle it."

Jackson sent Ty a dark, dangerous look, those ice cold eyes chilling him. "Back off, Derrick. Go home. I think you've caused enough trouble for one night."

Tyson watched as Jackson gathered Libby's slight weight into his arms. She hung limp, lifeless, her cloud of dark hair falling over his arm like skeins of silk. Ty paced along beside the deputy. "All I wanted to do was get Jonas help." He defended himself. He didn't give a damn what Jackson thought of him, but he needed to tell Libby.

He followed Jackson to the deputy's vehicle. He'd never felt so helpless in his life, or so unsure. He always knew exactly what he was doing and why he was doing it, but he just didn't have a clue about the situation he was in. He needed to protect Libby, even if it was from herself and he could see now that her family not only encouraged her behavior but would fight him if he tried to take her out of the situation.

Matt Granite and Aleksandr Volstov blocked him from reaching in and pulling Libby out of the police car. "You'd better go," Aleksandr said. "You don't want to make any enemies."

Anger flashed through Ty with such ferocity he could barely contain it. He stepped closer to the Russian, uncaring the man was an Interpol agent and had been trained since childhood in more ways to kill a man than Ty might ever know. "You back off. All of you. I'm not afraid of you and you're not warning me off of Libby. She needs help and all of you are idiots."

"So you're going to save her from her family," Matt said.

There was warning in Matt's stance, enough to remind Tyson he was a former army ranger. Ty shrugged off Sam's restraining hand. "Hell, yes, I'm going to save her from her family. They're fruitcakes and you're just as bad, encouraging them to believe in witchcraft. It's a bunch of garbage and you know it. Get the hell out of my way, Granite. You don't impress me all that much either."

Sam yanked on his arm, staring at him as if he'd grown two heads. Tyson couldn't blame him. He didn't believe in fighting—it was stupid and childish—but he wasn't afraid at the prospect of a fight. He had excelled in several forms of martial arts, but when he sparred, it was to teach or to be taught, or he simply ended the fight as fast as possible with a knockout. There was no in between. Yet now, he was virtually picking a fight with the Drake sisters' fiancés.

He shrugged Sam off a second time and stood solidly in Matt Granite's path, nose to nose, chest to chest, like a primitive jungle animal. "You're not taking her with you." Adrenaline surged through his body and at that moment he knew he was more dangerous than he'd ever been in his life.

"I'm arresting your ass," the deputy behind him announced.

Tyson didn't turn his head, didn't take his eyes off Matt, ready to fight.

Sam threw his arms around his cousin, pinning his arms to his sides. "He's upset over Jonas," he explained to the deputy. "He's not thinking right. I'll take him home. Come on, Ty. We've got to get out of here. No woman is worth getting arrested over."

That was the trouble. Libby was worth it and someone needed to save her from her family and from herself. Tyson Derrick was the man to do it, too. When he put his mind to something, he was unswerving.

"You can let go, Sam." It wouldn't help if he was in jail and Jackson was glowering at him, mean as a snake, ready to give the word. He would have to use finesse, plan his battle carefully. "I'm leaving."

8

SAM stood in the basement, right at the bottom of the stairs, hands on hip glaring at his cousin. "Did you forget something?"

Tyson didn't look up, didn't acknowledge his cousin's presence, continuing to frown with total concentration into a microscope.

Sam stomped farther into the room, careful to avoid the long rows of equipment, computers and big bulky machines. Tyson rarely spent large amounts of money, but when he did, it was usually on the best equipment possible for his laboratory. "Damn it, Ty, stop playing the mad scientist. You had a date tonight."

Tyson glanced up, the lines in his face grim. "No, I didn't. I made it clear to you I had no intention of dating that moron you were trying to set me up with. I'm busy, Sam. I've got work to do. I stand down here staring at all of this and all I can think about is that Drake woman."

"You're sulking, Ty. You've been down here day and night and I know you haven't slept—or eaten. What good is it going to do to make yourself sick? And over what? Libby Drake? No woman is worth this. She's become another one of your obsessive puzzles."

When there was no response, Sam sighed and changed tactics, his voice becoming coaxing. "You need to get out. The doctors won't sign a release to let you work as a firefighter, so we should plan other things to get you out of the house."

"You go, Sam, I've got a lot of work to do." Tyson wasn't going to admit to his cousin he'd been to Libby's house every day like some obsessed stalker and had been turned away by her sisters. He couldn't stop himself any more than he could stop investigating why the new drug, PDG-ibenregen, which BioLab had in second stage clinical trials, was producing depression in a certain age group of participants. Harry Jenkins wasn't paying attention, thinking the incidents small and random, but to Tyson, they were a glaring red flag and he wouldn't—*couldn't*—stop until he found the answer.

Sam swore under his breath. "You're obsessive, you know that? Totally a wackjob, and you need to find a way to get over it."

For one horrible moment, Ty was certain Sam knew about his numerous trips to the Drake home. He *felt* like a wackjob. He was used to his single-minded compulsion, his *need* to find answers and the thrill when he was on the right track, but that trait in him had never transferred to a human until Libby Drake had laughed in the streets of Sea Haven so many years ago and caught his attention. He couldn't allow Sam to know just how Libby had consumed his mind over the years. He didn't even know how it happened—or when it was that he decided to pursue her. Nor did he know exactly what he was going to do with her once he succeeded. It just was something he had to do. It was just like how his research took him over, only this was more potent. And like with his research, there was no possibility of failure in his mind.

"If you keep this up, you're going to end up in the hospital for malnutrition and I'm going to have to take care of you."

The concern in Sam's voice gave Tyson pause. He frowned up at his cousin, as usual feeling guilt for allowing Sam to try to take care of him. Sam tried so hard to understand him, but obviously it was impossible. "I promise to break for food. You go have fun on your date."

Sam scratched his head, the frown still very much in evidence. "I overheard the phone call with what's his name from BioLab. He didn't sound happy with you."

"Harry." Tyson supplied the name, waving his hand in a dismissing gesture. "Don't worry about it. We don't get along. I think he does shoddy work and he thinks I'm a glory hound. He knows, but refuses to acknowledge, that there are problems with the new PDG drug. He likes shortcuts and unfortunately the marketing department likes them as well. If they can get this new drug on the market, the company stands to make millions immediately."

"Has it ever occurred to you that old Harry might get very angry with you cutting into his territory? If this thing is worth so much money to your company maybe the safe thing to do is back off and see what happens. You could be wrong."

"I'm not wrong. Look at what happened to Drew Madison. He was taking the drug and he falls into the age group that seems to be having problems."

"We don't know that Drew's fall wasn't an accident." Sam took a step toward his cousin and halted again. "I don't like any of this, Ty. You're getting messages from Edward Martinelli . . ."

"A totally unrelated matter," Tyson assured him. "We're playing phone tag is all. I called him and asked him to get back to me as soon as possible. You know Ed. We've gone caving together. Hell, you've even played cards with him."

"I know he's trouble, Ty. Your head may be in the laboratory all the time, but even you know he's got unsavory connections. If he's a major stockholder in your company and you're on the verge of losing them a huge profit, you're likely to get fitted with cement boots."

"Ed may have relatives involved in crime, but I've known

him for years, Sam. He's a legitimate businessman. Ed inherited his business from his parents, neither of whom were mobsters."

"You can't be that naïve, Ty. No doubt he's using his business to launder money and I know for a fact he's very involved in the gambling world. He's got his fingers into all kinds of things."

Tyson sank into a chair, looking tired. "I've known Ed a long time. His parents and mine were close friends. In fact, one of the reasons I went to work for BioLab was because Ed's family persuaded my parents they would give me anything I wanted in the way of equipment and room to work on what I wanted if I joined them. And they offered a more than generous salary. My parents for once were thrilled with me. BioLab has always kept its promises to me."

"Come on, Ty. Your parents believed what they wanted to believe. Ed's father was indicted how many times?"

"But he was acquitted."

"Once the witness disappeared and another time he was killed."

"An accident."

"Electrocuted in a safe house with cops guarding him."

Sudden amusement crossed Tyson's face. "Precisely the point. He was well guarded and the idiot took a radio or something like it into the bathtub with him. He deserved to die if he was that stupid."

Sam rolled his eyes. "You're not that naïve."

"No, I'm not. Come on, Sam, those are urban legends. It never happened. And there was only one time, not two, that anyone brought charges against Ed's father. There was a bookkeeper who went to the feds and claimed he had proof the Martinellis were fronting for the mob. The newspapers had a field day, but when the case was dropped for lack of evidence, no one retracted the accusations. The witness didn't die, he slunk away because he was lying through his teeth. He was angry because he was fired for embezzling. No one reported that either."

"I don't care about all that. Maybe the father wasn't

involved with the mob, but Ed Martinelli is. His pharmaceutical company probably launders money for his other businesses and if you're in his way, he's going to hurt you. Stop investigating this drug thing and work on your inhibitor or whatever it is."

There was a small silence. Tyson sighed heavily. "Out with it, Sam. You know too much about Ed for this to be a casual conversation. What's wrong?"

"Nothing. I just don't want you talking to him. I don't want you doing anything to put yourself on his radar. He plays rough."

"How much do you owe him?" Ty asked bluntly.

Sam swore softly under his breath. "It's my problem, I'll work it out. I'm not kidding, Ty, don't talk to him. Stay completely away from him."

"That's bullshit. Is he threatening you?" Tyson stood up so fast the chair hit the floor with a loud thud. "Damn it, it is my problem if he's really threatening you. I introduced you to him. Just pay him the money and get it over with."

"He won't take the money now, Ty. Let it go. I didn't want you to know because it's my problem and you're a hothead when it comes to things like this. You know me. I always say I'm going to quit playing cards, but then I think one more game. I'll take care of it the way I always do."

"What do you mean he won't take the money?"

Sam shook his head. "He told me this morning that he'll wipe out the debt if you'll arrange for him to talk with Libby Drake. If not, he can't guarantee my safety."

"He said that?" Fury swept through Tyson. At last, someone to focus his anger on. "He actually threatened you?" Tyson began to pace back and forth, unable to contain the energy and adrenaline flooding his body. His fingers curled into two tight fists.

"Not in so many words. He's too clever for that. I don't want you approaching Libby about it. I'm the one dumb enough to get myself into a tight place and I can find a way out of it."

"I'm calling the son of a bitch, Sam. We were *friends*."

Even as he said it, Tyson wondered how true it was. Yes, they'd grown up together, but even as a child, Ty had been detached from others around him. Ed had enjoyed their outdoor trips, but they didn't move in the same social circles. Hell, Ty didn't have a social circle. "Leave it to me. I'll take care of it."

"No! Stay away from him. You already came close to dying." Sam paled considerably. "You don't think he could have had anything to do with your harness failing, do you?" He covered his face briefly. "Maybe you're already in danger because of me."

"I doubt he could have gotten to the harnesses, Sam."

"Well, if he did, no one's likely to ever know it, now that the evidence has disappeared. I still can't believe it disappeared right out of Jonas's car in front of everyone."

Tyson shook his head. "No one's seen it. Most likely a kid in the crowd took it out of the Jeep before the police had the area roped off. Everyone was so curious and a kid would be tempted to take a souvenir, at least Jackson said so when I called him to ask about it. Jonas is still in ICU and I doubt if anyone's been able to question him yet."

"So much for the Drake sisters and their miracles," Sam said. "You dodged a bullet on that one."

Tyson turned back to his work, hiding his expression. "You know, Sam, it seems a little strange that someone would attack the sheriff without a reason. I think someone wanted that harness." Ty voiced the conclusion his mind just wouldn't let go of.

"I doubt his attackers knew he was a sheriff. He wasn't in uniform and he wasn't in a marked car. There were a lot of people around. It was dark, but you'd think someone would have noticed." Sam shrugged. "If Edward Martinelli's people had anything to do with it, they could probably pull it off though. They're pros."

"Jackson said the area was roped off as soon as possible and the forensic people went over everything so maybe they'll turn up fingerprints, or whatever they do. I just don't see how anyone could have gotten near the Jeep without someone noticing."

"When did you talk to Jackson?" Sam asked.

"I wanted to know what happened to the harness. Brannigan called twice about it as well as talking to you and I thought we needed to make certain we followed up so I called this morning."

"Well, it's scary that it disappeared like that," Sam said. "We're all using those harnesses and if one was defective, we're all in danger. Everyone's nervous about it. The CDF has been testing the harnesses and so is the manufacturer. So far, no one's found any problems. I don't know, Ty, whoever has to be the next dope on a rope isn't going to be happy and I can't really blame them."

"It had better not be you," Tyson said, meaning it. "I can't afford to lose you, Sam. You're the only family I have."

There was an awkward silence. Sam flashed a sudden grin. "You mean I'm the only one who'll put up with you." The smile slowly faded. "Seriously, Ty, don't contact Martinelli. I'm not up to planning another funeral."

"I put in a call to him first on another matter, Sam. He knows I want to talk to him, but I'll avoid him until I calm down." Tyson glanced at his watch. "Aren't you late for your date?"

"Damn, she's going to be angry." Sam struggled to sound upbeat, abandoning his argument with Tyson. When Ty dug in his heels there was no swaying him. "Since you're not going with me to foot tonight's bill, and you're getting all sappy on me, I could use some cash. Do you have any on you?"

"I thought you said you just pulled out a huge stash and put it in the upstairs office just for incidentals. Use that."

"I didn't pull out enough for a date."

Ty patted his pockets with a small frown. "I think I left my wallet upstairs. I have no idea what's in it, but you should have plenty in your account if I don't have enough cash on me."

"I think I'm overdrawn. I haven't had a chance to make any deposits with everything going on."

Tyson shrugged. "Just use the family account then." He turned away from Sam on the pretext of getting back to work, but he was furious that Edward Martinelli had virtually threatened his cousin. Sam might not want him to get involved, but he was definitely going to be sorting out the problem. Martinelli had endangered the two people in the world that mattered to Tyson—Sam and Libby.

He had no idea why Libby had always been so important to him, but since the moment he'd first laid eyes on her, she'd always been there, at the back of his mind, not dominating his thoughts, but never forgotten.

It had been like that for him since the day he'd seen her with the accident victim at Harvard. Before that, he'd been happy enough to just watch her, see the expressions chasing across her face, listen to the sound of her laughter. Libby Drake was meant for him. She didn't even know how much a part of his life she'd become.

"YOU can't see her," Sarah said, her voice low but firm. She planted herself squarely in the doorway to prevent Tyson from getting around her.

Ty glared at her, not in the least intimidated by the oldest Drake sister. Their clash had become a daily ritual. "I'm beginning to think you're holding her prisoner in this house. I want to see her with my own eyes to make certain she's all right."

"Has it occurred to you that she might not want to see you?" Sarah asked bluntly.

"I have no idea why you're being so hostile." He itched to shake the woman. She just stood there studying him as if he were a foul smelling bug under a microscope. He had always enjoyed watching the Drake sisters together, but now he just wanted the eldest to disappear. He let his breath out slowly and changed tactics. "I only want to see her for a few minutes just to make certain she's all right. I'm not kidnapping her." He'd considered it just to get her away from her family.

Sarah raised her eyebrow. "It must have crossed your mind if you think you have to assure me you aren't here to kidnap my sister."

"Why are you so hostile?" Tyson repeated. "I'm not exactly a stranger to you."

"The gate was locked. How did you get here?"

He rolled his eyes, sick of the delays and her obstinacy. He had no patience for what he considered total idiocy. It was difficult enough to work on the niceties without having to put up with Sarah Drake's obstinacy. He *detested* having to be socially correct just to get past the door to see Libby—and the more difficult they made it for him, the more he dug in his heels, determined to visit her.

"I drove my car, parked it below in the drive and walked right up. The padlock was on the ground and the gate was open. In any case, Sarah, the fence isn't all that high and I've been known to go mountain and rock climbing. I doubt if your little gate or fence would stop me."

Sarah stared at him as if he'd grown two heads. "The padlock was on the ground?"

He clenched his teeth. "You aren't slow-witted are you? Because if you are, I'll speak more distinctly and enunciate every word."

Her gaze narrowed. "If you're trying to be funny, you aren't succeeding."

"I want to see Libby now." He tried not to sound belligerent, but his tone made even him flinch. He was definitely at the end of what little patience he possessed.

Movement behind Sarah caught his eye and he stepped closer, expecting Sarah to give way, but she held her ground dead center in the doorway.

"Quit skulking like a little coward, Libby," he said. "I'm tempted to pick your sister up and toss her into the shrubs."

Sarah snorted derisively, but stepped back when Libby squeezed by her.

Libby's appearance shocked him. She had always been petite, but now she was gaunt, so thin and pale she looked a wraith. There were dark circles under her eyes and shadows in them—but she was glaring at him. "Are you threatening Sarah?"

"Not yet, but I was considering it."

"Sarah would flatten you if you touched her," Libby said.

"Maybe, but you don't look in any condition to flatten me, so I'll take my chances with you." He lifted her into his arms, removing her from the doorway and striding right into the house.

He felt a curious shift under his feet as he entered, but before he could think about it Libby turned into a bundle of fury, thumping hard on his chest. He waited for the pain from his broken sternum to jar him, but surprisingly, he felt nothing at all.

"What the hell do you think you're doing? I'm not some rag doll for you to toss over your shoulder so you can strut around like a he-man."

It took great effort not to smile. He liked her furious; she seemed to get that way only around him, and that was far better than no reaction. Tyson put her down in the middle of the living room, steadying her as she rocked away from him. He searched for some way to break the ice and, as always, obscure facts were the first thing that came to mind. "Did you know that Shamans used dolls for healing? Some painted dolls red in order to raise the dead. And in parts of Alaska, the Shaman carved a woman's figurine to cure infertility."

"*Tyson.*" Libby interrupted him, fists on hips, her head tipped back to look up at him. "You've finally gone completely insane. You force your way into my home, toss me over your shoulder like some ridiculous caveman—"

He held up his hand to stop her. "There's no need for melodrama. Stick to the facts, Libby. First off, I didn't force my way in, I stepped across the threshold like any other man. Second, I didn't toss you over my shoulder. I cradled you against me with enormous care, despite my broken ribs, I might add."

As he talked, he walked around the room, examining first the mosaic on the floor and then studying the walls.

Sarah rolled her eyes. "He's all yours, Lib. If you need me, just call. I'll be with Kate up in her room. Getting rid of bodies is a specialty of hers. Just a little thought to leave you with."

Tyson frowned after her. "I thought Kate was a writer."

"Of murder mysteries," Libby said with exaggerated patience.

"Oh, that's right. I read one of her books once. It wasn't a bad story."

Libby gritted her teeth. "Did you come here for a reason, or just to annoy me?"

He heaved a sigh. It wasn't going very well. "Of course I came here for a reason. I just gave your sister a compliment. I don't see how that could possibly annoy you unless—" He drew the word out, his face brightening. "You can't be jealous? Kate's engaged and I'm pretty old-fashioned about that kind of thing. If a woman's engaged she's off-limits."

"Good to know." Libby gave up and sank into a comfortable chair, watching him prowl around her house, a bit reminiscent of Sherlock Holmes. "Are you looking for something?"

His gaze went back to the mosaic on the floor. "I don't know, bat wings and eye of newt. The supermodel with a cauldron."

Libby hissed her breath out between clenched teeth. If she wasn't careful her teeth were going to shatter from the pressure. "My sister's name is Hannah and at the moment she's at the hospital with Jonas where she's been for the last week and a half, night and day along with one of my other sisters. Tyson, I'm running out of patience."

He wasn't scoring any points with her. He didn't seem to be able to censor himself, although he was trying. He was just so shaken up by the sight of her starkly white face. She seemed almost ethereal, as if a good wind could blow her away. And she held herself stiffly, her arms wrapped around her middle, as if her chest was sore. There was wariness in her eyes and he realized the things he'd said so abruptly about her sister had really hurt her.

Tyson turned around, his piercing blue eyes resting on her face, his expression suddenly lost. "I came to see how you were doing. You scared the hell out of me, Libby, and your sisters wouldn't tell me how you were doing." He stepped closer, towering over her, shadows stealing into the depths of his eyes. "*Ten* days. I haven't been able to sleep or eat or even work the way I should. You put me through hell."

Libby opened her mouth to respond and abruptly closed it. Part of her wanted to yell at him to just go away, but he looked and sounded so vulnerable.

He raked both hands through his hair in frustration. "I'm so inadequate at this. I say and do all the wrong things, Libby, and I can see it upsets you." He picked up a thin blanket that was lying over the back of a chair and tucked it around her.

The action was so unexpected and his hands so gentle, that for a moment she couldn't speak. She stared up at him, shaking her head while she tried to hold on to her annoyance. "Why are you so angry at my family?"

There was a small silence. Tyson dropped into a chair opposite her. "The modern term family comes from the Latin word *famulus*, which means servant. In Arabia at the time of Mohammad, the word for marriage was *nikah,* which literally meant sexual intercourse. In the Koran, it was also used to mean contract. Marriage was conceived of as a contract for sexual intercourse."

Libby's eyebrow shot up. "I'm not touching that one, Ty. I don't even want to know what you meant by that."

He shrugged. "I didn't mean anything in particular, I just thought you might find it interesting."

Libby let her breath out in a slow rush of air. Tyson used facts as a defense mechanism. The moment he was uncomfortable with anything, he threw out random facts, distracting himself and anyone around him. He'd probably been doing it since childhood when his parents weren't really interested in the things he wanted to talk to them about, so he'd developed a way to shift his brain from emotional to intellectual instantly to protect himself.

Libby's heart went out to him. She didn't want to feel the way she did, all soft inside when what he really needed was a lesson in manners. "Why do you care at all, Ty? You've hardly spoken to me over the years."

"I've spoken to you, you just never heard me."

Libby frowned. She'd been attracted to him for years. Secretly maybe, but she would have noticed if he'd shown an interest in her. "That's not true."

"It's true, you just didn't notice someone like me."

"Someone like you?"

"You're repeating things. Do you need something? Water? Tea? You always drink tea. You look more like a ghost than you usually do." He jumped up again and rested his palm against her forehead.

Libby jerked her head away, scowling. "A ghost? I look more like a ghost than I usually do?"

He crouched down in front of her so they were eye to eye. Up close she could see he looked haggard and worn and his concern for her was etched into the lines of his face. "You're repeating everything I say." He enunciated each word carefully.

"Because I can't believe you would say such a thing, even if you're thinking it."

He rocked back on his heels. "What did I say wrong this time?"

"Do you think a woman wants to be called a ghost? News flash, buddy, women don't take that as a compliment. It makes me feel like a zombie walking."

"That's silly," Ty replied, exasperated. "You know you're beautiful, Libby. You can't possibly think anything else. You're incredibly intelligent, you actually understand what I say when I'm talking to you and when you smile, everyone around you wants to smile with you. You *are* pale right now. I'm thinking of calling a doctor and having you examined. What's wrong with everyone here that they don't see you're ill? You need someone to take care of you."

Libby knew her mouth had fallen open. She could only stare for a long moment, hoping a fly didn't buzz by. The man was impossible. He was always either saying something that made her want to hit him—or something that made her want to kiss him. Right now she wasn't certain which she wanted to do the most.

"I *am* a doctor," she reminded him, striving for a balance. There was no maintaining any kind of equilibrium around Tyson. She felt too much compassion, too much physical attraction and she was so annoyed she wanted to scream. No one in her life had ever torn her in so many directions. "If I needed treatment, I'd get it, Ty. And my sisters love me very much. They definitely would make certain I received any medical care needed." The moment the words left her mouth she thought of Hannah. She hadn't seen her sister losing weight and she certainly hadn't helped her.

Tyson caught her chin, the pad of his thumb running over her lips. "Now you're looking sad. You have the most expressive face. I used to sit in class and stare at you. I could for hours, you know, even when you're looking at me like I'm crazy. Why are you so sad all of a sudden?"

"I was just thinking I should have helped one of my sisters with a problem she has. She always looks after all of us and we didn't notice when she needed us most."

He patted her knee. "Tell me what she needs and I'll take care of it for you."

"Why would you want to do that?"

"So you won't worry anymore."

Libby shook her head. "I have no idea what to think about you, Ty. My family is my life. I've seen the way you curl your lip when you talk about us and I know you think we're all con artists. And then you go and say something like that." She drew a deep breath. "I love my sisters and my parents. They're part of me—a big part of who I am."

"I know that." He sighed and stood up. Things hadn't gone at all the way he needed them to go. "Do you mind if I come back to see you again tomorrow? We can go for a walk."

"Did you really go without eating or sleeping?"

"That's not nearly as important as the fact that I couldn't work. Nothing interferes with my work. Well, with the exception of you."

He ran his hands through his hair again, leaving him looking more like a rumpled professor than ever. She pressed a hand to her stomach, not liking the feeling of her insides melting. "You couldn't work?"

His eyes narrowed again, his gaze on her face. "You sound faint. Should I get your sister for you?"

"You couldn't work because of me?" If he spouted a factoid instead of answering her, she might really name him as a candidate for a rocket to Mars. On the other hand, if he answered, she was going to do something stupid like kiss him again.

"Damn it, no, I couldn't. Work is important to me. I don't need you doing this to yourself so I have to be obsessed over your health. You're a doctor, Libby, you should know better."

There wasn't going to be any kissing. She raised her voice. "Sarah? Do we have any Tums in the house?"

"You don't use too many antacids, do you? You certainly don't want to end up with kidney stones. The most common elements of calculi are calcium, oxalate, phosphate and uric acid."

Libby turned her face away from him, afraid the laughter was far too close. He'd done it again. She doubted if he was even aware of it. "Thanks for that information. As a doctor, it's certain to come in handy."

He frowned at her. "I'm going to let you rest, Libby. I need to actually get some work done, but I'm coming over tomorrow to take you for a walk."

"How can you work when you have broken ribs?" Her palm brushed lightly over his ribs, generating that same heat he'd felt before when she touched him.

He covered her hand with his, held it tightly against him. "Not for the forestry. I have a lab in my basement and I've got a project I'm interested in."

"Really?" Her face lit up with interest. "Tell me about it."

"Tomorrow. I want to see if I can get anywhere tonight. Maybe now that I don't have to worry your sisters locked you in the tower and let you die, I can get something done." He stood up, reluctantly letting her hand go as he bent over her to brush a kiss on top of her head. "I'm coming over tomorrow, Libby, so tell the guardian to let me in."

"If you're referring to my sister, her name is Sarah."

"You have a lot of sisters." He strode out of the house, pausing at the door to look back at her.

Libby could feel her heart beating way too fast. His expression was so—hungry. Caring. Longing. Even more than that, he looked protective of her.

"You'd better get some rest."

"I will, Ty," she assured him. When he closed the door she let out her breath, hardly realizing she was holding it.

"Is he gone?" Sarah asked, venturing into the room.

"Yes."

"Baby." Sarah rubbed the top of Libby's head affectionately. "The man is just plain maddening. I can feel how attracted you are to him, but he's just too weird."

"He's brilliant. He can speak several languages, talk about any subject I want to discuss and he's very, very hot. And a good kisser." Libby looked up at Sarah, feeling a little lost. "He's brilliant and that's like an aphrodisiac to me."

"Or more likely it's the wounded bird syndrome."

"What in the world is that?"

"Your continual need to help those in need. If anyone is in need, it's Tyson Derrick."

Libby made a face. "Now you have me being the good girl again. Libby the saint. I'd much rather the attraction be all about sex. Libby the bad girl is much more to my liking."

Sarah groaned. "Yes, because all bad girls like to be told you're so pale you look more of a ghost than usual. I nearly choked to death on that one, and Hannah would have turned him into a toad on the spot."

Libby burst out laughing. "The man can really hand out those compliments, can't he? The worst of it is, I'm actually starting to find it endearing."

Sarah rolled her eyes. "You're so sunk. And that just makes my point. You couldn't be bad if you tried, it isn't in your nature. No one else on the face of this planet would find that man endearing. He's like some kind of porcupine. Touch him and you come away with a hand full of quills."

"He's really quite sweet."

"The man analyzes feelings, he doesn't actually feel them."

"You're wrong, Sarah, and he's not 'the man.' His name is Ty or Tyson."

"I'm sorry, hon." Sarah ruffled her hair. "Drink your tea."

"I know nothing can come of it," Libby said. She realized she sounded regretful and frowned.

"Not necessarily," Sarah said, ashamed of herself when she could see the naked longing on her sister's face. It was just that she wanted to love all of her sister's choices. She couldn't imagine loving Tyson Derrick. "The lock fell from the gate and the house let him in. There was no resistance, Libby, did you notice that?"

"I was too busy noticing how hard his body is. It isn't fair, Sarah, he should either have brains or brawn, but not both."

Sarah laughed. "Elle wasn't happy that we kept him away from you. She said we should let nature take its course."

"What does that mean?" Libby was horrified. "What does she know?"

"Elle never says exactly what she means, but she was very adamant. It's hard for her to maintain a balance of giving people privacy, free agency and warning us off doing something stupid because she knows things we don't."

"Her life is so difficult, Sarah. I worry about her. She told me she doesn't want to have children."

Sarah put down her cup of tea, shocked. "She did? Why? She carries all the gifts. Without her, the Drake legacy would most likely end."

Libby sighed. "She's so sad. I think it's such a burden for her. I told her to talk to Mom. Mom had to learn how to cope with knowing what everyone is thinking and feeling all the time. I try to help, but Elle won't let me."

"You shouldn't be helping anyone for a while, Libby. You need to strike some kind of balance. You give too much of yourself to everyone. If you keep letting people take pieces of you, eventually there'll be nothing left. You know better than to take on someone's illness or injuries."

"It was Jonas. I had no choice." Libby defended herself.

"You did it twice. Healing infections is one thing, you're merely using energy to heal, but taking on something of that magnitude, you're absorbing the injuries. You could die. Why did you heal Tyson Derrick?"

Libby looked down at her hands. "I didn't have a choice, Sarah. I couldn't stop myself. I had no intention of healing him, but I was pulled there and then it was happening. He doesn't even know it."

"He doesn't want to know it because he'd have to believe in something he can't prove," Sarah said. "It's easier to believe we're con artists."

"He doesn't believe that," Libby insisted. "He's a scientist. He thinks differently."

"Magic is science. He just can't explain it, but it's all about energy and the universe. He doesn't fit with us, with our magic."

"Maybe not," Libby admitted and blew on her tea to avoid her sister's eyes.

9

LIBBY tried to hide her excitement and nervousness from her sisters as she surreptitiously glanced at the clock in her living room. Tyson was going to be there any minute. She'd really tried this time with her appearance. She was always pale, but she used foundation, hoping to give herself more color. She'd even applied more eye makeup than usual. She still wore a comfortable pair of jeans, but her top was clinging under her light sweater.

The pull of being with him didn't make sense to her, unless, as Sarah pointed out, it was the wounded bird syndrome. Libby walked over to the couch and put her arm around Hannah's neck to lean down and kiss her on top of her head.

"You're so tired, hon. Can't you go to sleep? I can help you if you'd let me."

Hannah caught her hand. "No, you can't. You have to stop using energy for a long while, even for the minor things. I'm drinking chamomile tea and at least I'm home where I can relax. Jonas is breathing on his own." Without warning, Hannah choked back a sob and put her hands over her face to hide the tears.

Libby sat beside her and put her arms around Hannah. At once the warm light burst out of her, seeking to comfort her sister, to ease her pain. Hannah pulled away abruptly. "Libby! You're supposed to be resting."

"Not when you need me," Libby said firmly. "I've never seen you so . . ." She trailed off searching for the right word. "Broken."

"I just never expected him to get hurt. Not just hurt, but someone almost killed him. Why, Libby? Why would someone do that to Jonas? He's a good man and he genuinely cares about other people all the time. You saw him the other night so upset over a case of parental abuse. He puts everyone else before himself."

"I know, honey," Libby said. Hannah looked gaunt, her eyes red with dark circles under them. "It's been bad, but he's going to live. He'll be back bossing us around very soon."

Hannah flashed a wan smile. "I never thought I'd ever want to hear his annoying arrogant bossiness again, but I can't wait."

Libby forced a bright laugh. "And once he does, you'll want to turn him into a toad again."

Instead of making Hannah laugh, she burst into tears. "I said I wanted him on a rocket to Mars. I was experimenting with spells to keep him out of the house. I never meant for him to get hurt. It was all supposed to be in fun."

"Hannah! For heaven sake, you can't think that you're responsible for someone shooting him. He's in law enforcement. His job is dangerous."

"He always seemed so invincible. I thought we'd always have him around." Hannah ducked her head, staring down at her hands. "Even if he got married, I thought he'd still come around because he loves all of you."

Libby went very still, took a deep breath and let it out. Hannah's pain was palpable. "Jonas loves you, Hannah. There's no question about that."

Hannah leaned her head against Libby's shoulder. "He doesn't, you know. He thinks I'm useless."

Libby wanted to cry for her sister. "Hannah, do you think you're useless? Certainly Jonas doesn't think so. Is it possible that you're putting your own feelings on him?"

"You obviously haven't heard him with me," Hannah said.

"He doesn't like your job. Has it occurred to you that he doesn't like other men looking at you? Not in magazines or on television, especially when you're modeling skimpy clothes? I think all his comments stem from jealousy. Jonas is the type of man to protect those he loves. He can't protect you when you're all over the cover of magazines and he hates the idea of total strangers looking at your body."

Hannah glanced up as Joley came into the room. "He isn't mean to Joley and she has men ogling her all the time."

"No, but he lectures her frequently and he always checks with her security people even though she hates it. And would you want to confront Joley all the time? She's as mean as a snake if you rile her up."

"Hey now!" Joley flung herself onto the couch on the other side of Hannah, catching her hand. "I think a snake is an insult. I'm more like a tigress, or something else fierce with claws."

Hannah laughed in spite of herself. "You're not mean, Joley. You just pretend to be. You have a soft heart."

Joley leaned over and kissed her sister on the cheek. "You keep thinking that, hon, but keep it quiet around Mom and Dad. I carefully cultivated the image and I like it. How's Jonas?"

"He's doing better," Hannah said. "I couldn't keep my eyes open and Kate said she'd stay with Abigail and watch over him until I get back."

"I'm fixing you soup," Joley offered.

"But you don't cook," Hannah said.

Joley shrugged with a small grin. "It's in a can, babe, not your from-scratch soup. Even I can manage to heat up a can of soup."

"Joley, that's so sweet. You don't have to do that."

"I already did. You look as if you haven't had anything

to eat this past week. You need nutrition. Lots and lots of nutrition."

"I haven't been able to sleep since Jonas was shot. I try, but I just keep seeing him lying on the ground covered in blood. I don't think I'll ever be able to get that image of him out of my head." Hannah's hand trembled as she rubbed at her mouth. "Why would someone do that to him? Why?"

Libby shook her head. "We'll probably never know, honey. You're overtired and you need to sleep."

"I didn't want to leave him, but I needed to come home. Kate and Abbey said they'd take care of him," Hannah repeated, sounding lost.

Joley exchanged a long look with Libby. "You're not doing anything wrong by coming home. You've been at the hospital for over a week. You have to take care of yourself or you won't be of any use to Jonas. Come into the kitchen and let me get you some soup." She tugged at Hannah until her sister stood. It was only then that she noticed Libby was wearing makeup. "You can't be going to work yet, Libby. You need at least another week to recover."

Libby tried to look nonchalant. "No, I'm just going out for a walk, maybe head into town to say hello to Inez at the grocery store. I need fresh air."

Joley snorted. "You have to learn to lie, big sister. You're totally blushing."

Hannah studied the scarlet color creeping into Libby's cheeks. "You're seeing him, aren't you, Libby? Tyson Derrick, the man who put the new birthmark on your neck."

"I'm sooo telling Mom," Joley said.

A small smile stole over Libby's face. "Maybe she'll think I'm the bad girl," she said hopefully. "What do you think?"

"Sorry, love, not with me in the house." Joley flashed an engaging smile. "Mom's bound to have read at least one of the gossip mags and I think I've got some love triangle going at the moment." She suddenly looked hopeful. "Or maybe it's a threesome."

"Joley." Hannah wrinkled her nose. "That's just *eww.*"

"Well, it would be nice if my life was as exciting in real life as it is in other people's imaginations."

"I think Libby's life is becoming exciting," Hannah said.

"If Hot Lips is hanging around there's no question things are going to be heating up, but I thought Sarah tried to run him off."

"He doesn't run off very easily," Libby said, a small part of her secretly pleased that he wasn't intimated by her family. Libby was surprised at how eager she was to see Tyson. She'd thought about him all night, even resolved to tell him she wasn't going to go out with him, but the resolve had dwindled away in the morning. She sat for a long time watching the pounding sea as the wind kicked up the ocean into rough, foaming waves as she thought about Tyson Derrick. The more she thought about him, the more she was convinced that he needed her.

"Good for him," Joley said, approval in her voice. "You need a strong man."

"Me? Need *him*? It's the other way around. He analyzes feelings but he either doesn't feel anything for people or doesn't recognize when he does. He's isolated himself from the world. And he uses extreme recreation, such as race car driving, just to make himself feel alive. He's always okay with commenting on people and observing them, but he certainly doesn't want to get involved."

"Except with you."

Libby blushed again. When he looked at her, there was unmistakable desire in his eyes. Raw hunger. Longing. Need. Everything in her rose up to respond. "We actually have a lot in common, although Sarah doesn't think so. We're both calm and it takes a lot to get us upset, although I've noticed I'm more emotional around him. He has a knack for getting under my skin like no one else and I seem to bring out a temper in him. I absolutely love his mind."

Libby caught her sisters exchanging a look. "I do. I can't help it. He's a genius and can talk to me about the things that really appeal to me, but he's disconnected to people and even to his own feelings. He had a rotten childhood. I think he needs me, but really, I don't see why you think I need him."

"Because you live your life for everyone else and you don't have boundaries," Jolcy said. "You're so smart, Libby, but you're too compassionate. You let too many people take pieces out of you. You can't say no. You need someone strong to step in and protect you. We try, but even we have a tendency to use you up. You can't say no and you need someone to provide a balance for you."

"I do not." Libby was indignant.

Hannah nodded her agreement with Joley. "She's right. You need a strong man in your life, one not afraid of anyone, especially us."

Joley glanced out the window and whistled. "Speak of the devil. Oh my, Lib, the man is looking good today."

Hannah and Joley crowded each other for space at the window.

"Get away from there before he sees you," Libby said, mortified, yet she could feel laughter bubbling up. Her sisters loved to tease her, but already Tyson thought her family was a bunch of fruitcakes. She didn't need him to catch them gawking at him. She bared her teeth at her two younger sisters, hoping to look fierce. "Back off, both of you. Go into the kitchen."

"Look at that chest, Hannah. Oh, my. I feel positively faint," Joley said, nudging the tall blond.

A faint answering smile appeared on Hannah's face, the first real one since Jonas had been shot. "I like the way his muscles are rippling."

"You can't see rippling muscles," Libby objected, straining to see.

"You just aren't looking hard enough," Joley said. "And he's wearing tight jeans. Ooh la la." She fanned herself with her hand. "Libby. You go girl."

"That's it. Get into the kitchen." Libby pointed out the direction for them, trying to look stern. "Both of you."

Joley and Hannah went, laughing out loud, peeking

through the archway to watch as Libby hurried to the front door.

Libby opened the door on the first knock. The moment she saw him up close her breath hitched in her throat. He did look hot in a pair of tight jeans and an open-throated shirt. His black hair spilled across his forehead and his blue eyes drifted over her face with a small hint of possession. Her heart quickened at his intent look. His smile broke out, a flash of white teeth, a hint of a dimple, his eyes lighting up. There was no way to stop her own answering smile. "You made it."

"Of course." He took her hand and pulled her to him, reaching past her to close the door behind her firmly. The action brought her body against his. "Are you feeling better?"

He was solid, his body muscular, and she could feel his heat. A small tremor went through her. Her womb contracted. Tyson even smelled good. Manly. She wanted to roll her eyes at her own thoughts. "Yes, much better. What about you, did you get any sleep?" Her voice was disgusting, all husky and silly and beyond her control.

"I got some work done and that's what really counts."

Catching movement at the window, Libby stepped away from Tyson. "What are you working on?"

Ty retained possession of her hand, tugging to get her to follow him down the stairs. He wanted to get her away from the influence of her family home. There was an indefinable power he could feel in spite of his determination not to credit the Drakes with being truly different. "I have some concerns with the PDG-ibenregen drug. I believe there's a problem with it, even though everyone else thinks it's just fine. Well," he hedged, "they want to believe it's just fine."

"The new drug is based on your original research on cell regeneration, isn't it?" Libby asked. She was all too aware of his hand holding hers and the brush of his body against hers as they walked. "I was very interested in the new cancer drug when I heard it was based on your earlier work, but to be honest, I thought they went to trial too soon."

"Exactly," he agreed. "I can't get anyone to listen to me.

I've received several calls from Joe Fields telling me to back off."

"He's the one you mentioned you noticed in the hospital," Libby said. She flashed him a smile. "See? I usually remember things."

"That's the one. He's been a bit unhappy because his old friend Harry, the biochemist on the project, has his nose out of joint."

"You really don't like Harry, do you?"

"He does shoddy work," Tyson said. "I have no tolerance or respect for anyone who is in such a hurry they can't finish the job right. He doesn't research for love of science or to help people, he's a glory hound. He wants everyone to know his name."

"He's jealous of you," Libby guessed.

They walked along the trail leading up above the ocean where she could see the sea seemed to meet the horizon. The waves were calmer without the cool wind. "It feels good to be out of the house."

Tyson took a deep breath and stopped her, swinging around so his body was directly in front of hers. His fingers tightened around her hand, threatening to crush her bones. "Here's the thing, Libby. I've thought a great deal about this. I don't believe in magic. It doesn't make sense to anyone with a logical brain. Whatever you and your sisters do isn't real. I don't know if your family originally used sleight of hand to con people, but whatever the origins, I've observed you enough to know you believe you're able to heal people."

Libby opened her mouth to speak but he shook his head and pulled her hand to his chest. "Just hear me out. I think you're experiencing psychosomatic symptoms, much like a false pregnancy, but we can work on that together. I know I can help you see that no one can really heal anyone with magic. You're smart. You'll see it in time."

She could only stare dumbly, torn between wanting to laugh and to cry. He was so earnest, his expression grave and his blue eyes holding her gaze captive. "I'll see that I make myself ill pretending to heal people?" Obviously she could pick them. If only he would just keep his mouth closed she might get somewhere with him.

"Putting it that way sounds bad. It's more like you've been brainwashed, programmed to believe it and your brain tricks your body into experiencing the symptoms. And that can be dangerous to your health."

He tightened his fingers around hers when she tried to move away from him. "Don't, Libby, don't pull away. I've thought this whole thing through. I want a relationship with you. You're able to understand me, we're interested in the same things and I think you're an incredible woman. I'm willing to pay the price of accepting your family. It really is worth the sacrifice to be able to see you."

Her eyebrow shot up. "How courageous of you to take on my crackpot, con-artist family." She tilted her head to one side. "So I don't really heal people, but I've convinced myself so strongly that I can that I manifest psychosomatic symptoms of the people I think I've healed. That's what you think really happens, huh?"

"Yes. If you just open your mind to the possibility, I'm certain it would make more sense to you. You're a scientist, Libby, a doctor. You *want* to heal people because you're so compassionate, but no one can really do that. Haven't you ever watched the faith healers in the tents and realized they're bilking the public?"

"How do you know they are?" She started walking back toward her house, this time holding his hand so *he* wouldn't let go.

"It's been proven time and time again. The faith healers have been investigated and debunked. Seriously, Libby, I could show you many of the reports. I looked them up over this past week and prepared them in a file for you. It's all there in black and white."

"You did that for me?" She smiled her sweetest smile, wandering slowly up the path to her house. "Tyson Derrick, how considerate of you. I had no idea you were such a thoughtful man."

He let his breath out. "I was afraid you'd be upset, Libby. I was prepared for you to take this in a negative way, but I should have realized you'd reason it out." He stopped on the path to their house. "You want to go home already? I'd like to spend more time with you."

She tugged until he followed her again. "I want you to come in and get to know my sisters. If we're going to spend time together and you're willing to pay that price, now would be a good time to start. Everyone is home with the exception of Kate and Abigail. They're at the hospital with Jonas. Hannah needed to rest, so she's here." She smiled up again, batting her lashes a bit. "She really doesn't use a cauldron—much."

"I wasn't thinking of actually spending time with them. Just more like nodding to them as I picked you up and dropped you off." Ty reluctantly followed her up the steps to the porch. "I'm not the easiest person in the world to be around." He stopped her before she could pull open the door, wrapping his arms around her, dreading going into the house.

"Who told you that?" Libby looked up at him, her voice edged with anger. She might think it, but she didn't want anyone else telling him that.

"Sam." He bent his head toward hers, dropping his tone to a husky whisper. "I love that about you, Libby. I've seen you get that fierce, protective look on your face over your sisters. You don't need to protect me, but you have no idea how much I appreciate the fact that you'd want to."

Libby's heart turned over. She was leading him like a lamb to the slaughter, which he absolutely deserved, but now he had to go and say something so sweet and make her feel guilty. "Sam doesn't always know what he's talking about, Ty."

"I don't know about that, Libby. He's one of the few people in Sea Haven who shares my opinion of your family's whole hocus-pocus thing. It seems to me that that makes him a lot more insightful than most people around here."

Libby narrowed her eyes. "Oh, *really?*"

Tyson nodded, his expression utterly sincere. "Yes. You see, I've been thinking about this a lot. You're too close to your family to see the truth. You're too emotionally involved to think logically about them."

"I see." Libby reached behind and pushed open the door. "Come on in, Ty, I think it's time you face a little realism yourself."

Libby could see Elle kneeling by the fireplace as they entered. "Elle. Tyson says he doesn't believe in our magic. He thinks you've all brainwashed me into believing things that don't exist."

Elle sat back on her knees and shot Tyson a long speculative look. "Oh? Really?" *What do you want to do?* Elle asked immediately. She was such a strong telepath that her sisters could speak to her without much effort.

He doesn't believe in magic. I think he needs to see the Drake family as we really are and not how he imagines us to be.

Yikes. Are you sure? Elle started laughing. *He might have nightmares for the rest of his life.*

Absolutely. If I don't, I'll never be able to live with myself. Is Hannah in bed?

Libby tugged Tyson into the entryway and shut the door so that he was trapped inside. "Come in and sit down."

"Hannah," Elle raised her voice. "We have company. Glad you stopped by, Tyson," she added and waved her hand toward him. "Take a seat."

A large comfortable arm chair slid across the floor to hit him hard in the back of the legs. His knees buckled and he landed in the chair. It went flying back to its normal spot, stopping so abruptly he was nearly pitched out of the seat.

"Ha. Ha. Very funny. I'll bet that does wonders to convince the locals, doesn't it." He felt along the sides of the chair for a runner. Libby wasn't at all happy about the things he'd said. He should have known. She was loyal to a fault and loved her sisters. Ty shook his head. "I guess I deserved that. Are you going to tell me how you did it?"

"I thought I'd let you figure it out," Libby said and sank

onto the floor opposite him. "Would you care for tea or coffee?"

"You always drink tea."

She waved a graceful hand toward the kitchen. "I think something soothing for me." At once the kettle whistled.

He sat back. If Libby wanted to put on a show for him, fine. It wouldn't take him long to figure out her methods and prove his point. "Anything you're having is fine."

Hannah walked into the living room and smiled at him. She looked tired and almost as pale as Libby. "Hi, Tyson. I'm glad you've decided to join us." She sat on the floor beside Elle. "Do you like cookies? I'm just baking them now so they'll be fresh out of the oven."

Joley hurried in. "I heard we were having a party. I'm Joley."

Up close she looked even more beautiful than in the magazines or on the cover of her CDs. Tyson thought he might be a little overwhelmed when he met her as she was one of his favorite singers, but the first thing that really struck him about Joley was the way she looked at her sisters. They all looked at one another with tremendous affection and a secret kind of mischief. He was fairly certain he was going to take the brunt of whatever joke they might be concocting.

"Good to meet you. I'm Tyson Derrick."

"The scientist." Joley made it a statement.

"That would be me."

"Tyson doesn't believe in magic," Libby announced. "He has a theory, which, by the way, is a very good one and makes perfect sense. I think it's very sweet of him to worry about me."

"I don't blame him for being worried about you," Sarah said as she entered the room. She sat on the floor with her sisters. "You still need to rest, Libby."

Tyson could see that they were comfortable on the floor, sitting in a loose semicircle, relaxed as they faced him.

Before he could reply, Sarah waved her hands toward the curtains at the windows and they danced across the glass. He shook his head. They were really determined to put on a show, but after he discovered how they did it, he might rig the house he shared with his cousin to do the same, just for the convenience of it. "A remote control on the drapes? I've heard about it, but haven't seen one quite like that. I particularly like the moving chair. I could use one in my lab to follow me around."

"Do you take milk in your tea?" Libby asked.

"I've never tried it that way, but I'm certainly game." No matter what she was planning, he could take it. She wasn't going to scare him off, not with a remote control device for the living room drapes and a moving chair. "Libby tells me you were at the hospital with Jonas, Hannah. How is he doing?"

Joley and Elle both reached over and put a hand on Hannah's legs. She lifted her chin a little and managed a small, strained smile. "He's breathing on his own, although he isn't really fully awake. They've been keeping him unconscious." There was a small hitch in her voice.

Tyson looked quickly at Libby. "He will be all right, won't he?"

Sarah answered, "Yes, of course. We wouldn't allow anything to happen to Jonas. He's family. We love him very much."

Tyson sighed and looked down at his hands. Maybe they all believed they were magic. They'd been tricking the public for so long, they had convinced themselves, just as he suspected. It wasn't just Libby, it was all of them. "When will he be able to get out of ICU?"

"Maybe another week," Hannah said.

Tyson caught movement out of the corner of his eye and turned his head to see several steaming mugs floating through the air. His breath caught in his lungs. There didn't seem a way to rig mugs of tea to glide through the air. He watched as each sister held out her hand to catch the handle of a cup floating past. The last mug came toward him, a slow lazy drift through the air. He narrowed his eyes, observing the air around the mug, studying it to see if it stayed on the same course or moved up and down.

He wasn't going to be intimidated by mere tricks. Trying to look casual, Tyson caught the steaming mug of tea by the handle as if he'd been doing it every day of his life. He shifted forward so he could sweep around it with his right hand, testing for hidden wires. His hand went through the air with ease and when he pulled the mug to him, there was no slight tug that he could feel that might indicate it was being released from a hidden mechanism. He settled back and took a blasé sip, his mind whirling with possibilities.

He eyed Libby. She seemed to be engrossed in her tea, nodding to something Sarah said that he missed. His mouth had gone dry and his heart beat that little bit too fast. He had watched more than one magician performing on a stage and never once had he thought it was real. He was aware of mirrors and illusions, but he had just plucked a floating mug right out of the air. He had tested for wires, for any kind of hidden device and there hadn't been one.

"Would you care for a cookie to go with your tea?" Hannah asked politely.

Before he could say no, a plate drifted out of the kitchen. Piled high with cookies, it didn't even take the same route as the teacups had. He shrunk back a little in his chair, choking on tea. It nearly went up his nose. There had to be a rational explanation. The plate hovered right in front of him, the cookies smelling like heaven and looking too good to be true.

He brought his hand under the plate and shoved, tipping the plate, spilling the cookies. He'd meant to examine the bottom of the plate, but he let go, staring in shock at the cookies spread out like a cascading waterfall in the air. They hovered there, unmoving, not hitting the floor. One by one they restacked themselves onto the plate. Before the last cookie could find its way to the plate, Joley snapped her fingers and held out her hand. Tyson watched with horrified eyes as the cookie zipped across the room straight to her.

Joley snatched it out of the air and took a bite. "This is awesome, Hannah. You outdid yourself. Did you use the new sugar cookie recipe you were telling us about?"

"Holy crap," Tyson burst out. "This isn't funny anymore. You nearly gave me a heart attack. How the hell did you all do that?"

Libby tilted her head to one side so that her hair slid over one eye leaving her looking mysterious and maybe that little bit like a witch. He'd never noticed that before.

"I don't actually know. I'm hoping you can explain it to us since you know so much more than we do. We've always been able to do things, but maybe we just *think* we can. Maybe we're deluding ourselves that the tea and cookies float in from the kitchen and that Sarah closed the drapes and Elle moved the chair."

"Or that I know exactly what you're thinking right now," Elle said. "I wouldn't mind if you managed to get rid of that for me. It's very uncomfortable knowing too much about people and feeling their emotions all the time."

"So what am I thinking right now?" Tyson challenged.

"You want to think we're all crazy, but the possibility that it's true excites you. You'd like blood samples and even to hook a couple of us up to an EEG monitor so you can scan our brains to see if activity changes when we do whatever it is we do. You're mostly excited about the possibilities to science. You're having a difficult time reconciling the two as they seem complete opposites. They aren't, you know. Magic is really energy which you've really known and have considered all along, but threw out the idea of as preposterous."

"You want to hook up our brains and study the activity?" Libby echoed.

Tyson leaned forward, his eyes glittering with sudden excitement. "Libby, she was dead on. She's either the real thing or she really has superb insight into people. I do want a blood sample and maybe even tissue samples. I'd like to know if there's anything different in your genetic makeup."

Libby put a hand to her heart. "You're so romantic, Ty. Whenever you talk like that I want to just fling myself into your arms."

"You're being sarcastic and whoever is controlling the cookie platter, send it my way. They smell good." He shook his head. "You of all people, Libby, should recognize the importance of this to science. If your family can really do such things as telekinesis and healing, which by the way, there is absolutely no proof of, it would be a remarkable discovery."

Sudden temper flashed through Libby. She'd been feeling somewhat amused and even a small bit guilty, but now she just wanted to throttle him. "I not only opened up my life to you, Tyson Derrick, I asked my family to do the same. Now you're looking at us as if we're a bunch of your little pet rats. Worse, you still doubt I can do what is so much a part of me. If you deny my ability to heal, you're denying me, who I am."

Elle, I need a very sharp knife.

You can't kill him.

Libby glared at her younger sister, jumped up and stalked into the kitchen. Ty frowned and leapt up to follow her.

"Do you have to be so emotional over everything, Libby? It's only logical for me to be excited about a discovery of this magnitude."

"You think I'm *emotional*? *Emotional*?" She repeated. Maybe she was acting a little out of character, but he was driving her to it. "For the last several days you've made it clear you thought my family was conning people out of money, although we've *never* taken a penny using our gifts. You have to be shown the truth in order to believe we might actually be able to do what everyone else says we can and then you want to study us for the pure love of science." She turned away from the counter, knife in her hand.

Tyson's expression hardened. "What the hell do you think you're doing?"

"Proving to you I can do what I say I can."

He took another step until he was within striking distance. "Give me the knife right now, Libby."

She scowled and lifted her left hand palm up, putting the tip of the blade against her skin. Tyson moved so fast she was shocked when his fingers settled around her wrist like a vice, jerking her arm up and away from her palm.

"I was only going to make a small cut so you could see for yourself."

"No, you aren't." He tossed the knife into the sink and tugged on her wrist until she came up against his body. "You are not going to cut yourself to prove a point. If it's that important, I believe you. Okay? I believe you, Libby. Your sisters can float cookies, read minds and you can heal." His voice trailed off as realization donned. Each time she brushed his ribs, there was less pain. His sternum hadn't hurt for a while now. He hadn't even noticed, but now that he was contemplating the possibility that her family was for real, he realized it was true. There had been bruises on his ribs and shoulder, ugly purple splotches, and they had faded away far too quickly. He swallowed, going pale. "You can . . . *heal* people. Me. Jonas."

Fear blossomed as he stared down at her face. The pale skin. The dark circles. Her fragile, ethereal appearance. Her *ghostly* appearance. She'd nearly died saving Jonas. That's why he hadn't been able to see her all those days. Her family had kept everyone away because *Libby was dying.* Had the same thing happened when she'd healed him of a brain injury?

He pulled out a kitchen chair and sank into it, his legs weak, as he remembered her staggering out of his room. "Oh, God, Libby." He covered his eyes with his hands, trying to wipe away the memory of the agony on her face that day at the hospital. "You almost died, didn't you?"

Libby wanted to comfort him. He looked so completely shocked, almost horrified by the dawning knowledge. Ty looked like a man who'd taken a body blow.

He shook his head, standing up. "I can't think about what you've done, or how it affects you. Not right now. It's too much. Believe me, I was impressed enough with the cookies." He lifted his head to study her, his gaze dark with sudden intrigue, emotions fading to the background where Tyson was most comfortable with them.

Libby could actually see the change take place. The scientist was back and he was looking at her with a quizzical contemplation. She backed away from him. "Whatever you're thinking, just stop now before you get yourself in more trouble. You aren't conducting a study on us."

"Just think about it logically, Libby. If it was turned around, wouldn't you want to figure out how it's done? There has to be a high level of activity in the brain and we have instruments to measure and map it out."

"I'm not a freaking study of yours, Ty." Libby tried to pull away from him so he wouldn't see the tears swimming in her eyes.

"Of course you're not. Damn it, Libby, don't you cry. I wouldn't have the least idea what to do and I've already said and done enough idiotic things today. I'm a little out of my element." His heart was still pounding with the realization of his discovery. He was desperately trying to lock away the knowledge that she could heal and that she was risking her own health in doing so. He needed to be alone to think about that one. Now she was going to cry. He was beginning to sweat.

"You've just admitted you're an intelligent man. Am I supposed to believe you can't figure out how to talk decently to a woman? Figure it out, Ty, because I'm not waiting around while you do."

In desperation, he framed her face with both hands and bent his head down to hers, his mouth taking possession. If he couldn't find the right words to say, he was determined to show her exactly how he felt. Libby held herself stiff at first, although her lips were soft and she opened her mouth to his when he tugged on her lower lip. Heat blossomed and spread, from him to her. Electricity arced, small sizzling licks along his veins, from her to him. Her body softened, melted into his so he could feel her imprinted on his skin. Hell, maybe all the way to his bones.

Her mouth was hot and exciting, and so responsive Tyson forgot he was in her house with her sisters close by. One hand tangled in the silk of her hair and the other slid down the curve of her spine. He swore the earth spun on its axis.

"Libby!" The protest came from a distance.

Tyson caught Libby's soft sigh and drew it into his lungs. His arms tightened, his body reluctant to step away from hers. He rested his forehead against hers, breathing deep. "I'm coming back for you tomorrow."

"Okay."

"I'll be on the motorcycle so dress warm."

"Okay."

He lifted her chin and brushed her mouth with his. "I'll wait a day or two before I creep in and take everyone's blood."

She flashed him a small grin. "Good of you. My sisters will appreciate it."

Joley raised her voice. "Your sisters would appreciate a little break from the hormone rush."

"I'm going now," Tyson announced and forced his body away from Libby.

10

"YOU can't go with him on a motorcycle and that's all there is to it," Sarah said. "What are you thinking, Libby? Have you lost your mind?"

"I've been on a motorcycle," Joley pointed out. "In fact I've been the driver."

"You aren't helping, Joley." Sarah flashed her rebel sister a stern look meant to repress. "Motorcycles are dangerous."

"So are airplanes and cars and mountain climbing. Walking across the street can be dangerous," Joley said, clearly not impressed by Sarah's reprimand. "Heck, going out on a stage to sing can be dangerous."

Sarah swung her attention instantly from Libby to Joley. "What does that mean?"

"It means life can be dangerous, Sarah, but we don't go through it sitting in a closet because we're afraid of every little thing."

"Tyson Derrick is a crazy man. Do you really want Libby racing around on the back of his motorcycle? That's nuts."

Libby drew up her knees and glanced at the clock. The argument was moot as far as she was concerned anyway. The man had kissed her senseless and somehow she'd agreed to try a small slow run on his motorcycle to "really see the beauty of the coast." She sighed. It sounded like something a bad girl might do. Her own small rebellion against always doing the perfect and right thing. The *responsible* thing. Now, what did it matter?

She could feel tears burning close. The man made her cry twice now. Wouldn't it be really horrible if he was right? If she was completely emotional? He was over an hour late and all of her sisters were acutely aware of her misery. It was making them edgy. Both Sarah and Joley were trying to protect her, each in their own way. But she didn't need it. She could protect herself from the idiot with the brilliant brain. *How dare he stand her up*?

"I'm certain Ty would be very careful with Libby," Joley said. "He obviously cares about her." She glared at Sarah, willing her to back off. Libby looked so miserable that if Tyson didn't show his face in the next five minutes, Joley was personally going to see to it he didn't date *anyone* for a very long time.

Libby stood up abruptly. "I'm going over to his house. He's already over an hour late. I'm not sitting here waiting for him. I'm going to tell him what a jerk he is and not to ever call me or come by again."

"Just call him," Sarah advised. "Why put yourself through seeing him in person? Just stay away from him and save yourself the heartache." She wanted to gather her younger sister into her arms and hold her until that look of rejection and hurt was gone forever.

"No, I have to do this in person, Sarah," Libby said. "He's different. I know you have a hard time with him, and at times like this I can't tell you why I've always been drawn to him, but I have. I like talking to him and I understand him even when he's not saying things right, which is most of the time. We mesh when we're together."

"He needs you," Elle said in a soft voice. "And you need him. I'm sorry he hurt you, Libby. I know it can't be intentional. I wouldn't have let him near you if he wasn't sincere in his feelings. He has the most analytical brain I've ever come across and he computes at a very rapid rate of speed. It must drive him crazy sometimes. But not with you. He wasn't being analytical no matter how hard he tried. You tap into the human side of him and he's very aware of it and aware of how much he needs you."

"Then why is he trying to change her?" Sarah asked.

"He's uncomfortable with emotion, Sarah," Elle said.

Elle sounded tired and Libby put her arm around her youngest sister. At once a soothing warmth flowed from one to the other. Elle rested her head briefly on Libby's shoulder.

"Well, he'd better get comfortable with it a little faster," Sarah bit out between her teeth. "Damon was uncomfortable with emotion but he didn't stand me up or dislike my family because they were a little different."

"A little?" Joley echoed. "We're freakin' weird and you know it. You can't blame the man for not believing we do what we do. Face it, Sarah, he had every reason to think we're a family of con artists and yet he still wanted to see Libby. That should tell you something about the way the man feels about her. It has to be genuine."

Libby caught up her purse. "We don't argue and fight with one another as a rule. I'm not letting Tyson Derrick ruin the way we are with one another."

"Libby, honey." Sarah hurried to throw her arms around her sister. "No one could change how close we are. If Tyson Derrick is your choice, I'll not only accept him, but I'll come to love him. You have to know that. I'm just worried about you and how he makes you feel about yourself. I'm overprotective, that's all. You're not only beautiful on the outside, but on the inside as well. You don't see it in yourself but you light up a room just by walking into it. If he doesn't see that, he doesn't deserve you."

Libby hugged her back and stepped away. "I know I at least deserve more than a man who stands me up on a date."

Libby could feel her sisters watching her as she slid into her car and closed the door with controlled violence. She did have a temper that flared up as strong and as passionate as her sisters, she just couldn't sustain it for any length of time. She always made excuses for everyone. She thought of herself as strong. When it was necessary she could stand up to anyone for her patients or her family. Even for herself. She just always was able to see other people's point of view. But that didn't make her a doormat and if Ty thought she could be walked on simply because he had a brain and was the hottest kisser in town, he was sadly mistaken.

She drove straight to the house Ida Chapman had bequeathed to her son and her nephew. It was a huge home on a beautiful piece of property, high on a bluff so the residents could see the rolling ocean from the long bank of windows in the front. She parked at the entrance to the double garage and stalked up to the front door. Leaning heavily on the doorbell didn't do her much good.

Libby walked around to the garage entrance to see if Tyson's car was parked in the building. The door was slightly ajar and she slipped inside. The lighting was dim and she took two steps before her eyes adjusted and she became aware of two men at the far end of the garage near Tyson's car. Both straightened up and turned to face her. Neither man was familiar to her and the way they turned suggested stealth or guilt.

Libby's heart fluttered wildly. She took two cautious steps backward. She could never get into her car and drive away before they could stop her so she whirled and ran back up the steps to Tyson's house, praying the front door was unlocked. She heard the pounding of footsteps behind her as she yanked open the door, slamming it behind her, trying to lock it quickly.

"Wait!" Libby heard the hoarse cry behind her. Visions of Jonas's body lying on the side of the road and the threat of Edward Martinelli were enough to keep her self preservation alarm shrieking.

"Tyson! Sam! Help!" She screamed the names at the top of her lungs. "Call nine-one-one. Tyson!" The doorknob twisted before she could engage the lock and she sprang away from the door, running through the living room toward what she hoped was the kitchen. She had no idea of the layout of the house, but nearly everyone had a phone in the kitchen.

She found a door, tore it open, hearing the men running through the house just behind her. A lighted staircase led to the basement below. Tyson's laboratory. Libby ducked inside and closed the door, running down the stairs just as Tyson came rushing toward her. He caught her in his arms and held her tight. "What is it? What are you doing here? Tell me what's happened."

The door at the top of the stairs opened and the two men began to descend cautiously. Tyson thrust Libby behind him, his body shielding hers. Sam stepped into view, trailing behind the two men. "I heard Libby scream and ran downstairs to find these two in our house, Ty."

"Harry Jenkins and Joe Fields." Ty identified them, his voice low and furious. "What the hell are you doing in my house? And what did you do to Libby?" He took a step forward, his fingers curling tightly into two hard fists.

Harry and Joe exchanged a long nervous look. Harry took a slight step toward Tyson, one hand coming up in a conciliatory manner. "We didn't mean to scare her. She startled us, Ty. We were having a look around and she walked in on us."

"What do you mean 'having a look around?' " Sam demanded. "You just thought you could walk into our house unannounced? Who are these two idiots, Ty? Should I call the sheriff?"

"There's no need for that," Joe said. "We wanted a word with Ty and we inadvertently frightened the lady. It was unintentional."

"And we weren't in the house," Harry added. "We were in the garage."

"So you were skulking around my garage?" Tyson asked. "And then you chase Libby into my house? What the hell is going on?"

"We knocked for half an hour, Ty," Harry said, running a finger around the collar of his shirt. "No one came to the door, so I checked inside the garage to see if your vehicles were there, but I couldn't find a light switch. I could see the car but not your motorcycle so we went all the way in. We drove all this way to talk to you in person and we didn't want to just turn around and go back. You told me a year or so ago that you had a laboratory in your home. You're deaf in your lab so I just figured if you didn't answer you might still be here."

"So you chased Libby?"

"Come on, Ty," Harry burst out, exasperated. "You know I'm not some psycho killer. I was trying to reassure her we weren't stealing anything." He paced down one of the three long aisles between the rows of worktables, eyeing the various pieces of equipment. "I said I was sorry, what more do you want?"

"I want you to apologize to Libby for scaring the hell out of her. And I want you to acknowledge to me that you understand I will beat you to a bloody pulp if you ever come near her again."

Libby's fingers twisted in the back of Ty's shirt. He was a man of science, certainly not a violent man, but his tone made her shiver. He sounded cold and mean and downright dangerous.

Ty must have felt the small shudder that went through her because he turned to sweep her under the protection of his shoulder. His eyes glittered with menace and Libby realized that there was another side to Tyson Derrick that she didn't know.

"I'm not kidding about the apology, Harry. I'd better hear one from both of you or Sam's calling the sheriff and I'm pressing charges for breaking and entering."

Harry glared at him from two worktables down. "I'm sorry—what is your name?"

"Her name is Dr. Drake."

The steel in Ty's voice made her wince again.

"I'm sorry, Dr. Drake," Harry said. "I certainly didn't mean to frighten you. I'm Harry Jenkins and I work with Ty at BioLab. This is my colleague, Joe Fields. I'm a biochemist and Joe is in marketing."

"I second the apology sincerely," Joe said. "I tried to call out to you, but you were already out the door before we could get around the cars."

Before Libby could respond, Sam interrupted. "You've been calling night and day, Jenkins. What the hell is so important that you had to break into our house?"

"You must be Sam, Ty's cousin." Harry wandered around the laboratory restlessly, bending once to put his eye to the microscope. "You've got some great equipment here, Ty."

"Let's have it, Harry," Ty said. "What's so important?"

Harry scowled at him. "You know what's important, Ty. I received a little visit from the director. He *questioned* my reports. He *questioned* me, you son of a bitch, just like he always does when you step in to play the heroic savior of all the projects in the lab. His shining star. I want you to back off on this. This is my baby. I put my sweat and blood into this drug and you aren't going to take it away from me."

"Your reports aren't accurate, Harry," Ty said, ignoring the other man's rising tone. "I went to you first and tried to tell you, but you refused to listen. Look at *all* the data, not just the part that supports your theories."

"We stand to lose millions, possibly billions, if you keep interfering," Joe said. "BioLab is one hundred percent behind this drug. It's going to save thousands of lives and you know it."

"I know it's going to kill people."

Harry slapped his hand down on the table, rocking some of the glass. "This is so like you, Derrick. You always have to be in the spotlight. You know I have a winner here and you just can't stand it."

Tyson wrapped his arm around Libby's waist. He knew what was coming, he'd been through it many times before with other biochemists when he refused to compromise. He laced his fingers through hers, hoping she would understand. He shrugged. "Harry, why do we always have to go through the same arguments? You and I both know you took a shortcut. You used my research as a platform."

"Which is perfectly legitimate. You don't own that research, Derrick. I knew this was about your ego." Harry snarled. "You don't want anyone to touch the research and possibly improve on what you did."

"I want any place I work to be known for good solid research, Harry. And solid researchers don't overlook obvious flaws simply because they don't want to take the time to fix it." Tyson glared at him as the man peered at the data on the screen of one of the computers. "Get the hell away from there."

"You're working on *my* drug right here. Who gave you access to my files? I knew it. You have a spy on my team."

"Don't be ridiculous, Harry. I don't need a spy to figure out what you did. What I'm trying to do is figure out what you didn't do."

"I'm getting a court order to insist you leave my work alone," Harry said.

Tyson gave a snort of derision. "You do that, Harry."

Joe held up his hand. "Let's all calm down."

"I'm perfectly calm," Ty said. "Considering the two of you have trespassed on private property and Harry here is threatening me."

Joe forced a small smile. "Harry needs to calm down. No one wants to get a court order, Ty. We're reasonable men. You've been working long enough for BioLab to know the company would never put out an unsafe drug. The studies are amazing. This drug can really save lives and we're all excited about it."

"What about the deaths, Fielding? Are you excited about them, too?"

Joe waved his hand. "Only a very small percentage of the test subjects have died Ty, and in each case, the patient took his own life. You know as well as I do suicide is not uncommon among chronically ill people. That's a sad fact of life, but BioLab can't be held responsible for patients who decide to end their life during trials."

"Don't you even want to investigate the possibility that not only is something wrong with the drug the way it is, but that it can be fixed?" Tyson asked. "If Harry wants to be named as founder of a drug that saves millions of lives, hold him accountable. Don't let him turn in second-rate work."

"Second-rate work!" Harry thundered. "You son of a bitch." He rushed Tyson, attempting to tackle him.

Ty stepped to the side, avoiding the charging man with ease, his movement unexpectedly graceful. Harry landed heavily on the floor at his feet.

"Surely you weren't thinking of attacking me, Harry?" Ty asked, amusement plain in his voice. "You're a grown man. Have a little dignity."

Libby backed away farther as Harry glowered up at Tyson. There had been a definite taunt in Tyson's voice.

Harry scrambled to his feet, fists clenched. "You think you're so superior, Derrick. You always have. You think your money makes you better than everyone else?"

"Money?" Tyson echoed. He clearly hadn't considered the money. "Work ethics, Harry, the love of science. Try sheer brains."

Harry went berserk again, swinging wildly at Tyson who deflected several punches and tapped Harry's cheek lightly twice. That only seemed to enrage Harry more.

Joe Fields stepped in, catching Harry and dragging him away. "He obviously could beat you to a bloody pulp if he wanted, Harry. This isn't helping. We came here to talk this out reasonably."

"How can anyone be reasonable with that smug bastard?" Harry asked. His gaze flicked to Libby. "The only reason anyone would want to be around him is for his money. Nothing else could possibly make him bearable."

Libby's gaze shifted to Tyson's face. A muscle jerked in his jaw and his eyes went icy, but other than that, it was nearly impossible outwardly to tell if Harry's arrow had found a mark—but she *felt* the jab of pain. Harry scored a much larger hit than he realized. The revelation struck Libby. Tyson didn't believe he was lovable. And why should he? His parents hadn't understood or wanted him, and even Sam told him how difficult he was to be around. Her heart ached for him. He stood tall and straight, his shoulders square, staring down Harry Jenkins.

"You can say whatever you like about me, Harry, but it won't change the facts. The drug is flawed and it's going to kill people. You have no intention of fixing it. You want respect for your work, but you're never going to get it unless you get over your shoddy work practices. The drug might eventually be an amazing discovery, but not in its present form. You're rushing something for glory."

"Like you care about the people dying," Harry snapped back. "You could care less if half the population of the world died from the plague. Don't go trying to portray yourself as the savior of the world."

"Stop," Libby burst out, taking a step forward. She marched back down the aisle between the worktables until she planted herself in front of Tyson, her fists on her hips. "That's enough. You didn't come here to talk reasonably about a drug that obviously, *obviously* has a major side effect on a certain age group of patients. I heard rumors about the side effects months ago, but not once since barging into this house have you even asked Ty about his concerns or his findings. Neither of you. That certainly doesn't show the least bit of responsibility to me. You can stand here until Christmas, calling Ty all kinds of names, but if he believes there is something wrong with the drug, you can bet there is. And you can't keep a thing like that secret."

Joe Fields shook his head. "Dr. Drake, this has gone badly, but we did come to try to resolve this situation. I'm sure you can understand the reactions of a man when he sees someone stealing his work."

"*Stealing*?" Libby shook off Ty's restraining hand. "Ty wouldn't steal a glass of water if he were dying of thirst in the desert. Harry Jenkins used Ty's research as a foundation. Ty did all the hard work and Jenkins jumped onboard as soon as he saw Ty had something important."

"I think we'd better leave," Fields said. "We're not going to solve this by arguing. I'm sorry you both feel this way, but if you persist, Derrick, you'll be hearing from our lawyers."

Tyson took an aggressive step forward, setting Libby to one side as he confronted Fields. "Either you both think I'm stupid or you've forgotten we all work for BioLab and they own all intellectual rights to the drug, research, everything. I'd have to show intent to harm BioLab for you to get lawyers involved, but hey, I'd love for this to go public."

Fields tugged hard on Harry, practically dragging him up the stairs. Tyson jerked his head at Sam to indicate that he wanted him to escort them through the house. Sam nodded and trailed after the two men.

Tyson stood for a long moment staring up the staircase before turning to Libby. "I'm sorry about that. Harry Jenkins can be very unpleasant."

"They scared the hell out of me."

"I know. I could see it on your face. Thank you for sticking up for me. It isn't often that happens and I really appreciate it."

"Aren't you going to ask me why I stopped by?" Libby challenged him.

His fingers tangled in her hair. "I managed to work that out while I was pretending to listen to Harry and Joe. I'm sorry, Libby." He turned to wave his arms to encompass the lab. "I've been breaking down the PDG drug, component by component, and time got away from me. I can't tell you how sorry I am. I set the alarm, but if it went off, I didn't hear it."

"You set an alarm to remember we had a date?" She glanced at the clock by the stairway. A tray of untouched food was beside it, right where Sam must have placed it earlier in the day.

He sighed. "That sounds so bad. I mean it, Libby, I'm really sorry. It won't . . ."

She put her fingers over his lips. "Don't tell me it won't happen again. Of course it will happen again. It's just a fact of your life that whatever you're working on can consume you completely. Where's another lab coat? I want to see what you found."

Tyson stood in stunned silence. *No one* had ever reacted that way. And no one had ever asked to share his passion with him. "Are you sure?" He could barely get the words out and his tone was husky to his own ears.

"Before Irene ever mentioned the trial to me, I was reading as much as I could about the drug. It sounded so promising that I researched it as thoroughly as possible. Several colleagues of mine contributed what they knew or thought, and I began to get a very uneasy feeling. That's why when Irene asked about putting Drew in the program I asked her to wait a bit longer until we knew more."

"You were right to be suspicious," Ty said. "The side effects for young people are very different from the side effects for adults, yet they're using the drug for both. The adults seem to be able to handle it, but the kids are definitely having a problem." He reached over her head to drag a lab coat from a shelf. "Here, put this on."

"And then we're going to go out and get you food, Ty," Libby said. "You can't go without eating, it isn't good for you."

"You sound like Sam," Tyson said as he led her toward the back of the room where he had his work set up. "He's all about getting me fat."

"He brought you lunch earlier."

"Did he?" Ty looked around with a faint frown on his face. "I don't remember. Poor Sam. I must drive him crazy. He takes the time to make food for me and I don't even notice him. I'm the only family he's got and I'm not very good."

Libby rubbed his arm. "Family loves unconditionally."

Their gazes collided. "Not my family."

She flinched at the grimness in his tone. "Isn't that the way you love Sam?"

He turned to examine the data on the screen of his computer. "Yes."

Libby smiled to herself. His voice was gruff. He was uncomfortable with anything to do with his emotions. "Then most definitely you know how to love unconditionally."

Tyson drummed his fingers on the tabletop, peering closer at the computer, clearly uncomfortable. "I know the problem is in the components, but I haven't isolated it yet. Old Harry could be a great biochemist. He's got the right idea, but something is off and I just can't get it."

"Most research focuses on adults, not adolescents. Much more research on the adolescent brain is needed. We need large focus studies of treatment conducted," Libby suggested.

Tyson nodded his head in agreement. "I spoke to the head office about that just the other day. They don't seem to understand that brains that aren't fully developed react differently to meds than adult brains."

"Maybe they don't want to know, Ty," Libby said carefully. "There are too few researchers focusing on children and most are working for pharmaceutical companies. Maybe the answer is for a non-pharmaceutical company to conduct the studies."

He shook his head. "I don't believe that, Libby. The men and women on my team are dedicated to what they do, not to the money for the company. They want to find ways to help. I think we need to show the importance for adolescents. People have the unrealistic idea that teens aren't vulnerable to disease and mental illness. Maybe they just don't want the facts in their face so they overlook that particular segment in research, but the reaction these kids are having to this drug is a prime example of why we need to concentrate on the adolescent brain."

Libby pushed a hip against him to move him so she could see the data as well. "We should talk to Drew and get his mother's consent to draw his blood."

"And get the reports on him from this study," Tyson agreed. "That would be very helpful. Do you think Irene will give us her consent?"

"She's called the house numerous times and she was very apologetic."

"She should be. She bashed you over the head."

"Not just for that. I doubt she would have hurt me if I hadn't already been having a difficult time, but she actually sold Drew's remarkable story of my putting him into remission to a tabloid."

Tyson stiffened, straightening to frown at her. "She claimed you healed Drew and sold the story to a tabloid?" He repeated it slowly and Libby could feel the tension in the room go up noticeably.

She swallowed hard. Tyson might be on his way to accepting the magical talents of the Drakes, but he wasn't totally there yet. It made him very uncomfortable and she didn't like the feeling of walking on eggshells when she talked to him about it. "You know, Ty, I live with unexplained things every day. They're commonplace in my life. If we can't talk about it, then there's no point continuing to try to have a relationship."

His eyes narrowed and he caught her chin in his hand. "I'm not *trying* to have a relationship with you; Libby, I'm *in* a relationship with you. I've wanted you as far back as I can remember. Maybe I didn't always recognize that it was you that I wanted, but you were important to me and I couldn't stop thinking, or fantasizing about you. Your family doesn't scare me. I have a lot of failings, but I'm tenacious. I know we're right together. Maybe you don't yet, but I do."

"I love my family, Ty. I'm always going to love them and I'll always need to be close to them. There's no getting away from that."

"I know. I can see that every time I look at you with them. If I seemed a bit upset it wasn't over your family, it was the fact that Irene would sell out not only a friend, as you obviously are to her, but her own son. I'm certain the notoriety didn't help his condition."

Tyson bent his head to kiss her again, because he couldn't resist. Her eyes widened with shock and took on a slow, sensual burn that caused a heated meltdown to his insides. He threw caution to the wind. His palm curled around the nape of her neck to drag her closer, fingers twisting in the wealth of thick, dark hair so he could pull back her head to the perfect angle, to give his mouth access to her. She was everything he'd ever wanted, ever dreamed or fantasized about. He wanted her with every fiber of his body, every cell of his being.

He kissed her, savoring the taste of her, aggressive in his

pursuit. He wanted her to feel the things he couldn't seem to convey to her with words. It wasn't only about the excitement of her body. She'd found some weakness and invaded his mind, wrapped herself inside him. She'd been there much longer than he'd ever acknowledged.

"Sometimes, at night, before I go to sleep, I hear you laugh," he murmured against her lips. He ached with wanting her, with his need of her. "I lie there wishing you were with me."

His mouth was driving her crazy, making the world slide away until she could think of nothing but him. Her arms slid around his neck, her body became liquid heat, pliable, flowing, alive with need. She could feel every muscle in his body, taste his hunger, his passion. One hand tangled in her hair, the other shaped the curve of her waist, her hip, slid under her blouse to stroke bare skin. She swore the pads of his fingers sent tiny electrical pulses streaking through her body to find every nerve ending.

She burrowed her hands under his shirt, wanting to get closer to him, surprised by the feel of hard muscle as she ran her palms gently over his chest. She was drowning in his kisses, aching for him, returning kiss for kiss as the voltage went up several kilowatts and spread with the force of thermonuclear energy through her body.

Tyson tore his mouth from hers, breathing deeply to regain control. "We can't stay here, Libby."

She blinked up at him, a little dazed by her reaction to him. "We can't?"

"No, Sam could walk in any time and I'm not going to be able to keep my hands off you." Tyson looked down at her, arms still holding her tightly against him, pressing his body into hers. "Come on, I've got a few special places I'd like you to see. We can go on the motorcycle. You're already dressed for it."

Libby slid her arms around his waist. It was silly, really, she was very independent, but Tyson made her feel protected and safe when he held her so close. And she couldn't suppress a small guilty thrill that went through her at the possessive way he looked at her. "I worked up my courage hours ago, Ty, but I've lost it again. I've seen too many head injuries from motorcycles."

"You said you'd go with me." His chin nuzzled the top of her head.

"That was before, when you kissed me until I couldn't think."

He pulled back to look at her, a slow smile lighting his face. "You couldn't think?"

"No. I was lucky to know my own name," Libby admitted, laughing softly.

As Libby hugged Tyson hard around his waist, she felt waves of animosity surrounding her. Glancing up, she encountered Sam scowling down at them from the landing. He reached out and touched the clock sitting on the small telephone table beside the stairs, but he was looking at her, and it wasn't a pleasant perusal. In that unguarded moment, she knew Sam felt the same way about Tyson and Libby dating as Sarah did—he was totally against it.

Sam's eyes met hers, his animosity plain. She couldn't really blame him if Tyson really hadn't been eating or sleeping or even working because of her, but it was uncomfortable to know someone didn't like her. She'd never known that to happen before. Instantly she tried to pull free from Ty, but he tightened his hold as he looked up at his cousin with a small grin.

"Hey, Sam, I was just about to leave with Libby on the bike. Are you going out tonight?"

"Ty, I'd like to talk to you for a minute," Sam said, his voice grim.

"Sure. This will only take a second, Libby," Tyson assured her as he went up to the top of the stairs.

Libby watched the two men go into the hallway. Neither closed the door. Their voices carried clearly back down to her.

"You aren't going to take her out on your motorcycle, are you?" Sam demanded. "Are you crazy? If something goes wrong she's liable to sue you."

"What's wrong, Sam?" Tyson asked.

"Good old Harry is a first-class bastard, Ty, but he asked a good question. What is she doing with you? You're worth a lot of money. You don't think she knows that?"

Libby's breath caught in her throat. No one had ever accused her of being a gold digger before. She was going to tell Sam to shove it. She took a step toward the stairs.

"So, what you're saying, Sam, is that a woman couldn't possibly want to be with me for any other reason than my money? What? Am I really that screwed up?"

"I'm not saying that, but come on, Ty. Libby Drake? She agrees to go riding on a motorcycle because you kiss her and she can't think? That's a load of crap and you're smart enough to know it. The perfect woman is not about to go out with anyone who isn't perfection unless she has an ulterior motive."

"You're so certain it can't be because she respects who I am? That just maybe she finds me interesting and unique? Isn't that possible?"

The hurt in Tyson's voice stopped Libby. His parents had rejected him and now Sam, his only family, had said the one thing guaranteed to break Ty's heart. Her temper flared and she practically flung herself up the stairs, uncaring that they would be embarrassed to be overheard. She deliberately wrapped her arm around Tyson's waist as she glared at Sam.

"I couldn't help overhearing, Sam. I assure you, I make more than a decent living for myself. I don't need Tyson's money."

"Right," Sam said, sarcasm dripping from his voice. "And right now you're more than willing to sign a prenuptial agreement."

"For a motorcycle ride?"

"Yeah, that's what I thought," Sam snapped.

"Enough, Sam," Tyson said. He took Libby's arm. "We're heading out and I'm not certain what time I'll be home."

11

TYSON didn't say anything as she climbed on the motorcycle behind him and wrapped her arms around his waist. His gloved hand rubbed briefly over hers and then he looked straight ahead.

Libby pressed her face against Tyson's back as the motorcycle roared to life. Her heart thundered in her ears and she closed her eyes. It was silly to be afraid, especially when he had promised to go very slow, but she was already regretting her decision. That little niggling doubt was beginning to edge into her mind, growing stronger and more fearful as the road sped past the cycle's wheels.

But worse than her nervousness about riding the motorcycle was the way her mind kept coming back again and again to Sam's hurtful accusations and the realization that he didn't like her and didn't want her to have anything to do with Ty.

She tried to shrug it off as Joley would have done, with a casual toss of her head. *He doesn't like me? Well, screw him!* But Libby wasn't Joley and she couldn't just forget it. Sam's accusations had hurt. Being disliked *hurt.*

Oh, for heaven's sake. Why was it so necessary that everyone like her? Yes, she was mortified and humiliated that Sam thought she was after Ty's money, but while she was sitting here wallowing in her own pity party, she could feel Tyson's much deeper pain radiating from him. She *felt* his pain, the ache in his heart. There was no way to take back Sam's cutting remarks. She could only do her best to soothe Ty with warm waves of energy and burrow close in an effort to comfort him. She knew he doubted himself—and her.

With her body pressed up against Ty's, her arms around him and the bike vibrating between her thighs, she eventually began to relax and allow herself the luxury of enjoying being alone with him in the night. She took the opportunity to look around her, to see what he loved so much about riding on a motorcycle.

The sea air felt cool on her face and when she lifted her chin, tears formed in her eyes from the wind. They were out riding on Highway One, moving through the switchbacks above the sea. She looked down at the frothing water, amazed at how close the ocean seemed, dazzled by the way the spray looked like gems thrown into the moonlit sky. The water frothed and folded over, rushing at the rocks and then receding. The bike sped past the stretch of rocks and shore near the seal rookery.

Tyson pulled onto one of the many roads that wound up toward the higher bluffs. She was familiar with the coastline and knew the views were breathtaking from the few enormous properties in the area. He slowed as they approached an imposing set of six-foot iron gates. Pulling out a small remote from his pocket, he pointed it and the gates swung inward and he proceeded down a long drive. Impressive grounds flanked the driveway on either side, rolling lawns dotted with lush banks of flowers and shrubs, all meticulously setting off the huge two-story house at the end of the drive. The entire front of the house was glass. It rose up over the cliff, facing out to sea, designed to blend in with the landscape around it.

Tyson stopped a few yards from the circle leading to the

triple garage. He pulled off his helmet and looked down at her. "What do you think, Libby? Isn't this beautiful?"

It wasn't just the ocean views, or the house built with the line of the coast in mind, and the series of wide covered decks, but also the gardens surrounding the house, the windswept trees and the wildness of the boulders and meadows. The pathways were well lit and led into small private alcoves, a flower garden bursting with blossoms leading to the sea itself. This wasn't just beauty. It was . . . serenity.

Libby slid off the motorcycle and removed her own helmet, waiting a moment to get her legs back under her as she turned in a circle to take in the house and grounds. "It is beautiful, Ty. I had no idea this was here."

"It has a separate guest house. I really liked that about it. The house is on two acres. The land is mostly rolling hills and meadows."

"Are you thinking of buying it?" She hadn't noticed a For Sale sign at the entrance.

"I already bought it. The day after Jonas was shot. I thought a lot about you, Libby, and how we're so different from other people and it occurred to me that you needed me. I've never been needed."

The breath stilled in her lungs. Libby slowly tilted her head to look up at him. "I need you?"

He took her hand. "Yes, you do. After I realized maybe your family might be gifted, it shook my confidence for a minute or two . . ."

"That long?" Libby's smile was faint. She felt faint. She wasn't ready for what he was going to say. The underlying pain in his heart was apparent to her, although she was certain he wasn't admitting it to himself. She wanted to run, but she wanted to hold him, to keep him safe.

Tyson tucked her hair behind her ear. "You don't know how to say no to people. They use you up, Libby. I'm very good at saying no. You fly all over the world helping out, but you really don't have a home or a life for yourself. I can offer you those things. I can offer this." His hand swept around to include the gardens and house. "I can offer you a sanctuary."

Libby couldn't look away from his face. His features were etched with lines she'd never noticed before. His eyes were dark with shadows. He looked curiously vulnerable and yet very determined. It took everything she had not to wrap her arms around him and hold him close to her.

"Tyson, you hardly know me," she said as gently as she could, all the while remembering that her sisters had said nearly the same thing to her. He was right. She might not want to admit it to herself, but she did have a difficult time setting boundaries.

He shook his head. "You're wrong, Libby. I do know you." He sighed. "Here's the thing, Libby. I've never felt happy before. I didn't realize it. I knew something was missing, but I didn't know I wasn't happy until I actually sat down with you and talked. Being with you makes me happy. I feel good about myself. I don't actually think that much about myself, or life in general for the most part, and then when I'm with you, there I am. All the adrenaline rushes in the world just don't compare to the way you make me feel."

Libby could see it was a terrible struggle for Tyson to choose his words with care in an attempt to convince her he meant what he said. And what was he saying? Surely he wasn't proposing. "I'm not positive where you're going with this, Ty. Obviously I enjoy being with you or I wouldn't keep saying yes when you ask me out."

"But then you didn't really say yes. I tricked you the first time and bullied you and then seduced you."

He let go of her hand and walked along the circular drive toward the path that led to the bluff. Libby followed behind him, hating that she was enough of an empath that she could feel the ache in his heart. It seemed an intrusion on his carefully constructed world. He didn't let people in and yet he was wide open to her.

"Tyson," she told him softly, "if I didn't want to be with you, I assure you, I wouldn't be. Each one of those times we spent together, I came of my own free will because I *wanted* to be with you."

Looking around at the beautiful house, the grounds, the

view of the sea, Libby knew this was everything she could have ever wanted in a home. The path made of marble ended in a wide circle at the edge of the cliff. A wrought iron fence provided a barrier, but it was a perfect vista for the incredible view. She stood beside Ty, aching for him, wanting to find the right words to stop whatever storm was coming. She could feel the tension in him, feel it building around them, so she felt edgy and restless.

"I bought this house for you, Libby." He sounded bleak, almost harsh, the expression in his eyes desolate.

Her heart boomed nearly as loudly as the sea below them. "Why, Ty? Why would you do that?"

"I wanted you to see all of me, not just the person the rest of the world sees." His smile was grim. "I do have good parts in me somewhere."

"Do you think I need you to buy me a house to see what's inside of you, Ty?" She wrapped her fingers around his wrist and gave a little tug until he turned to face her. "I'm looking at you, Tyson Derrick, and believe me, I see who you are."

"You deserve the best in the world, Libby."

A small smile curved her mouth, but failed to reach her eyes. "Maybe you should see the real me. You're so worried I won't see all sides of you, but I think you're only seeing what you want to see of me. I'm not perfect and I never will be. And you're right, I don't know how to say no to people even when I should—especially when I should." She ducked her head. "Healing comes with a price. Most of the time, I don't take on the injury, I just send the energy needed to promote healing. That weakens me, but it isn't that dangerous. My sisters are tied to me, just as I am to them. If I choose to heal someone who is mortally wounded . . ."

"Like Jonas." *Like me.* He couldn't even think about what she'd risked for him.

She nodded. "Like Jonas, then I endanger not only my life, but the lives of my sisters as well. I'm usually very cautious, but it can be difficult to say no or to turn my back when a parent is begging me, or a child is injured beyond normal aid—or if it is someone who I feel affection for."

"You aren't God, Libby, any more than I am. We do what we can and live with everything else." And if he had anything to do with it, she would never put her life or health in jeopardy again.

"I've been to Africa, Ty, and many other countries where they have no food or medicine, where children can't go to school and be educated. It's difficult to see and feel so many children, so many people just thrown away as if they don't matter."

He framed her face with his hands, bending down slightly until his head was nearly touching hers. "It won't help them to hurt yourself, Libby. You're a doctor and in that capacity alone you can do tremendous good. And you don't have to apologize for the way you are or explain it to me. I just know I'm supposed to be with you. I know I can make your life better in so many ways." It seemed so much easier to talk to her there in the dark, with the ocean booming below and the night sky scattered with stars. She was restful and yet exciting. She was also a mixture of compassion and steel that intrigued him.

"I know what Harry and Sam said upset you, Ty," Libby said. "I have no interest in your money."

"That doesn't make me as happy as you think it would. If you were interested in money, I'd have something to offer you."

He was like a small boy offering her his treasures, one by one, in an attempt to entice her to stay with him. She wanted to wrap her arms around him and hold him safe forever. "I thought you said I needed you."

"You do, but you probably aren't ready to admit that yet."

She shrugged. "I don't know. Thinking about needing someone in my life other than my family makes me feel more vulnerable than I've ever felt before. We have a prophecy in our family about a gate and finding our true love." She laughed softly. "My sisters and I padlocked the gate just to make certain we were safe."

He touched her face, his gloved finger tracing a path over her cheekbone. "You locked out your true loves? You're dashing all my illusions. Aren't women born wanting marriage?"

Libby burst out laughing. "I think men want to believe that, but no, surprisingly enough, many of us like our independence and view marriage as a male institution."

He threw both hands into the air. "Now you're really shaking me. How is marriage a male's institution?"

"All the advantages are on his side. We women earn money and run our own lives now. If we take on a male, we have to still do all the other wifely chores as well as earn the money." She grinned at him. "How is that appealing?"

"Fine, I'll learn to cook."

"You'll never learn to cook, Ty, so don't even go there."

"Can't you wiggle your nose or something and have dinner on the table?"

"You sound so hopeful. I think Hannah can do that. Maybe you're going for the wrong sister." The smile faded from her face. "I thought about you so often, but you seemed to disapprove of me. I had no idea you looked at me."

"How could I not look at you? Come on, Libby, you're beautiful and intelligent and sexy as hell. Any man in his right mind would be looking at you. I just didn't think in terms of permanency."

"You mean you thought my entire family was a group of charlatans."

"Well, yes. How in the world did you ever come to accept that you could manipulate energy in some way without trying to find a scientific explanation for it? I would have been conducting experiments every day until I figured it out."

"Not if you grew up with it as commonplace. The talents have been in my family for generations. No one thinks about how we do it, just that we do and we have to learn to control and accept the gifts from the time we're children. It isn't all that easy, so the wonder of our talent sometimes gets lost in the wielding of it."

"You should feel special, gifted."

Libby turned in his arms, sinking back against him to look out over the ocean. "Not most of the time. Most of the time what we do is taken for granted, just a part of our lives we don't think about. When we were children, we felt different, apart." She glanced up at him. "Probably the way you felt when you realized you thought and learned on an entirely different level than most people."

He rubbed his chin on the top of her head. "Superior maybe. I was pretty full of myself growing up. I think I had a chip on my shoulder."

"You're bossy and a bit on the arrogant side."

"I'm right. And you need me to help shield you a little bit from all the demands you place on yourself."

"I do?" She laughed softly. "That's the arrogance talking."

"No, it isn't. Don't you want a family? Children? Do you see yourself without a family? Striking a balance is a good thing, Libby."

"With you telling me what that balance is?"

He shrugged. "Someone needs to, Libby."

She pulled out of his arms, spinning around to glare at him. "Has it occurred to you I've done a pretty good job of running my life so far without anyone telling me what to do?"

"I didn't think it would fly, but I thought I'd give it a shot."

He gave her a lopsided grin that tugged at her heart. Libby shook her head. Sadness lurked in the shadows in his eyes. Always there. No one else seemed to see it, not even Tyson, but it never went away. Something deep inside her responded, needed to take away that look of lonely pain and replace it with something altogether different. "Someone has to take you in hand, Ty. It may as well be me."

"Let's go look at the house."

"No way. If I go up there you're going to try to seduce me and I get weak every time you kiss me."

"I'm going to seduce you whether we're in the house or out here, so you may as well be somewhere warm." His voice roughened, a seduction in itself.

A tremor went through Libby, her body tightening with

instant response. It wasn't going to take much on his part. She felt she'd wanted him her entire life. Alone, in the middle of the night when her life was empty and she *felt* empty, she dreamt of this one man, fantasized a thousand ways of pleasing him. Of having him for herself. Even when she'd cried at a perceived slight or a careless word from him, she'd still dreamt of his hands stroking her body and his mouth taking control of hers.

Tyson groaned as he swept her into his arms. "You can't look at me like that and not expect me to take you up on it." The naked longing on her face was his undoing. He began walking her backwards up the path toward the double doors. He didn't give her time to think about it, kissing her over and over. Erotic, hot, arousing kisses as he shoved her leather jacket off her shoulders, so that it fell unnoticed on the walkway.

He opened the door and pushed her inside, following after her, crowding her up against the far wall, his arms caging her in as he leaned his weight against her, his mouth already devouring hers. Libby might not want his money, but she wanted his kisses and there were other ways to make sure she didn't want to leave him. He had tonight to convince her she belonged with him, and he meant to take every advantage, keep her off balance and unthinking until she was so wrapped up in him she'd stay with him forever.

Behind them, the door swung closed and she was his. How long had he waited for this moment? Years. He had wanted Libby for far too long and his control was fast slipping away. Her mouth was dark and hot and moist and the taste and feel of her was wildly addicting. He needed her skin beneath him, all of it, her body open to his, wanting his. No one in his life that he could ever remember had been his alone and he wanted Libby. This one woman. It was all he was asking, all he would take. This one gift for himself.

"I can't breathe, Ty," she whispered against his neck, her fingers biting into his shoulders. "I really can't."

"You don't have to breathe, Libby, I'll breathe for you," he answered, ravenous for her. He needed her the same way, needed her willing to do anything for him. God help him, he needed her. That was all there was to it. Reality. He was locked away from the rest of the world in a dark place where nothing could touch him until there was Libby. She was his passport, his sunlight, his one way out of solitary confinement—the dungeon that was his life. Libby with her sexy mouth and her sultry eyes and skin that cried out to be touched. If he didn't have her tonight, he wouldn't survive.

He kept her pinned against the wall, holding her in place with his mouth on hers, while he tossed his jacket aside and managed to get out of his shirt. He was fast losing his ability to think clearly. There were so many sensations crowding in, his body harder and fuller than it had ever been. He'd always approached sex as a science, the art of anatomy, the top of his class. It was all about the right spots, the right touch, skill, but most of all control. But everything was all different with Libby.

"Don't say yes if you plan on walking away from me, Libby. I don't work that way." His voice was harsh, strained, even as he tugged the blouse over her head to toss it away from them. He didn't wait for her reply, already leaning into her to find her neck, her throat with the heat of his mouth as he flicked away the catch on her bra. He slid his palms up her waist to cup the slight weight of her breasts in his hands, his eyes closing to savor the feel of her satiny skin. It was softer than he'd ever imagined.

Nothing he'd done before had prepared him for his reaction to her. His heart pounded with need, his body trembled with it, and air refused to pass through his lungs. Somehow, Libby managed to shatter his iron control. He kissed his way down her neck to the edge of the swell of her breasts before opening his eyes.

"You are so damned beautiful," he said. "Kick off your shoes, and get rid of your jeans. Hurry, baby, I'm burning up."

Libby felt helpless to resist the command in his voice, the aching hunger that roughened his voice or the intensity burning in the depths of his eyes. His hands were so sure on her body, no hesitation, no holding back, possessive and authoritative as if he knew exactly what he was doing and where he was taking them.

She couldn't look away from his gaze as she managed to struggle out of her shoes and drop her hands to her jeans. Her breath caught in her throat. She was already throbbing for him, her desire past any point she'd ever been before. She just wanted to give herself to him, and give herself up to the pleasures his mouth, teeth, tongue, hands and body could give her. She wanted him for herself with almost a desperation.

Holding his gaze, she slowly began to peel off her jeans and underwear, stepping out of them and letting them drop to the floor. Libby lifted her chin, as his blue eyes shifted to inspect her naked body. His gaze slid over her small, pert breasts to the tucked-in waist and flat belly, then lower still until she saw him still, his breath stopping abruptly, his tongue touching suddenly dry lips. She loved the shudder that went through his body, the lust that darkened his eyes when he saw she was smooth and soft everywhere.

Ty drew off his boots and socks and threw them a distance from them. "Now my jeans, Libby."

She couldn't tear her gaze from his as she did as he said. Each brush of her fingers against the bulge stretching the front of the material sent another shudder of pleasure through his body. Her entire body tingled, pulsed with life, was aware only of him. Slowly, loving the expression on his face, she unzipped his jeans and put both hands into the waistband to begin pulling the denim down.

She had to work to get his jeans off and in doing so she found herself staring in awe at his heavy erection. The breath rushed from her lungs and a soft moan escaped. His shaft jumped in response. She straightened slowly, leaning back against the wall and allowed her gaze to drift over his naked body, inch by slow inch.

"I want to feel your hands on me," he said. "Now, Libby, wrap your fingers around me."

His voice was so hoarse, so rough, she felt a tremor run

down her spine. She cupped his sac in her palms, slid her fingers in a long caress over him, shaped the thick shaft and ran fingertips over the engorged head. The heat was astounding.

At the first touch of her hands, he lost all control and with a groan of pure carnality, he lowered his mouth to her nipple. A strangled groan escaped her as she arched her body into his, one hand stroking down the silken length of him, while the other clutched his hair. Her breathing turned ragged. He used his tongue, stroking as he suckled, wringing a shocked gasp of pleasure from her.

His hand slid up the inside of her thigh, knuckles brushing the sensitive bare mound between her legs. Her skin was softer than he'd ever imagined. She was so moist and ready and he hadn't even gotten started. "I could eat you alive, Libby."

She ran her hands over his chest, up to his neck and pressed close to him. "Now you get hungry."

"Don't worry." Tyson lifted her easily into his arms. "I've got plans to take care of that." He laid her on the rug in front of the fireplace, his body stretched out beside hers, his hand covering the perfection of that soft mound. At his touch, her body jerked and a soft cry escaped. He leaned over her to catch her next sob of excitement with his lips as he slowly sank one finger into her inviting wet channel.

He loved her mouth. He'd dreamt of her mouth, the shape and fullness, the way she could look so sultry one moment, pouting and laughing the next. He tugged at her lower lip with his teeth, his tongue shaping the curves and sucking lightly while she moaned softly. It aroused him even more to watch the expressions chasing across her face, the naked need and stark emotion. For him. All for him.

Libby couldn't look away from the harsh lines in Tyson's face. His expression should have been sculpted for all time, pure sensuality, a dark promise of pleasure. He swept his tongue over her nipple, a curling flame that seemed to sink through her skin to rush straight to her groin. Her muscles clamped around his fingers. He pressed kisses down her belly, alternating with licks and tiny teasing bites until she thrashed under his lips and teeth, thinking the pleasure was nearly unbearable.

He moved down farther, pushing her thighs apart, leaning close to nuzzle her bare mound. The sensations on the swollen nerve endings caused her to gasp, to jerk her hips as another small cry escaped. Libby couldn't seem to catch her breath. He watched her, his gaze hot, his tongue tasting his own lips before he settled between her thighs. The sensual look on his face sent her pulse careening out of control.

"Ty. I don't think I can take this."

His small smile was all knowing. "I think you're going to come apart in my arms, Libby. Just give yourself to me."

Control. He was telling her he wanted control. Libby closed her eyes, fingers digging into the thick rug beneath her as he lowered his head and licked across her sensitive mound. Her entire body jerked. The hell with control. Libby Drake was going over to the bad girl side. *Nothing* had ever felt so good. Nothing had ever made her feel so alive, so beautiful, so wanted, so sexy. Or rather, no *one* ever had. Stretched out naked on the thick rug with Tyson between her thighs, she gave herself up to the sheer beauty of just feeling.

Tyson breathed on her shivering body and his tongue moved over her again in another long stroke, curled and caressed, dipped deep and then she heard herself crying his name as he suckled hard, tongue stabbing deep, rasping and rubbing over her most sensitive spot. She couldn't stay still, thrashing under him, her head falling back and forth, her lungs burning, *burning* for air, while her body tightened and tightened, straining and building until she though she'd explode.

"Tyson!" She caught his dark hair in her fist and yanked. "You're killing me."

"It's all good, baby," he encouraged. "I want you ready for me." His fingers pushed deep, found gold and she bucked, her back arching, as wave after wave of orgasms rocked her from head to toe.

Tyson shifted instantly, moving between her legs, thrusting deep into her silken sheath. Her muscles gripped him, fought his entry in spite of her slickness, but gave way as he powered deeper, pushing through the tight, hot folds. There was unexpected resistance and then he sank into her, holding still for a moment, savoring the absolute pleasure of being inside Libby Drake.

He leaned his head towards hers, his arms bracing him above her, his mouth seeking the sweet addicting taste of hers. His hips began to pick up a hard, quick tempo, as he lifted his head to watch the pleasure bursting through her. Passion raced through his body with the force and heat of a firestorm. No fire he'd ever fought had seemed so hot. Flames licked over his skin and burned through his gut and in his groin as the strokes grew harder and deeper and more forceful. All the while he watched her face, devouring the pleasure washing over her.

Her nails bit into his shoulder, her fingers dug into his back, once she lifted her head to press a string of kisses along his chest. Each touch drove him closer to insanity. Her fingers brushed his skin, so did the silk of her hair. Her gaze locked with his, glazed, dark with sensual need, alight with something that sent the fire crowning, flashing, searing his soul. He didn't dare believe she could love him, but she felt emotion, not just lust, and it was enough for him.

"You're so tight, Libby, and so damned hot I think I'm going to come out of this scorched for life."

Nothing in his life, not even his most erotic fantasies had prepared him for sharing Libby's body. She gasped his name again, the small, helpless plea for release tearing his last thread of control so that he caught her hips in his arms, holding her still while he plunged deep, over and over, the passion washing through him, sizzling and cracking and roaring like thunder in his ears. He felt her spasm around him, grip tightly, her soft cries mingling with his strangled one. The sensations started somewhere in his toes and slammed through his body with such force, he thought he might not survive the pleasure.

Libby dug her nails into his back, holding on to the only anchor she had as her body fragmented and the earth spun away. She lay underneath him, feeling as if her heart might explode out of her body, uncaring that it was pounding way too fast and that her lungs burned for air. Ripple after ripple shook her, and she clutched at Tyson, shocked that she could feel so much so fast, that her untutored body could respond with such powerful orgasms. She was a doctor. How often had she counseled women that it could take awhile before one had an orgasm—or multiple orgasms.

She ran her fingers through his hair, small little caresses meant to convey the enormity of what she was feeling.

Tyson lifted his head, easing his weight off of her. "You might have mentioned you wanted me to go slow, Libby. By the time I realized, it was too late."

Libby smiled up at him. "I think we can agree that things went rather well for our first time. Well, I may have rug burn."

He brushed the hair from her face, fingers lingering on her skin. "You look very satisfied. Sleepy, but satisfied. I love that I put that look on your face."

"We're going to have a bit of a mess on the rug."

"I'll get another one," he said, rolling over, taking her with him so she was lying on top of him, her head on his shoulder. "I don't want to squish you."

Libby closed her eyes, loving the feel of his arms around her, of his body beneath hers, legs and arms tangled together. She let herself look around the room, something she hadn't even done up until now. It was enormous. The floor was light wood to capture the sunlight that would pour through the wall of glass facing the sea. The view was spectacular. Outside, the waves rushed toward the rocky beach beneath the bluff, soothing them both until she began to drift toward sleep.

Tyson held her close. She seemed so fragile and delicate in his arms. He had a much larger frame and he was definitely endowed. He'd been afraid of hurting her, yet she'd been eager for him, not in the least fearful. He had never imagined Libby Drake draped naked over him, her mouth pressed to his chest, and her body moving with restless abandon under his. He let her sleep for a half an hour before he moved out from under her to find a towel and clean them both up. He already wanted her again. Maybe he was destined to spend the rest of his life in a semihard state.

Libby woke to his kisses. Soft. Gentle. Tender. She kissed him back and smiled, wrapping her arm around his neck. "This is a wonderful way to wake up."

"I was missing you."

She laughed, her eyes sparkling at him. "What's it been, an entire hour?"

It gave him secret pleasure that he knew she would laugh at his remark. "I was going cross-eyed staring at you."

She leaned into him again and brushed a kiss across his mouth before wiggling free. "Bathroom."

He pointed. Libby was shocked that she didn't feel in the least bit embarrassed to walk around in front of him totally naked—in fact she enjoyed feeling his gaze on her. When she returned she deliberately walked past him to the window where the moonlight could shine down on her as she looked out to sea.

His gaze grew hot. Predatory. "You're killing me, Lib. I can't look at you without getting hard."

Libby laughed softly, feeling sexy for the first time in her life. It was a feeling she could get used to. "Really?" Deliberately she allowed her gaze to drift over his body, teasing him, provoking him. *Flirting.* She'd never flirted. She didn't even know how.

He came across the floor like a tiger, pouncing on her, spinning her around until she was pressed up against the glass. Both of his hands covered her breasts, his erection already thick and hard, pressed against her buttocks. "Really," he answered, bending his head to her shoulders, giving her teasing little bites that sent shivers down her back. He applied pressure, slowly bending her forward to drop kisses and bites down her spinal column. He paused to swirl his tongue over the rug burns on her back.

She pressed the palm of her hand up against the glass to steady herself, turning to look over her shoulder at Ty. His face was etched with passion, with lust, his eyes so dark with desire her breath left her lungs in a rush and her body dampened and contracted in anticipation. "You can't possibly want me again."

"You're so beautiful, Libby," he answered. He loved her naked, surrounded by the plush white rug and the open glass gleaming behind her. He hadn't yet turned on the electricity to the house but lights weren't needed. The moon spilled enough light over her body to see her curves, and the clouds threw intriguing shadows over her soft, inviting skin. Her hair was a cascade of midnight black silk falling over her shoulder and swinging free. He stroked the curve of her bottom, the inside of her thighs, moved his hand to find her slick with response. "That's what I'm looking for, baby," he approved, his voice going hoarse.

He loved the marks of possession he could see on her skin. His marks. His woman. The way she responded to him, the way she looked at him, her breathless little cries when he stroked her with his fingers, all of it was amazing to him, a new wondrous world he wanted to dwell in for the rest of his life.

She groaned aloud, her hips pushing back against him. He pushed two fingers into her, stroked and caressed until she was riding his hand with a small mindless sob. Her sheath was hot and silky, her muscles clamping tightly around him so that his own body hardened all the more. Blood rushed and pounded and he lifted his hand to slowly lick her taste from his fingers.

Libby couldn't look away from him, loving the way he made her feel so sexy, so completely his. Every touch, every look was so intense. Tyson was a single-minded man. When he researched, he gave his all. She should have known he would be a thorough, dominant lover, in the same way he approached everything else in his life. He wanted her to feel pleasure, not just that, sheer ecstasy, and he set about it with that same purpose he did all things.

She watched his face as he caught her hips and pushed the broad head of his shaft against her bare entrance. He felt like a brand burning through her skin, pushing through tight muscles with exquisite care, invading her body inch by slow inch. She wanted to scream with pleasure, her body shaking under his caressing hands. His fingers tugged at her nipples, every stroke of his strong fingers sending electric shocks straight to her hot tight sheath.

Libby gasped for breath, pushing back with every powerful stroke. He rode her hard and fast, and then suddenly, when she was certain she would burst into flames, slowed to long, lingering strokes that nearly sent her over the edge, only to build up the speed and fierceness of his possession a second time. Every muscle, every cell seemed to coil in readiness, needing, begging for release, but he kept her on the edge, until she was certain she couldn't take the intense pleasure another moment.

Something dark moved in her mind, past the bright colors and the erotic bliss rushing through her. A tendril of insubstantial smoke, no more, but goose bumps formed on her skin. She opened her eyes and looked out the window into the cloak of darkness shrouding the house. Tyson's fingers dug into her hips, dragging her into him, sending the heat spiraling through her body until the breath slammed out of her lungs and she couldn't form a coherent thought.

But there it was again. Something moving in her mind, past all the pleasure, a twisted shadow that grew larger and larger. She thought to pause, to catch her breath, take a moment to clear her mind, but it was too late, her body betraying her, her orgasm ripping through her with such force she nearly fell, forced to clutch the glass to save herself from falling. Behind her, Tyson's fingers dug deep into her flesh, holding her to him while he emptied himself into her, his guttural cry ringing through the room. Everything around her spun out of control as her body fragmented. For one moment, Libby felt as if she could touch the sky.

She gasped for breath, as he helped her to stand, as he took her into his arms, bending her back over his arm so his mouth could find her sensitive breast. Her eyes closed and she gave herself up to the soaring pleasure. The shadow moved again, blocking the sky, slamming her back to earth so hard her eyes snapped open and she looked around her wildly.

Libby stepped away from Tyson quickly, feeling waves of animosity, ugly hatred, a dark malevolent presence watching. *Watching* them through the glass. Whatever, *whoever,* was outside had seen Tyson taking her with such ferocity and hunger, had intruded on what should have been one of the most wonderful moments of her life. The thought sickened her. A beautiful, private time was shattered by something so ugly, so deviant she backed away from the glass, her hand going protectively to her throat.

"Someone's out there, Ty. He can see us." She reached out to him with shaking hands, still backing up to the wall, trying to draw him with her. "We should call the sheriff."

He turned toward the window, looking so fierce, Libby caught his arm to hold him back. "Are you certain?" His tone was low, but there was a controlled fury radiating from him.

She nodded. "I'm really afraid, Ty. Don't get too close to the window. What if he has a gun?"

He pulled her into the protection of his arms, his body shielding hers from view. "I'm not going to let anything happen to us, Libby."

"I feel his hatred."

"Who is it?"

She shook her head. "I don't know. I can't tell other than he's male and he wants me—us—dead. Please call the sheriff."

"I haven't turned on the phone here yet." He gathered up her clothes and handed them to her. They were far enough back into the room that he doubted anyone could see them. "Get dressed."

"He saw us."

"Maybe not. He couldn't have been there the entire time or you would have felt uneasy." Tyson yanked on his jeans. "Wouldn't you?"

"I don't know." She choked back a small sob. Her body still burned from Ty's possession of her. She felt his brand in places she hadn't known existed, delicious sore places that still throbbed and pulsed with too much pleasure, yet someone might have been a witness to those beautiful, perfect, private moments. The idea sickened her so that her stomach churned and she pressed a hand to her mouth. "I was feeling, not thinking, Ty. I doubt if I could have told you my name."

He caught her chin with hard fingers, forcing her to meet the turbulent fury in his eyes. "What we have together no one can take away from us, Libby. Do you understand me? I don't care if a hundred people saw us together. I made love to you tonight. They can call it anything they want, but that was me, giving you everything I could of myself." He leaned down to claim her mouth, both palms framing her face, holding her still for his kiss before pulling her shirt over her head. "Do you understand what I'm saying? He's not taking you away from me, not by harming either of us, or not by trying to humiliate or embarrass us. And personally, Libby, I don't give a damn if anyone sees us together."

Libby stared up at him, shocked at the hard truth on his face. She dragged her jeans on. For some reason, his seething rage calmed her. She even managed a faint smile. "I'm a little more modest."

He wiped away her tears with the pad of his thumb. "That's a good thing—with any other man. I don't share well."

"Do you think someone's trying to kill us, Ty?"

"Not so far, baby. Just stay calm. I'm going to go out first . . ."

"No!" Libby shook her head. "No way."

"I'm going to get the bike and bring it to the door and then we're out of here. I'm not going to stay trapped like a rat in a cage. I'll go out the back way and work my way around to the bike."

"I don't know where he is."

"You said he was watching us. If he was, he had to be in the front, maybe up by the circular viewing area overlooking the ocean. And if he had a gun, he should have used it right then."

She curled her fingers around his sleeve, hoping to keep him inside. Pressed back against the wall where she was certain the watcher wouldn't be able to see them, she closed her eyes and tried to clear her mind, to reach for more of the energy the unseen man was giving off.

The energy was already dispersing. Whoever he was, the man was gone and the malevolence he left behind faded quickly. Libby let her breath out slowly. "He's gone."

Tyson frowned. "Are you sure? Are you sure anyone was here?"

"Let's go. I want to go home. My sisters are going to be frantic."

"I thought you had telepathy." Tyson yanked open the door and peered outside. He didn't know what to think, whether or not Libby had simply frightened herself, but she'd seemed so certain, so scared.

"Elle does, not me. And she can't just find me anywhere." She looked around her. "Do you see my jacket?"

"It's right here, where I tossed it—" Ty's voice broke off as his gaze dropped to the walkway where he'd slid the jacket from her shoulders. Adrenaline exploded through his body, needing an outlet.

The jacket lay in strips, shredded and stabbed repeatedly, viciously, the leather in pieces.

12

"WHAT is it?" Libby asked, trying to get around Tyson to see. Instead of stepping out of the doorway to make room for her, he stepped back into her, forcing her back into the room.

"Are you absolutely certain he's gone?" he demanded. Tyson shook with rage. It swept through his body and into every muscle. He wanted to smash something. In all his life, he'd never felt helpless. His intellect and his physical abilities had always given him supreme confidence in virtually any situation, yet the unseen enemy clearly threatening Libby was out of his reach. She looked so pale and frightened that his guts twisted inside.

She studied his grim face. "Tell me, Ty."

He shrugged out of his jacket and held it. "Put this on." When she began to shake her head, his expression hardened. "I'm not arguing. Put it on." He forced gentleness into his tone. "We're getting out of here. I want you to stay put while I get the bike. Don't leave this house until I'm at the door ready to go."

She blinked up at him, opened her mouth and then closed it. She wasn't going to argue with a possible killer on the loose. She was still feeling the aftereffects of the waves of hatred and malice. Libby slipped her arms into the jacket and stood quietly trembling while he zipped it up.

Tyson leaned down and brushed a kiss over her mouth. "We'll be fine, baby. I'm just going to be gone a couple of minutes. Keep the door closed behind me." His fingers slid into her hair and tugged once before he slipped out the front.

Libby rested her head against the closed door, listening hard for any sound. It was the longest few minutes of her life before she heard the roar of the motorcycle. The sound increased in volume and she knew he was right outside the door. She yanked it open and, slamming it behind her, raced toward him.

Tyson handed her a helmet and waited until she was on the back of the bike, secure with her arms around him before taking off down the drive. Libby laid her head against Ty's back and closed her eyes.

The motorcycle sped down the coastal highway a little faster than before, but not so fast it was reckless. Tendrils of fog reached out in the darkness from over the sea to creep toward land. The cycle shot past several wisps and suddenly, with no warning, the back wheel began to slip out from under them.

Libby controlled a scream of fear as the motorcycle went into a slide across the highway, heading straight for the narrow shoulder and flimsy fence, the only barriers between them and a long rocky drop toward the sea.

"Tyson!" she cried. Her arms instinctively tightened around his waist. She could sense his sudden fear for her as he frantically tried to control the skid.

As if in slow motion, the bike tipped to one side and began to slide across the road. She felt the crush of weight on her leg and hip, the rough road tearing at her clothing and flesh as they skidded along the surface, dragged by the bike. She couldn't hang on to Tyson, ripping fingernails as he was torn from her arms and disappeared out of her sight. She felt herself falling, tumbling sideways off the bike to land on the road surface hard, coming to an abrupt stop, gravel embedded in her skin.

"Tyson!" Libby screamed, fighting the dazed shock accompanying an accident, pushing herself up to look around her frantically. He had given her his heavy leather jacket, protecting her skin, but he was sitting up a distance from her, taking off his helmet, one arm dripping blood from shoulder to hand, his head swiveling around as he called out to her.

"Just stay there," Libby commanded. "For once, do what *I* say."

It was like trying to ward off a hurricane. Tyson was up and running to her, catching her in his arms to ease her back down onto the dirt at the shoulder of the road. Immediately his hands were skimming over her body, checking for signs of damage.

Libby pushed at his chest to back him off, but he didn't appear to notice, frantic to make certain she was alright. "*I'm* the doctor," she snapped. "And I'm fine. I want to check you."

"Damn it. This is impossible," Tyson said. "Totally impossible."

"We must have hit oil. There's grease all over my leg." She pointed to her jeans. Part of the material had shredded and along with the oil stains, there was the darkening stain of blood. "I think the oil plug loosened and came out."

Tyson bent over his leg to inspect the gravel pitted in her flesh. He had a fair amount in his hand and arm, but his much heavier jeans had saved his leg. "I work on my motorcycle myself. There is no damned way that plug would come loose."

"Not even with the vibrations as we rode down the highway?"

"No way, Libby. I know that for a fact. If that's what happened, then someone tampered with the bike."

Libby rubbed at her pounding temples. It wasn't such a stretch to think that someone had sabotaged Tyson's bike. "This evening in the garage when I saw Harry Jenkins and Joe Fielding they looked very guilty. When they saw me they both sort of straightened up, looked at one another and for some reason it really scared me."

"Like tonight?"

She shook her head, winced when he touched her leg and jerked it away from him. "That hurt. I'll take care of it when we get home. And no, it wasn't the same as tonight. Tonight felt . . ." Libby searched for a word, shrugged her shoulders and sighed. "Malicious is all I can think of. There was hatred. Whoever it was wanted us dead."

"You don't have any old boyfriends, do you?" He drew her leg into his lap and stroked a finger down her calf just above the raw streak.

His voice was so gentle, so teasing, Libby smiled in spite of herself. "I was thinking maybe an old girlfriend of yours."

His lips twisted into a lopsided grin that made her heart beat faster. "I didn't have girlfriends, only you."

"Yes, you did. You didn't get to be such a great lover by reading a book. And I'd be pretty jealous if a man made love to me like that and then left me for another woman."

"Why Libby Drake, I do believe you're threatening me."

She jerked her leg away a second time, or attempted to, when he lightly brushed away a piece of gravel. "Ow! If you don't stop I'm definitely going to threaten you. I have to call my sisters."

"We're in for a walk. The cell phones don't work along this section of road."

"Who needs a cell phone when I have the wind?"

She turned to face the direction of her home, lifting her arms into the air. She closed her eyes, visualizing her sisters, knowing they would be on the captain's walk, waiting for any clue that would give them a direction to find her. She'd always had that safety net, the love of her family solidly behind her. She focused and reached for them, arms up to the stars, calling the wind, directing it home with her message of need.

Tyson watched the concentration on her face with interest. Almost at once he felt the wind begin to pick up, driving at them from the sea and heading away toward Libby's home. The wind shifted suddenly, racing back towards them at a furious rate of speed and he swore he heard feminine voices. The wind enveloped him, surrounded Libby like a living blanket, whirling and spinning as if inspecting them. It left just as fast in a sudden rush, back towards the house again.

"Your family must wreak havoc with meteorologists."

Libby laughed, relief spreading through her, easing the tension that had drawn her so tight. "I never thought of that. You're becoming a believer."

"I still want to hook you up to a scan and collect all the data. Only now I'm going to be fantasizing all sorts of interesting things while I'm studying you."

"You're *not* hooking me up to a machine, Ty," she said, trying to look stern.

He flashed a small grin and went back to inspect his motorcycle. There was oil all over the back wheel and just as he suspected, a puddle leaking from the bike onto the ground. He swore softly as Libby came up beside him. When she slipped her hand into the crook of his arm, he glanced down at her. "Someone is trying to kill me, Libby."

"Or both of us," she said.

"Or both," he conceded, "but I think I'm the primary target." He gave her a grim look. "The fall I took during the heli-rescue is starting to seem a little suspicious right about now. All along, I've been wondering how my safety harness could have failed the way it did. We triple check that gear, Libby, because we know our lives depend on it."

"You think someone tampered with your safety harness?"

"I do. How they got to it and what they did to it, I don't know, but I don't think it was an accident. And I'm beginning to think it was no accident that Jonas was shot while taking the broken harness back for testing. The harness disappeared right out of his squad car while everyone was trying to save his life."

"Why would someone want you dead?"

"A lot of people might want me dead. I step on toes, Libby. I'm not very careful what I say and I don't have tolerance for idiots."

"You mean like Harry Jenkins."

"I also called Edward Martinelli and told him to back off."

"You didn't!" She shook her head. "But you had the accident *before* there was any reason to connect us. He wouldn't have had a reason to want you dead."

"That's not exactly true." He took her hand and led her to the side of the road so they could sit down. Libby didn't realize it, but she was shaking, and probably not from the cold. Already he could see lights in the distance, blinking on and off around the hairpin turns. "I've spoken to Ed about you many times in casual conversations. He had to know I was interested. And my cousin, Sam, owes him a great deal of money. Sam gambles and apparently he lost heavily to Ed. Ed's been threatening him and Sam didn't tell me about it until recently."

"Is it more money than you can pay for him?" Libby asked.

"No. He won't take the money. He wants me, or Sam, to persuade you to talk to him. He says he needs your expertise and no one else will do."

"But you didn't tell me. And neither did Sam."

"Hell, no, we weren't going to tell you. We don't want you anywhere near that bastard. Sam got himself into trouble and if it's a money thing, money can fix it. I only told you so you'd see Ed could have wanted me out of the way."

"Why would he want you out of the way though?"

"Ed knows I never stop if pushed. He's known me since I was a child. Sam can't sustain anything for very long. Of the two of us, he'd want to deal with Sam. I just don't back off once I'm dug in on something." He ran his fingertip down the back of her hand, all the way across to caress her fingers. He curled his hand around hers to press her palm to his heart. "Does that scare you, Libby?"

"No. I can handle you, Tyson. Even when you pull your superior act." How could she not, when he looked at her as if she were the only woman in the world. His eyes devoured her, ate her alive. She'd never, in all the years she'd known him, seen him look that way at anyone else—nor seen anyone look at her that way either.

"You're turning me on, going all dominatrix on me." He leaned over to kiss her. "Your mouth drives me crazy. Every time you do that little thing . . ."

"What little thing?"

He grinned at her. "That. You do this little sexy pout with your lips and all I can think about is kissing you until you're so hot and wet for me I can have you right there and then, or better yet"—his hand slid over the front of his jeans—"I can watch you put those lips to good use."

She tried to stop the slow burn creeping through her body to center deep and low. His voice had gone rough again, and he sucked her finger deep into his mouth.

"Well, try to control yourself, the troops have arrived."

The car screeched to a halt just as the passenger door opened and Elle Drake leapt out to fling herself at Libby. Libby barely had time enough to stand and catch her. Tears poured down Elle's face. "I couldn't find you. I tried, Libby, but I couldn't find you."

"I'm okay, baby. *Ssh.* It's all right. We're both all right." Libby soothed her. "This isn't your fault, Elle."

Sarah slammed the car door and ran to her sisters, her arms around both of them. "We were so afraid, Libby. We even tried reading the mosaic, but we couldn't find you."

A second vehicle pulled up behind the Drakes' and Jackson emerged. "You two all right?" His sharp glance raked them both, then settled on Elle's tear-stained face.

Tyson nodded. "Someone tampered with my motorcycle and earlier they were watching us at my house." He turned to Libby. "You go on home with your sisters and I'll stay here with Jackson."

"Are you certain?" Libby asked. "I should take a look at your arm first."

"It's nothing, a scratch. Go on home and let me take care of this."

Jackson pulled his gaze away from Elle to study Tyson. "Go on, Libby. I can take your statement later."

Tyson leaned down to brush a kiss across Libby's mouth. "I'll see you first thing tomorrow."

"If you're certain," Libby said. She followed her sisters to the car.

"What is it?" Jackson asked.

Tyson met the deputy's eyes with a long, level look, allowing him to glimpse the pent-up rage looking for a way to break free. "I took Libby to the house I just purchased. We were up there for a while and she became certain someone was watching us through the front glass. The property is fenced in and gated. I thought we were safe, although I don't have a security system in place. I dropped Libby's jacket outside on the walkway and when I went to get it so we could leave, I found it ripped to shreds. The cuts were too clean to have been made with anything but a knife. I'm telling you straight up, Jackson, you'd better find the son of a bitch before I do."

Jackson ignored the threat. "Do you think these attempts are directed at you? Or is this about her?"

Tyson shrugged, looked down to see his fists were clenched and made an attempt to open his hands. "I don't have a clue which one of us. I'm in love with her and maybe that's drawn her into danger. I just don't know." He raked his fingers through his hair in agitation. "There were a couple of men in my garage earlier this evening who chased Libby into the house. They had access to my motorcycle as did whoever was at the new house tonight."

Jackson nodded, careful to take down the details. He glanced at the Drake car as Sarah pulled a U-turn and came up along side of them. She leaned out the window.

"Libby's worried about Ty. She wants him to come by the house and let her clean his arm. She says he'll get an infection if he doesn't take care of it."

Tyson stepped up to the car on the passenger side so he could put his head inside and kiss Libby again. "Sam's good with scrapes, Libby. I want you home and safe now. Get moving." He glanced up and down the highway as if he might spot a threat to her.

Libby didn't want to cling to him so she forced a smile. "Great, you're already trying to get rid of me. I'll see you soon."

Tyson nodded and stepped away from the car.

Libby sank back into her seat with a small frown. "I missed something important, something he doesn't want me to know about. I have a feeling it has something to do with my leather jacket."

"You're wearing his." Sarah glanced at her.

Libby nodded. "I dropped mine outside his house. He owns this absolutely beautiful house and we were going in and I dropped the jacket on the walkway. When we left the house, I was running, so I didn't notice it until we were driving out. I just caught a glimpse but it seemed to be in pieces."

"Pieces?" Elle echoed.

"I think it may have been."

Sarah's gaze jumped to the mirror to meet Elle's vivid green eyes. "I don't like this at all, Lib. We all felt the danger to you. It was incredibly strong this time."

"More to the point it was sharp and spiteful. Very directed."

"At me? Or Ty?" Libby swiveled around in the seat to look at her youngest sister.

Elle shrugged. "I don't know. It felt like you, but I'm tied to you. I couldn't tell. And how in the world would they know you'd even get on his motorcycle?"

Sarah sniffed. "Most people would never consider that a woman of your intellect would even get on the thing."

Libby turned her head to stare out the window with a small secret smile on her face. Libby the bad girl. Her first lecture from big sister. She was grown and a doctor, but it felt like an earth-shattering achievement. Danger and making love and riding on a motorcycle. She wouldn't take back a single second of her night with Tyson Derrick.

"Just in case you'd like to know, Lib," Elle said, studying her fingernails, "Sarah not only has been on a motorcycle, she owns one and drives it."

"*For work!* For work, you wench," Sarah emphasized. "I'm in security and I do all sorts of things for the job. Libby's a doctor and much more—fragile."

Libby whipped her head around. "I'm *so* not fragile. I'm

a *doctor.* I don't hang out in a high-rise either, Sarah, I fly to Third World countries where people don't have medicine and their world is filled with power hungry murderers. I am not a pansy."

Sarah held up one hand in surrender as she maneuvered through a switchback. "I didn't mean to offend you, Libby. I was being protective."

"Well, don't. Why is it everyone thinks I need protection? Hannah and Joley both need more protection than I do. You do, too, Sarah. I don't do anything that warrants protection."

Sarah flashed a small grin. "You go out with Tyson Derrick."

Libby huffed out a breath and tried not to smile. She did more than go out with him. She hugged the knowledge to herself. "I do, don't I?"

Elle shook her head in disgust and settled back in her seat with a slight frown. "Another one bites the dust. Just so you know, Hannah isn't going to be happy with you. You were her last line of defense."

Libby bit her lip. "I know she won't be happy. I think deep down she knows she should be with Jonas, but she can't accept him. He's too dominating. She's afraid she can't stand up to him and eventually he'll realize she isn't the strong woman he wants, but someone weak."

"Hannah isn't weak," Sarah denied, shock in her voice.

"Of course she isn't," Libby said. "Hannah *thinks* she is and that's all that matters. She isn't like the rest of us and she knows it. She never has been."

"She believes we'll all have families and she'll be alone in our house," Elle added. "She laughs about it, saying she'll be the strange old lady with cats, but she isn't laughing on the inside."

"And she isn't eating either," Libby said. "We have to find a way to help her."

"Joley's been trying to get her to eat a little," Sarah confided.

"Joley?" Libby was amazed, but then, on second thought,

realized it was like Joley. She talked a good game, and played the part of the musician for the crowd and her adoring fans, but she loved her sisters just as fiercely as they loved her. And Hannah *was* different. She was the fragile one, even though she would deny it with her last breath. "Of course Joley would notice and try to do something about it. How many accidents have there been in the kitchen?"

All three girls laughed and it helped to dispel the terrible tension. Libby let her breath out slowly as the house came into view. The lights were blazing in welcome, the heavy gates wide open. Hannah and Joley waited on the wide verandah with anxious expressions and even Sarah's guard dogs ran in circles barking a welcome. The moment Libby was out of the car, Hannah and Joley nearly knocked her flat as they dragged her into their arms.

"I was so afraid," Hannah said, somewhere between laughter and tears. "Don't you ever scare us like that again."

"You aren't hurt, are you?" Joley stared at her leg and took her hand, turning it over to wince at the gravel embedded there.

"It's painful, but I heal fast."

Hannah stepped back to stare at her. "Libby, you have been with that man. I thought he had broken ribs. I was sure you were safe."

Joley nudged her taller sister. "You mean you thought *you* were safe. Libby is a fallen woman."

Libby carefully folded Tyson's jacket and set it on a chair with a loving caress her sisters couldn't miss. "I made certain I didn't expend a lot of energy, but I sped up his healing every time I saw him. Just a little touch here and there." She gave them a dreamy smile.

"Stop mooning, you goose, and let's get you cleaned up." Hannah put a hand on Libby's back, felt her wince as she yanked up her shirt. She whistled and pulled the material back in place. "You've been having a good time, haven't you?" She gestured toward a chair and waited until Libby removed her jeans so she could kneel by her to begin the difficult job of cleaning her leg. Joley started to work on her palm.

"I'm going to marry that man," Libby announced.

Sarah turned back from the window to face her. Hannah covered her mouth to keep the gasp from being heard. Joley and Elle exchanged a long look of near despair.

"Are you certain, Libby? You haven't been seeing him that long."

"Longer than you think," Libby said. "I remember watching him argue with a professor at Harvard. I knew he was right, but the professor was so arrogant and Ty was making a mortal enemy. I wouldn't have done it. I would have agreed and taken the good grade and simply have quietly known I was right. It was the principle, the fact that Professor Harding was teaching an entire class something inaccurate. Tyson didn't care if that man could fail him, it mattered that the material was taught correctly. I knew then, at that moment, that he was someone special. He stands up, Sarah."

"Can you stand up to him? A man should make you feel good about yourself, Libby. I saw your face when you talked to him back in school. He made you cry."

Libby nodded. "I know. I just didn't understand him back then. He thought I had all kinds of confidence, that I was some sort of royalty. Why do people think that of us? I know Jonas does with Hannah, and for years I've heard how popular we were. I didn't feel popular in school. Did any of you? Ow!" She glared at Joley and jerked her hand away.

"What does that mean anyway?" Joley asked. "I was leader of the pack. Does that make me popular? I just couldn't take having rules. And stop being a baby. You're a doctor, for heaven's sake, it's supposed to hurt."

"You still hate rules," Sarah said, frowning. "I don't know how you do it, Joley, and you still stay as sweet and as innocent as you do."

Joley made a face. "Ugg. *Never* repeat that in public. Or in front of Mom or Dad. That's just wrong, Sarah."

"All the girls hated me," Hannah said. "I walked into a room and they immediately got really nasty looks on their faces. I was so painfully shy I couldn't have talked to them anyway, but it made it worse. They all thought I was stuck up and haughty. I didn't even know what haughty was the first time I overheard someone call me that." She poured a dark-looking liquid into a bowl. "This is going to hurt, honey, so take a deep breath. We want it clean though."

Tears swam in Libby's eyes for a moment as the antiseptic flowed over her leg, but she choked back the gasp and rubbed Hannah's shoulder in commiseration. "School was rough on you, Hannah. I didn't pay all that much attention to what other people thought of me. I had all of you and I was perfectly happy."

"That's because everyone loved you, Libby," Joley said. "And if they didn't, they were afraid I'd beat them up. And I would have, too. If Jackson doesn't figure out who is threatening you, I'm going to have to do the investigating myself." She passed Hannah the tube of antibiotic cream.

"That will win you points with both Jonas and Jackson," Sarah said.

Elle made a face. "Big bad Jackson. Guess we should all hide in the closet so we don't ruffle his feathers."

"What is it with you and Jackson?" Hannah asked.

Elle shrugged, turning her face away from her sisters. "He's driving me crazy."

"He never talks," Sarah pointed out. "How in the world could he drive you crazy?"

"He doesn't talk to you, Sarah. That doesn't mean he doesn't talk to me."

The sisters exchanged puzzled looks. "When?"

"All the time."

Hannah stood up and crossed the room to wrap her arm around her youngest sister. "What does he say to you, Elle?"

Elle let her breath out slowly and turned back to them. "He doesn't approve of me."

"What a shocker," Joley said, curling her legs under her. "Jonas doesn't approve of any of us, especially Hannah, and no one approves of me. Elle, sweetheart, tell the guy to drop dead. That's what I do."

Elle flashed a small smile. "Believe me, I do."

Hannah shook her head. "She doesn't mean he speaks to

her as in physical talking, do you, Elle? He's telepathic, isn't he?"

Elle's hand went to her throat and she pulled away from her sister, her face going pale. "How did you know?"

Hannah ignored the question. "Can you shield yourself from him?"

Elle shook her head slowly. "I've tried. He's too strong."

"What does he want?" Sarah said. "You should have told us right away, Elle. Jonas would make him stop."

"No, don't say anything to Jonas," Elle said. "He won't stop and Jonas would try to make him. It would ruin their friendship."

"Have you told him to stop?" Sarah asked.

Libby saw the utter weariness and despair on Elle's face, her eyes so dark and shadowed it broke Libby's heart. "We can help you, Elle. Let us help you for a little while. You'll figure things out in your own time. No one has the right to rush you or dictate to you." She sank to her knees in front of her youngest sister. "Abbey should have the wedding she wants, not what the world wants for her. And you deserve that as well. You have the right to choose."

"Do I? Do any of us? Do we really have the freedom or does destiny decide for us?" Elle whispered, her voice strangled. "Because the only choice is whether we carry on the legacy or we end it. That's a hell of a responsibility."

"Every seventh daughter before you has had to make that decision," Libby said, her voice gentle, "and you have to make your choice, Elle. You have that right. But you don't need outside pressures, not from anyone. We can help you." She took Elle's hand and held out her other hand to Sarah. Sarah took Libby's hand and held out her other one to Joley.

Joley brushed a kiss on top of Elle's head as she linked hands with Hannah. "You don't always have to be strong, honey. That's why you have us. Together, we're pretty much unbeatable. Let's see him get past this shield." She hesitated and then shrugged. "While we're at it, let's add me into the circle, too. I could use a little boost to stay protected."

Silence followed her seemingly casual statement. The admission coming from Joley was shocking. She rolled her eyes then winked at Elle. "See, little sister, you don't always know everything, do you?"

"I thought I did."

"What is it, Joley?" Sarah asked warily. "We don't know any other telepaths."

There was a small silence. Joley began to rub her hand against her thigh as if it bothered her. It was a gesture they were all becoming too familiar with.

"Ilya Prakenskii." Elle whispered the name. "He has to be a telepath."

Joley shrugged. "Don't look so scared for me."

"We owe him," Sarah said. "We all swore we'd answer his call when the time came. What does he want?"

Joley made a face. "Who knows, who cares. The man can burn in hell for all I care. He'd better stay away from me or he'll find out what hell really is."

Libby tightened her fingers on Elle. "Let's do this, but with everybody. We all need a little extra strength. Tomorrow morning Abbey and Kate will be back. Before Hannah leaves for the hospital we'll perform the ritual just to make certain we're all in top form."

"You think it will take all of us?" Hannah asked. "I don't like the idea of leaving Jonas alone even for a couple of hours."

"He's in a good hospital," Libby assured her. "And he's improving every day."

Hannah flashed a small smile. "I forget anyone but you can actually doctor someone, Libby."

Libby laughed. "San Francisco has great hospitals and doctors."

"So what have we learned tonight?" Sarah asked, looking around the circle.

"We're all really good at keeping secrets," Libby said.

"Everyone but you," Hannah teased. "You have whisker burns all over your face. And little bruises on your arms and skid marks on your back, you little hussy."

She had whisker burns other places as well, but she wasn't

volunteering the information. Libby smirked. "Yes, I do. And I'm planning on going back for more."

"Do you really love him?" Sarah asked.

"I'm falling so hard, so fast, I don't even know what hit me," Libby admitted, "but you know something? For the first time in my life I feel complete. He makes me feel beautiful when I know I'm not. He makes me feel sexy when for sure I'm not and he looks at me like I'm the only one in the world." A slow smile spread over her face and lit up her eyes. "And he's *brilliant.* The man is so damned brainy I'm in heaven."

"You're a brain groupie," Hannah pointed out. "And I'm so happy for you."

"Me, too," Libby said. "And on that note I'm going to bed."

"Aren't we going to talk about who might want you dead?" Sarah asked.

"Nope. I'm going to bed and I'll worry about it tomorrow." Libby blew kisses to her sisters as she climbed the stairs to her room.

She could still feel him in her body, on her skin, taste him in her mouth. Slowly she peeled off her clothes and looked at the marks of his possession on her body. There were faint smudges on her skin. She turned to look at her back and burst out laughing, feeling silly, but very happy. Hannah was right, she had rug burn on her back.

"Little Hagatha," she whispered affectionately and lay down in her bed naked, feeling the cool sheets on her body, wishing Tyson was beside her.

Libby lay thinking about Tyson, her body aching all over again. She went over every detail of their evening, wanting to keep it forever etched into her mind. The beauty of his lovemaking, the perfection, the sheer ecstasy she'd never imagined. She should have realized Ty would be a dominant in all things, he was used to being the one in charge. He certainly saw to her every need. Her heart jumped, fingers sliding on the cool sheets under her. Everything had been for her. Tyson had given, taken charge, controlled, but he had taken nothing for himself. Of course he'd achieved a shattering orgasm, but he couldn't have felt the way she did—complete. Sated. *Loved.*

Tyson had made her feel sexy for the first time in her life. He'd made her feel as if she were the only woman he could want to be with. He looked at her with longing, with a burning lust, but also with something much deeper.

And she'd responded without giving him anything back.

He was that little boy with his box of treasures again. His intellect. His house. His incredible sexual expertise. Even the motorcycle ride, his gift to the good girl so she could play bad girl. Libby groaned softly and covered her face with her hands. She hadn't seen it and she should have. He said she needed him. Well, maybe she did, but he needed her more. He needed someone to love him.

13

"WHAT the hell are you doing down here, Tyson? It's ten o'clock in the morning and you haven't been to bed. You were in an accident last night, ripped up your leg and arm, not to mention bruises, and you've got some mad chemist gunning for you." Sam sank down onto the bottom stair of the basement and shook his head. "You're a lost cause, bro. I swear you are. I'm getting gray hair trying to look out for you, man."

Tyson looked up from the latest sheets of data the computer had spilled out, squinting at his cousin. "I thought you'd sleep in, Sam. You were up as late as I was."

"Not quite, you bonehead." Sam grinned at him. "You didn't actually go to bed."

Tyson shrugged. "I tried. I can't sleep without her."

"Her?" Sam's eyebrow shot up. "Libby Drake? Look, Ty. I'm going to give you some advice here and for once in your life, will you please listen to me? Fuck her brains out and get it out of your system. Shower her with presents if it makes you feel less guilty, but for God's sake, don't fall into the trap of thinking you're in love and you want to marry her.

You don't exactly date a lot of women. If she's that great in the sack, by all means, have fun, but the truth is, that rush you're feeling is going to go away and you're going to be left with a big financial mess and a clingy woman."

Tyson looked back down at his data without answering.

"At least tell me you used protection."

"I don't have a disease and neither does she."

"How the hell do you know what she has or doesn't have?" Sam said, his disgust plain. "And I'm not talking disease, you moron, I'm talking pregnancy. The oldest trap in the world for a man with money. She's a damned doctor. She knows whether or not she can get pregnant probably right down to the minute."

Tyson whirled around to pin his cousin with an icy, warning stare. "I hope to hell she does get pregnant, Sam. If all I have to offer her is money, then, damn it, it's all hers. I'm in love with her." He'd never said the words aloud. He hadn't let himself think about the emotion. Loving Libby Drake, if she didn't love him back, it would tear out his heart. He wasn't the kind of man who would recover.

"That is such bullshit. You don't even know what love is, Ty. I feel like I'm talking to a damned sixteen-year-old greenhorn having his first sexual encounter. So she's a great fuck. That's all she is and that's all she'll ever be. You don't fall in love with them, you get your rocks off and leave it at that."

"What the hell is wrong with you?" Tyson demanded. "You've known how I felt about Libby for a long time. I told you a few weeks ago I planned on pursuing her."

Sam clenched his fists in utter frustration. "I thought you'd be normal, Ty. I should have known better. You think every man in this town hasn't fantasized one time or another about one of the Drakes getting them off? Personally, I'd love to have Joley lying flat on her back, legs in the air, begging me for it, but you know what? Even if that happened, I'd fuck her and walk away. I'd go back to the firehouse and have my bragging rights for weeks until everyone was sick of every detail, but jealous as hell. The point is, *I'd walk away.* You don't get caught in the sex trap. That's for kids. Little boys who don't know better."

"You have an interesting philosophy, Sam, a great way to live. It isn't my way."

"You don't have a life. You've never had a life. You live like a mole with no friends most of the time. You can't be bothered with boring details such as actually paying bills or buying groceries. How long you think old Libby is going to stick around once you put a ring on her finger and she has access to all that money? Hell, Ty. Your own parents couldn't deal with you. You think Libby really wants *you*?"

"It's possible."

Sam snorted. "She'd be panting after me if I had control of the checkbook. You think she hasn't looked at me? I know when a woman wants me. I have women calling here night and day, not you. You think you're so damned smart." He sneered. "You're as dumb as a rock. I go out with ten different women, do whatever I want to them and they beg me, *beg* me to take them out again and they even pay for it. You don't see me having to dangle my money or my damned pompous Noble Prize in front of some slut's nose to get her to spread her legs."

Tyson took a step forward and stopped himself. A muscle ticked in his jaw and his fingers curled tightly at his sides. This was Sam. Sam sometimes lost his temper and said a lot of crap, apologizing profusely a few minutes later. Beating Sam to a bloody pulp wasn't the thing to do, no matter how badly Ty needed to do it.

Tyson had always known he held himself tightly under control, but the utter fury sweeping through him was like some terrible destructive storm, bent on destroying anything around him—or anyone. He knew he couldn't hold himself in check with Sam standing in front of him in spite of all his reasoning. "Get the fuck out of here," he bit out, taking another step toward his cousin. "Right now I want to tear your head off and stuff it in a garbage can. I mean it, Sam. Get out of my sight before I do something I don't want to do."

Sam leapt to his feet. The look on Tyson's face was

enough to know he was in serious trouble. Tyson was a strong man with enough lethal training behind him to be intimidating during any given situation, but riled, he looked deadly. Sam rushed up the stairs and slammed the door behind him. Tyson heard a chair crash against it and bump back down, splintering along the way.

Swearing, Sam took two steps before he realized he wasn't alone. He stopped abruptly, towering over Libby Drake. His hands opened and closed, clenching into two tight fists.

"What the hell are you doing skulking around my house? Looking for cash lying around? Or just trying to drive a wedge between my cousin and me?"

"I'd say you were doing a pretty good job of that all by yourself," Libby replied. Her palm itched to slap his face. She couldn't imagine how Tyson would feel after listening to Sam shove it in his face that no one had ever really cared about him as a person. "Ty gave me a key and asked me to come over this morning."

"Great, I have to actually watch you seducing my cousin into making a fool out of himself. Women like you are a dime a dozen. You may as well be whoring on a street corner. At least a streetwalker is honest."

Libby tilted her chin, wishing she were taller. No one had ever looked at her with such a mixture of contempt and loathing. "You can't even consider, not for one minute, that I might love Ty for himself."

Sam snorted. "Yeah. He's such a lovable guy. And so suave with women. Hell, he wouldn't know how to please a woman if you gave him a map of her body and big red arrows pointing out the hot zones. He's rude to everybody. Because he's such a fuckin' genius, everyone is supposed to jump when he says so. Yeah, Libby, I believe you're really falling in love with him and that paltry little estate worth upwards of forty million doesn't in any way have anything to do with you taking off your clothes for him. You disgust me."

"I thought you loved him."

"I do love him. Why do you think I'm going to fight you

with everything I have to keep you from ruining him? Just because I know what he's like doesn't mean I don't care about him. I've been looking after him since he was a kid. He *needs* me. You're a sweet piece of ass, probably his first, and the rockets are going off for him, but you aren't going to get away with it."

Libby found herself shaking. She'd never been so insulted, or so despised. The bad girl image wasn't all it was cracked up to be. After listening to Sam's idea of relationships with women, the terrible things he'd said about her, she wasn't even certain she could face Tyson; but now it was even worse. An estate upwards of forty million? No wonder Sam thought the worst of her, but why didn't he think the best of Tyson?

"Well, this piece of ass is going to the lab, get out of my way."

Instead of moving, Sam planted himself squarely in front of the door. "Maybe you want to be with a real man, one who knows what he's doing."

She shook her head. "No, thanks. Your idea of a good time and mine are very different, but I'll ask Joley what she thinks about your oh-so-generous offer."

"You fucking bitch." He took a step closer to her, his face a mask of rage. Hard fingers bit into her shoulders, nearly pulverizing her bones as he shook her. The more he shook her, the more his anger seemed to increase and the harder he slammed her around.

It wasn't even the physical confrontation that was frightening, it was the anger radiating from him. Libby just didn't have the nature for such deep hostility. For a moment she imagined his hands creeping up to her neck and him strangling her. A small sound escaped, whether a plea or a protest, she wasn't certain, but she forced her shocked body to move, trying to imagine what Joley or Elle would do in the situation. She managed a kick to the shins and another squeak.

The door behind Sam flung open, hitting Sam in the back, driving him into Libby. She stumbled backward under his weight and went down hard, sitting on the tiled kitchen floor, staring up in shocked surprise at Tyson. He looked like an avenging angel. If he had come up with the idea of making peace with his cousin, the thought was gone in a single heartbeat.

He actually roared. Libby heard it. Dark, demonic shadows clouded his face and sparks glittered in the depths of his eyes. He spun Sam around, his shoulder heaving. Sam's head jerked back and Libby heard the sharp crack of fist breaking bone. Sam grunted. Tyson hit him a second time, driving him backwards so that he stumbled over Libby, stepping hard on her thigh; he caught himself and took a couple steps to her left.

Tyson yanked her to her feet and shoved her back behind him. "Get out of here, Libby." His voice was low and utterly cold.

"Stop. Both of you," Libby demanded, horrified. "This is crazy. Sam's nose is broken. Let me take a look at it and both of you calm down."

Was this the kind of thing that happened to Joley? It sickened Libby. She'd never even witnessed a fistfight, not even in school. It was much more primitive and raw then she ever imagined.

"I'm not asking, Libby. Get the hell out of here before you get hurt. You've got bruises all over you. No one, *no one,* puts their hands on you, related or not."

The entire time Tyson didn't take his eyes off his cousin. Cold. Angry. The tension rose until Libby wanted to scream. She thought she knew Tyson, but realized the man who was always so unfailingly gentle with her, was quite capable of extreme violence.

Sam pressed his back against the counter and shook his head, one hand to his nose, the other up in surrender. "I'm not fighting with you, Ty. I've made enough of a jackass of myself. I don't know what the hell got into me." He shook his head again and walked around the island counter to the sink, running water on a paper towel. "I must have sounded like a raving lunatic. I don't need help, I've had a broken nose before."

Tyson glared at his cousin. "You were hurting her, Sam. *Hurting* her."

"Was I, Libby?" Sam pressed his fingers to his nose, trying to stem the flow of blood. "I'm sorry, I lost my mind. I just don't do change well. That's no excuse, but I've been looking out for Tyson for so long I almost forget he's a grown man. My mother used to tell me he's different, that it was up to me to watch over him and I guess I took it a little too seriously."

"Different doesn't mean slow, Sam," Tyson pointed out.

Libby made no attempt to walk over to help Sam. She couldn't tell exactly why when her instincts insisted. She stood behind Ty and watched his cousin's face. The anger was gone to be replaced by the easygoing charm, but she could still feel his hands on her shoulders, fingers digging all the way to the bone.

"If you're all right, Sam, I promised Irene I'd be seeing Drew today." She glanced at her watch, eager to get out of his presence. She might be able to see his point of view another time, she might even be able to eventually see his side, but she was never going to be friends with Sam Chapman, Tyson's only relative and the only person in the world he loved, and that was heartbreaking. Libby felt she was letting Tyson down. "I can meet you over at the Madisons', Ty, if you still want to come."

Tyson reached out to wrap his hand around the nape of her neck, holding her still. "I'm coming with you now. I've wanted to drive your car."

"What makes you think I'm letting you drive my car?"

He held his hand out for the keys. "Because that poor car deserves to be driven by someone who goes more than thirty miles an hour." He snapped his fingers, palm up. "It begs me every time I get close to it."

Libby dropped the keys obediently into his hand for two reasons. He never took his eyes from Sam, never once looked at her, but kept his cousin pinned with a dark promise of retribution. She didn't want to leave him there. And Sam was watching. She wasn't denying Tyson in front of Sam.

Ty swept his arm around her, turning his back on Sam. "Let's get out of here."

Libby didn't say anything until they were out on the highway. Tyson drove like he did everything, with complete commitment and focus. He stared straight ahead, hands loose on the wheel and gear shift, the car smoother going through the tight turns than it had ever been.

"Are you all right, Ty?" Libby ventured. His jaw was set, his expression blank, but his eyes were alive with pain. She wanted to cry for him.

"You're the one he was trying to slam into the wall."

She winced at the clipped grimness in his voice. "People say things in anger they don't mean. He's worried about you and I can't blame him."

He glanced at her, a brief sideways flick of his eyes as the Porsche slid smoothly through a series of S turns. "Don't do that. Don't make excuses for him. People are responsible for what they do whether they're emotionally upset like Irene, drunk, or angry. He could have hurt you. You're not exactly big, Libby."

Too much pain filled the small confines of the car. She opened the window and drew fresh air into her lungs. "It's not true, you know."

His gaze slid sideways again and then back to the road. "That you're not a hundred pounds soaking wet?"

"The things he said. About the money. About someone not wanting you for yourself. About someone loving you. I don't care about the money."

A muscle jerked in the side of his jaw. "I know the money doesn't mean anything to you, Libby. I've watched you too long to think you were ever after my money. You don't have to tell me that."

Abruptly he pulled the small sportster onto the shoulder of the road, put his head down, brow on the steering wheel, breathing deeply.

Libby put her hand on his shoulder. "Talk to me."

He shook his head. "The things he said . . ."

"None of it was true."

Head still on the wheel, he turned to look at her, anguish in his eyes. "What do I do that's so wrong all the time? I've seen exasperation in your eyes, the same as I've seen in Sam's, in my parents. What is it I do that you don't do, that Sam doesn't? The rest of the world? What makes me so damned unlovable?"

Libby brushed caressing fingers through his hair. "People can love someone and still be exasperated, Ty. They can get angry and have terrible fights. You've removed yourself emotionally from the world for so long you don't recognize things that are normal. It's when you feel very strong emotions that you can have passionate reactions. Believe me, my parents were often exasperated with Joley, but she is very, very loved."

"I don't feel sorry for myself, Libby. I never thought how much my life was missing until recently."

Libby leaned closer to him, rubbed her cheek against his shoulder. "Maybe you aren't for everyone, Ty. Neither am I. Most couples find one another because they're right for one another. Maybe someone else couldn't live with you forgetting dates."

"I've never remembered my own birthday let alone someone else's."

She laughed softly. "Somehow, hon, that doesn't surprise me in the least. I can live with reminding you about the big things."

"What if we have children?" He put his palm on her stomach. "What if you're already pregnant? I'd make a terrible parent. I'd probably forget to come to their birth."

"Fortunately, I'm a doctor, so I'd get through it and then I'd skin you alive and you'd remember for the second one. And just for your information, I'm on birth control. I suppose it wasn't very responsible of us to not talk about all of that before we jumped into having sex."

"I made love to you, Libby. I didn't fuck you and I didn't have sex with you, I made love to you. I'm in love with you. Whatever else is going on, at least believe that."

"I may not be experienced sexually, Ty, but I think I know

the difference. You didn't have to reassure me." He was still radiating so much pain that Libby needed to get out of the car. But she didn't want to take the chance he might view her distance as a rejection. The things Sam said, the way his cousin had treated him, brought his childhood, so carefully hidden away, straight to the surface.

"He hurt you, Libby."

"He hurt you, Ty," she pointed out gently. "Your parents hurt you. People we love can do that. We give them power over us by loving them. That's part of living. You can't sit on the sidelines and you can't hide in a laboratory forever. Life is messy, Tyson. If you don't trust me with your love, you're never going to know if we work or not. Whatever Sam thinks, or Sarah thinks, ultimately doesn't matter. It's what we think."

His hands fisted in her hair and he pulled her close to him, holding her head still. "I think I want you more than I've ever wanted anything else in my life. What do you think, Libby?"

His piercing blue eyes blazed down into hers and she felt that same curious melting sensation she always felt when she looked at him. More than that, more than the ache between her legs and the tightness in her breasts, was the feeling of rightness. Love could be overwhelming and for a long moment she could only look at him.

Tyson never took his gaze from her face. Didn't blink. His world, his future, the rest of his life had come down to this one strange moment, sitting on the side of the road. Her delicate scent drifted to him and her hair felt like crushed silk in his hands. Libby Drake, with her large bedroom eyes and her sensual mouth and her innate innocence. She couldn't hide her thoughts from him if she tried. She had the most expressive face of any person he'd ever met.

And there was love in her eyes. There was no mistaking that. He might not have ever seen it before, but it was unmistakable and quickened his heartbeat until his pulse was thundering in his ears and tears burned close behind his eyes. To prevent making a fool of himself, he leaned down and took the words as they formed, from her mouth. Tasted them. Savored them. Held them inside of him.

Emotion rose from some well deep inside he'd slammed shut a long time ago. It flooded his body, his mind, his heart, until he shook with it. He kissed her until he thought he'd choke on tears. He didn't know if the tears were for his past, finally shed, or tears for his future, but he turned his face away from her and started the Porsche.

"I can't talk about this, Libby," he said, keeping his face averted. "So don't start."

Libby put her hand over his as he shifted. "You can't talk about loving me?"

The little smile in her voice twisted that emotional knot in his gut tighter. "I mean it, Lib. I'm not going to be one of those mushy men women push around." He injected command into his voice, but he sounded raspy instead, not quite striking the right note.

She burst out laughing, that soft sound that seemed to be music to his ears—and his body. "You mean you're never going to tell me you love me?"

"I just did. I said it and that should be enough."

"For the rest of my life?"

"Well, how many times exactly is a man supposed to say it to a woman?"

"In an entire lifetime? Or in a few years before they divorce because he never says it and she doesn't know?"

His gaze narrowed as he flicked it over her. "There is not going to be a divorce and she should know if she's smart like you. Being nice isn't my forte, as much as I hate to admit Sam might be right in any way, but . . . I'm not about to screw this up."

She hid a smile. "Well, I guess you're going to have to make the supreme sacrifice then, and say it at least three times a day. And there's going to be kisses involved."

"Kisses I can handle. I'll be happy to make love to you three times a day, but why do we have to talk about it?" He shook his head. "We're going to do some negotiating on that one."

He pulled the car into Irene Madison's driveway and turned to look at her. "And you're going to marry me. None of this living together first to see if we're compatible. I'm not compatible with anyone, so there's no point in you trying to find that out. You're just going to have to make it permanent and find a way to cope."

"Gee, honey, I'm overwhelmed with your sweet talk. You're sweeping me off my feet."

"You're being sarcastic and I'm being serious. I want to get married as quickly as possible. I have a private plane somewhere." He looked around as if he might spot it out the window.

"A plane?" she echoed faintly. "Somewhere?"

"Yes, we could fly to Reno."

"No, we couldn't. I have this enormous family, Ty. I'm not flying to Reno. You don't actually have a pilot's license, do you?"

"Sure."

"Get out of the car. We're not talking anymore." She pushed the door open and stepped out before he could stop her. What in the world was she thinking? Tyson Derrick was going to make her crazy.

Tyson draped his arm possessively around her shoulders as they approached the house. Just before they got to the door, he pulled her to a stop. "Listen to me, Libby. I don't care what state we find this boy in. Don't risk your health or that of your sisters to ease him. Jonas is still in the hospital. All of you seem to be running on empty. If you start to feel overwhelmed and on the verge of doing something you shouldn't, give me a sign and I'll get us out of there."

Libby scowled at him. "Don't think you're going to get all bossy on me. I don't go for the he-man type."

His sudden grin was almost boyish, the smile lighting his eyes. "Yes, you do. You just never admitted it to yourself before now. I'm very bossy."

"So am I."

"But I'm always right," he said smugly and knocked on

the door. As the door began to open he put his mouth against her ear. "Because I'm *brilliant.*"

He flicked his tongue over an ultrasensitive spot, sending chills down her spine. Libby lifted her shoulder and gave him a warning glare.

"Libby. Tyson Derrick." Irene stepped back, her expression wary, ashamed, hopeful. "Please come in."

Ty allowed his arm to slip off Libby's shoulder, but he ran his fingers down her arm until he captured her hand, tugging her close to his side. Irene didn't have her purse handy, but if she decided to bash Libby, he was ready.

A small girlish giggle escaped from Libby. She leaned into him, her lips brushing his ear. "Stop looking so intimidating. The poor woman is terrified of you."

"Good. You seem to incite people toward violence. I think looking intimidating might be helpful in these situations."

She laughed and squeezed his hand. Tyson found himself wondering how she did it. Turned everything around so that he was having fun. Felt light. Playful. He wanted to swing her into his arms and kiss her right there in front of Irene because he was happy.

"Irene, Tyson works for BioLab and is a biochemist. He researches drugs all the time. In fact, his original work is the platform for the PDG drug. Like me, he's concerned that the drug in development for cancer patients performs differently on the adolescent brain. There's no significant proof of that. The clinical trials have been conducted with mainly adults. There have been only a very few patients in the trials who have developed severe depression with suicidal tendencies, but all have been teens."

Tyson leaned forward. "We know the adolescent brain isn't fully developed. I think it reacts differently than an adult brain to the stimulation of the drug. This particular drug was derived from a plant in the rain forest of Peru and . . ."

Libby squeezed his knee, flashed a smile at Irene and broke in. "How much do you actually know about clinical trials?"

Irene ducked her head again, twisting her fingers together.

"Next to nothing," she admitted. "We need money desperately and Drew has been so tired of not being able to be like other kids. When I read about this, it seemed like such a miracle."

"Prior to a clinical trial a drug or procedure is tested on animal and human cells. If the drug shows no serious concerns then they'll go into phase one of the clinical trials." Libby tried to judge Irene's reaction, but it was impossible. The woman bustled around rather than sitting still, pouring tea, cutting coffee cake and handing them plates and forks. "Phase one is anywhere from around twenty to eighty people. About seventy percent of all drugs pass this initial testing. They look for things like safety, how it's metabolized or absorbed, the best way to administer it, that sort of thing. Very few teens are ever asked to participate and certainly a test study of concentrated numbers of teenagers wouldn't be done except in very rare cases."

"I was told all that had been done and they were in the next phase. That they had already determined it was safe," Irene protested.

Libby glanced at Tyson. He raised his eyebrow. "Mrs. Madison. Irene. A trial that small cannot possibly determine the safety and side effects to a large number of individuals, especially to the adolescent brain. In a phase two trial, such as the one your son is participating in, the drug is given to a larger group of people. They're looking to further evaluate its safety and effectiveness. It's still an experiment, Irene. They have little idea of how the drug is going to interact with an adolescent brain."

Irene pressed her fingertips to her face, hiding her expression. "I'm sorry, Libby, I should have listened to you."

"You can leave a trial anytime you want, Irene. Surely you've pulled him out by now."

"I haven't done anything. He isn't taking the drug, but he seems so different, so discouraged. I just wanted to find a way to end this all. I'm going to lose my house, everything we have, and he still isn't better. I've done everything I can think of to do."

"You should have told us about the financial difficulties,

Irene," Libby said gently. "As a community, we all would have helped. Let me take this to Inez. You know she's a wonderful organizer. Joley can probably help raise money. We have resources as a community to help."

"I just didn't feel I could ask," Irene said.

"But you felt you could sell Libby out to the sharks?" Tyson asked, his voice a low whiplash of recrimination.

Libby was so startled she nearly dropped her teacup. She flashed him a chastising look, but Tyson ignored her, pinning the other woman with his piercing, icy gaze. "If you have a problem, Irene, taking it to your friends seems a better alternative than deliberately exposing a friend to what may be dangerous and unwanted attention."

"It was so much money. A man called me and said he had heard all sorts of stories about Libby. He offered me money just to tell him."

"What man?" Tyson asked, ignoring Libby digging her fingers into his thigh.

"He said his name was Edward Martinelli. I just told him a little about the Drakes and how over the years they'd put Drew's leukemia into remission over and over. He sent me a check for five thousand dollars. I'd never seen so much money. So I began to think if he would pay me for the story, maybe others would, too."

"And they did."

"Only if I had pictures and some kind of proof. I had the hospital records and many pictures of Libby with Drew. They gave me ten thousand once I came up with a picture of Joley and Libby together with Drew. Fifteen thousand dollars was too much money to pass up. We had so many bills and I was afraid of losing the house. It was a godsend." She ducked her head. "I didn't know the headlines would sound so lurid. *'Goddess and Queen of Debauched.'* That was so terrible."

Libby hated the way the gossip rags were so fixated on Joley all of a sudden.

"It was a betrayal, Irene," Tyson said, his voice so hard Libby winced. "It was wrong and you knew it was wrong and that's part of the reason you were so angry when you attacked Libby. You felt guilty."

"I did. I do." Irene began to sob.

Libby immediately went to her and put her arms around her. "It's going to be okay. Let the community help raise money for the bills. Take Drew out of the test program immediately and sign a release for Ty and me to have access to the data."

"We could use Drew's blood as well," Tyson added.

"Now? You want to take his blood now?" Irene asked.

"It's important, Irene, or we wouldn't ask. We need to analyze the data and try to figure out specifically what is wrong for this one age group of patients. The drug is highly promising and if I can just put my finger on that one small glitch, we might have a real opportunity for success. Without that specific data, I can't get anywhere."

Irene took the consent form from Libby and slowly began to read it over. Twice, tears welled up in her eyes and she blew her nose. "Go ahead, Libby, he wants to talk to you anyway. He's so angry with me for what I did. Take his blood if it will help."

Libby patted Irene's knee, flashed a warning look at Tyson and hurried down the hall to Drew's bedroom. She heard the doorbell ringing but ignored it as she knocked on the teenager's door.

Drew lay on the bed staring up at the ceiling. His leg was in traction and he looked utterly miserable. He brightened when he saw her. "Libby. I was hoping you'd come to see me."

"Tyson Derrick is here, too," she said, not wanting him to think she was hiding anything from him. "He's the firefighter who rescued you."

"And fell," Drew said glumly.

"You do know it wasn't your fault, don't you?" Libby asked. "Surely someone explained what happened to you."

Tyson joined her, holding up the paper in triumph. He held out his hand to Drew. "How are you? I'll have to sign your leg there. It's a long-standing tradition."

"The drug you took has certain side effects, Drew," Libby said. "One of them is severe depression. I hope you've stopped taking it."

Drew nodded. "I couldn't stop myself. Now I just feel stupid and angry and embarrassed. Pete wanted to see me, but I wouldn't let him in." He looked up at Tyson. "I'm really sorry. You almost died because of me."

"Not because of you," Tyson said, seating himself on the edge of the bed.

Libby had never heard his voice so gentle.

"I'm a biochemist, Drew. I only fight fires during the high season. More than most people, I know the effects of drugs on people. You were using an untested product. You *were* the test. It isn't safe yet, but I'm going to try to fix that. In the meantime, don't cut yourself off from your friends and family. You need them to help keep up your spirits for the long fight."

Before Drew could respond, there was a commotion in the hallway. Irene raised her voice and a man's voice snapped something back. Something hit the wall and the room shook. Tyson jerked open the door, one hand behind him to hold Libby back.

"Harry Jenkins." He greeted his nemesis, his voice mild. "Always a pleasure to see you. We were just leaving. Have you come to see Drew?" He flashed a small, taunting smile.

Libby caught his belt in warning. He was still smoldering from the night before, from the things Sam said; now he had a target. She tried to remind him the boy and his mother were watching. Tyson didn't seem to care.

Harry's face turned a mottled purple. "You! I should have known you'd be here. Mrs. Madison, I hope he's not bothering you. You don't have to talk to him."

Libby quickly turned back to Drew and deftly took a vial of blood while Tyson stood squarely in the door, preventing Harry from seeing what she was doing. Surprisingly, Drew flashed her a conspiratorial grin and stayed quiet until she was finished. She winked at him and tapped Tyson on the shoulder. Irene hovered behind Harry, wringing her hands together.

"I'll visit you later," Tyson said to the boy. "Libby and I have a lot of work to do." He reached behind him to urge her through the doorway, forcing Harry to step back.

The man followed them out the door. "I can't believe you'd go this far, Derrick," he said. "You're interfering with a legitimate study and it's against the law."

"Not if I have the mother's permission," Tyson said, his smirk plain.

Harry took an aggressive step forward. "You think you're going to get away with this, but you aren't. I have resources you haven't dreamed of."

"Do your worst, Harry," Tyson encouraged him. "You should be in the lab, not dogging my every step. What the hell are you doing in Sea Haven anyway?"

"Protecting my interests. I'm not letting you ruin my entire career, you and that doctor friend of yours. We'll see how highly everyone thinks of the two of you when you are exposed for what you really are."

Tyson slid behind the wheel of the Porsche and adjusted his sunglasses. "I'm going to be spending a few days in the lab, Libby. You feel like helping?"

"Absolutely."

14

TYSON was a tyrant in the laboratory. He ordered Libby around as if she were his assistant, didn't acknowledge anything she said and was so focused on his work he didn't see or hear anything else around him. She lay down twice on his futon and fell asleep, but in forty-eight hours he didn't stop once. She fed him eggs while he examined several compounds. He didn't seem to notice, opening his mouth on command and chewing when she told him to. His eyes were continually glued to his computer. Libby found him absolutely fascinating.

His mind seemed to work at three times the speed of anyone else she'd ever met and he was definitely on the track of something. Tyson reminded her of a hound dog on the scent trail. Nothing else seemed to matter to him—not even her. It should have hurt her feelings, but she was too impressed with his single-minded purpose. He poured over the data, compared notes, went back to his original earlier experiments, often muttered to himself and ran tests over and over. Sometimes he'd become excited and show her things, only to break off in mid-sentence, frowning and turning away to check something else.

Several times a day Sam brought them food, food she hand-fed to Ty to get him to eat, although sometimes even that didn't work and he ignored the offer. Sam apologized every single time he saw her for his outburst, but Libby couldn't help but feel uneasy around him. Tyson never looked up or acknowledged his presence.

"Has he eaten anything at all?" Sam asked.

Libby shook her head. "Very little. He's possessed."

"He's still not speaking to me." Sam looked tired. "He's pretty stubborn. He can hold a grudge a long time and I guess, this time, I deserve it. At least you should eat something, Libby. I've got the late shift later this evening. I won't see you for a while."

"I'm going to head out, too, maybe take the day and get a few things done, but I'll check on him tonight," Libby promised.

"Thanks." Sam disappeared up the stairs and with a little sigh, she gathered up her things and began to follow him, careful to be quiet.

"Where are you going?" Tyson spun around instantly, giving lie to the belief he wasn't aware of her presence while he was working. He was definitely paying attention and it startled her.

"I figure after two days, Ty, I need a shower. Technically I'm on vacation, but I usually put in a shift at the hospital and I'm not getting any sleep here." She indicated the computer. "You have fun and I'll come back in a day or two." She flashed him an encouraging smile.

Tyson stretched and came across the room with long, ground-eating strides. "Give me a second and I'll go with you. I need a break anyway." He reached her side, circled her neck with his arm and kissed her. Instead of his hard, hungry kisses, he was gentle, tender even, and it turned her heart over. "I like you in my lab."

She laughed. "Because I was such a big help to you."

"Actually you have been. Remember when we talked about the plants in the rain forest of Peru and how many of them have a symbiotic relationship with insects or plants around them? I haven't been able to get that out of my mind."

He followed her out of the basement, blinking a little in the light, reminding her of an owl. She smirked at him. "Just out of curiosity, Tyson, are you aware that owls see in black and white?"

A slow grin spread across his face, wiping away the weariness. "Do I remind you of an owl?"

"Just thought you might be interested—for future reference." She grinned back at him, almost daring him to come up with a matching fact.

He scratched his head. "Owls' irises dilate and contract independently in the two eyes. Fascinating creatures. BioLab is working on a retina retainer drop. It will hold the retina's shape to stop eyesight from worsening. They're only a couple of years out before they'll have it ready for humans." He held out his hand. "Do you want to go home? Hopefully your sisters have food and drink around."

Libby went with him out to her car and didn't protest when he produced the keys and slid into the driver's seat. He loved driving the Porsche and she loved giving him that small pleasure. "I thought you were totally oblivious to my presence, Ty."

"I always know when you're in a room with me. I have Libby Drake radar. In college I could spot you walking clear across campus. I'm not going to miss you in the same room." He glanced at her and then back to the road. "I know I'm not very talkative when I work."

She laughed. She couldn't help it. "You don't talk at all. Or you start to talk and forget and stop in the middle of it because you've thought of some great idea."

There was a long silence as he handled the Porsche through several tight turns on the narrow highway. Libby rolled down her window to watch the scenery flashing by. Several miles went by before he spoke.

"I'm sorry. I'll try to get better."

She glanced at him sharply, hearing the wariness in his voice. He thought he'd upset her, because he usually managed to upset the people around him with his tunnel vision. "Don't be sorry." She flashed him a reassuring smile. "When I'm at work, no one expects me to entertain them. I found it all very interesting. I know you're going to be able to figure out why the drug is reacting differently on the adolescent brain."

He frowned. "That may take some time. I might be able to figure out how to stop it from happening, but the why of it is going to be more difficult."

"That doesn't make sense. Don't you have to know why before you can fix it?"

Tyson shook his head as he pulled into the Drakes' long drive. He waited until he parked the car and stopped the engine. "It doesn't always work that way, Libby. Research is often discovering something by accident."

"Maybe, but you don't seem to do anything by accident." She got out of the car and walked with him up to the house. "Everything you do is careful, Tyson. You're thinking it through."

"Harry was close, but he was just in too much of a hurry. He lets the marketing people pressure him." His grin looked a bit like a hungry shark. "They stay away from me."

"I'll bet they do. You aren't at your most courteous when you're working."

He frowned again, looking more rumpled than ever as he pushed his hands through his hair in agitation and genuine concern. "Was I rude to you, Libby?"

She leaned into him and kissed his blue-shadowed jaw. "No, Ty, you weren't rude to me. Believe me, if you ever are, you'll hear about it."

His smile flashed, making him look younger and far more boyish. "Good."

Before Libby could open the door, it opened from the inside and she found herself staring at all of her sisters. None of them were smiling. She frowned. "You weren't worried, were you? I called a couple of times and left messages on the answering machine saying I was all right." She stepped into the house. "Oh, God. Nothing happened to Jonas, did it?"

Sarah closed the door behind them. "Jonas is fine, Libby."

"We got your message," Joley added.

Libby stopped in her tracks to stare at her younger sister. "Joley! You dyed your hair." Joley was a natural blond, her hair nearly platinum, the closest of all the sisters to Hannah's hair color. She often dyed, streaked and rinsed it with various colors, but never midnight black. She looked like Libby now, with her pale skin and large, mysterious eyes. "Mom is going to kill you. Why did you do that before the wedding? Please tell me you're not going into a Goth phase right before everyone gets married."

There was a small silence. Libby became aware of the tension in the room. She glanced at Tyson, suddenly uneasy.

He reached out and took her hand, his thumb running in a small caress of reassurance over her skin. "What is it?"

"I think you'd both better see this," Sarah said. "Why don't you sit down and have a cup of tea? There's a gossip rag you need to take a look at. It arrived on our doorstep with a little note." She handed Tyson the note.

It was on plain typing paper. A single word said, "Enjoy." There was a smiley face stickered beside it. Tyson turned it over and over in his hands, not certain why such a simple thing felt sinister, but it did. He exchanged a worried glance with Libby.

Libby reached for the gossip rag. "I'm not going to like this, am I?" she asked Joley.

Joley put a hand on her shoulder as if to steady her.

Libby lifted the fold one of her sisters had carefully creased and nearly dropped the paper as the photo swam into focus. She stared in utter horror at the front page photograph. It was taken at Tyson's new home through the panels of glass and showed an obviously naked woman wrapped in the arms of a very naked man. The headline read: *Drake Lovenest.*

For a terrible moment Libby couldn't think. She couldn't get enough air into her lungs to breathe. She could only stare in horror at the picture of her first sexual encounter now available for the entire world to see. She looked like a porn star.

There would be no way to identify Tyson—his head was down, his tongue lapping at her breast—but her head was thrown back, her arms cradling him to her. Black hair hung down her back, her eyes were closed in ecstasy.

"Oh my God. This can't be happening. Mom and Dad are going to see this. All of my patients." Libby choked on bile rising in her throat. "I'm going to be sick." She jumped up and raced for the bathroom, dropping the paper on the floor.

Tyson picked it up, studying the one large photo before turning to the inside where the headlines promised more. The other pictures were grainier and somewhat fuzzy, impossible to identify, but equally as revealing. He became aware of the slow burn of ice cold rage spreading through his system. His temper had always been slow moving, but now it burned like a wildfire out of control when lost. This was different. This was something far deadlier.

He lifted his head slowly and looked around the room at the sober faces of Libby's sisters. His gaze settled on Joley with the wealth of midnight black hair streaming down her back and curling around her face. She looked exotic. He'd never noticed she had the same sultry mouth as Libby. His breath hitched. "You dyed your hair so you would look like Libby. So everyone would think this was you and not your sister, didn't you?"

Joley shrugged, struggling to look casual. He caught the gleam of tears in her eyes before she turned away. "I'm used to it. Any publicity in my business is still publicity, negative or not. I don't like it, but this will kill Libby. She isn't tough enough to take the jokes and innuendoes. People are very cruel and she doesn't have a tough skin. The late-night talk show hosts are going to have a field day."

"And you have a tough skin?" Tyson wanted to smash something. Joley Drake was making a huge sacrifice for her sister. She wasn't nearly as tough as she pretended to be. He could see her hands were trembling, but she sank gracefully onto the floor in front of the sofa and reached for the cup of tea Sarah handed her.

"This is a big deal, Ty," Joley warned. "The magazines

have been trying for a couple of years to find dirt on me. Lately they've really worked at it. This isn't going to die down right away and you have to keep Libby from telling the truth. They'd crucify her."

"What does the article say?"

"Look at the headlines. They're following up on the faith healer article, and wondering if the Goddess, that would be Libby, or the Queen of Debauchery, that would be me, was caught in a love nest. It went so far as to imply there was more than one man there. They've even circled a picture they believe is proof of the second man. Libby's name is mentioned, but of course, the real speculation is whether it's me or not. Hannah is too tall. They can't implicate her, so with my hair dyed, everyone will believe it's me. I've instructed my publicist not to comment."

"You can't do this, Joley," Tyson said. "I appreciate that you'd want to, but Libby won't let you and neither will I. We didn't do anything wrong. We were in the privacy of my home."

"I think you need a really good security system," Sarah said. "If you don't mind, I'm going to put one in for you."

Tyson rubbed his hand over his jaw. "I doubt she's ever going to want to go back to that house." His mind raced a million miles an hour with ideas of retribution, but there wasn't a single idea of how he could change what had happened. He looked around the room at the faces of Libby's sisters. All of them, even Sarah, looked sympathetic.

And Joley. She sat by herself, one leg drawn up, her head on her knee, the black waves of hair cascading down to draw a veil over her face.

"Joley." He said her name softly. "No one has the right to do this to anyone. It doesn't matter what your profession is, they shouldn't hunt you down and peek like voyeurs into your private life."

She sighed and lifted her head, a wan smile on her face, one that didn't reach her eyes. "Maybe they shouldn't, Ty, but they do. I'm not letting them hurt Libby. My career can take this." She shrugged. "Who knows, maybe it will benefit from it, but not Libby's. She has to maintain a certain reputation."

"You hate this." She did. He could feel her misery. All of their collective misery and somehow, instead of condemning him, they made him feel a part of their protective circle.

"I hate that my beloved sister has to endure dirt like this because of who I am. No one from a slander rag would even know our names if I wasn't Joley Drake."

"Baby," Sarah said, "that isn't true. Hannah is famous and so is Kate."

"Yes, but they weren't stupid enough to be photographed with Rob Ryan. He's married with a couple of kids and since Rob just made another blockbuster movie, the paparazzi are out for blood. That's why I've been in all the rags lately. It's been a regular 'Get Joley Fest' lately and now it's spilled over to my family."

The bitterness in her voice had Elle wrapping her arms around her sister protectively. Tears streaked her face and Tyson remembered Libby had said she was an empath. If that were so, she would be feeling the pain each person was feeling.

"What were you doing with the movie star?" Tyson asked.

"Walking through the hotel. We ran into one another, had lunch and that was the entire extent of our fling. Well, I signed a couple of CDs for his kids."

"Have you warned Mom and Dad?" Libby asked. She came into the room, her chin up, green eyes alive with pride.

Tyson went to her and when she tried to sidestep, he simply gathered her into his arms. She went stiff, but he persisted, holding her close to him, determined they'd weather this firestorm together.

"I wanted you to know first," Sarah said. "It's impossible to tell from the picture that it's you, not with Joley dying her hair."

Libby jerked out of Tyson's arms. "I'm *not* letting Joley take the fall for this. No way. Joley, you can just dye your hair blond again. If you take the blame those pictures won't stay in the tatty little gossip papers no one believes. They'll get sold to the more reputable magazines. They'll be on television. You won't be able to get away from them."

"I knew that's what you'd say, Libby," Joley said. "So I made certain it was a done deal. Even if you call the paper and say it was you in the picture, they'll believe you're just trying to clear my name. I'm not letting anyone drag you through the mud."

"I am going to call them and clear this up."

Joley waved toward the phone. "The number's right there. Talk to Kingsley. He's a decent enough guy and at least he'll listen, but I'm telling you it won't do you one bit of good."

"What did you do?" Libby demanded.

"I called in a few favors. A few people called a few mags and helped the story along with hints and well-placed lies."

"This isn't your fault, Joley," Tyson protested. "No one did this because of you. Whoever took these pictures tried to kill us the other night by tampering with my motorcycle. If I'd been going the speed I usually go, it may have worked. They're after me. Or Libby. Or both of us, but not you. You didn't do this."

"They found a medium to hurt my sister that wouldn't be there if it wasn't for who I am and what I do."

"Sarah." Libby appealed to her eldest sister. When it came down to tough decisions, Sarah was the one they all listened to.

"You're a doctor, Libby."

Libby clenched her fists. "So what? Does that mean I have to let my baby sister take the blame for something I did? It isn't going to happen." She caught up the newspaper and stomped over to the phone.

Kate handed Tyson a cup of tea. "Sit down, Ty. Let Libby rage a little bit. She needs to get it out of her system. Are you hungry?"

Libby turned around. "I'm on hold, waiting for this Kingsley person. Yes, he's hungry. He hasn't really eaten for forty-eight hours."

Kate smiled at him. "Breakfast or lunch? You're at the in-between time."

"Breakfast. But, really, you don't have to do that."

"It's no trouble at all." Kate disappeared into the other room.

Tyson watched Libby as she adamantly explained to the reporter the pictures were of her, not her sister and to retract any mention of Joley immediately. He sighed. Joley was right. The magazines were interested in anything to do with Joley, not with her older sister. From her end of the conversation, it was fairly clear that no one was going to listen to Libby.

Libby slammed down the phone in a fit of temper. "Moron. He doesn't want the truth. He thinks it's admirable—*admirable*—of me to want to protect my sister. No matter how many times I said it was the other way around, he refused to hear it." She looked at her younger sister, despair in her eyes. "It isn't right that you're being accused of this."

"As long as Mom and Dad know that none of us, not you or Ty or anyone else, did anything wrong, I'll be fine," Joley said. "Libby, think for a minute. Don't just react. I've had a lot of time to think about this. People make up lies about me all the time. According to the press, I've done everything but strip naked and have orgies backstage after a concert."

"Well, now reporters and your fans will think they have proof," Libby pointed out. She flung herself into a chair and looked around the room at her sisters. "This is acceptable to you all?"

"It isn't to me," Tyson said. "I could come forward and identify myself as the man and name Libby as the woman."

"Don't you dare," Joley hissed. "They'll never believe it was Libby and they'll just think I've seduced my sister's fiancé. I refuse to look that low. You are her fiancé, aren't you?"

"Yes," Ty said. "Of course."

"No," Libby denied. "He hasn't asked me yet, so stop jumping the gun."

"We're getting married. I wanted to go to Reno, but she says no, she has to have a wedding. What do you think?"

"He didn't ask me," Libby insisted.

Kate handed Tyson a plate of food. "I think you should get married here, Ty," she said. "Abigail and Aleksandr are having a small private ceremony. There's no reason that you and Libby can't do the same, unless of course you want to join Sarah and me in a big wedding. You're certainly welcome to do that."

Tyson shuddered. "I think Abbey has the right idea. Private for me."

"He *didn't* ask me," Libby wailed. "Is anyone listening? Where's Hannah? I need her."

"You can't turn your fiancé into a toad," Sarah said.

Libby bared her teeth at her sister. "You're all finding this very amusing, aren't you? I'll have you know that Tyson Derrick may seem the bookish, geeky, nerd type, just because he's a biochemist and is a bit on the brainiac side . . ."

"A bit?" Tyson's eyebrow shot up. "*Brilliant* is how she normally thinks of me."

She flashed him a glare. "But he turns into a bossy caveman every chance he gets. He actually tries to tell me what to do."

"Imagine that," Sarah said. "But I don't think there is any question of you two getting married, baby sister. Everyone else in the world may think those pictures are of Joley, but Mom and Dad are going to know Libby the good girl has become Libby the bad girl overnight. When you told us you wanted to change your image, you weren't kidding around." She smirked at Tyson. "And they're going to be well aware who managed that little change."

He puffed out his chest. "True. That was all the brilliant one." He saluted Kate. "The eggs are great."

"Brilliant one my butt," Libby muttered. "This bad girl thing is harder than it looks. And true bad girls don't get married, they have flings. *And* if you're so proud of yourself, Ty, you can be the one to show Mom and Dad the pictures."

Tyson choked on his eggs. Kate patted his back and Sarah

handed him a glass of water. "I don't know the first thing about talking to parents. I didn't have a lot of practice. I'm thinking you'll be better at it, Libby."

"And if we do get married—and I'm stressing the *if,* as you haven't asked me yet—I want an ironclad prenuptial agreement stating that your money isn't mine."

"That's just bullshit. Once we're married, everything I have becomes yours. That's the way it's supposed to work. As for asking, if I asked, you'd have the opportunity to say no and I'm not taking any chances. The potatoes are dynamite, Kate. Does Libby cook like this?"

"No, I don't," Libby snapped, hands on hips.

"Hence the reason you need my money. You can use it to pay for the cook," Tyson said, striving to look practical.

Libby glanced over at Joley, the smile fading from her face. "I don't know what to do. It feels wrong to me to let this happen."

"Let it go, Libby," Joley advised. "Maybe we should concentrate on thinking who might have done this."

"Irene received around fifteen thousand dollars for her story and pictures of Libby and Joley from a magazine. If she did it once, and she admits she has many bills, she might try again. This story was probably worth a fortune," Tyson said.

"I tried to get the source," Joley admitted. "I even promised Kingsley an exclusive if he gave up the source, but he refused."

"Not Irene," Libby said. "She was so upset."

"That was guilt," Tyson pointed out. "Pure guilt. Harry Jenkins is out to get me. If he can ruin our reputations in the scientific and medical communities, maybe that would score him a victory."

"He goes on the list, too," Sarah said.

"And Edward Martinelli," Elle added. "Remember the pictures of Libby healing Tyson in the hospital? They threatened to put them in a magazine."

"Good grief." Kate frowned. "I've never heard of so many people out for blood. Anyone else?"

"Sam doesn't like me," Libby ventured, not looking at Tyson.

"And Sarah doesn't care much for me," Tyson added with a careless shrug, "but somehow I believe she'd think more in terms of toads than scandal rags."

"I'm imaginative," Sarah said. "And you're beginning to grow on me."

Tyson found himself smiling. Even happy in spite of the unfortunate and bizarre events. There was something about the acceptance into Libby's family that made him feel different. Libby made him feel whole. They made him feel accepted. The easy teasing was strange, but he found he enjoyed it. "Well, considering that Libby loves her family and I intend to be a permanent part of it, it's probably best you learn to appreciate my finer points."

"You have finer points?" Sarah challenged. "What are they?"

Tyson grinned, not in the least offended, and passed the empty plate to Kate. "Aside from the fact that I adore your sister, I'm a walking encyclopedia and every family needs one."

"That certainly will come in useful for me when I'm researching for a book," Kate said. "Very helpful stuff, Sarah."

"You know anything about security systems?" Sarah asked.

"Some. I can brush up. Mostly I've always had an interest in electronics."

"Is there anything you can't do?" Libby asked, feigning exasperation.

"I minored in quite a few subjects," he explained. "I get bored easily, once I'm fairly familiar with something. I can't sleep very well and if I read something I remember it, so I spend a lot of nights reading textbooks."

"Wow," Joley exclaimed, her smile wide and for the first time, real. "You really are a geek, aren't you? I've never really known a geek very well—with the exception of Libby, but she doesn't count because she's my sister."

"So out of all the suspects"—Sarah brought the conversation back on track—"which one does your gut say is responsible for getting these pictures in a magazine?"

He hesitated, a slight frown on his face. "That's a good question, Sarah, and I wish I had an answer. I'm used to people not liking me, but as far as I know, I've never had anyone want to kill me or smear my reputation. Someone tampered with my motorcycle and I think whoever took those pictures had to be the one who rigged my bike."

Sarah looked at Libby. She put her hands in the air. "The only one I can think would be after me personally is Edward Martinelli and I've never met him. I guess I need to talk to the man. At least face-to-face I might be able to judge if he's really trying to kill me."

"You're not serious," Tyson said. There was a warning note in his voice.

"Be still my heart." Joley clutched her chest and fell backward on the couch. "Who knew the scientific types could go all caveman on a girl?"

"It's annoying," Libby protested.

"It's sexy as hell and you know it," Joley said.

"I'd like to see someone get caveman with you, Joley." Libby nudged her hard. "You'd flatten the poor guy. He wouldn't know what hit him."

Joley grinned, not bothering to deny it. "The thrill would still be there for one small second before I annihilated him. I do love a strong man. You go, Tyson."

"Stop encouraging him in Neanderthal behavior. Just because you're kinky doesn't mean the rest of us are."

"No," Sarah denied. "We are."

"You're *not* helping," Libby said, glaring at her sisters. "Ty, don't listen to any of them. They're all little Hagathas."

He burst out laughing, the sound startling him. He was in the middle of a group of crazy sisters and they were talking sheer nonsense and he was actually enjoying himself. He'd never felt part of anything—not even at the fire station in the midst of the camaraderie. He was always too odd. The Drakes didn't seem to care that he was odd. Even Sarah was coming around. "Hagatha?"

"That's what we call each other when we're being, er, witchy," Libby explained. "Speaking of witches, Hannah must be at the hospital with Jonas again. How's he doing? I planned on seeing him not tomorrow, but the day after. That should give me plenty of time to rest before I give him another boost."

Tyson's gaze narrowed on her face and the smile faded. "What do you mean by giving him a little boost?"

Libby frowned at the edge to his voice. "Jonas was very seriously injured. By rights he should be dead."

"He would be if Libby hadn't healed him," Kate informed him. "Even Elle and Hannah together could never have saved him. Only Libby."

"And it nearly killed her," Sarah added soberly.

"Which is precisely why she doesn't need to be doing it again," Tyson said. He scowled at them. "Jonas is in the hospital getting excellent medical care. My understanding is that he's out of danger and is expected to make a full recovery."

"In time," Libby interrupted.

"A full recovery," Tyson repeated. "You don't have to risk your own health to speed up his recovery process. You saved his life. That should be enough, and I'll bet, if you ask him, he'd tell you not to take the risk."

"It isn't the same thing," Libby explained. The commanding note in his voice might be a thrill to Joley, but it was beginning to set her teeth on edge. Tyson wasn't joking. He meant what he said and he was, without so many words, attempting to forbid her to further aid Jonas.

"Jonas is family, Ty," she reminded him quietly. "I would never let him suffer if I can help him, any more than I would one of my sisters or you."

Tyson opened his mouth to protest, but closed it abruptly as realization swept through him for the first time. His ribs didn't hurt. He couldn't remember when they'd stopped hurting. His arm and hand no longer ached. When had she done that? Without any fanfare, without any discussion, Libby had completely healed him . . . from the smallest bruise and scratch, to torn muscles and cracked ribs. And he hadn't even noticed.

"Libby Drake." His gaze narrowed on her face, his features settling into hard lines. "Come here."

Joley let out a groan. "My heart can't take this. I'm ready to swoon!"

In spite of his resolve to stop Libby from endangering herself, Tyson couldn't stop the laughter from exploding out of him. Not mild amusement, but full-blown belly laughs. Joley was just too dramatic with her eyes dancing with mischief and her infectious smile. She looked so much like Libby, and he found he was rapidly developing a fondness for her, which was no small thing considering he simply didn't like that many people. She was outrageous and loved to tease, but she also genuinely loved Libby. And her absolute resolve to protect her older sister had won his respect and admiration.

He forced a tough expression. "You're cramping my caveman style, Joley. She isn't going to take me seriously if you keep that up."

Libby made a face at him. "I'm *never* going to take you seriously, if *you* keep it up. I can't remember a time in my life anyone dictated to me. You're so bossy."

"And he really means it," Joley said. "Isn't that cool? This is going to be so fun to watch, you being bossed around by science man."

"Science man?" Tyson echoed. He shook his head. "Are you always like this?"

Libby laughed, that lighthearted sound that always lifted him up toward the sky. "We're being very good at the moment, so we don't run you off. We get much, much worse."

"That's a scary thought." When had the atmosphere in the home gone from horror, shock and tears to laughter? He was beginning to suspect the true magic of the Drakes was their closeness, and their strength together rather than some mysterious supernatural force.

"Wait until Elle starts asking you how to make bombs. She

likes blowing things up. And don't give her any information, either," Sarah added, "because she's lethal enough as it is."

Elle teased with the others, but her eyes never laughed. He found himself a little worried about Libby's youngest sister. He looked around the room and wondered how he got there. In all his fantasies, he'd never considered he'd ever be a part of, or accepted by, the Drake sisters. His worst and very secret nightmare had been that Sam would have managed to date one of them. Not Libby. Tyson couldn't even allow that to happen in his nightmare.

It was acceptance he craved and hadn't even realized it until that moment. He thought he was above that need.

Libby brushed her hand over his jaw, and he wrapped his arm around her, bringing her down to his lap, struggling for a moment not to be overwhelmed by unexpected emotion.

"What is it, baby?" she asked, her voice low and intimate and caressing.

He felt the sound of her, the touch of her inside him. She could disarm him so easily with her voice; her touch. It didn't bode well for his caveman image. "I like your family." His tone was huskier than he intended and to cover the surge of emotion, he brought her hand to his mouth and nibbled on her fingers.

Libby looked around the room at her sisters. "I like them, too."

15

TYSON stopped abruptly on the walkway to the Chapman home, pushing Libby behind him. "The front door's open," he whispered. "Sam would never leave that door open. Go back to the car and if I'm not out in a couple of minutes, get out of here and call the sheriff."

He squeezed her fingers to reassure her and slipped inside his house. Faintly, he could hear raised voices and he followed the sound through the house into the kitchen. The door to his laboratory was wide open and he could hear Sam cursing.

Tyson hurried down the stairs to find Harry Jenkins bending over Sam who was on the floor. There was blood on Sam's face, one eye was black and swollen nearly closed. Tyson reached for Harry's collar and jerked him backward, tossing him hard against one of the many tables bolted into the floor. Harry yelled something unintelligible, but Tyson was on him, yanking him to his feet.

"Stop!" Sam yelled. "No, Ty. It wasn't him. Martinelli's men were here."

Tyson reluctantly let go of Harry to turn back and help his cousin off the floor. As Ty gripped Sam and drew him up, Sam's eyes went wide, the only warning, but Tyson whipped his head to one side. Even with the quick movement, Harry clipped him on the jaw with his fist.

"You son of a bitch, you sent the cops after me," Harry accused him, backpedaling as Tyson came at him again. He held up both hands. "You deserved that. They held me for hours. Do you have any idea how humiliating that can be? You're the one who should be locked up."

Tyson glared at Harry. "This time maybe they'll throw the key away. What the hell are you doing here?"

"What do you think? You had the cops haul me out of my hotel room in front of everyone and take me in for questioning. I had to call the lawyers from the lab." Harry took a step toward Tyson. "You went too far this time."

"How'd you get down here?" Tyson asked as he inspected his cousin's face.

Guilt crept into Harry's expression. "I wanted to see what you were doing. I have the right to see."

Sam rubbed the bridge of his broken nose. "I caught him down here with a baseball bat. He was about to have a go at your computer when Martinelli's men jumped me. Harry hid under the table while they pummeled me." Sam righted one of the chairs in front of the four computers and sat down. "Martinelli means business, Ty. I think he might have me killed if I don't do what he wants."

"I hid under the table because they had guns." Harry defended himself. "It wasn't my affair. I wasn't about to get shot over some gambling debt."

"You're a real humanitarian, Harry," Tyson said, contemptuously. "You don't mind breaking into my house and vandalizing my work, but you won't aid Sam when someone is assaulting him."

"It isn't your work," Harry objected. "It's *my* work. And I'm not letting you steal it this time."

Tyson ignored Harry's outburst as he examined Sam's puffy face. "How many of them?"

"Two. There might have been a third looking out. I had the feeling they were hoping to find you home tonight, not me. I was running late for work, but I came down here to get the dishes and throw them in the sink. I knew you'd forget. Then Harry showed up with his baseball bat and Martinelli's crew came a few minutes later."

"Who broke all that glass?" Tyson stared Harry down as he asked.

"Not me," Harry denied.

"Martinelli's men were smashing things," Sam confirmed.

"Why didn't you just pay them off?" Tyson asked. "The equipment down here is worth a fortune, not to mention if they destroyed any part of my research."

"I offered the money to them, but they said no, the deal was Martinelli would forgive the debt if Libby talked to him. I tried to explain I didn't have any control over Libby, but they seemed very aware that you do." Sam leaned his head into the heel of his hand. "I've got to get to work, Ty. Look at me."

"Harry, get out of here and don't come back to my home. If you do, I'm having you arrested. You might also consider updating your resumé because the next time I talk with Edward, your name is going to come up."

Harry's face turned bright red. He huffed out his breath, choking as he tried to respond. "You can't do that. You wouldn't dare."

"Not only can I, Harry, but I'll take great pleasure in it. Get the hell out of my house. And leave the baseball bat."

Harry spit on the floor. "You're disgusting, Derrick. You'd do anything at all to be the big man. Well, I know all about your little love nest and I saw the papers with the pictures of you starring in your own porn movie, having a threesome with some hot little rock star. I'll bet the doc doesn't know you're two-timing her."

Sam waited until Harry had stormed up the stairs before he lifted one eyebrow. "Porn movie? Threesomes? Why the hell wasn't I invited? I used to have all the fun, now you're turning into a regular playboy hustler." He flashed a wan grin, then flinched when it pulled on his swollen, cut mouth.

"Yeah, that would be me, playboy of the century," Tyson replied, wrapping his arm around his cousin. "Let's get you up the stairs. Did they break anything?"

"I don't think so, but I'm as sore as hell."

"I'll bet Libby's already called nine-one-one. I left her outside and told her to call if I didn't come back right away," Tyson said. "Damn, that's all we need, the cops showing up and asking about gambling debts."

"I'm sorry, Ty. I've been asking around about the Gambler's Anonymous meetings. It's not like they have anything like that around Sea Haven."

"Don't worry about it, Sam. We'll take care of this. I'm going to talk to Ed myself."

"I think you're becoming a violent man, Ty," Sam said, another grin slipping through. "You sound as mean as a snake."

"I'm beginning to feel violent. Ed should have taken the money. I'm getting tired of threats against Libby and you. If someone wants to come after me, fine, but they'd better leave my family out of it."

Sam hunched into a chair in the kitchen. "Man, I think someone got in a couple of really good kicks. Maybe your girlfriend can work her supposed magic on me. I could use it. I think I'll just sit here and rest while you go get her."

Tyson hesitated. Sam was rocking back and forth, his arms hugging his midsection. He was afraid Sam might have internal damage. "I'll just be a couple of minutes. Don't try to do anything."

"I was thinking of dancing on the counter," Sam quipped and waved him off.

Tyson hurried back outside. Libby had the car running and was pacing back and forth. She ran to him and threw her arms around him. "You scared me, especially when Harry came out. He was so angry, Ty. He really hates you."

"Did he touch you?"

Libby shook her head. "No, he just called you a lot of names. What happened down there?"

Tyson swept his arm around her and guided her up the stairs to the front door.

"Sam's hurt. Apparently he had a visit from Ed Martinelli's men. They beat the hell out of him and that coward Harry just let them do it. Did you call the sheriff?"

"Yes, you were gone for what seemed forever. Should I tell them not to come?" She hurried through the living room. "How hurt is he? Should we call an ambulance?"

He shook his head. "Bruises and one eye swelling shut, but they kicked him. You'll have to see if he has internal injuries. I want to make out a complaint against Martinelli's men. I ought to have Harry arrested for breaking and entering. He brought a baseball bat with him and he was going to destroy my laboratory, but Martinelli's men did it for him."

"Oh, no, Ty, not all your work." Libby entered the kitchen and went straight to Sam. He looked pale, sweaty and was breathing hard. "Maybe you should help him lie down on the couch in the living room, Tyson. I can examine him there. Sam, can you breathe all right?"

He nodded. "There's a first aid kit in the lab, if you think you'll need it, Libby. It's in the second cupboard at the back of the lab."

"I can get it," Tyson said.

"I don't think I can walk into the living room," Sam protested. "You're going to have to help me."

"Take him on in," Libby directed. "It should only take me a minute to get the kit. I'll need some towels and water, too."

She didn't wait for Tyson to agree, but headed down the basement stairs. The lights were still on and she could see glass smashed on the floor and books and equipment on the floor. Careful not to disturb anything in case the sheriff wanted pictures for evidence, she kept to the outside edge of the room as she made her way to the bank of cupboards at the back of the laboratory. There were cabinets and cupboards completely along the back wall. She chose the right side to start looking.

She couldn't believe someone would be so stupid as to destroy such important work. Why would Martinelli do something so damaging when he was in pharmaceuticals? It made no sense to her. Even Harry made no sense. People could be so illogical at times. Did Martinelli really think by harming others and threatening her family she would want to help him? And why in the world didn't Harry just try to figure out what was wrong with the drug, or even ask Tyson what he thought the problem was?

She flung open the double cupboard doors. She wasn't tall enough to see what was on the floor-to-ceiling shelves. Frustrated, she dragged a chair over.

"Libby? Did you find it?" Tyson called down to her from the top of the stairs. In the distance she could hear the phone ringing and a siren.

She stepped up on the chair. "It's right here. Is Sam all right?"

Tyson took two steps down, ducking his head for a better look at her. He frowned. "Get the hell off that chair. I'll get it. It's on the shelf on the other side."

He was in midstep when a blast blew through the left side of the laboratory, lifting Libby and slamming her backward several feet, shattering the windows and knocking him onto his backside. The concussion was deafening in the confines of the basement. At once flames licked up the walls and danced across the floor. The explosion triggered the overhead sprinklers so that water rained down, adding to the chaos.

"Libby!" He shouted her name, trying to peer through the swirling smoke and water to see her body. The world seemed to stop. His heart thundered in his ears and deep inside, where no one could hear, he was screaming in protest, in stark ugly fear.

She lay unmoving, curled up in a ball on the floor under an overturned table. One of the larger pieces of equipment was on its side, leaning against the table she was under.

"Tyson!" Sam was behind him, struggling down the stairs, holding his ribs, but following his cousin. "What the hell happened? Where's Libby?"

"She isn't moving, Sam." Raw fear edged Tyson's voice

as he bolted down the stairs, jumping the last few feet to scramble through the rubble.

"Don't worry, Ty. We'll get her out."

"She's not moving," Ty repeated, terror ripping through his body. He'd never experienced panic, not in any situation he'd ever been in, but on some level he recognized he was close. And terror was mixing with rage, a lethal combination. He shook with it, felt it eating at his gut and battering at his mind. This couldn't be happening. Not to Libby.

He shoved chairs, a computer, glass even, out of his way to get to her. She lay like a broken doll, hair spilling across her pale face, hands over her head as if at the last moment she flung her arms up to protect herself. Her arms looked singed. Tyson dropped to his knees, uncaring of the glass and wreckage. "Libby. Baby. Open your eyes." He ran his hands over her body. She seemed so delicate, so small and fragile. She didn't move, but when he checked her airway, she was breathing. "She's alive," he announced to Sam. There were no visible signs of damage other than a few cuts, none of which appeared deep, and the singed hairs on her arms.

Sam examined the bulky stability chamber that lay partially across the table pinning Libby's legs. "This is what saved her. It was directly in front of her and took most of the blast. I've never seen anyone so lucky. If she's breathing and her heart is fine, help me get this thing upright. We can lift the table off her and get her out of here. She's moving her legs so they can't be damaged either. I can get the rest of the fire out if we move fast."

"Derrick?" The basement door opened and feet pounded down the stairs. The police had arrived with Jackson in the lead. "What the hell is going on?" Jackson took one look at Libby beneath the table and signaled to Sam to help him lift the incubator upright.

It was a struggle to remove the bulky chamber, but they managed to shift it enough to get to the broken table. "Get the fire out, Sam." Jackson crouched down on the other side of Libby, taking her limp hand.

"No broken bones that I can find," Tyson reported. "I think the blast knocked her out. I can't seem to find any real damage, unless she has a concussion."

"What about her neck or a spinal injury? Can we move her?"

Libby moaned, both hands coming up in a defensive position. Tyson trapped her arms to hold her still.

"You're all right, baby, but don't move. I have to make certain you haven't injured your neck."

Libby blinked up at him, looking dazed. She struggled to sit up. Tyson pressed her to the floor.

"Libby, stay put."

"I can't hear very well."

"That will go away."

"My neck is fine. I have a hell of a headache though and my ears are ringing. What happened?"

Tyson lifted her into his arms, cradling her close, his lungs fighting for air. He would never get over the sight of her flying through the air to land in a crumpled heap. He knew it would haunt his sleep and eat away at him during his waking hours. "Harry Jenkins was here in the lab just a few minutes ago," he said to Jackson. "And quite a bit of the damage to my equipment was done prior to the explosion by a couple of men Ed Martinelli sent to beat up Sam."

Jackson turned his cold gaze on Sam. "Now, why would they want to do that?"

"I owe Martinelli a lot of money," Sam admitted. "I tried to pay him off, but now he's decided he doesn't want the money. He wants to talk to Libby instead."

"Is there a possibility that the explosion was an accident? A couple of chemicals were accidentally mixed together that shouldn't have been?" Jackson persisted.

"First of all, I don't 'accidentally' mix anything. And I wasn't doing that kind of experiment," Tyson denied. "I was analyzing reports and a very long list of compounds, but I hadn't mixed anything together in weeks. In any case, the blast was definitely directed. It came from the left and you can see the pattern of damage. Someone set it."

"Could Sam be a target?"

"Not in my lab. He might come down a couple of times a day to bring me a meal or tell me he's leaving, but he doesn't hang out there. Neither does Libby. No one would have known she'd be here." Tyson gently laid Libby on the sofa, stretching out her legs and putting a pillow under her head. "I want to take you to the hospital, just to check you out, Libby," he added.

"That's not necessary," Libby said. "My ears are the worst. The rest of me just feels a little battered."

"I think it's too dangerous for any of you to be around me. I can't protect you or Sam from whatever's happening here."

Jackson ran his hands over Libby's legs and arms, not in the least intimidated by Tyson's scowl of irritation. "You may as well stop giving me the evil eye, Derrick. Elle's upset and wants me to show her Libby's not hurt."

"I told you she wasn't. You don't need to be touching her."

"Elle wants to know for herself, so you'll just have to deal with it. That's what the rest of us have to do with the Drakes."

Sam came in, seating himself in a chair. "The fire's out, but it's a mess down there. Whatever you were working on is toast, Ty." He indicated Libby. "How bad is she hurt?"

Libby pushed Jackson away from her. "I'm fine, except I can't hear very well. Everything sounds muffled and I've got a terrible ringing in my ears. Do you think Harry did this to prevent you from finding out he's testing a drug before it should be given to humans?"

"There really is something wrong with the drug?" Sam asked.

Tyson nodded. "I can make it safer, but we need studies done on the adolescent brain. It isn't just this drug that has side effects specific to a young age. I was close to figuring out how to solve the problem."

"Really?" Sam said again. "I just thought maybe you were tweaking Harry because he's such a jerk. Is there any way to recover what you lost?"

"I always back everything up a couple of different ways. I'll check my equipment and see if I got lucky. What about you? You moved that heavy incubator. Your ribs aren't broken, are they?"

Jackson glanced at Sam, one eyebrow raised. "Your face is a mess. You think they broke your ribs, too?"

"Libby had gone to the laboratory to get the first aid kit," Tyson explained. "Martinelli's men kicked the hell out of him."

"I'm going to go talk to him," Libby announced decisively. "I'm going to see Jonas, so I may as well drop in on Martinelli and see what he wants. At least he'll have to forgive Sam's debt and won't have a reason for sending his men around here again."

"I'm having a word with Martinelli's men myself," Jackson said.

"No!" Sam shook his head vehemently. "That will just make them madder. Tyson, tell him I'm not willing to press charges. Look how angry Harry was just with being questioned. He brought a baseball bat with him. He planned to tear up the laboratory or hell, maybe even use it on you, Ty."

"Harry Jenkins brought a baseball bat into the laboratory with the intent of destroying your research?" Jackson asked.

"And he broke into the house, too," Sam pointed out. "He hid under a table while Martinelli's men beat the shit out of me."

Libby sat up slowly, reaching for Tyson to steady herself. She leaned her head on his shoulder. "Life around you is certainly exciting."

His hand came up to the nape of her neck. "It's not the kind of excitement I want for you."

"What does Martinelli want from you, Libby?" Jackson asked.

"I don't know. My guess is that someone in his family is ill and he thinks I can perform a miracle for him."

"I wonder why he'd think that," Sam said, sarcasm dripping from his voice.

"Shut up, Sam," Ty advised. "I'm running on a thin edge

and if you say anything else to Libby, your other eye is going to be swollen shut."

"Oh, for heaven's sake." Exasperated, Libby swung her legs over the couch to put her feet solidly on the floor. "The last thing we need around here is more violence." She pushed her hair out of her face and looked at Jackson. "Don't you think it's a little bizarre that I'm always around when these things are happening?"

"Who would want you dead, Libby?" Jackson asked.

"I don't know, but I'm going to find out."

Jackson's expression settled into hard lines. "You'll leave the investigation to the sheriff."

Libby rolled her eyes. "You've been around Jonas too long, Jackson. How's the investigation coming on who tried to kill him?"

"Why don't all of you get your things and get out of here for a while?" Jackson countered. "We need to take a look downstairs and gather as much evidence as possible."

Libby frowned at Jackson. "You could just tell me if you'd found something instead of acting all mysterious. My hearing's coming back, thank God, and I'm leaving."

"Let's head back to the house, Libby. I want to make certain nobody broke in and that it's locked up properly. I haven't gone back since the other night. We left in such a hurry and afterward I was talking with Jackson and I don't remember if I locked it or not."

"The house?" Libby hesitated. She didn't know how she felt about the house. Could she go indoors and ever feel safe again—or would she always be afraid someone was watching them?

Tyson curled his fingers around the nape of her neck in a gentle massage to ease the tension out of her. "It's all right, Libby. I'm going to put the house back up for sale right away. I'm not going to have you uncomfortable in your own home."

Libby blinked up at him, shock registering on her face. "You can't sell it, Ty. It's the most beautiful piece of property I've ever seen."

"It doesn't matter how beautiful it is, if you're uncomfortable there. A home should be a safe haven. Like your family home. You and your sisters feel safe and protected and at peace there."

She smiled up at him, surprised that he would have noticed. "Don't sell the house, Ty. Give it a little while and see if I feel differently." She stood up, pushing past Jackson. "I'm going to go see Jonas. Is there anything you want me to tell him?"

"Tell him you plan on seeing Martinelli."

"Very funny, Jackson." Libby took a tentative step. Her legs felt rubbery. The ringing in her ears faded a little, but she still felt shaky. "We don't know if he's the one doing this, but if he is, maybe he'll stop."

"My bet's on Harry," Tyson said. "He has motive and opportunity."

"I'll be talking to him," Jackson replied, "but don't jump to any conclusions."

Libby patted the chair in front of her and looked at Sam expectantly. He gave her a faint grin. "Are you sure it's safe? Isn't this what we were doing before the explosion?"

"I'm going to do a once-over again, just to make sure the fire's completely out," Tyson said. "You two don't move. I'm afraid if I take my eyes off of you, something bad is going to happen."

"I'll go with you," Jackson said.

Libby shook her head. "Your poor face, Sam. I hope Jackson finds those men and locks them up. Are the ribs still hurting?"

"They're sore," he acknowledged. "But I'm having a difficult time seeing and my nose and jaw hurt worse."

"That's a good thing. They didn't break your jaw, but I need to fix your nose." Without waiting, she applied pressure, snapping it back in alignment.

Stoically Sam endured her washing wounds and taping his nose. "Thanks, Libby. You didn't have to help me."

"I'm a doctor."

"You know what I mean."

"Don't worry about it, Sam." Libby patted his arm.

The ringing in her ears was definitely going away, but her headache throbbed and pounded. She wanted to quit smiling and go home where she could shut out the world for a few minutes. She pulled on her sweater and caught up her purse. Tyson could catch up with her later if he wanted.

She cried for no reason at all on the way back to her house. Elle came out as she parked the car and put her arms around Libby.

"Are you all right?"

"I don't know," Libby answered honestly. "For the first time in my life, I'm really afraid. Why would anyone want Ty dead? Whoever it is seems to be escalating their behavior. If it's the same person who shot Jonas, there's a good chance they're going to step out of a doorway and just shoot Ty down. Why, Elle? Even Harry doesn't have a good enough reason in my opinion."

"That's because you don't know how to hate, Libby," Elle said gently. "You aren't a violent person and you don't understand that kind of reasoning."

"Is it Harry, Elle?" Libby clung to her youngest sister. "Is Harry trying to kill Tyson?"

"I wish I knew. We don't want to lose you and I see danger surrounding you. All of us do, yet we can't pinpoint it. Even Jackson feels it, Libby. You have to be more careful."

"How do I do that? I don't know why or how or when. None of this makes any sense. Part of me thinks someone is out to kill Tyson, but there's another part that won't be quiet. And it's telling me in a very loud voice, that someone wants me dead."

Elle paused before opening the door. "If you feel that, Libby, you can't ignore it. Even if everyone around you is telling you something different. You have to believe in your gifts, all of them."

"What gifts? I can heal. The rest of you have all these interesting things you can do. Have you ever seen me levitate anything?"

"No, but you call and send the wind. You reach out and

I can find you. And obviously you have a major warning system. Don't discount it because you can't figure out what's happening."

"I know I shouldn't ask you, Elle, but does Tyson feel towards me even half of what I feel about him?"

Elle shoved open the door. She had a very strict policy of privacy towards others. Reading thoughts and emotions without wanting to do so was a tiring and voyeuristic experience, one she didn't care for. All of her sisters were aware of her rules. "I wouldn't ever allow you to marry the wrong man. Tyson Derrick loves you so much that when I think about it too much I cry."

Libby hugged her again. "I'm sorry, I shouldn't have asked. I'm so confused right now."

"And embarrassed by the tabloid," Elle added. "Don't let that affect your relationship."

Libby covered her face. "It was so *horrible*. I can't get the idea out of my head that someone was watching us the entire time. Tyson was so good to me. So caring of how I felt, and it seemed so perfect and right and some stranger took it away from us."

Joley looked up from her guitar. "Don't do that, Libby. Don't let someone turn something beautiful into something ugly. You didn't do anything wrong. You love Tyson. You're meant to be together. Everyone knows it. Let it go."

"I called Mom and she was upset for us, but she said the same thing," Libby admitted. "In all honesty, Joley, it makes it worse that everyone thinks it's you and not me. I feel so guilty on top of feeling utterly humiliated."

"What did Mom say?"

"She said you were a wonderful sister and I should cherish you. She was proud of both of us and she knew it would be difficult for both of us."

Joley blinked and bent her head over the guitar so that the riot of black hair fell around her, hiding her expression. "Well, I am wonderful. We all know that." Her voice sounded a little choked.

Elle leaned over the back of Joley's chair to watch her

fingers flash over the strings of the perfectly tuned instrument. "It's always fascinated me how talented you are musically."

"Not how wonderful?" Joley teased.

"That, too. I tried to play the guitar. I practiced for an entire summer."

Joley swiveled around in her chair. "Really?"

Elle nodded. "It brought you such peace. I could feel it radiating out of you, so much happiness even when you were a bit melancholy and I thought it might do the same for me, maybe all of us." She laughed. "I was more annoyed than joyful. I couldn't play the thing to save my life."

Libby burst out laughing. "Elle, you're so good at everything. You couldn't play the guitar?"

"Stop laughing, Hagatha," Elle said. "It's not funny. All the guitar did was buzz at me. I'm the queen of mosquito noises."

Joley shook her head. "You could learn, Elle. I'll teach you if you want."

"Guitars despise me. They are not my friend. I'm quite happy to listen to you play. Let's go out on the deck and look at the moon and you can play for us. I love it when we do that."

Joley reached out suddenly to touch her younger sister. Elle drew back quickly, but Libby saw Joley wince from the contact. Joley glanced at Libby, entreaty in her eyes. Libby smiled at them both. "What a great idea. Who else is here? Joley, why don't you get the others while Elle and I make sure we have enough chairs." As she spoke she casually circled Elle's shoulders with her arm and felt the well of warm, healing energy burst free. It moved through her body and into Elle's.

"It's a full moon tonight, isn't it?" Joley asked as she stepped over to the stairs to call her other sisters down.

"Yes," Libby said. "Well, almost full. And very little fog. A little cool and windy, but it's beautiful."

They sat together for an hour, simply listening to the surf below and the cry of the birds as they sought refuge for the night. Peace seeped into Libby, a small bit at a time. The Drake home was a sanctuary for them, a place to retreat and revitalize.

"I feel Hannah," Elle said suddenly. She closed her eyes and put her hand on Joley's shoulder, amplifying the connection. "She's standing by an open window looking towards us and she's crying."

"Is it Jonas?" Sarah asked.

Elle shook her head. "No, she's just feeling alone without us, and Jonas isn't a very good patient. He's been particularly difficult and taking it out on her."

Libby stepped out to the railing facing the sea, her sisters behind her. At once she felt the power of the Drake women flowing around her. It was often that way, particularly in the evenings, watching a sunset or in the moonlight. Energy leapt between them and crackled in the air. Joley picked out a soft melody on her guitar, accompanying the crashing waves. The ocean appeared wild, the serenity gone, waves slamming hard against the cliffs and spraying high into the air.

Sarah stepped to the railing and lifted her arms to the sky. Light from the moon spilled down on her fingertips as she wove the beams into fine nets connecting each of her sisters. She whispered softly, the rhythm following Joley's guitar riff and the rhythm of the sea. Kate stepped up beside her sister, shoulder to shoulder, and lifted her arms. The wind answered, surrounding the women, a soft, gentle breeze completely at odds with the power of the ocean beneath them.

Joley began to sing. A song of nature, of unity, of strength and power weaving a bond so tight none could break it. Although her voice was soft and melodious, the clarity rang above the crashing boom of the waves. The wind increased, catching the notes and taking them up towards the stars.

Abigail joined in to harmonize the chorus, the purity of her voice carried on the wind to the water below and the sea creatures answered, rising to perform an acrobatic ballet, leaping, spinning and somersaulting in unison.

Libby turned south, toward a city miles away where Hannah stood alone in a hospital room keeping vigil over Jonas. Libby lifted her arms to the wind, adding her power and healing energy to the gathering strength.

Elle was last. She stood close to Joley, lifting her face so that the moon bathed her in light, so that the beams from Sarah's fingers seemed to surround her. Power glittered like small sparkling gems over their heads. She turned, facing in Hannah's direction, feeling with her mind, a conduit of power, reaching for Hannah, knowing Hannah was reaching back. She waited until the connection grew strong, until the wind increased, whipping at them and Joley's fingers flashed over the guitar drawing out such a melody of power and energy that it fed the wind, fed the intensity until small charges of lightning sizzled across the sky.

Elle joined their minds, heightening the strength and love as they all poured their emotions into the collective universal pool. She threw her arms forward, commanding the wind, and it raced away, out of the ocean, carrying the message to their absent sister.

The music softened. Joley's voice faded away to a last haunting note. They stood waiting beneath the bright moon. And it came back to them. A soft feminine voice on the wind, whispering love and thanks. Libby blew a kiss out over the sea and smiled at her sisters. "I needed you all. Evidently so did Hannah."

"Me, too," Elle added.

"I was feeling a bit melancholy myself," Joley admitted.

Sarah smiled at them. "The best part of being a Drake is having all of you."

16

LIBBY stared out the window as Tyson parked the car in the hospital lot. She wanted him. Every single cell in her body was acutely aware of him. She had been afraid the experience of having her first time caught in a photograph for the world to see would inhibit her for all time, but she had awakened in her bed with Tyson lying beside her. His body had been wrapped around hers, his arms protective as they held her. There was nothing sexual and everything caring and shielding in his body language. Perhaps if he had been aroused and pressuring her, it would have been different, but he had slipped onto her bed, atop the comforter and simply held her close to him.

"You were very sweet to me last night. Did you sleep at all?"

Tyson glanced at her. She'd been so quiet on the drive to San Francisco. It worried him that she might be reconsidering her commitment to him. He wouldn't blame her if she did, but he knew he'd never recover. "I didn't want to sleep. I needed to watch over you, Libby. I've had too many scares lately." He turned off the engine and reached along the back of the seat to wrap his hand around the nape of her neck. "I hope you don't mind. I had to be with you last night."

"I didn't mind at all. To be honest, I expected you earlier."

His fingers brushed against her neck, did a slow massage. "I thought you might need a little time with your sisters. You've had so many things happen lately and I wanted you to have some time to talk things out with them."

He was always such an unexpected surprise to her. She had never considered him thoughtful, yet, with her, he was. "How'd you get into the house?"

"Elle opened the door and asked me the same thing. She thought the gate had been locked, but it swung open when I approached. I found the padlock on the ground."

Libby's heart did a peculiar flip. "The padlock was on the ground?"

"I closed the gate and locked it. You should be more careful. Sarah's dogs didn't even bark at me. I thought they were supposed to be great guard dogs. Neither animal so much as growled. Whoever trained those dogs ripped Sarah off. And if you have an alarm system, I didn't trigger it."

"Did Elle open the door before you knocked?"

His fingers slid into her hair. "Yes."

"Our alarm system was working just fine. And the gate opened because it was you." She flashed a small smile. "The gate and house welcomes those who belong."

"I definitely belong." He rubbed the silky black strands between the pad of his thumb and index finger.

Her smile widened. "That's my man. Totally sure of himself."

"I'm not, you know. I have a few questions that don't seem to go away. For instance, you aren't thinking of breaking up with me, are you? You've been so quiet and distant the entire drive, and you didn't say much this morning when you woke up."

She touched his jaw, a soft, tentative brush of her fingers. "I woke up and saw your face and thought I wanted to wake up like that every morning. You were looking at me and I can't even begin to describe the look you had on your face." Love. Adoration. Neither word could come close to the stark intensity she saw shining in the depths of his eyes. She had known it wouldn't matter how many photographs had been taken or how embarrassed she was. She wanted Tyson Derrick in her life. Not just now, but forever.

"You looked so beautiful."

She shook her head. "My hair was wild and I didn't have any makeup on, but I appreciate that you'd say so."

"You don't need makeup and I love your hair. I've told you that before, Libby." He slid out of the car and went around to her door, opening it before she had the seat belt undone. "Women are weird, you know that, don't you?"

She took his hand and hid her smile at his expression. "We're weird? How so?"

"I just don't understand how a woman can be so beautiful but worry constantly about her hair or nails or clothes. Who the hell cares?"

"You don't care whether or not I look nice?"

"Well, of course it's a plus, Libby, but I didn't fall for your looks." He frowned. "Well, okay, if we're being honest, I noticed your smile. And your mouth. You've got a killer mouth. And your eyes are really pretty." He started through the parking garage toward the hospital.

"So you do think about my looks," Libby pointed out.

"Not the way you do. And I love your hair, frizzy or not. It's so damn soft and smells good all the time." His fingers disappeared into the mass of silky strands. "I spent half the night just inhaling the scent of your hair."

"Ty." She stopped and faced him, her arms circling his waist. "Did you read a book on what to say to women? Because when you want to be, you're incredibly romantic."

"And I'm incredibly good in bed." He bent to brush a kiss across the tip of her nose. "I want you to remember that."

"I remember." She let her arms drop and took his hand so she could walk with him to the hospital entrance. "How many books did you read?"

He shrugged. "All of them."

Libby burst out laughing. "You nut."

"They paid off," he said smugly.

Libby was still laughing when they entered Jonas's room. The sheriff had finally been moved from ICU. Hannah rose immediately to hug Libby, clinging a little to her.

"Thank you for last night," she greeted in a whisper, glancing toward the bed. "He's been in a really bad mood."

"Stop whispering," Jonas snapped. "I'm not a child."

"I wouldn't have known from the way you were acting," Hannah said. "Libby's come all this way to see you. The least you could do was to be civil."

"Great. Stay across the room, Libby. I'm not having you touch me."

Libby studied the haggard face. She'd never seen Jonas look so pale, his face carved of stone, the angles and planes sharp, the lines of suffering etched deep. She blew him a kiss. "I love you, too, grumpy." She picked up the chart strapped to the back of his bed and began reading through the information.

"You're not my doctor."

"Jonas, stop it," Hannah ordered. "I mean it. You don't have to be so nasty all the time."

"No one asked you to stay, baby doll. In fact, it's damned difficult having you in the room watching me as if I were a little baby every minute."

Hannah shook her head and reached for her purse. "He's all yours, Libby. I'm going home." She turned her back on Jonas and walked out, her head high, but Libby caught the sheen of tears in her eyes.

"Did that make you feel better, Jonas?" Libby asked. "You're such an ass, even when you're hurt."

He sighed. "*Especially* when I'm hurt. She didn't have to run like a rabbit. I keep expecting her to hit me over the head when I'm mean, but she never does."

"In case no one has explained it to you, you nearly died. Hannah's been sitting with you night and day since it happened. And if she hadn't, you'd be dead. Didn't your doctor tell you it was a miracle you lived? Because if he didn't, he should have."

"I know. I detest her sitting there fading away while she gives me her energy. You think I can't see her getting weaker while I'm getting stronger? I feel helpless laying here like some impotent lump while she waits on me hand and foot all the while giving me her strength." He slammed both fists into the mattress. "I have to get out of here, Libby, or I'll go crazy."

"Well, Jonas," she said, seating herself on the edge of the bed, "I think you just prolonged your stay by several days, maybe weeks. Without Hannah, your recovery will be normal and with being shot four times, it won't be easy. And when you're actually out of here, you'll have physical therapy to do. So just so you know, you might want to eat a little crow and ask Hannah to come back."

"You're supposed to be a doctor, Libby. Your bedside manner stinks."

"Yes, well, your manners have always stunk so I guess that makes us even. I've got a bit of a problem and I thought I'd run it by you."

"Thank God. Something besides did I pee today. You've got to get me the hell out of here, Libby."

"You already said that. Pay attention. Someone is trying to kill me. Or maybe Ty. Or both of us." She related every incident, starting with Tyson's accident during the rescue, pointing out the harness was gone and ending with the explosion in the laboratory. She told him about Harry and ended by admitting she planned to talk to Edward Martinelli.

Jonas was silent for a few minutes. "Libby, whoever this person is has been escalating their behavior. It would be too big of a coincidence to think that there are two killers working separately, one after Ty and one after you. I just can't buy it."

"So you think the killer is after Ty."

"Don't jump to conclusions," Jonas cautioned. "Take it one step at a time. I haven't seen all the forensics yet, but it's very possible you're both in danger. Ty, you've been around those safety harnesses for years. How could one of them be sabotaged? If it wasn't an accident, and the first attack was on you, then we at least know where to start."

Ty frowned and rubbed the bridge of his nose. "If it was cut, I would have noticed before I ever put it on. The harnesses are examined over and over. Before and after each use. And believe me, I'm meticulous about that. Our lives depend on our equipment and all of us are careful."

"So you didn't notice anything at all out of the ordinary."

Ty shook his head slowly, still frowning. "When I go up, I get an unbelievable adrenaline rush. Everything is very vivid. Colors. Smells." He stopped abruptly.

"What is it?"

"I remember thinking I smelled chloroform."

"Certainly chloroform wouldn't do anything to a safety harness," Libby said.

"What other chemical smells like chloroform that would?" Jonas asked. "The suit looked as if something had chewed through it. The threads were gone completely. I could tell Brannigan thought it looked suspicious."

"Something that would dissolve material," Tyson mused. "Harry would have access to all kinds of chemicals and he'd certainly know what each one would do. For that matter, even Joe Fielding might. And Ed Martinelli. I don't think we're narrowing the field of suspects."

"No, but we at least are aware that your harness could have been tampered with and how they might have done it," Jonas pointed out. "Do you remember smelling anything else?"

Tyson shrugged. "The usual things I think. Cologne. Aftershave. I smelled garlic. Nothing else to identify a chemical."

"Some chemicals give off a garlicky smell, Ty," Libby reminded him.

"Who would have access to the harness?"

Tyson sighed and ran his hand through his hair, leaving him looking a bit rumpled. "I suppose anyone really. No one is supposed to go to the heliport, but it isn't high security. We have a gate, but it's open most of the time. If we're busy working, I think someone might be able to slip in easy enough."

"And the attacks began on both of you after you started seeing one another," Jonas mused aloud. "Let me think on this, Libby. You two concentrate on the chemical. If you think of something that would eat through the material that smells like chloroform, let me know. And be careful when you talk to Martinelli. I'm not going to tell you it's a bad idea, because you're going to do it anyway, but let him know up front that I know where you are."

Libby leaned over to brush a kiss across his brow. "Get better fast, Jonas."

Tyson wrapped his arm around her waist, his touch a shade possessive. Libby shot him an amused look.

"If Hannah's still out there, send her back in," Jonas instructed.

"No way. You're too abusive," Libby protested. "You deserve to lie here alone and think about what a jerk you are."

"I know, but send her in anyway." Jonas caught Libby's hand when she scowled at him and went to turn away. "She said she was leaving, but she'd wait for you. Come on, Lib, give me a break. She looks so damned skinny and pale and worn out and it just makes me mad. She doesn't take care of herself."

"So have her go home and we'll watch out for her."

"No, you won't. She'll watch out for all of you. At least when she's with me she has to eat. If she doesn't, I don't." He smirked at her. "It works every time. She falls for the pathetic look."

"She needs sleep."

"I'll get her to lie down on the bed with me. I don't want to be alone."

"You're such a baby. Fine, I'll ask her to come back, but you'd better treat her right and I'm going to tell her to leave the second you get nasty with her," Libby warned him.

Jonas waved his hand at her. Libby glanced up at Tyson as she followed him out the door. "He's never had patience for inactivity. I remember years ago when he came down with some virus and was running a high fever. All of us sat on him to keep him down. I can't imagine how poor Hannah puts up with his bad temper." She glared at him. "I wouldn't."

He held up both hands in surrender. "I wouldn't expect you to."

Hannah stood up as they approached her. "I waited to see if you were all right, Libby. I've had all these terrible fears for your safety and I keep calling home. Sarah told me about all the accidents. It's so scary."

"We'll figure it out eventually," Libby said. "How's it going here? I can see Jonas is in rare form. He's as mean as a snake."

Hannah rubbed her temples. "It's hard on him to just lie there, especially with you in danger. He hates it. He's not very nice to the nurses or to anyone else. He calls Jackson three times a day for updates. I don't know what he's going to do when he starts feeling even a little better."

"If he gets nasty with you, Hannah, leave. He's begging for you to come back now, but if you do and he starts getting abusive, leave him. He's out of danger unless he gets an infection, so he should be fine a day or two without one of us here. I know you're feeding him strength to heal him faster, but he has no right to upset you."

Hannah gave her sister a faint smile. "He's upset me for years. I doubt if he can suddenly change overnight."

"Well, let him try. Seriously, Hannah, he's wearing you out."

Hannah leaned over to kiss Libby on the cheek. "I promise I'll leave the next time he yells at me." She glanced at her watch. "Probably in an hour."

Libby laughed. "That's so Jonas. I'll see you later." She took Tyson's hand and with a small wave, walked out.

"She did look tired," Tyson observed.

"She's not getting any sleep. Hannah's a homebody. She

travels for her work, but as soon as possible she goes home. She sleeps better and is much more relaxed."

"It's incredibly nice of her to stay with Jonas."

"We try to keep one of us with him at all times. Hannah is very connected to him in spite of all their bickering. She's always loved him, but they just fight all the time."

"Why? He's got that look when he's around her, the one warning other men off. If she loves him and he feels that way, what's the problem?" He opened the door to the passenger side of the car.

Libby snapped her seat belt in place. "They're both stubborn and complicated and refuse to admit how they feel. They'll work it out eventually."

Tyson slipped into the driver's seat. "Are you going to come home with me? I've got a surprise for you. At least I hope I do."

"What have you done?"

"It wouldn't be much of a surprise if I told you, now would it?"

Libby found herself laughing all over again. "Just being with you makes me happy, Ty."

"Even though I forget our dates? You know I'm going to forget birthdays and anniversaries. I'll be terrible at that."

"You're so silly. We haven't gotten that far so there's no need to worry."

"I plan far in advance." He slipped his hand into his pocket and pulled out a small box. "I found this just before I bought the house."

Libby stared at him for a long time before she took it out of his hand. He wasn't looking at her, but kept his eyes straight ahead, his other hand gripping the steering wheel so hard his knuckles were white. Heart pounding, she opened the lid. The ring burst into fiery brilliance the moment the sun hit it, sparkling from every exquisitely cut facet. Her breath caught in her throat. "It's beautiful. More than that. I've never seen anything like it." And he'd paid a fortune for it. Libby loved jewelry, particularly diamonds, and she knew she was looking at an ideal, flawless stone. "Ty." She could only breathe his name, shocked at the perfection of the ring. It was designed for a small, petite hand, and pale skin. For her. He'd had it made for her. She hugged the knowledge to herself, once again shocked by his thoughtfulness.

"Well?"

"I can't speak. It's so incredible."

"Say yes, Libby. I could use a yes right about now."

"You didn't ask me."

"You're going to make me ask you?"

She laughed softly, hearing the note of exasperation in his voice. "I'm an old-fashioned girl."

"I'd rather just tell you and start off the right way."

"That might get you hit over the head."

Tyson drove for several miles in silence. A muscle ticked in his jaw. Libby was not going to help him out. She remained quiet. Waiting. He sighed. "Libby, are you going to marry me?"

She didn't hesitate or try to keep him in suspense. "Yes, Ty. I am."

He let his breath out slowly. "You sure? I'm not very social."

"That isn't exactly news."

"Put the ring on your finger."

Libby wasn't surprised when the ring fit perfectly. She held out her hand so he could see. "It's beautiful."

He caught her hand and kissed her fingers. "I don't want you to make up your mind about the house until we give it another try. Promise me you'll keep an open mind." He pulled the car onto a long winding drive leading up to high gates.

"This is where Martinelli lives?"

He glanced at her, quickly recognizing the apprehension in her voice. "You don't have to go in, Libby. I can talk to him myself."

"No, no. I need to do this. I want to look at him while I'm talking to him. It's easier to read someone face-to-face."

"You're not afraid, are you? Ed wouldn't be so stupid as to try to harm you in his own house, especially when he knows the police are aware we're talking to him. When I set up the appointment with him, I made certain he knew we were letting everyone know where we were."

"He has to be involved in something dirty if he sent men to your house to beat up Sam," Libby pointed out. She waited until Tyson leaned out the window to speak into the camera box.

The gates swung open and Tyson drove them up to the house. He'd obviously been there before and knew exactly where he was going. The house was large, Spanish style with a huge courtyard. The grounds were well kept, with flowers and shrubs everywhere. Ed Martinelli held the door open, waiting for them as they came up his walkway.

"Finally, Miss Drake. Thank you for coming." He held out his hand to Tyson. "I can't thank you enough for bringing her to me."

"You can thank me by telling me why the hell you sent a couple of men to beat the hell out of my cousin." Tyson took an aggressive step forward despite Libby's restraining hand. "And it's *Doctor* Drake."

Martinelli looked puzzled. "I don't know what you're talking about, Ty. I sent John Sandoval to ask her to speak with me. I tried to reach her by phone, but didn't get anywhere. When you called me and told me what they'd done, I pulled them out of Sea Haven immediately." He looked at Libby. "Please accept my sincere apologies, Dr. Drake. John takes his job very seriously."

"They had guns," Tyson said.

"I can only repeat my apology, Ty. They're bodyguards. They carry guns. If it makes you feel any better they were fired. I was desperate and I sent men I thought I could trust to handle a delicate situation. When they made it worse, I asked Sam to arrange a meeting and offered to exchange his gambling debt for a chance to talk to Dr. Drake." He stepped back and gestured toward the entryway. "Please come in."

Tyson stepped into the cool interior. "You're telling me you didn't have a couple of your men beat up Sam?"

"You've known me for years. Nearly my entire life. You know I don't operate that way. Sam owes me money. He has before and he will again. Why would I want him hurt? He's your cousin. If there was a problem, I'd go to you and we'd work it out."

"If you didn't send the men after Sam," Tyson asked, "who the hell did?"

Libby remained silent, her fingers curled around Ty's hand, her gaze sharp and clear on Edward Martinelli's face. He looked worn and tired. She could feel waves of distress pouring off of him.

"I have no idea, Ty." He spread his hands in front of him, looking defeated. "I have three uncles involved in criminal activities. I can't help who my father was any more than he could help who his brothers are. Periodically they send bodyguards around to protect my family. I don't ask questions and I don't refuse them. Whatever is happening in their lives, I don't want my family hurt. It may be wrong of me, but I'm not willing to take a chance. I live my life as best I can." He waved his hand toward the sofa, an invitation to sit.

Tyson settled his body close to Libby, his posture protective, his fingers threaded through hers. "If you're not involved in anything, Ed, why does Sam owe you money?"

"Because I have a great deal and he asked me for it. He's always paid me back. And there's always you if he doesn't. You've spent your entire life bailing him out. Everyone knows you're good for the money." Ed switched his attention to Libby. "I had to find a way to talk to you. Ty told me how stupid John was in approaching you. I have no excuses, but I hope you'll at least hear what I have to say without prejudice."

"I'm here, Mr. Martinelli," Libby pointed out.

"I heard you were able to heal people." His gaze shifted, obviously embarrassed. "I've never believed in that sort of thing, but I'm so desperate at this point I'd take my wife and son to a tent in the woods if I thought it would help."

"I take it they're ill?"

He nodded, rubbing his hand over his face. "For the last few years, my wife has had an autoimmune disease. At least that's what the doctors tell me. She gets so tired sometimes she can hardly function. It started up about three years ago and they diagnosed her with everything from Lyme disease to chronic fatigue syndrome. When Robbie first started showing signs about a month ago, I thought it was the same thing, or maybe mono. But the doctors thought I was overreacting. Since then he's gotten so much worse, but no one seems to be able to figure out what's wrong with him. I find doctors so frustrating. They know they're sick but they have no idea with what so they've given us ten diagnoses, none correct. But he's going to die. I see him slipping away from us every day. My wife is beside herself and so am I."

"Have you taken them to a place like the Mayo clinic for a diagnosis?"

He shook his head. "I gave up on doctors. I just feel so damned helpless. Can you just look at him?"

"He's here?" Libby asked incredulously. "Not in a hospital?"

"I've hired a full-time nurse for him, but after his doctor and two others diagnosed him as autoimmune, I brought him home. I have his records."

"I'd like to see those before I see him."

Edward immediately picked up a large envelope from his coffee table and handed it to her. Libby began a methodical read through the thick file. "He has bouts of fever, itching, headache and joint pain that moves around." She read aloud, her voice thoughtful, lines appearing between her eyebrows as she frowned. "I see here that you've never been to Africa. I know you travel extensively."

"Why does everyone keep asking us that? No, I've never been near Africa and neither has my wife."

"Has anyone checked your wife's heart?"

"This is about our son. My wife isn't nearly as bad."

"Chances are whatever is wrong with your wife is also what's wrong with your son. Give me another couple of minutes and I'd like to examine him as well as your wife if she's available."

"She's with Robbie. She hardly leaves his side." Ed rubbed his hands over his face and peered through his fingers at Tyson.

"I don't have a lot of time to devote to threatening people. I don't know why someone might be after Sam, but the only conversation we had was when I begged him to talk to Dr. Drake. I put in numerous calls to you and never got through. With Eva and Robbie sick, I just don't think about much else."

"I don't check the messages."

"Can she heal people?"

Tyson winced at the plea in Edward's voice. He glanced at Libby. There was no question she was feeling his pain and frustration—his desperation. He had always been able to read Libby's expressions, her face was so transparent to him, and she was definitely forming an opinion. Libby had worked for Doctors Without Borders as well as WHO. She'd worked for the Centers for Disease Control and she'd seen both domestic and exotic illnesses, far more than most doctors. He wondered if her healing ability aided her in diagnosing, but had no chance to ask her.

"Mr. Martinelli," Libby began, an edge of desperation in her voice.

"Libby," Tyson interrupted decisively, interjecting a note of warning.

Tyson found himself responding to the pain and weariness so evident in Edward. And he could see how it would be so difficult for Libby to walk away from a situation like this one, but she wasn't recovered from healing Jonas—or him. He couldn't let her risk her own health or possibly even her life. "Libby's a brilliant doctor, Ed. If it's possible to figure out what's going on, I have every faith in her that she'll be the one to do it."

Libby's eyes met his and his heart nearly stopped at the look she gave him. He'd never seen love in another's eyes, not directed at him. He had the sudden urge to drag her into his arms and kiss her, just for looking at him that way. He was smart enough to acknowledge to himself that there was a part of him that felt he was unlovable and no amount of telling himself to grow up would get him over those childhood feelings of rejection. He was beginning to believe Libby

Drake could love him, and all of his careful planning to get her to see she needed him was every bit as important as he'd first thought.

Edward shook his head. "I've lost all faith in doctors."

"Don't give up yet, Mr. Martinelli," Libby said, standing up. "Please let me see your son. Has your wife and or your son ever traveled with you to a foreign country?"

"Not Robbie. We haven't been out of the country since before he was born."

"Which country?"

"I traveled in South America. I wanted to see the rain forest. Eva flew to Mexico to meet me when my trip to the rain forest was over, and no, she wasn't bitten by any bugs. She wasn't near any bugs. I was very conscious of her health and kept her in the best hotel available. We've had the same questions asked over and over by the doctors."

"It's the only way we can get a clear diagnosis, Mr. Martinelli." Libby preceded him into the room where a nurse sat beside a bed and a young woman lay beside a small boy. He was about five and very pale and weak. Eva Martinelli looked just as weak.

"This is Dr. Drake, Eva. She's come to take a look at both you and Robbie," Ed said, his voice gentle.

"Don't get up, Mrs. Martinelli," Libby said, her smile easy as she pulled gloves out of the small bag she'd brought with her. "I won't disturb him too much."

She approached the bed, noting the woman's breathing. "Have you been short of breath for a long time?" Libby slid her hands down Eva's neck, feeling the swelling in the cervical glands. "On this trip you made to Mexico to meet with your husband some years ago, you don't recall being bitten by anything at all? Nothing unusual happened?"

"Nothing to do with bugs," Eva said.

Libby paused, her hands sliding down to the deeper glands. "What do you mean? What did happen on that trip?"

"I flew to Mexico to meet Ed. I wanted to swim with the dolphins. I love the water and we have a favorite place we enjoy going."

Libby nodded encouragingly as she moved to the sleeping child, her hands sliding over his neck to feel similar swelling in the glands.

"Eva's leg was cut open on a piece of metal embedded in the wall of a swimming pool just below the surface of the water. We were at the estate of some friends of ours and the cut was very deep. We barely got her to the hospital in time."

Libby straightened up and turned to face Eva. "You suffered severe blood loss?"

Eva nodded. "It was just a cut though. It didn't get infected."

"But you had a blood transfusion."

"I don't have AIDS. They checked us for AIDS."

"I don't believe you have AIDS, Mrs. Martinelli, but I believe I've seen your symptoms many times before. The signs are very indicative of Chagas's disease. You can get Chagas three different ways and one of them is through a blood transfusion. The symptoms often don't show up, particularly in an adult, for years. Adults many times get a more chronic form where a child can often get an acute form. You both will need some tests run immediately."

"But I thought the blood was screened for everything," Ed protested.

"I obviously could be wrong," Libby said, although she was certain she wasn't. The swelling in the cervical glands was very symptomatic of Chagas. "But the disease is very easy to misdiagnose. Did you tell the doctors about the transfusion in Mexico?"

Eva exchanged a long look with her husband. "We talked about South America quite a bit, but not Mexico. The subject didn't come up."

"Someone mentioned Chagas once," Ed said, "but she was never exposed to the bug that carries it."

"I think she should be tested and Robbie as well. She obviously was transfused before she ever conceived him. If I'm correct, Mr. Martinelli, time is of the essence to get treatment for them both, particularly Robbie. I'd like to call their doctor if you don't mind and arrange things immediately."

"I don't want to put them through a lot of tests again and then have the doctors say they have no idea."

"Chagas is present in eighteen countries on the American continent. In the early eighties, over seventeen million people were infected. Even now with all the work being done to eradicate the problem we see between seven hundred to eight hundred thousand new cases per year. I'm telling you, I've seen this over and over. Get them to the hospital and get treatment started. If you let me use your phone, I'll speak with their doctor and we can get things rolling."

17

"OKAY, woman," Tyson said, as he unlocked the door to the enormous glass front house, "I was very impressed."

"It wasn't all that difficult. I've seen Chagas's disease many times, and when I touched Mrs. Martinelli, I knew she was having heart problems. It wasn't such a big jump, especially since I knew Ed often went to foreign countries doing wild things with you. I was thinking foreign diseases as soon as he told me about his wife."

"You thought about trying to heal them," Tyson said, holding open the door, waiting for her to make the move to go inside. "Just like you wanted to do with Jonas."

"I was giving Jonas a boost, it isn't the same thing."

He made a huffing sound, which Libby ignored as she forced herself to step over the threshold. It was utterly silly to feel exposed in the house, but she did. She had loved the property from the first moment Tyson had driven her along the winding driveway and the first glimpse of the house had been breathtaking. It meant even more to her that he had found the place himself and purchased it for her. She wanted to feel safety and peace, instead of the current heart-pounding fear that someone was watching their every move.

"I did think about it, but you gave me your best imitation of intimidation and I was able to be sensible."

His eyebrow shot up. "*Imitation*? I scare everyone at the lab with that look. A little more respect, Drake."

"I thought if you kissed me, you couldn't call me Drake anymore."

"Are you angling for a kiss?"

"Yes."

"Well, then, why didn't you just say so?" He caught her chin in his hand to lift her face to his. She felt the long slow kiss all the way to her toes. Her reluctance to enter the house faded away instead of increasing as she thought it might. Every time he touched her, the world fell away so that she could only feel the ebb and flow of passion, and a rush of love so deep it shook her. She hadn't known she was falling that hard. It hadn't come fast as she'd always imagined love would, but had happened slowly over time. All those years of watching him, thinking about him, she had tied herself to him without even knowing.

When he lifted his head, she stared up at him feeling a little bemused. "That book you read on kissing? I'd like a copy."

"You kiss just fine, baby."

"I was going to frame it and hang it on the wall over the fireplace in a place of honor. In fact, let's keep the entire collection of your 'how to' books on the shelf where we can refer to them often."

He grinned at her. "I like the idea." Tyson gestured toward the living room.

Libby took a breath, forced air through her lungs and walked through the cool marble entryway into the enormous glass living room. She halted abruptly. Where before the unfinished room had been a lovely but bare hardwood floor and plush throw rugs, now neat groupings of furniture filled the space, leaving openness, but eradicating emptiness. A long, wide couch curved around the corner in soft buttered leather.

Several recliners and low slung coffee tables formed intimate, relaxing spaces. She halted abruptly. "Who did this?"

He shrugged. "I picked out the furniture a while back and had it delivered yesterday. If you don't like it, you can have them take it back and pick something different. I just wanted to make the house seem more like a home than an empty building. And you won't have to worry about voyeurs. Sarah put in an alarm system. We have cameras for outside. And I had these drapes installed for you." He looked really pleased as he crossed to the wall opposite the glass. "I remembered Sarah waving her arms and closing the drapes and it gave me the idea."

He pushed a button on the wall and drapes slowly descended from above the panels of glass. "We can close them from just about anywhere in the room, on either story so you'll have privacy whenever you want. There are several remote controls as well."

Libby blinked back the tears she felt burning so close. She had always known Tyson was a genius and that he was wired far differently than most people. He seemed shut off from his emotions most of the time, and he was often socially inept. So it had never occurred to her that he could be so thoughtful. Yet more and more, he was proving it was a fundamental part of his character. "This is wonderful. I can't believe you were able to do it so fast."

He gestured around the room, a small, almost shy boyish grin on his face. "You really like it? When I bought the house I had the drapes custom ordered and asked for a quick delivery. When things got out of hand the other day, I called them up and offered them a lot more money to speed things up." His grin widened. "I'm getting this money thing down."

"Ty, you didn't have to do that." She could barely speak around the lump in her throat.

He suddenly looked a little lost. "I can't take all the credit. You know, Libby, I'm not very good at this kind of thing, even though I want to be. I've never noticed things like drapes before. The realtor pointed out to me that the sun might be too much at times through the glass. She actually handled finding the place that did the drapes and then I couldn't find her number at first to ask her to get them moving faster."

A smile began somewhere deep at his confession. He sounded like that little boy again, the one that popped out occasionally and was so endearing to her. Meticulously honest. Expecting a reprimand or worse, a rejection.

"How did you find her number?"

He squirmed, looking a little embarrassed. "That's not really important." He dismissed the subject with a wave of his hand. "The drapes look good, don't they?"

"You've already confessed to me that you didn't do it yourself. It doesn't negate your thoughtfulness in realizing I would need the protection." She put her hands on her hips, looking up at his face. "Confession is good for you."

He rubbed the bridge of his nose and shoved both hands through his hair until he was so rumpled her body began to tingle, acutely aware of his. She loved his many different sides, but this—this helpless, mystified side of him—was one of her favorites.

"I called Elle."

She blinked, unable to believe her ears. "You called Elle?"

"You heard me."

"After all those years of thinking we were charlatans? You called Elle?"

"I couldn't ask Sam because I didn't tell him about the house." He defended himself. "He's not been very happy with my decisions lately. I've always ignored the details of life, like paying bills and reading anything the lawyers send, at least as much as I could, but the past few months I've worked at not putting so much on Sam's shoulders. He's had to take care of too many details and I realized it wasn't fair to him."

Libby sank into one of the plush recliners just because it looked so inviting. The room was set up with small conversation areas and the recliner in front of the fireplace provided the most intimate space. She waited until Tyson sat across from her.

"Didn't it worry you that Sam had a gambling problem with all that money around him all the time?"

"I knew he gambled, but didn't realize the extent of the amounts until recently. I didn't know he was borrowing money from Ed."

"Did you believe Martinelli when he said he didn't send those men after Sam?" Libby asked.

Tyson hesitated briefly before he nodded his head slowly. "I've known Ed a lot of years, Libby. I've never believed all the rumors about his family. I've met his uncles, and I know how difficult all the rumors were for his family."

"I believed him, too." Libby leaned back, frowning slightly as she thought the situation over. "The men could have gone after Sam if they were employed by Ed's uncles, all on their own."

"That doesn't make much sense, Libby," Tyson insisted. "It seems a bit of a coincidence that Harry showed up at the same time and was in my lab hiding under a table. He didn't try to call the police or help Sam in any way and a few minutes later there was an explosion in the lab."

"How would he know about Sam's gambling debts?"

"Information like that wouldn't be all that hard to come by."

"I guess you're right." Libby sighed. "I don't like knowing someone may want me—or both of us—dead."

"Baby, honestly, I don't think anyone wants you dead. I think it's me they're after. You just fell in love with the wrong man."

"Really? I don't think so." She stood up and went to him, framing his face with her hands to lean in and kiss him. "I think I found exactly the right man for me."

Tyson closed his eyes, savoring the taste and texture of her. Satin lips, full and soft, her mouth so warm and welcoming. Her hands slid down his neck to his shirt, slipping the buttons open one by one. At once his body responded, right along with his aching heart and burning lungs. Every brush of her fingers against his skin heated his blood and sent it roaring through his body. He could barely breathe with wanting her. When she had his shirt open she nibbled her way down his throat to his flat nipples, teasing with her tongue and teeth.

Tyson stretched his legs out in front of him, seeking to accommodate the growing bulge in his jeans. Her hands were at his belt buckle, loosening, sliding his zipper open as she kissed her way down his belly. He reached for her, wanting to touch her, wanting to take control when he was fast losing his.

Libby stepped back, a small smile on her face. She took her time undoing the buttons on her silk blouse before letting it float to the floor. Tyson kicked off his shoes and stood up, his gaze darkening as she unhooked her lacy bra and allowed it to drop on top of her blouse. His shirt joined hers on the floor. As fast as possible the rest of his clothes followed. He kept his eyes on her as she slowly tugged at her gray slacks, sliding them over her hips to pool on the floor where she added the small scrap of underwear.

She crooked her little finger at him. "Come here."

"There?"

She pointed to a spot in front of her and dropped to her knees. "Right here."

"Baby, you're killing me." Tyson's body thickened and lengthened even more, as he approached her. He swept his hand over her dark hair. "I love your mouth."

"You're going to love it more," she murmured as she took his shaft in her hands. She knelt even closer, nearly wedging herself between his legs so she tipped her head back, looking up at him. "I've been reading a few books myself lately."

Tyson's knees went weak. She looked beautiful kneeling there, her hands stroking and caressing, her eyes dark with a mixture of lust and love. The combination was so heady he fisted her hair, pulling her mouth closer to him.

Tyson was far larger and thicker than Libby had expected, much more intimidating, but he was beautiful, his body hardened by the continual training and extreme activities he chose to participate in. She wanted to taste him. To shape his body with her own hands. She wanted to show him love and lust could be the same thing. That she loved his body the way he loved hers. That she wanted his pleasure as much as he wanted hers. It was his turn this time, to experience someone wanting to fulfill his every desire. The look in his eyes as he gazed down at her, mesmerized, filled her with a mixture of joy and power.

Libby moistened her lips with her tongue, holding his gaze, letting him see her eagerness. She felt his shaft jump in her hands. Her tongue flicked out again, a long lick up the shaft and around the mushrooming head. She was rewarded immediately with the sound of his breath exploding out of his lungs. Holding his gaze with her own, she curled her tongue around him, long slow licks that left him gasping. Her nails grazed gently along soft skin, fingers stroking his tightening sac.

Deliberately she made him wait, drawing out the anticipation, her tongue teasing and tormenting, tasting his salty tang as his fingers tightened in her hair and his hips began a slow nearly helpless thrust. One moment her grip was firm with long hard strokes, then she switched to a lighter hold and shorter strokes. She lapped at him like a kitten with a bowl of cream, then licked as if he were an ice cream cone.

Watching his every reaction, she slid her lips around the broad head and engulfed him completely. She concentrated wholly on him, on bringing him as much pleasure as possible. She closed her lips as far as possible down his shaft, creating steady suction while she slid her mouth up and down, tickling with her tongue just beneath the base of his head with every up stroke.

Libby loved the sound of his moans, the way his shaft grew harder and his hips pushed deeper. She felt greedy with power, passionate with the sheer pleasure of loving him. The more he enjoyed her mouth and hands, the more she wanted to prolong it, to give him the ultimate experience. She found herself taking him deeper in her throat than she ever thought she could, his obvious enjoyment feeding her own.

Tyson couldn't take his eyes off of her. Her pleasure in his body heightened his excitement. She was like a beautiful seductress, her eyes cloudy with hunger for him. She seemed more than eager, tasting and teasing, licking and humming softly so the vibration raced over his cock and down to his balls until he thought he would explode with the sheer ecstasy of it. He couldn't prevent the groans escaping or the way his fingers tightened in her hair. He couldn't stop himself from thrusting into the silky cavern of her mouth, feeling her tongue stroking and caressing, her hands lovingly moving over him.

He felt his body tighten to the point of pain and he fought it, not wanting this moment to ever end, but her throat closed around him and then her mouth teased and suckled and he felt the explosion begin somewhere in his toes and roar through his body with such force he couldn't believe it. He threw his head back, almost growling with the raw bliss rushing through him. He couldn't think, his head spinning, his body jerking and thrusting, his hands dragging her closer, needing the feel of the tight, hot mouth.

"Son of a bitch, Libby," he managed when his first coherent thought finally formed. "You nearly killed me."

She sank back on her heels. "I know." She was pleased with herself. "We'll frame that book, too."

"Hell, yes, we will." He loosened his fingers in her hair, struggling for breath. She was just kneeling there, her smile wide and her eyes bright with satisfaction and love. She looked utterly happy and he hadn't even touched her body. He had to turn his head away, afraid of showing too much. No gift would ever be so important, so treasured by him. She hadn't asked anything for herself, but her pleasure in the giving, in his body was nakedly obvious. Libby was so very transparent.

Tyson caught her arm to lift her to her feet, enfolding her close to him. "That was an incredibly selfless act, Libby."

She laughed. "Silly. It was selfish. I *loved* it." Her hand stroked down his chest, rested a little possessively on his shaft. "I'm very good at the things I love."

He swooped her up to hold her against his chest. "We actually have a bed. Since we've never tried one, I thought it might be a good idea."

The bedrooms were on the lower floor and he carried her down the spiral staircase. Not once did he turn on a light, but seemed to know his way through the house to the master bedroom. He laid Libby on the bed. "I finally had the electricity turned on, but I'd rather use candles."

She caught his arm. "I'll light them." Libby cupped her hands around her lips and blew softly toward the wick. A small flame flickered and she waved, creating a slight stir in the air. At once the candle sprang to life.

"Okay, that's very handy. Can you teach me how to do it?"

Libby laid back, her hair spilling across the pillow, without a stitch on, wondering how she could feel so completely at ease with him. "I wouldn't know how to teach it. I think we're just born able to do certain things."

He stretched out beside her, slightly on his side, head propped up with his hand. "Will our children be able to do that?"

Libby shook her head. "Nope, not like we have it. Elle's children will."

"What if something happened and Elle couldn't have children, would the magic just die out?" He dipped his head to flick her taut nipple with his tongue, drawing a quick inhale from her. "Because that would be a shame."

Libby smiled. He was talking, but he had that look on his face of utter concentration and he seemed far more interested in her body than the conversation. Even his voice was beginning to fade and that was all right with her. Every cell in her body was alive and pulsing with need. She was acutely aware of his fingers splayed wide on her belly and the brush of his hair against her breast. Every curl of his tongue sent heat radiating through her straight to the welcoming dampness between her legs. Libby wrapped her arms around him, holding his head to her, giving herself up to the slow leisurely pace he set as he explored her body.

"I love this little ridge right here, your hip bone." He rubbed the pads of his fingers over the bone. "Do you know how often I'd find myself staring at your hips and imagining myself lying just like this, your legs open and my face buried between them? I wanted to taste you so bad, Libby. I'd go to bed thinking about you and wake up with such a hard-on I thought I'd explode. I still can't believe you're here with me."

She tugged hard on his hair until he yelped. "I'm here, but I can't believe you were having erotic fantasies about me. I certainly never thought of myself as sexy and I never would have guessed you were looking at me that way."

Tyson retaliated by nipping the inside of her thigh. "I was looking at you. I realized somewhere in the second year of college that I was fixating on you. I didn't want to be a stalker—even in mind only—so I forced myself to stay away."

"Come here." She crooked her finger at him again.

"Where?"

"Right here." She patted her belly and widened her legs to accommodate his larger frame.

Tyson lifted his body over hers and settled down on her like a blanket, sliding his body deep inside hers. "You feel so good." It was an understatement, but it was the best he could do under the circumstances. His brain was malfunctioning again, wires crossing and electricity arcing so that every circuit was fried. And it was perfectly okay with him.

He began to move, long, slow strokes, watching her face closely to see her reaction to every pressure, every caress. He wanted to know her body, know what made her gasp, what forced those small moans from her throat and especially what had her bucking her hips and crying his name.

In the end, when she was nearly sobbing and he could no longer remember his own name, he allowed them both release, taking them over the edge so that they clung to one another, barely able to move.

Libby felt like spaghetti, so relaxed she wasn't certain she could make her way to the shower. She lay beneath him, holding him to her. "I love you, Tyson Derrick. I love you more than you'll ever know."

He kept his face buried in the softness of her neck, struggling to keep the tears burning behind his eyelids from being shed. Why did she have to go and say things like that when he had no idea how to respond? He tried to think back over his life, to remember if and when someone had said they loved him. "My Aunt Ida."

"What?"

"She said it to me once when I was very ill. I remember she came to my room and sat with me because my fever was so high. She told me she loved me."

"Of course she loved you. She left you a share of the house. She wouldn't have done that if she didn't think of you as her son."

"You're good for me, Libby."

"Silly man. I know that. I'm going to take a shower."

"I forgot we'd need towels."

She laughed as he eased his body away from hers. "You remembered candles but forgot the towels. I guess you hit all the essentials. I'll just drip dry."

"I'll be happy to lick the water off of you."

"Thank you. I may take you up on that." Libby slid off the bed and made her way to the large bathroom with the double shower and the glass doors. "Whoever built this house wasn't in the least bit modest, was he?"

She didn't wait for Tyson's answer, but stepped beneath the spray of water, allowing it to run over her skin like a downpour of rain. Even something so simple as a shower felt sensual. Tyson had changed her entire world, especially how she felt about herself. She rinsed her hair and wrung it out as best she could.

"I'm going to need a sheet," she announced as she returned.

"I thought I was going to be your towel."

"Take a shower, crazy man."

Libby laid down on the cool sheets and let the air dry her

body as she listened to Tyson whistling in the shower. He was happy. She knew he was happy and she'd contributed to that, to making him feel loved and wanted. There was satisfaction in that knowledge.

She let herself drift on a tide of elation waiting for his return. She was nearly asleep when he came back, droplets of water running down his skin.

"Do you mind if I pull the drapes back?" Tyson asked, padding across the floor on bare feet. "I love looking out at the ocean."

Libby propped her head up on one hand. His thoughtfulness on asking her only made her love him more. "I definitely don't feel anyone hanging around the house. By all means, open the drapes." He looked delicious standing by the window with his hair slicked back and the small beads of water running into intriguing places.

The view of the shimmering sea was extraordinary. The moon was nearly full and spilled light across the water making it sparkle like a thousand gems.

"Look at the ocean, baby," Tyson said, opening the wide sliding glass door so the cool night breeze swept into the room. "The moon has such an amazing effect on the water. Do you realize that the sun has only a forty-six percent gravitational force on the earth? That makes the moon the single most important factor for creating tides."

He turned his head to look at her as she sat up, pushing her midnight black hair from around her face. There in the moonlight she looked otherworldly, a little fey, a little bit witch with her enormous eyes, generous mouth and pale skin.

Libby smiled at him. "The earth and the moon are attracted to one another, like magnets. The moon tries to pull everything on earth to bring it closer, but the earth is able to hold onto everything but water."

He walked back to her and bent down to kiss her temple before seating himself on the bed beside her, staring out the window. "Water is constantly moving so the earth can't hold onto it." He wrapped his arm around her. "I'm going to hold you still so there's no chance the moon will make a grab for you." He pretended to frown. "You don't fly on a broomstick across the moon, do you?"

She kept a straight face. "That requires levitation and only Hannah is really adept at that, although Jolcy might be as well."

He yanked his arm away, narrowing his eyes, studying her face. "You're lying through your teeth."

"Am I?"

"Why would anyone fly around the moon anyway?" he challenged.

She shrugged casually. "To make certain the tides are behaving the way they should. That's a witch's job, you know."

A small smile flirted with his mouth. "And all this time I thought the full moon caused those high and low tides and the quarter moons rendered the tides less dramatic."

"Did you learn all that in science class? We were already busy making certain the sun and moon lined up for the strong gravitational pull. It was all the Drake sisters." She leaned close to him to rub her face over his shoulder, wanting the skin to skin contact. Her tongue darted out and she caught several drops of water in her mouth. "In case you didn't know, we have a symbiotic relationship with the moon and the sun."

"I'm just learning so much tonight. It must be like the clown fish and the sea anemone—a very dangerous relationship."

She nodded seriously.

His grin turned mischievous and his eyebrow went up, alerting her to a possible trap. "You're aware the clown fish is covered in a slimy mucus and if the mucus gets wiped off before the clown fish returns to the host anemone it will be stung or even killed by the anemone's tentacles. I can't imagine you slimy, but I'm willing to try a little olive oil." He wiggled his eyebrows at her.

"Aw, but then you have it all wrong. We, meaning the Drake sisters, represent the anemone with the tentacles. We send the clown fish out with his bright colors to attract unsuspecting prey." Her hand slid over his bare chest and dropped to his flat stomach where her fingertips began to walk lower. "The clown fish lures our prey back to us and we strike with our tentacles." Her fingers brushed his shaft, stroked teasingly. "We kill and eat our fill and the poor clown fish gets our leftovers. I do so love a symbiotic relationship." She bent her head to flick, first his nipples with her tongue, then his belly button. Her hair slid over his most sensitive parts and in spite of everything he felt himself stirring again.

"I can imagine you with all kinds of tentacles." His cock jerked as her breath bathed him in warmth. "Poor unsuspecting fish."

She laughed and sat back up. "It gets worse. The clown fish not only feeds on plankton crustaceans and algae that live and grow in the reef, but also eats away debris and nibbles off the dead tentacles of the host anemone."

"I'm sure as hell not going to be the clown fish, especially if he eats dead tentacles and algae. If it wasn't for marine algae, we wouldn't be able to breathe."

"And you think the poor clown fish is devouring it at an enormous rate, threatening the oxygen in the world?" Her tone was innocent, but the mouth engulfing his shaft was sinful and greedy with passionate teasing.

Tyson looked down at her head in his lap and realized he'd never recognized the fun of teasing, sexually or otherwise. It was one of the things that had left him so socially inept. But here he was, flames licking over his skin and streaking through his bloodstream, and he had a big smile not only on his face, but also deep inside where he'd never looked before because it had always been too damned painful.

He found himself struggling to draw air into his lungs and it made him laugh. "See? The clown fish is a definite threat. I can't breathe."

Her tongue swirled and she sat up again, her grin smug. "Poor baby. Never think you can win a discussion with a Drake."

"That's because you cheat." He wrapped his hand around the nape of her neck and tugged in an effort to urge her back to his lap.

Libby resisted. "I'm breathing here, buddy." She waved her arm toward the ocean. "Marine plants and algae provide much of the world's oxygen supply and take in huge amounts of carbon dioxide. With the clown fish disturbing the natural balance, I can't breathe." She pretended to choke, falling slightly forward, allowing his hand to guide her head to his hardening erection.

"You can't possibly be serious. Men aren't supposed to be able to have multiple orgasms. At least not this many." She licked the water from him.

"Are you certain? I wouldn't want to injure anything valuable."

He was already hard as a rock and with her teasing breath and lapping tongue gliding over him and the sound of the ocean in the background, he felt entirely at peace. He closed his eyes, savoring the moment, the absolute feeling of being loved and accepted, of being the object of Libby's pleasure.

His hands tangled in her hair and he tugged until she brought her head up, her sparkling gaze meeting his much more serious one. "Libby. I need to tell you . . ." He choked, just the way he knew he would. He never realized he was an emotional man, but she sat there with her damp hair spilling around her and her eyes so expressive with her feelings and he felt like a fool trying to find the right words to describe a feeling so big, so intense, nothing could really describe it.

Libby wrapped her arms around his neck and leaned against him, her lips moving over his throat and chin. "I'm an empath, Ty."

"Thank God, because I swear I want you to feel what's inside of me."

"You need sleep. You never seem to sleep."

"That's because you have the most beautiful mouth on the face of the planet."

"Maybe so, but I'm going to make certain you eat and sleep properly, Ty, even when you're working."

"Did you know that if you get the recommended eight hours of sleep a night, that in one year you'll have slept away over two thousand nine hundred hours."

Libby made a face at him as she slid down in the bed and patted the sheet next to her. "Lie down."

Tyson did so, turning to hold her in his arms. His mind was racing, first with thoughts of her, of how much she meant to him, how much she'd changed his life, changed *him*. From there it went to how her family had accepted him, how he was learning to laugh and tease. He might never be social, but he would have his moments and he certainly would always enjoy the banter between Libby and her sisters, especially if he were included.

He thought about how Libby teased him, their conversations which would be strange to anyone else, but were so much a part of who he was. Facts were always interesting to him. Facts and science. She'd even managed to turn a clown fish and an anemone into a fascinating, fun discussion.

He sat up abruptly, staring down at her face. Her lashes were two thick crescents and her breathing was even, but she smiled and settled her fingers around his wrist. Even her beauty, the sight of her body, couldn't stop his mind from racing at a hundred miles an hour now. He was on to something. He was certain of it.

"What are you doing?" Libby asked, her voice drowsy.

"I'm just watching you while I think."

She opened her eyes at the distracted, almost elated note in his voice. "You've thought of something."

"Not quite, but the data I need is there, working its way to me. Go to sleep, baby." He brushed back her hair and bent to kiss her. "I'm going to think this through and then try to get a little work done."

"How?" She touched the back of his hand with her fingertips. "Didn't the explosion destroy everything?"

"I back up everything. I have several computers at BioLab

and I sent everything there as well. I never know where I'm going to be so I make certain I can access it from everywhere I am just in case I get inspiration."

"So your work wasn't destroyed?" A slow smile broke out on her face. "You really are a genius, aren't you?"

"And thorough. I don't take chances with my work, or my woman."

"Do you have to go back to BioLab to access it?"

"Before I set up anything else, I started setting up a laboratory here. I only have a computer in it at the moment, but I can get everything I need into the computer."

"What are you considering that is so different from what you'd been thinking before?"

"Something we were joking about earlier. A symbiotic relationship. The clown fish and the sea anemone have one, but you know, so do many other things, including plants. Some plants are dangerous, and poisonous, just like the anemone, but often growing right near them is a plant or fungus that can provide an antidote for the poison."

Relationship dawned immediately. "You used a plant for your original work, didn't you?"

He nodded. "That's how the drug got part of its name. I used the *Ibenkiki cyperus* from the rain forest in eastern Peru. The bottom line, Libby, is when something isn't working you go back to the beginning."

"To the *Ibenkiki cyperus* plant?"

"To the rain forest."

"You really do need to sleep, Ty."

"Not while I'm working. When I figure this out, I'll crash and sleep for a couple of days." He bent to kiss her again. "I'll stay here until you fall asleep."

There was no point in arguing with him. She could see how Sam could become so frustrated trying to take care of Ty, but she felt Tyson's need for his work. His mind refused to let him go, refused to allow him to relax. His brain was working too fast, making leaps and pushing him to continue. There would be no rest for Tyson until he solved the puzzle.

If she accepted Tyson, she'd have to accept all of him. And his brilliant mind was the biggest part of him. It was what drove him and always would. Libby touched his face and then turned on her side, curling up beneath the sheets, closing her eyes. The last thing she thought of before she drifted off was how lucky she was to have him.

18

LIBBY woke to find Tyson gone. She lay for a moment staring up at the ceiling, feeling inexplicably happy. He was somewhere in the house and she had a good idea what he was doing, she'd just have to find the room. Whatever he'd been working out last night, he'd obviously decided he was on the right track.

Wrapping herself in a sheet she walked through the house. Light was beginning to filter in through the windows, turning the rooms to a soft dove gray. She should have asked for a tour earlier, but they hadn't been able to keep their hands off each other and had barely managed to find the bedroom. It was a little spooky walking down the wide hall and peeking into the various rooms.

Tyson had told her the house was five thousand square feet without the garages and she felt a little lost. She was used to a big house having grown up at the Drake family home, but the house seemed enormous without her sisters as she walked on the hardwood floors. The only two rooms she knew had furniture were the living room and master bedroom. She paused in the large kitchen to look around. Like all of the rooms, it was wide, open and gleaming. The tile was cool under her feet, looked like marble and picked up the colors in the counters. It was definitely her dream home and she still had to pinch herself to believe it wasn't all a hallucination.

"What are you doing up, baby?" Tyson asked, coming up behind her. He wrapped his arms around her and kissed the back of her neck. "You should be sound asleep. Didn't I wear you out? I was doing my best."

She reached behind her to find his neck, tilting her head back as she brought his face down so she could indulge in one of his long, sinfully sexy kisses. "I don't ever wear out. You've been up for hours, haven't you?"

"After you went to sleep I got thinking about our conversation and the more I did, the more this idea just wouldn't let go." He kissed the corner of her mouth, swirling his tongue along the seam of her lips, kissed a path down to her throat where he nuzzled his face for a long moment, simply inhaling her scent. "How the hell do you manage to smell so good?"

"What do I smell like?"

"Sin. Sex. And peaches. Rain. It turns me on." He pressed his body close to hers so she could feel his heavy erection.

"I woke up turned on. I knew the moment you were gone you'd thought of something brilliant. I have to say, that's a total turn-on."

He lifted her to the kitchen counter, spreading her knees so she could wrap her legs around him. "So you like brainy men?"

"Check for yourself," she invited, dropping the sheet.

He slid his fingers over her soft mound, a slow exploration, dipping deep into the moist heat to find her slick and ready for him. "So you're a brain groupie."

"Absolutely."

He ducked his head to swipe over her hot bare lips with his tongue, savoring the taste of her, the fact that she wanted him every bit as much as he wanted her. He thrust against her clit, tormenting until her muscles clenched and she moaned softly, fingers digging into his shoulders. He straightened and caught her around her hips. "I'm keeping you out of the BioLab, where all the smart men are, but you can hang around my private laboratory. That way, when I'm on to something exciting you can strip naked for me."

She slid her arms around his neck and wrapped her legs around his waist, sliding forward until she could feel the head of his shaft pressed tightly against her, demanding entrance. "I'll strip naked for you anytime without you being on to something exciting," she confessed. She settled over him, closing her eyes as she felt him invading her, pushing through soft, tight folds to bury himself deep.

"I'm still not letting you near BioLab."

"Aren't you the smartest man there?" She lifted herself, began a slow, sensual ride, head thrown back, utter bliss transparent on her face.

"Hell, yes," he answered, drinking her in. He'd never get enough of seeing her like that, wrapped up in sex, wrapped around him, that look of ecstasy on her face.

"Well, then, you have no worries. I go for the man with the brains." She opened her eyes and smiled at him, arms tightening around his neck. "Silly. I love you. I don't care how brainy any other man is."

His hands dug into her hips as he thrust hard. Waves of pleasure washed over him. "I should have gone after you the very first time I realized I loved watching you."

"You're a little slow, Ty, but I'll forgive you."

"Slow?" He thrust harder, deeper, picking up the rhythm until she was gasping and clutching at him. "I. Don't. Think. So." He gasped out each word.

She laid her head on his shoulder, inhaling the scent of him, feeling surrounded by his body, by his love. Every hard stroke of his body drove him deeper into hers. She could feel every sensitive nerve ending rippling with pleasure. He was thick, driving through her tight folds, stimulating knots of nerves she hadn't known existed so that she gasped for air with each penetration.

His fingers gripped her, lifting her to bring her body down over him as his hips thrust upward and his speed increased. Libby moved, tightening her muscles deliberately, using her body as if she were slow dancing seductively on a pole. The more his breath turned ragged, the more she responded by grinding down over him, and milking him with her tight, inner muscles.

The orgasm rushed over both of them, taking them by surprise with its intensity. They clung to one another, trying to slow their hearts and recover their ability to breathe. Instead of allowing her legs to fall naturally to the floor, he eased her back onto the counter, kissing her over and over.

She lost herself in his passion, her body still sizzling with pleasure, rippling around his with strong aftershocks. "I'm sure this is unsanitary," she pointed out when she could talk again.

"We aren't using it for anything else," he said, reaching for a roll of paper towels. "I think this room is perfect."

"Sanitary or not, I'm fixing you food and you're going to eat it, Ty, so you may as well resign yourself to telling me all about your new ideas on the drug before you disappear again. I'll leave you alone after you eat so you can work your little heart out."

"I thought you said you didn't cook."

She gave him a little smirk. "I didn't say it would be good, only that you had to eat it."

"Fortunately for me, and maybe our kitchen, I forgot to buy groceries."

"Nothing?"

"Only the essentials."

"And that would be?" Libby asked.

He shrugged with a small grin. "Coffee and paper towels. I'm messy." He pointed to the coffee maker already filled with the dark liquid and then to her wet thighs.

"You crazy man. I'll run to the nearest diner and get you something much more nutritious and substantial."

He poured himself a cup of coffee. "I already had

something nutritious and substantial. You're enough for me to live on. If you want to just lie on the counter, I'll do my best to devour you." He wiggled his eyebrows suggestively.

"You know," she said casually. "I've been thinking of doing another article for the *American Medical Journal*."

"Really? On what?"

"Male multiple orgasms. You'd make a fantastic study. I'm thinking if we have sex a few times with you hooked up to an EEG . . ." She broke off with a little laughing cry of alarm as he put down his coffee mug and swooped down on her. "I was joking. It was a joke!"

He wrapped his arm around her neck and ruffled her hair, ducking his head to kiss her again. "Get dressed and quit trying to tempt me. You can drop me at the other house, that way we'll both have a car. I need to talk to Sam and make a few phone calls. I have things at the lab I'm hoping didn't get ruined in the explosion. Most of the blast went to the left side of the room, damaging everything there, but if I'm lucky a few things escaped. We can meet back here later this evening."

Libby noticed he hadn't mentioned food again. He was obviously eager to test whatever theory he'd come up with. She waited until they were both dressed and in the car, heading down the highway toward the Chapman house before she said, "You didn't tell me what you think about the drug."

He shoved his hand through his hair, a habit she'd noted when he was excited or agitated. "I think Harry was definitely on the right track. There's a good chance that this drug can be used to at least keep the cancer cells from growing—much like hormone therapy for breast cancer. The problem is that the risk to adolescents is too high."

"And you think you've discovered the answer to the problem?"

"Depression can be caused by a chemical imbalance in the brain, right? We know that already. Serotonin helps sends electrical messages from one nerve cell to the other. In the process serotonin is released from the sender nerve cell to the receiver nerve cell where it is either released or travels back to the original sender cell. Depression can occur when the serotonin levels are out of balance."

"Which is why antidepressants work."

He held up his hand. "But not always the same in adolescent brains as in adult brains, right? There are problems even with those drugs."

"That's true."

"Near where the *Ibenkiki cyperus* plant grows in the Peruvian rain forest is a fungus called the Balansia fungus. It contains alkaloids and naturally infests the *Ibenkiki* plant. I thought the Balansia is the source of the medicinal properties, but Harry discounted my findings and only used parts of the *Ibenkiki* without Balansia. His theory is that the fungus is much like an invading cancer, taking over the cells of the plant."

Libby frowned. "You're talking about ergot alkaloids. Many of the ergot alkaloids have a poisonous effect on the central nervous system. It can be very, very dangerous. That's how LSD was discovered. And I have to tell you I suspect, along with many others, that that's what led to the frenzy of witch trials here in America in the 1600's. The colonists ate poisoned rye and people hallucinated and went a little off the deep end. And before you argue with me, I'm very well aware, dopamine is a derivative and is used to treat Parkinson's disease and that ergot fungus is the base for many of the drugs fighting migraines."

"It's all about serotonin. Don't you see that? It makes perfect sense. I know I'm right, Libby. I always feel it when I'm on the right track and this is it. The drug has to contain a certain amount of Balansia. We have to determine those amounts. The chemistry of the brain, particularly that of the adolescent brain, remains an essential field for investigation."

She pulled into the driveway of his house. "Good luck, Ty. If you don't meet me at the house tonight, I'll come looking for you."

"I'll be there. I've got a few errands to run, but I can't really work here in such a mess. I might be back and forth though, trying to salvage what I can." He leaned over to kiss her.

"I'll pick up some groceries this afternoon and stock the house with a few supplies," Libby promised.

Tyson slipped out of the car, his mind already racing with the possibilities. There was so much to do. First and foremost, he was going to call Edward Martinelli and let him know about the potential to fix any problems with the drug.

Sam was lying on the couch, holding an ice pack to his face when Tyson let himself in. He shoved the pack under a pillow and managed a wan grin. "I didn't expect you. I took a couple of days off work. I figured black eyes and a broken nose and sore ribs were just a bit too much. I doubt I'd be of much use."

Tyson hesitated, struggling to shift gears, trying to think of everyday details instead of allowing his racing mind to dictate that he ignore his cousin's needs. "Did you eat? I can get you food or something to drink," he offered.

Sam's mouth gaped open. "What?"

"I was just worried maybe you hadn't eaten," Tyson persisted, feeling a bit like a fool. "I can make you something."

"Like what?" Sam challenged.

Tyson shrugged. "Eggs with curry in them."

"Curry?" Sam echoed faintly.

"Curcumin is the yellow pigment used in curry spice and currently is being investigated for its potential in prevention of Alzheimer's disease. The curcumin appears to block and break up brain plaques that cause the disease."

Sam stared at him for a long time. "You're giving me a headache, Ty. I don't want eggs with or without curry. I'm going to take a couple of sleeping pills and sleep the day away."

Tyson nodded and started out of the room.

"Where were you last night? You didn't call and I was worried. I knew you were going to talk to Ed."

"I'm sorry." Tyson rubbed the bridge of his nose. "Ed said he never sent those men after you. I'm wondering if Harry had something to do with it. And yesterday I asked Libby to marry me."

There was dead silence. The clock ticked loudly. Sam sat straighter, twisting his fingers together hard before looking up. "Are you sure that's what you want, Ty?"

"I've known for a while. I bought a house close by. Things won't change that much, Sam. I'm only here three months out of the year as it is."

Sam sighed. "If you're really sure, there isn't much I can say. I hope you're happy with her. I really do." His face brightened a bit, although his smile was still strained. "At least I can attend all the Drake family get-togethers. That's something to look forward to. The guys at the firehouse are going to be jealous." He stood up and made his way to the stairs leading up to the bedrooms. "What are you doing today?"

"I've gotten a lead on what might be causing problems with this drug. I need to salvage some of my equipment if possible, so I'll probably be in and out this afternoon taking things to the other house where I can work."

"Don't worry, I won't hear a thing once I take those pills. I've only used them once and I was dead to the world." He went halfway up the stairs and paused again. "Ty?" He waited until Tyson turned around. "I am happy for you. If Libby Drake makes you happy, then I'm all for her."

Tyson stood there, feeling a bit awkward, trying to hide the flood of emotion that acceptance from Sam had brought. He flashed a wide smile hoping it conveyed even a tenth of what he felt. "Thanks, Sam."

Tyson called Edward Martinelli to get the okay to put his team on studying the healing properties of the Balansia fungus. He explained quickly his reasoning and that he wanted his team to study the brain of the adolescent, begin another study on serotonin receptor activity, and run analytical tests as well. He was rather proud of himself for remembering to ask how Martinelli's family was doing and wasn't surprised to hear Libby had been right. Both Eva and Robbie were in treatment for Chagas's disease.

He had to run down the members of his team, none of whom were happy that their vacations were being cut short, but most of them agreed to return to the laboratory and begin work. Tyson spent the rest of the afternoon and early evening sifting through the wreckage of his lab and packing Sam's truck to take the equipment to the new house.

It took longer to unpack the load at the house than he counted on and once he got there he could see that he had missed Libby. Towels hung in the bathrooms and there were groceries in the cupboard and refrigerator. Glancing at his watch, he realized he had time for one more load if he hurried.

As he returned to the Chapman house, he could see Harry pacing back and forth on the front porch. For the first time ever Tyson had actually remembered to lock the front door and for this he was grateful since Sam was sleeping unawares upstairs in his room.

Tyson sat in the truck, hands on the keys, debating whether he wanted to risk another unpleasant argument with Harry.

"Get the hell out of that truck, you coward." Harry jumped off the porch, ignoring the three stairs. "You stole my project right out from underneath me."

"I take it the director called you?" Tyson asked as he slid from the truck and shut the door. "You knew it was going to happen if you didn't look at the problems, Harry. Instead of spending all your time in Sea Haven, you should have been back at the lab working out the kinks with the drug. You knew when the first trial was completed that there were warning signs of trouble and instead of addressing them, you went on to the second trial. Not only did you endanger lives, but if you were interested in getting the drug on the market, you risked that as well."

Harry doubled his fists and glared at Tyson. "I'm getting out of BioLab. Martinelli backs you every time you want to run wild. All you have to do is call him and he calls the director and the rest of us have to kowtow to you. You think you're protected by him, but he can't hold your hand outside the lab. I'm taking you down, Derrick."

"Are you threatening to kill me?"

"I'm not stupid enough to threaten to kill you. You'd just run to your sheriff friend like a scared rabbit. Do I want you dead? Hell, yes! That would make my day. It would make my life complete and be a relief to the world. Believe me, I'd be ecstatic and so would most of the others working for BioLab. But before you ever die, I want you to lose everything important to you. Your godlike reputation. Your girlfriend. Your money. Your home. *Everything*. That's how much I hate your guts."

"Go away, Harry. Don't take shortcuts and you won't have the problems you're always running into."

Harry took a threatening step forward. "Don't give me any advice. The only reason a total antisocial misfit like you has a job anywhere is because you're Martinelli's stoolie."

Tyson shrugged his shoulders. "I can't help you, Harry, because you're not bright enough to figure it out. You worked for three different companies before you came to BioLab and I knew your sloppy rep before you were ever hired. It's a small community."

Harry spat on the lawn. "This isn't over. You've messed with the wrong man."

"Harry, that's just nasty, but you're in good company. Cobras, camels and llamas spit. There are quite a few animals that express anger that way."

Harry gestured rudely with his finger and stomped off. Tyson shook his head and went back into the house. Harry certainly was capable of slashing Libby's jacket to shreds and selling pictures to a magazine. He might even rig an explosion in the laboratory, but Tyson just didn't think he had the brains to rig an accident on a helicopter rescue. He paused halfway down the stairs. Maybe the harness had simply been defective. His fall could have truly been an accident. Harry certainly could have been behind everything else that had happened.

Tyson thought of Harry Jenkins as an unintelligent, inept biochemist, but he wasn't. The man was capable of good work, he just didn't have the patience it took for research.

Did that make him incapable of plotting murder? His brain chewed on the percentages as he began going through the mess in the laboratory.

LIBBY swept her hair back into a ponytail. She rarely wore her hair that way because it made her look too young, but she wanted to work a little in the garden. The Drakes grew herbs and flowers in abundance and she planned to do the same when she moved with Tyson to the new house. More than that, she wanted to feel grounded again. She'd spent so much time thinking of Tyson and none concentrating on any of the problems cropping up around them. She needed her mind clear.

"Are you going outside?" Elle asked. "It's getting dark."

"Right now," Libby answered, "I need to feel the soil in my hands just to connect with the earth. I've been floating on air all day, dreaming instead of getting anything done. It makes me feel so silly to be so sappy, but I can't help it."

"You're going to blind somebody with that rock on your finger," Elle teased, handing Libby a pair of gloves. "Cover it up!"

Libby held the ring up to allow the last rays of the sun to shine on the stones. "It's so beautiful. Ty does the most unexpected things. He'll forget everything and everyone while he's working, but when he pays attention, he's entirely focused. I love that and he makes me feel so incredibly special."

"That's because you are special." Elle pulled on a second pair of gloves. "I'm glad you've found Tyson and he loves you so much. I feel it when I'm close to both of you." She picked up the small bucket of tools. "I've never seen a more beautiful ring."

"He's such a surprise, Elle." Libby pulled on the gloves and followed her sister out to the courtyard where the flower beds were. "I never thought I could be this happy, even with everything else going on. I am worried about him though." She looked around her and lowered her voice to a conspiratorial whisper. "I have a really bad feeling I just can't shake."

"What is it, Lib?"

Libby sighed as she jerked a couple of weeds from the ground. "I feel so disloyal even thinking it, let alone saying it aloud."

"There's only the two of us."

"I don't like Sam and I don't think I ever will. It isn't just the fact that he obviously despises me, I can live with that. Sarah didn't like Tyson all that much, although she's really trying now, but Sam puts Ty down in little ways."

"He does?"

Libby nodded. "He's probably been doing it all of his life. Sam was popular in school and is still popular. He's used to being the center of attention and Ty probably was a drag on him. Sam's mother made him hang out with Ty all the time and like all kids he probably made fun of his cousin behind his back. But I don't think he's ever grown out of it. He has such a smug superiority sometimes, as if Ty is clueless and no one could actually love Tyson for anything but his money. I think he honestly believes that and it makes me angry. He actually said that to Ty."

"You don't think Sam genuinely loves Ty?"

"Yes, of course he does. He takes care of him, even bringing him food that Ty never seems to eat, but he has such a superior attitude and it bothers me."

"You've always been so empathic and sensitive, Libby. You hated it in school when one child picked on or bullied another, but many children—and adults—are competitive by nature. They need to feel superior in some way. You don't understand that kind of behavior and you never will." Elle threw several clumps of weeds on the growing pile. "We should have started earlier, it's getting too dark to see, although there's a full moon tonight and that will help."

"I know, it was just that I wanted to be out here with the plants for a few minutes. I thought I'd feel at peace again."

Elle reached out to her. "Sam is Tyson's only family, Libby."

"I know. I know. That's why I feel so guilty. I want to like him, I really do, and I've tried. It's just that I don't think he's really what he presents to the world. He isn't smooth and easygoing." She rubbed her face and smeared soil across it. "I should have guessed he wouldn't be. Neither is Ty. The temper must run in the family."

"Tyson has a temper?"

"Big time. Especially if someone isn't very nice to me. And Sam has it, too. He got so angry with me one day he shook me."

Elle glanced up sharply, storm clouds gathering in her eyes. "He physically shook you? The bastard. No wonder you don't like him. You should have told me. I would have paid him a visit."

Libby burst out laughing. "Talk about a temper. You don't have to visit him, Elle. Tyson did enough damage."

"Did he?" Elle asked curiously. "What did he do?"

"He hit him twice and broke his nose. It was awful." Libby ducked her head. "And I'm ashamed to say I didn't want to heal Sam at first."

"Ashamed? When he shook you?"

"He felt bad afterward. He apologized both to me and to Ty. Come on, Elle. I'll bet Jonas or even Jackson is capable of shaking one of us."

Elle huffed out her breath. "I don't want to think what Jonas might do, but Jackson's reactions to things are utterly primitive. He doesn't care about being thought of as a modern man and I'm certain he beats his chest on a regular basis." She smiled encouragingly at her sister. "Don't worry. You'll find a way to accept Sam, Libby. You're like that. You have a naturally compassionate nature and you're probably very protective of Ty. You're protective of all of us."

"Maybe. I hope so. It's not like I detest Sam or anything," Libby hastened to explain. "I'm sure it wasn't easy growing up with a boy genius several years younger but always ahead of you in class. Ty even admits he embarrassed Sam a lot. You know how boys have such egos."

Elle smiled at her sister. "I'm sure it won't take long before you'll be protective of Sam, too. And you know he'll be coming to all the family functions with Ty, so we'll help mellow him out. Joley always mellows the men out. They drool over her."

Libby winced. "He said a few disgusting things about Joley. Maybe that's what makes me dislike him. Well . . ." she hedged. "I suppose dislike is a strong word. I have mixed feelings. He definitely wants to go to bed with Joley and brag about it to his firefighter buddies."

"You can't be too angry with him over that. Half the men in the world want to go to bed with her. She oozes sex. She can't help it. That's just the way she's put together. She walks down the street and she stops traffic."

"She doesn't like it, does she?" Libby asked shrewdly.

Elle shrugged. "No, but she accepts it. We all have things we don't like but we live with. Joley isn't at all as she appears to the public, you know that. Her public image is just that, an image that sells her music. She's doing the rounds with the late-night talk shows to laugh at herself over this latest write-up. She won't say one way or the other if those pictures were of her, but it will give her more publicity and turn a bad thing into something positive. She knows what she's doing."

"I don't know how she manages with all the lies they tell about her." Libby shook her head. "I'm upset for her, more than *she* seems to be."

The door banged open and Kate waved to attract their attention. "Libby, you just got a garbled phone message. Something about Irene and Drew and you're to meet Tyson at the Chapman house."

Libby pulled off the gloves. "Was it Ty?"

Kate shrugged. "I don't know, but I assumed so. I asked him to repeat what he said, but he hung up."

Elle and Libby exchanged a long look and both laughed. "That sounds like Ty." They said it simultaneously and that had them laughing again.

Libby stood up and dusted off her jeans. "I hope Irene hasn't changed her mind. This morning, Tyson was so excited. He was absolutely certain he'd figured out why the drug wasn't working as well for adolescents and he was all set to conduct more experiments and write up a report for BioLab."

"I hope he found what he was looking for," Kate said. "If he did, would it help Drew, do you think?"

"He'd need to do a lot of testing before he'd trust a drug he came up with on the general public, especially teenagers, but he looked so excited, almost like a kid with his first bicycle." Libby leaned against the door. "I remember that look on his face in school sometimes. He'd just suddenly *get* something and be so eager to try it he couldn't contain himself. And he was always on the right track."

Elle suddenly reached out to hug her. "I'm so happy for you, Libby. You'll always have that, you know, the ability to share in his excitement of discovery. And he'll always be trying to figure out how you do your magic."

"I am happy," Libby admitted. "Who would have ever thought Tyson Derrick could make me feel like this?" She glanced at her watch. "It's getting late. I'd better go check on him. He didn't get any sleep last night. Once he decided he was on the right track he was working." She tossed her gloves into the tool basket and hurried into the house to find her car keys. She hadn't seen Tyson all day and she was eager to be with him. It might be silly if she thought about it too much, but she didn't care.

Libby hurried out to the Porsche and slid behind the wheel, smiling at the thought of how Tyson always grabbed the keys. He'd grown very fond of her Porsche and he definitely had a penchant for driving too fast. Each time he got behind the wheel, he pushed the speed just that little bit more. The next time, she resolved to take the car keys away from him until he could resist the temptation to speed.

She shifted as she came onto the narrow switchback climbing the mountain and as she did so, a shadow slid across the moon. At once her heart jumped and she glanced in her rearview mirror. A vehicle was pulling off the shoulder of the road. She hadn't seen it because the lights were off and it was parked beneath the massive shrubbery growing along the side of the mountain.

Again, her heart reacted, beginning to pound with real fear. The car paced along behind her at a safe distance, but for some reason she felt threatened. Apprehension didn't just creep over her, it hit her hard. Her mouth went dry and she felt panic welling up. Libby increased her speed. Her car was fast and built for taking the curves on the highway. And she knew the road. She'd grown up there. The Porsche should have easily outdistanced the other car, but when she looked in the rearview mirror, it was still maintaining the exact distance behind her.

Libby tried to tell herself her imagination was getting the better of her, but she couldn't convince herself. She debated trying a U-turn and making her way back to the Drake house, but she was only a couple of miles from the Chapman home and Tyson. She glanced in the mirror again and her heart leapt to her throat. The car was moving up on her fast. Too fast.

She fought down panic and forced her frozen body to perform. She had the better car. She wasn't the greatest driver in the world, but she should be able to outmaneuver the other driver until she reached Tyson's home.

"Don't freeze, don't panic," she chanted between chattering teeth as she dropped her hand to the gear shift and stepped on the gas.

The car behind her slid forward, running without lights, the bumper attempting to ram her, but just as it connected, sharply bumping her car, the Porsche sprang forward, pulling away. She felt the contact, her head snapping back, but because she was speeding away, he managed to barely tap her.

A sharp curve was coming up. Libby glanced in her mirror and a small moan of fear escaped. He was staying right with her. She was into the turn before she could blink, tires squealing, as the Porsche raced through the switchback at three times the speed she normally would have driven.

Her hands jerked on the wheel, sending her into the gravel on the shoulder of the road. She screamed as the Porsche went into a small slide heading right for the side of the mountain. Rocks spit into the air, hitting the sides and undercarriage of the car. Libby forced herself not to overcorrect, trusting the maneuverability as she eased the Porsche back onto the road. He was right behind her, nearly on top of her, the larger, heavier car gliding up like some avenging demon. He suddenly turned on his headlights, full blast, shooting them right into her eyes, blinding her.

"You're on a straight away," she reminded herself. "Hold the car steady." Even as the words escaped she was able to see again, and she pressed harder on the gas.

The Chapman house was very close, but it was set on a small knoll by the sea. The turn into the drive was sharp. She was coming up on it very fast. Too fast. She didn't dare miss it. She had no choice but to slow down and the larger car was right behind her. Gritting her teeth, Libby swung the wheel. The tires made a screaming sound and she felt the impact as the bigger car sideswiped the rear. The Porsche went into a spin, over the driveway and onto the lawn. Libby fought for control. Her Porsche hit Sam's truck, jolting her hard as it came to an abrupt stop.

Libby looked wildly around, but the larger car was gone, already down the highway. She sat for a moment, shaking so bad she was afraid her legs wouldn't hold her. Tears streaked her face and blurred her vision. With trembling hands she tried the door. Thankfully it opened and she staggered out.

19

LIBBY forced herself to breathe. She wiped off her tears and looked back at the road a second time, scanning anxiously up and down the highway. She couldn't even hear the engine of a car. Her heart thundered in her ears. There was no noise at all and she should have been able to hear the engine.

The absence of sound galvanized her into action. She ran to Tyson's front door, praying it was unlocked. Yanking it open, Libby stumbled inside, catching herself before she fell. The house was dark and seemed unoccupied. She slammed the door closed and snapped the lock in place before running to the kitchen. "Ty! Sam! Is anyone home? Ty! Where are you?" She was ashamed of the rising wail.

The door to the basement was open and a single light shone from the laboratory.

"Down here, baby," Ty called.

Fresh tears flooded her eyes and she ran down the stairs, banging the door closed behind her. Libby flung herself into Tyson's arms, nearly knocking him over.

Tyson held her trembling body close to him. "What is it?"

"Someone tried to run me off the road." Her voice was

muffled, her face buried against his chest. She clutched his shirt with both hands. "I got your call to come here and started right out and he pulled out of the bushes behind my car . . ."

"Wait a minute, Libby. Slow down. I didn't call you. I thought you were going to meet me at the other house."

Libby stilled, turned her face up to his. "I got a message saying to meet you here. Something about Irene and Drew."

"I'm calling the sheriff right now," Tyson said. "If Harry's behind this, he has to be stopped." He gestured with a bottle of colorless liquid he had just pulled from the rubble toward the phone. "I brought the phone down in case you called me."

It was a simple thing, but even in the midst of her fears, Libby felt a burst of warmth for his consideration. He'd probably never thought to remember such a simple thing before. "What is this?" she asked, taking the bottle from him.

Tyson reached for the phone. "I've been trying to gather up everything I might need for the other lab and salvage as much as I could. Everything's a mess. That was on the floor near the other chemicals. It's a wonder the entire house didn't blow up with the compounds I have down here." He hit the phone against the work table. "That's a bottle of methoxyethanol. I was wondering why I bought it." He looked up at her, his expression serious. "The phone's dead, Libby. Damn it. Let's get the hell out of here."

Above them, they both became aware of crackling noises coming from the kitchen. They exchanged a long look of knowledge and dread.

"Is there another way out?" Libby asked. "There has to be another way out."

"Don't panic." Tyson's voice was grim. He went up the stairs, his tread deliberately light. He put his hand against the door and quickly removed it. "He's started a fire, Libby, and this time, I don't think any sprinkler's going to put it out. I can already hear the flames in the kitchen and the door's hot."

"He's burning down the house on top of us?"

Tyson hurried down the stairs to her. "Listen to me, baby.

I have to get Sam out. He's upstairs asleep. He took sleeping pills and he's been out all day. You're going to have to go for help."

She wrapped her fingers in his shirt and held on. "We should stick together."

He shook his head, sweeping things off his table until he found the small flashlight he was looking for. "You know better." He pulled her over to a small door and handed her the light. "We've used this tunnel to get to the beach since we were little kids. If you run along the beach about a quarter of a mile, there's a path leading back up to the highway. The moon's full, Libby, that means the tides are unusually high, so be careful, don't get out beyond the first line of rocks."

He yanked open the door and pushed her into the narrow tunnel. "Go."

"Wait." Libby felt panic welling up. "What are you going to do? At least get out of the house this way."

"I won't have enough time to get to Sam. Don't worry about me. I know what I'm doing. Hurry, Lib. Get the fire department and the sheriff. Hell, get *everyone* here." He kissed her hard and shoved her away from him.

Libby hesitated, but he had a look of absolute, determined resolve. She turned and ran down the dark tunnel, clicking on the flashlight to show her the way. The tunnel was dank and musty, mostly held up with ancient timbers that didn't look too sturdy to her. It had to be part of an old smuggler's route, much like the one they discovered beneath the old mill Kate had bought a few months back.

The tunnel led steadily down toward the pounding sea. She could hear the ocean and feel the coolness of the night on her face. As she went down farther, the tunnel was extremely narrow until, as she rounded a bend, it widened into a small cave. Hesitating, she flashed the light over the ground. Her heart leapt in her throat and she stared at the large footprints in the dirt. They were fresh and they were everywhere. She turned to go back, but she heard the distinct sound of heavy breathing.

Libby froze. The breeze drifted to her from somewhere in the interior of the chamber. The draft felt like the sea, salty and cool, spreading out to waft through the tunnel and return to surround her, bringing back a scent she was familiar with. She held her breath, afraid to move or speak, afraid even to think.

"Liiiiibbeee." Icy fingers of fear went down her spine. The hair on the back of her neck stood up. Her heart thundered in her ears so loud she wasn't certain she heard that low whisper.

"Liiiiibbeee." Her name was drawn out a second time, a long eerie undertone floating on the breeze along with that scent. Libby pressed one hand against her mouth, afraid a sound might escape as she tried to reach into her memory to identify when she'd smelled that particular cologne.

Her mind seemed numb, sluggish with mounting terror. Terror kept her paralyzed, holding her in one spot while she fought to think. Maybe she just didn't want to know. Maybe the knowledge was too terrible and she couldn't face it. The thought crept in unbidden as the light wind touched her face. Because she knew exactly who crept through the tunnel stalking her. She had probably known all along but just couldn't face the truth.

"Tyson." She whispered his name, aching for him as the realization swept over her. For a moment heartbreak for him sent anger coursing through her. Just the knowledge alone would kill Tyson.

Her anger gave her courage. "Sam. I know you're there."

There was a heartbeat of silence. The disembodied voice came out of the darkness. "You just couldn't leave him alone."

Libby turned toward the cave, shielding the light as she swept the interior. She had no idea if Sam was behind her or in front of her. If she were lucky, she might find a place to hide. Once she knew his location, she could get past him and go for help. Tyson would be gone already, working his way through a burning house to try to save the very man who had worked so hard to kill him.

She spotted a crevice toward the left side of the cave. She was small and might fit. Libby skirted around an opening in the cave floor that, when she flashed the light, dropped straight down fifteen feet to a rocky surface. She clicked off the light and slid into the crevice, her heart pounding, her throat raw with fear.

"Libby. Oh, Libby. Don't you want to play with me? I saw how you liked to play with Ty."

His voice was chilling. Sam sounded as if he were enjoying the cat and mouse game, wanting to heighten her fear—and it was working. Had he sounded closer? She heard the drip of water. Was that his breathing? Libby closed her eyes, but that terrified her more and she snapped them open, her gaze darting around the small chamber. It was so dark. Too dark. Wrapping her fingers around the small flashlight, her only weapon should Sam find her, she held it in close to her body, concealed in her fist.

"I took a lot of pictures of you, Libby." The voice floated to her out of the cold and dark. "Standing there up against the glass, whoring yourself out for money."

Libby pressed her hand over her mouth to keep a sob from escaping. His voice was turning creepy. Evil. Hate spewed out of him, coloring his tone as he taunted her.

"You're such a little slut. I'll bet it turns you on knowing I was watching. You must have been pretty good for him to want to marry you. I never would have guessed."

His voice definitely sounded closer. There was a slight echo in the chamber. Did that mean he was standing near the entrance? Had he come from behind her, or ahead of her? She couldn't freeze up. She had to think, not panic. She wanted to scream for Tyson. For her sisters. She wanted Sam to go away. She couldn't answer him. She had to keep silent or it would give away her position.

Without warning a picture sprang to vivid life in her mind. Tyson battled his way through a burning house, flames all around him, above and below, streaking up the walls and running across the ceiling. The images were so dramatic that she knew she was sharing her mind with Elle. She clung to her sister, holding the connection tightly, terrified for Tyson, frightened for herself.

A light suddenly bounced through the chamber, swept past the crevice and continued in a circle. Libby shrank back as far as she could, choking back an audible gasp, unable to take her petrified gaze from Sam. She couldn't make out any features as he stood behind the light, but he seemed taller. Broader. Stronger. More a monster than a human being.

To her horror, the light swept in a second circle, went beyond her hiding place, hesitated, and slowly traveled back, to spotlight her. "There you are. I knew you couldn't have gone far." The voice sounded smug this time. Much more like Sam.

Libby struggled out of the crevice, standing upright to face him, chin up, eyes steady. Her hands shook, but she had the presence of mind to keep the small flashlight hidden, tucked safely in her fist against her leg. She was afraid to speak, knowing her voice would wobble, and she wanted to appear fearless.

He snickered. "You look like a deer caught in the headlights. Your eyes take up half your face you're so scared. How the hell could Ty ever fall for a little mousy thing like you?"

So much for looking fearless. Libby remained silent, trying to figure out how she could get around him to get back into the tunnel.

"I suppose Ty, ever the hero, is upstairs trying to save me." Sam sighed. "I tried to warn him. I tried to keep him safe. Burning is a hell of a way for him to die."

Her heart contracted painfully. Abruptly Sam switched off the light, leaving her in total darkness. She heard a whisper of movement and her sister's alarm echoing through her mind. Libby sprang forward, determined to get past Sam. She was small, she could be the little mouse he thought her and squeak by.

Sam caught her hair, yanked her backward. She stumbled, crying out at the pain. He transferred his hold to her wrist, dragging her to him. Libby slammed the bottom of the flashlight as hard as she could on the back of his hand, turned her wrist and drove the metal into his cheekbone. He let go of her, cursing, swinging his fists at her as he stumbled away from her. One punch caught her in the chest, knocking her back. It wasn't a hard blow—just enough to make her lose her balance, forcing her to take a couple of steps back. She hit air.

Frantically she threw out both arms, trying to find something to save her. She fell straight down through the hole in the floor of the cavern, to the rocky surface below. She hit hard, heard the crack of her bone as her leg snapped in two. The pain drove the breath from her body and tore a scream from her throat.

Mocking laughter floated down from above her and the sound steadied her. She drew in deep gulps of fresh ocean air. Looking around her, she could see that there was an opening cut into the cliff face by the continual assault of the water. It was only a few feet away, yet it might as well have been a mile. Her leg was bent at an awkward angle and she could see the bone jutting up through her skin. Her skin was clammy and she recognized signs of shock.

"Hurt yourself, did you?" Sam taunted. "Where's your hero now? Where are your sisters with all their magic? You're all alone. Mine to kill whenever I want."

Libby fought to stay conscious, to keep her mind clear. Sam was definitely a sociopath. She had been in his way all along and by refusing to give up Tyson, she had sealed her fate. Poor Ty. He had never realized how good old affable Sam, so charming and caring, turned into something altogether different when he was thwarted.

She reached out with her left hand, found a raised portion of rock and gripped it, gritting her teeth hard and dragging herself forward by inches. The edges of her tibula ground together. Sweat beaded on her body and for a moment, white spots danced in front of her eyes. She breathed deeply to keep from fainting.

She heard Sam moving above her, a strange brushing she couldn't quite identify. She turned her face up toward the hole, struggling to listen—to see. He was definitely up to something. Small rocks rained down on her, pelting her on the head and shoulders. She covered up with her arms, the movement jarring her. She *had* to move before he found anything bigger to dump on her.

She searched for another hand hold and finding none, she forced herself to drag her body closer to the wide opening on the cliff face. Tears streamed down her face and twice she threw up. If it had been a regular break instead of a compound fracture, she could have easily begun the healing process, but she had to press the bone back together and she knew the pain would be excruciating. She couldn't do that and risk passing out until she was safe from Sam.

The light shone down. "I see blood, Libby. Did you cut yourself? Are you slowly bleeding to death?"

Libby rested her head on a jutting rock, dragging air into her lungs, trying to breathe away the pain. "I'll bet you tortured little animals for your own enjoyment."

"I'd never do that. Not unless they were stupid enough to get in my way."

Libby pulled herself closer to the opening, away from the pool of light spilling down. She took the journey an inch at a time until she reached the very edge of the cliff. About six feet below her was the sea, waves crashing against the rock, spraying water, salt and foam into the small cavern. The walls were sheer in both directions. She was truly trapped with the water rising quickly.

She rested, deliberately tuning out the scraping sounds she heard coming from above her. Drawing a ragged breath, she faced the water and raised her hands to the skies, calling for the wind. She was shocked at the strength of the response. Her sisters were waiting, all of them; she felt the connection leaping from sister to sister.

A large rock crashed down from above. Sam flashed the beam of light around, trying to catch sight of her, but she was out of the reach of the illumination. She watched in horror as he dropped a rope through the opening.

The wind returned to her, howling with anger, shrieking

as it raced through the cavern. Fog and mist poured into the small confines, quickly filling it, surrounding Libby, brushing her face and body with small droplets of water. Feminine voices rose on the wind, calling out, weaving a spell of magic in the mist. Strength and resolve flowed into her. She took a deep breath, clung for one moment to the mind bond she had with Elle, and then put both hands over the jagged bone protruding through her skin, applying pressure and manipulating it back in place.

She thought she screamed. She heard screaming, but it came from a distance and she couldn't identify the voice as her own or one of her sisters. She vomited again, reduced to the dry heaves as she sobbed and sweat drenched her body. Once she almost passed out, only to be prodded awake by the relentless wind.

A wave crashed against the cliff sending icy water into the cavern. She gasped as it drenched her. She'd forgotten. The earth, sun and the moon were in a line. It was a full moon and the tide would be extremely high. She had to hurry. Once again she lifted her arms toward the opening, sending the wind back to her sisters, conveying the urgency of her situation.

The wind returned, stronger than ever. The mist and fog increased, rising to curl around the rope and rush upwards to the chamber above her. Sam cursed loudly as visibility plunged to zero. Libby tuned him out, focused completely on her own body and opened the well of healing energy deep inside of her.

Peering down, Sam saw a glow in the mist below him, but couldn't make out anything in the thick fog. He didn't have time to play with his prey much longer. He was going to have to go back and face the mess. *Damn her to hell.* Ty would be dead.

He swore again and took a hold of the rope. He was going to strangle the bitch and toss her body into the sea. She deserved it, too, for making him do this. It was her fault. Ty started talking bullshit, messing everything up and forcing Sam to take action. She'd used sex to get Ty's money, to weasel her way into his life. Tyson had been so obsessed with her, coming home this time, telling Sam his big plan—how he was going to court and marry Libby Drake.

After the initial rigging of Ty's harness had been unsuccessful, Sam realized it was Libby he needed to get rid of. He could keep Ty alive if the idiot would just stay out of the way and let things happen naturally. Sam had tried to be nice about it, but *no,* Libby just wouldn't go away.

Hand over hand, he went down the rope, the mist in his eyes nearly blinding him. It didn't feel right, almost as if the vapor was alive and something moved in the minute droplets of water. Had fingers brushed his skin? He slapped the air around him. He heard voices whispering. *Whispering.* The bitch was trying to trick him. That was all.

His feet touched the rocky surface. He heard her breathing, over by the opening. Good. It was less distance for him to have to drag her skinny body and throw it in the ocean for shark bait. He wished he hadn't thrown his gun away, but after shooting Jonas Harrington, he didn't dare keep it. It was at the bottom of the sea along with the safety harness. He should have thought to bring a knife, but the truth was, he wanted to feel his hands crushing her throat, feel her gasping her last breath and look into her eyes. She'd caused him to kill his own cousin. Damn, he might not ever get over that.

Another wave crashed through the chamber, the sound, a deadly roar. Icy water saturated his clothing, penetrating all the way to his skin. He shivered, gripping the rope. The mist and fog were woven so tight it was hard to breathe in the small cave. He coughed several times, trying to clear his throat. Sam found he was reluctant to let go of the rope even as the water receded from around his ankles, washing back into the sea.

"Hi, Sam." Libby greeted him softly.

The wind carried the greeting like a melody, whirling it around the small space. It seemed to echo so that he heard his name over and over. Sam shook his head. He thought she was over by the entrance to the water, but now he didn't know. He felt surrounded, as if many pairs of eyes were watching him. Anger began to rise and that wasn't good. He liked to be in total control.

Everyone, even his mother, thought Tyson was the smart one, the genius in the family, but Sam knew better. Tyson needed him. Ty couldn't take care of himself and he was easily manipulated. Sam had been managing him for years.

Sam took a step toward the hole in the cliff face and stopped. There she was, just to the left of him. He spun around, hands up, expecting an attack. The wind blew through the cave and a woman laughed softly from directly behind him. He whirled around, his anger mounting. The thick mist bit at his skin, small stings that began to burn from the salt in the water.

The wind began to move at a ferocious speed, tugging his clothes, pulling at his hair, driving him towards the cliff face. He wondered why the fog was so thick and didn't move. If anything, it drifted *against* the wind. Swearing, he reached for the rope. Libby could drown for all he cared. He was going to leave her there to die. If by some miracle she survived, well, she was trapped and he could come back and finish her off at his leisure.

He couldn't find the rope. He stumbled around, fighting down panic, his arms spread wide, hoping to walk into it. The chamber was not that large. There was no rope and no Libby.

Although noises seemed muffled in the fog, when he stood very still, he could sort through the various sounds. The ocean was building up its fury, the waves crashing hard, each one higher than the last. He heard soft, ragged breathing. Feminine voices. A siren's call to lure him to his doom.

Sam remained still. There was something else. Footsteps above them, heavy, running. A voice calling out.

Libby heard it, too. She had to warn him. Tyson had survived the burning house and he was looking for her. She broke away from the far side of the wall and ran for the middle of the chamber, uncaring that she put herself in danger. She would not let Sam kill Tyson. "Stay away, Ty! Stay out of here."

Sam tackled her from behind, using her voice to guide him through the stinging mist. He covered her mouth with his hand, pressing hard, holding her down. "Down here, Ty. Libby fell and I can't get her out. She's hurt and the tide is rising fast."

Libby bit his hand hard, but he held on grimly, refusing to let her warn Tyson. Sam managed to get to his knees, his hand clamped tightly on her mouth, the other pressed around her waist. She drove her elbow into his solar plexus, tried to snap a fist into his groin, but he twisted and the blow fell on his thigh.

He began to walk backward on his knees, taking her with him, dragging her through the swirling mist toward the elongated hole in the cliff. The roar of the water hit them hard, this time knee deep, slamming through the cave, reverberating throughout loudly enough to hurt their ears. Because they were so low to the ground, the force drove them both over, facedown, the water rushing over their heads and rolling them over.

Sam never once let go, his fingers digging hard into her face. He tried to let the water carry them closer to the entrance as it retreated, leaving them both shivering with cold. Libby grabbed at anything she could to slow Sam down, kicking and fighting every step. He knew the direction now, knew exactly where he could hurtle her into the roiling sea in spite of the thick fog.

"Libby?"

She renewed her efforts to fight. Tyson was close. Too close. She was certain he had found the rope. She made as much noise as she could, struggling against Sam's strength. He lifted her right off the ground so that her feet dangled in the air. She kicked out toward the wall of rock, driving them over backward so that Sam fell, still clutching her to him.

The hand came out of the mist. Fingers closed on Libby's arm and jerked hard. "Let her go, you son of a bitch. What the hell do you think you're doing?" Tyson's face emerged, skin streaked black, clothes covered in soot and smelling of smoke.

"I'm trying to save her life," Sam snapped, shoving Libby so hard she slammed into Tyson, knocking him off balance so that he staggered backward.

Tyson clamped his hands around Libby's waist and took her with him, thrusting her directly behind his larger body the moment he was stable. "I realized a couple of things when I was running through the house to get to you, Sam. Libby and I talked about being in the house I bought a couple of days ago right in front of you and you didn't say a word. You knew about the house before I told you." His voice almost broke.

Tyson still didn't want to believe the truth, not even now, when it was staring him in the face. He looked at his cousin. Sam. The one person in his life who had truly loved him. Truly cared. The one person he had grown up counting on—and yes, loving back. It wasn't just his heart hurting. Everything hurt. His throat felt raw and tears burned behind his eyes. A part of him wanted to smash everything around him, and another part wanted to cry forever. "But more importantly, I found methoxyethanol in the lab. It's a solvent, but not one I've ever used. I didn't buy it, Sam. And it smells like chloroform and also garlic, both of which I smelled in the helicopter before I went out on the rope. It would take about half an hour to eat through the fabric of the harness once you dumped it on there."

Sam held up his hand. "You wouldn't listen to me, Ty. I tried to tell you, but you're always so damned stubborn."

Ty glanced over his shoulder. "Libby, climb the rope."

"Not without you. I'm not getting separated again."

His features hardened. "Climb the damn rope now. We don't have much time and all of us have to get out of here. The next big wave is going to swamp this cave. We're waist deep in water or has anyone noticed? Your teeth are chattering and you're going to get hypothermia."

Libby still hesitated, not wanting to leave him alone with his cousin. He loved Sam. He wouldn't want to believe the things Sam was capable of, even if the evidence was staring him in the face. He loved Sam, his only living relative, the way she loved her sisters. Her heart was breaking for him.

"Do I have to throw you up to the top?" Ty's voice cut like a knife. He was somewhere between rage, resignation and anguish and wasn't certain he could hold onto his control. She looked small and broken. He felt broken. "Sam, how could you do this?"

It was that heartbreaking tone that did it for Libby. Tyson was shattered. Completely shattered and holding on by a thread. She lifted her arms to send the wind back to her sisters and with it, the thick mist. "Be right behind me, Ty," she pleaded.

Libby took the rope in her hands and began to pull her body up toward the hole in the ceiling. She'd never done anything like it in her life and realized it was going to be nearly impossible. Before she could say anything, she felt her sisters gathering strength. Energy. She felt it bursting through her muscles and stretching her reach, guiding her body straight to the rock floor. She pulled herself to safety and turned, lying on her stomach to look down at the two men.

"Tyson, get out of there. The water's filling the chamber."

Sam shook his head, stepping to his left, forcing Tyson to mirror him. "I don't understand how you could let her do this to us, Ty. Why would you do that? Why would you think it would be okay to bring her into our lives? Our world?"

"We'll discuss it later, Sam. We need to get out of here."

"She's poisoned your mind against me. That's what she's been doing all along. I saw it, but you just couldn't. You wanted me to stop taking care of the finances. You started checking credit cards. You paid attention to the cash. Why would you do that if she wasn't telling you I was taking your money? It was *our* money. We shared it, remember? I want to know why you listened to her."

"Come on, Sam. Let's get out of here." Tyson held out his hand.

Libby ground her teeth together to keep from screaming at him to just climb up the rope. Sam was stalling. He wasn't repentant. He was planning, scheming still. She felt his need to best everyone. Why couldn't Tyson feel it, too?

The sea was roaring again, water pouring in with each succeeding wave. "Please, Ty, please," she whispered.

A hand fell on her shoulder and she nearly jumped out of her skin. She turned around to find Jackson crouching beside her. He put his finger to his lips and gestured for her to get out of his way. He stretched out prone on the cave floor, placing his gun on the rock floor in easy reach beside his hand as he watched the two men below and the rising water.

Tears burned close. Of course Elle would send Jackson. Her sisters *always* came through. She sat down on the rocks and tried to see around Jackson's larger frame to where Tyson was moving back toward the rope.

"We've got to go now, Sam," Tyson prompted, feeling a little desperate. He couldn't leave his cousin. He had to find a way to bring him back. "We'll sort all this out up top."

Water swirled around Sam's waist, prodding him forward. He smiled and it chilled Tyson to the bone. "I'm not letting her have you, Ty. It's not going to happen."

"Your choice then, Sam." Tyson caught the rope and pulled himself up out of the water, hoping abandonment would force Sam into action. "Follow me or stay and die. You'll never last in the sea. The water's too cold and rough."

Sam timed his jump for the next wave. As it crashed into the cavern, he leapt on Ty, wrapping his arms around his legs with every intention of dragging him back into the cave. The water poured in with tremendous force, knocking into them, pushing them toward the back of the chamber.

Libby cried out and leapt toward the hole, instinctively reaching for Tyson. Jackson was already there, his hand catching Ty's wrist, locking on like a vise while the icy water filled the cave to the ceiling, completely covering the two men below and bursting up through the hole, to drench Jackson's face and shoulders.

Libby could see the strain on Jackson, his muscles bulging,

the veins standing out as he fought the suction of the water as it retreated, trying to take the men with it. He shifted, wedging his shoulders against the opening and reaching with his other hand to grip Tyson's forearm.

Sam struggled to hold on, choking and spitting sea water as the wave began to retreat, the suction dragging at him, trying to sweep him out of the chamber. His hold on Tyson's leg loosened and he fell into the whirling vortex caused as the water sucked back out of the cave. He rolled against the rocky floor as it took him to the long, narrow hole. Managing to grip the edges of the rock to keep from being forced out to the sea, he kicked to get to the surface. Only his head was above water now and the movement in the cave was strong enough to continually smash him against the rock wall.

Tyson felt Jackson straining to pull him up through the water. He turned to try to see Sam. Their eyes met across the small expanse of water and he knew he couldn't leave him there to drown.

Libby knew the moment Tyson made the decision to let go of Jackson and go back for his cousin. She felt the collective gasp of her sisters and her own body went rigid in denial. "No!" Libby screamed. "Jackson, don't let him go." She actually flung her body over the deputy's in an effort to catch Tyson's arm, her fingers brushing his wrist as he let go, slipping away from her.

Jackson swore, the sound bitter and angry. Libby burst into tears, covering her face with her hands, but unable to stop herself from watching the drama unfolding below her in the water-filled chamber. She peeked through her fingers to see Tyson swimming strongly toward his cousin. She knew the water was freezing. She was still shaking violently from the exposure, but Tyson made it to Sam's side and caught at his arm, signaling him to head toward the rope.

Sam nodded his head and the two fought their way through the water together, using sheer physical strength against the surging waves. They were running out of time. When the next large wave came, they would both be slammed into the rocks, drowned and swept out to sea.

The water swirled in the chamber, creating a whirlpool. Twice the two men were sucked down to the rocky floor but they fought their way back to the top, gasping for air, tilting their heads to the ceiling to manage to grab a few breaths. Sam wrapped his hands around the rope and reached back to draw Tyson to it as well. He began to climb fast, Tyson right behind him. Their combined weight helped to prevent them from being tossed around by the strong current and undertow.

By the time they neared the hole in the ceiling, both were weak from fighting the water, the icy cold and the sheer energy it took to go up the rope. Jackson caught Sam and dragged his body through the opening, falling back to make room for him. Sam was soaked, shaking with cold, teeth chattering, hardly able to move. He rolled to the right to make room for Tyson.

Tyson's head broke the surface of the water and he reached for the edges of the rock in an attempt to draw himself up. Sam continued his roll, coming up on one knee, the gun Jackson had set to one side in his hand, the barrel pointed straight at Libby.

There was a moment—a heartbeat of time when no one moved. Libby saw the utter resolve in Sam's eyes, the brutal triumph. Behind him, Tyson tried to heave his freezing body out of the water, but his movements were uncoordinated and slow. Sam's finger slowly squeezed the trigger.

Jackson drew his spare gun from his boot as he dove in front of Libby, slamming into her body and driving her sideways. The two explosions were simultaneous, deafening in the small confines of the cave. A small neat hole blossomed right between Sam's eyes and he went over backwards, almost into Tyson's arms.

The second bullet skimmed Jackson's shoulder, taking clothes and skin as it went by to smash into the rock behind him, ricocheting off to zing into the tunnel and embed in the dirt wall.

Water blasted up through the hole, completely soaking Tyson. Jackson made a grab for him and dragged him clear where he lay on the floor of the cave staring at his dead cousin's open eyes.

20

"LIBBY, what are you doing up?" Hannah asked. "It's nearly four A.M." She watched Libby pace back and forth across the living room floor. "Would you like me to make you a cup of tea?"

Libby shook her head. "I can't sleep, but you should go back to bed."

"You've been crying." Hannah waved her hand toward the kitchen. "You need something soothing. Have you slept at all since you last saw Tyson?"

Libby shook her head. "Not much. I try. I have a lot of nightmares."

Joley peeked into the room. "Are you having a private conversation, or can anyone join?"

Libby smiled in welcome. "I'd ask you what you're doing up, but you never go to bed. At least not until morning."

Joley shrugged and curled up in a wide recliner. "I've always been a bit of an insomniac. Don't you remember poor Mom trying to get me to bed?"

"You and Kate. She was always reading under the covers with a flashlight," Hannah remembered. "It drove Dad crazy."

"Hey!" Abigail walked in, carrying her pillow. "If you're having a get-together, I want to be included. Besides, the whales should be coming through in about an hour and a half. We can sit on the cliff and watch them."

"Only you would know precisely when a pod of whales would be swimming by," Hannah said. "We're always so lucky, we never miss them."

"We can't have you sitting down here alone," Elle said, joining them. "If you all were going to have a party, you should have invited me."

Libby's answering laugh was strained. "You're all crazy." She wasn't in the least surprised when Sarah and Kate arrived, complete with pillows.

When she'd first come downstairs, she hadn't bothered with the lights, but sat alone in the dark, crying. Restlessness had set in and she'd been unable to remain still, pacing back and forth like a caged lion. Now she felt exhausted with grief.

"Libby," Sarah said gently. "You're wearing yourself out."

"Ty didn't say a single word," Libby burst out. She'd been so determined to be stoic, but now, surrounded by her sisters, she had to tell them how she felt—what she feared. "Not one. Not to me and not to Jackson. He looked so devastated and so alone."

"Here, honey, drink this."

Rather absently, Libby took the cup of tea Hannah handed to her. "Ty put his arm around me, but he was so broken I could feel it. I tried to help him, but he was in shock and nothing I did penetrated enough to comfort him. I've never felt more useless. He lost so much. *Everything*. And I couldn't help at all." She blinked back tears. "Tyson walked away from me and he didn't look back."

Hannah dropped her hand on Libby's shoulder. "You were in shock yourself, Libby, and you'd just expended a tremendous amount of energy healing your compound fracture. You have to cut yourself a little slack."

"Not to mention fighting for your life," Joley pointed out.

"Thank heaven you taught me that smashing maneuver with the mace that time, Joley," Libby admitted, striving to steady herself. "I never would have gotten away otherwise. I used the flashlight." She took a sip of tea. At once the soothing blend helped to calm her.

She looked around the room suddenly aware of what she had. The true gift she'd been born into. Sarah and Abigail were lighting several aromatic candles. Kate added logs to the fire. Joley dimmed the lights. Elle and Hannah tossed pillows on the floor so they could all lie in their usual circle together. Everything Libby's sisters did was all for her. The house was warm and filled with love. Her sisters had all come together—gotten up at four in the morning just to support her—to make certain she was all right. She was surrounded by love every minute of her existence. Whenever she needed it or wanted it, all she had to do was reach out and any one, or all, of her sisters would be there for her.

Tears filled her eyes. Setting the cup of tea aside, she slipped onto the floor, and put her head down and cried. "It's been a week and he hasn't called me."

"Baby." Sarah stroked her head. Kate and Abbey rubbed her back. "He'll call. He'll sort it all out. You know Tyson. He's a thinker. He has to make it all right in his mind before he comes for you."

"It's just that I have everything that matters. And Ty has nothing. Everywhere I go, whatever I do, I have all of you behind me, supporting me." She touched Joley's hand. "Standing up for me and watching my back. He's never even had parents that understood him or made him feel loved. Sam was his everything, the one person Ty thought loved and cared for him. How can he ever be whole again?" Libby wiped at the tears running down her face. "You should have seen him. Felt him. He was absolutely shattered."

"Libby," Sarah said gently. "Tyson didn't lose everything. He still has you. He has to come to that realization and he has to do it on his own. You're the person who will give him the love and understanding he's never had. You're the person who will stand up for him and watch his back and support him. He hasn't lost everything; it only feels that way right now. But he's a strong man and he'll wake up one morning and know that you're his everything. And he'll come back to you. You have to believe that."

Libby wasn't so sure. Sarah hadn't seen Tyson. She hadn't looked into his eyes or felt his pain. "He didn't even look back at me when he walked away," she whispered. She ducked her head and let herself cry, let the love of her sisters ease the terrible heartache.

Sarah's two guard dogs rushed down the stairs into the living room and whined at the front door. Sarah glanced at Kate, one eyebrow raised. She went to the window to look out. "Libby. There's a man wandering around outside. He looks very lost and alone . . . and very much like Tyson."

Libby jumped to her feet.

"Look for yourself."

Libby rushed to the window, her sisters crowding around her. In the distance, on the path leading to the beach below, a man stood, hands in his pockets, staring out over the ocean. The breath rushed from her lungs. "That's Ty. I have to go to him."

Libby reached out to her sisters and squeezed their hands hard before racing outside. She ran down the walkway leading through the front garden to the courtyard overlooking the beach. She slowed down when she saw him, her heart pounding so hard she pressed her hand to her chest.

Tyson stood looking down at the sea. His tall frame was silhouetted against the sky and his hair blew in the breeze. His profile was to her and in that unguarded moment, she could read the unrelenting sorrow etched so deep into the lines on his face. As if sensing her presence, he turned to face her fully.

Her heart nearly stopped. She'd never seen such naked grief. Waves of anguish, of anger and confusion radiated from him, nearly overwhelming her. He looked utterly defeated, his face ravaged by the pain of his loss, of Sam's betrayal. In the week since she'd seen him, he'd lost weight, and there were deep lines of suffering carved into his face. His eyes were alive with heartbreak and dark with shadows.

Everything she was, the healer, his lover and friend, the woman in her, all responded with such intense compassion, such empathy, she had to fight back tears.

"Libby." He said her name as if it were a talisman.

She went to him and silently wrapped her arms around him. Tyson buried his face against her neck. A shudder ran through him and he gripped her so tightly she knew she'd have bruises later. A sob of anguish tore from his throat. Libby closed her eyes as she felt his tears on her neck.

"I'm here, Ty. I'll always be here," she whispered, her own tears streaming down her face. She held him in her arms and let him cry until he was worn out from his grief.

Tyson straightened, looked around him and blinked at her, as if he had no clue how he got there.

"Come on, let's go down to the beach," she urged, knowing he wouldn't want to face her family so ravaged.

Tyson took her hand as they walked side by side, the sand under their feet and clouds drifting overhead. As far as the eye could see, the ocean continued its ceaseless ebb and flow. They walked a mile before he spoke.

"I had nowhere else to go, Libby. The house is gone. Sam is dead. I didn't know what to do. I just stood in the morgue, staring at his body for hours and I didn't know what to do."

The wind touched their faces, ruffled their hair and tugged at their clothing as they continued down the beach. A seagull screamed overhead.

"Why didn't I know? I'm supposed to be a genius, and I didn't know. Didn't guess. He needed help. How could I have been so fucking blind that I missed that?"

She remained silent, knowing he had to be able to talk, to work things out for himself. He wasn't to blame. Sam was a sociopath. No one close to him had known—or guessed. Had Tyson known, he couldn't have done anything about it, no matter how smart he was. Sam had been beyond help.

Tyson stopped abruptly and faced her, both hands raking through his hair in agitation. "I failed him. I didn't see what was right in front of me. I was too busy with my research and I didn't care that he was stealing money from the estate. I never once addressed it with him. I should have, Libby. I didn't think it really mattered, but I should have called him on it. I let things go too far."

She put her hand over his heart in silent sympathy. The empath in her wanted to weep forever. The healer wanted to take it all away. The woman who loved him, let him talk, let him find his own way back. It was one of the most difficult things she'd ever done.

"Sam hired those men to beat him up. Jackson found the men. Sam *hired* them. My God." He shook his head. "I *failed* him, Libby. And I could do the same thing to you."

Tyson stared down at her, his mind reeling with the blows he'd taken recently. *He'd put her life in danger by his own blindness*. All of his life he'd had blinders on and now it was too late, the one man in his life he called family, the one he'd counted on, was dead. He couldn't bear to lose Libby, not out of neglect, not out of stupidity. He was supposed to be a damned genius and yet he'd observed *nothing*.

He framed Libby's face with his hands, thumbs sliding over her face in a long caress. "I couldn't bear that. I spent a lot of time thinking about my life and what it's been like the last few weeks with you. I'm a wreck, I know that and I'm coming to you with so much baggage I can't imagine why you'd want to take me on, but I need you, Libby. I swear, I'm losing my mind. I need you, baby. I need you with me."

He'd trained himself to believe he didn't need anybody, yet he couldn't function, couldn't think straight. His life was a mess. He had nothing to offer her, not even his mind anymore. It was as fucked up as the rest of him, but he needed her and if she turned her back on him like every other living person, he had no idea what he would do. He felt naked and vulnerable standing there, stripped of everything he was, everything he'd believed in, his very soul in tatters.

Libby brushed the tears from his face with such tenderness it turned his heart inside out. "You'll always be my choice, Ty. I love you with everything I am and I have absolute faith in you. Whatever happens, we'll handle it together."

"How could you have faith in me? I don't. I almost got you killed. Even there at the end, I went back for him and he would have murdered you right in front of my eyes." He would never be able to close his eyes at night without reliving that moment. "I couldn't lift my body out of the hole and get to you. I just hung there helpless, watching him pull that trigger."

Libby caught his face in her hands and forced his eyes to meet hers. "I love you *because* you went back for him. Because that's who you are, Ty. *That's* the man I'm in love with and will always be in love with."

"Are you sure, Libby? I don't know what the hell I'm offering you."

"I know *exactly* what you're offering. Tyson, you're everything I've ever wanted. No one has ever made me feel complete before. In all honesty, I didn't think it was possible, that maybe there was something wrong with me. When I'm with you, everything in my life is better."

Tyson swallowed hard, bent down to brush a kiss over her lips, his throat working as he fought back emotion.

"I love you, Ty. Nothing is going to change that. What happened with Sam was a terrible tragedy, but it isn't your fault."

She turned back in the direction of the path. It was high tide, the pull of the moon was strong, lending the sea a wild fury. They walked along the beach while the waves rushed at them, foaming and frothing, rolling over and over.

"Maybe not, Libby, but there were signs. If I'd been a different person—more attentive to people rather than to my work, I could have gotten him help. I should have seen it. He was gambling like crazy, using the credit cards at first, then dipping into the cash we kept at the house and eventually even the bank. He began embezzling, probably out of desperation."

Libby wrapped her arm around his waist, tucking herself beneath his shoulder in a gesture of solidarity. She did the best she could, warming him, staying close, trying to keep from interfering with her own diagnosis of Sam. Tyson didn't need to hear it. He needed to talk—and she let him.

"There were signs all along. As I became aware of his gambling problems, I decided it was unfair of me to put more temptation in his way by having him handle all the financial responsibilities for me. It was laziness on my part, letting him attend all the details, so I tried to pull it back over these last few months. I hired a full-time accountant to put us both on a budget. Sam didn't like it, but he went along with it."

"He must have been growing more desperate, afraid you'd find out the extent of his misappropriation of your money."

Tyson sighed heavily. "When I came back home this time, I told him I was planning to get married. As long as I was single, he had access to the money and no one else would inherit it. It was right after that the harness failed during the rescue."

Tyson turned his face away from her, toward the roaring sea, his expression bleak. He bent and picked up a piece of driftwood, hurling it out to sea with pent-up fury, watching the turbulent waves toss it around. He lifted his face to the sky and roared out his grief and rage, the sound tearing through him, a stark, raw agony that clawed and twisted until he thought he might go mad.

She couldn't bear his pain. Libby wrapped her arms around his neck a little desperately, turning her face up to his, willing him to kiss her. She couldn't heal a broken heart with the well of energy deep inside her, but love could do it. And she had more than enough love for him.

Tyson bent his head to hers. He watched her looking at him. He needed to see her eyes, be able to read what she was feeling. There were tears swimming in her eyes, but the love shone through. It was there just for him. She looked only at him that way. It was the one thing he had left to count on. He kissed her gently, tenderly, trying to convey without words what was inside of him.

His feelings for her were far more than just need. He knew that, but right now, when he was so empty, it was all he could focus on.

"You're all I need," she whispered, almost as if she could read his mind. Her hands fluttered to his throat, his raw, burning, *torn* throat and almost at once the pain was gone with just her touch. She slid her hands under his shirt, over his chest to find his wildly beating heart. "I love you so much, Ty. If you can't hold on to anything else right now, hold on to that with both hands."

"I wish I could tell you how much you mean to me, how much I love you, Libby."

"I feel your love for me, Ty."

Tyson kissed her again, his arms enfolding her closer, even while her body tried to shelter his. He realized she was attempting to protect him from the elements, her healing warmth already running through his body and her tenderness easing the pain in his heart. His hands found her hair, the hair he was so fond of and he inhaled the familiar scent. Midnight black, her hair was wild, the way he loved it, the strands soft and silky. He buried his face in it, tightening his arms, simply holding her while the wind blew around them. Holding her brought him a semblance of peace, easing the tight constriction in his chest.

"Come on, baby, let's get you out of the cold," he said.

"Abbey said the whales were coming. We can watch them from the cliffs if you'd like," she suggested, as they began walking again.

"Why is the sea so soothing?" he asked, as a sense of serenity began to tame the wild anger and unrelenting grief. He knew it wasn't the sea. It was the woman walking beside him. He felt the heat of her body reaching into the cold of his and slowly warming him.

"The sea reminds us we are only a small part of a much larger whole. The world doesn't revolve around us and we don't carry the responsibility of everything and everyone on our shoulders, which is a tremendous relief. We get so caught up in our lives that we began to think we're able to fix everything." She flashed him a small smile. "But then I also think the ocean is soothing because it's so incredibly beautiful."

They slowly climbed the stairs toward the top. Halfway to the top she gestured toward the beach chairs set out facing the sea. "Abbey says a pod of whales will be swimming by. It's an awesome sight."

She gestured toward the center of the row of chairs and Tyson sat down facing the water below. Already light was streaking through the gray of the sky. He tried to focus on the water below, but was mostly aware of Libby curling up beside him, close, almost in his chair, leaning her head on his shoulder. He slipped his arm around her, wanting to just hold her. Needing the closeness, still feeling lost and needing her as an anchor.

He was startled when Joley came up behind them and wrapped a blanket around them. "It's still a little chilly out here." She sank into the chair beside him.

Hannah handed him a steaming cup of tea while Elle gave one to Libby before both Drakes sat down.

"I found an extra pair of binoculars, Ty," Sarah said, handing them to him.

"I brought Libby's," Kate added.

"The whales are coming." Abigail pointed out to sea.

Tyson strained to identify the magnificent creatures, but he could only see the rush of the waves and the ever-moving surface of the water.

Joley began to play the guitar and the seven sisters began to sing softly, their voices drifting out over the ocean. Tyson felt the sudden surge of energy surrounding him, leaping from sister to sister. He felt power moving not only through them, but because of his connection with Libby, through him. More than that, he felt the strong bond of love, of camaraderie woven between the sisters.

He didn't take his eyes from the sea as dark shadows below the surface began to take shape, rising toward the melody. His breath caught in his throat as the whales emerged, blow holes spouting water high into the air. Several breached, their enormous bodies hitting the surface hard and sending up fountains of water. The ocean ballet was mesmerizing and he found himself leaning forward, holding his breath as he watched.

He had no idea how long he sat there before he began to realize he was surrounded by much more than the Drake sisters. He felt acceptance, the offer of family—of a circle of love so strong nothing could destroy it. Like Libby's healing touch, silent yet strong, the others were offering to let him join that unbreakable bond. The enormity of what they were giving him was overwhelming. *This* was what tied Jonas Harrington to them.

The ocean blurred for a moment while he breathed away the overwhelming emotions. He pulled Libby into his arms, onto his lap and kissed her hard. "I love you, Libby Drake," he whispered against her ear. "And I'm going to love your family, aren't I?" He had the feeling that he would have the same reactions as Jonas to much of what they did.

"Of course you are," Libby replied, her eyes shining at him. "This is where you belong, with me. With us. You always have."

Keep reading for an excerpt from

CONSPIRACY GAME

by

Christine Feehan

Coming in November from Jove Books

NIGHT fell fast in the jungle. Sitting in the middle of the enemy camp, surrounded by rebels, Jack Norton kept his head down, eyes closed, listening to the sounds coming out of the rainforest as he took stock of his situation. With his enhanced senses he could smell the enemy close to him, and even farther away, hidden in the dense, lush vegetation. He was fairly certain this was a satellite camp, one of many deep in the jungles of the Democratic Republic of Congo, somewhere west of Kinshasa.

He opened his eyes to narrow slits to look around him, to plan out each step of his escape, but even that tiny movement sent pain shooting through his skull. The agony from the last beating was nearly shattering, but he didn't dare lose consciousness. They would kill him next time, and next time was coming much quicker than he had anticipated. If he didn't find a way out soon, all the physical and psychic enhancements in the world wouldn't save him.

The rebels had every right to be angry with him. Jack's twin brother, Ken, and his paramilitary GhostWalker team had successfully extracted the rebel's first truly valuable American political prisoners. A United States Senator had been captured while traveling with a scientist and his aides.

The GhostWalkers had come in with deadly precision, rescued the senator, the scientist, his two aides, and the pilot, and left the camp in shambles. Ken had been captured and the rebels had had a field day torturing him. Jack had no choice but to go in after his brother.

The rebels weren't any happier with Jack for depriving them of their prisoner than they had been with Ken. Jack had laid down the covering fire as the GhostWalkers were extracting Ken and had taken a hit. The wound wasn't critical—he'd been testing his leg and it wasn't broken—but the bullet had driven his leg out from under him on impact. He'd waved his team off and resigned himself to the same torture his brother had endured—one more thing they shared as they had in their younger days.

The first beating hadn't been so bad—before Major Biyoya showed up. They'd kicked and punched him, stomping on his wounded leg a couple of times, but for the most part, they'd refrained from torturing him, waiting to find out what General Ekabela had in mind. The general had sent Biyoya.

The majority of the rebels were military trained, and many had at one time been of high rank in the government or military until one of the many coups, and now they were growing marijuana and wreaking havoc, raiding smaller towns and killing everyone who dared to oppose them or had the farms or land the rebels wanted. No one dared cross into their territory without permission. They were skilled with weapons and in guerrilla warfare—and they liked to torture and kill. They had a taste for it now, and the power drove them to continue. Even the UN avoided the area; if they did try to bring medicine and supplies to the villages, the rebels robbed them.

Jack opened his eyes enough to look down at his bare chest where Major Keon Biyoya had carved his name. Blood dripped and flies and other biting insects congregated for the feast. It wasn't the worst of the tortures by any means, nor the most humiliating. He had endured it stoically, removing himself from the pain as he had all of his life, but the fire of retribution burned in his belly.

Rage ran cold and deep, like a turbulent river hidden beneath the calm surface of his expressionless face. The dangerous emotion poured through his body and flooded his veins, building his adrenaline and strength. He deliberately fed it, recounting every detail of the last interrogation session with Biyoya. The cigarette burns, small circles marring his chest and shoulders. The whip marks that had peeled the skin from his back. Biyoya had taken his time carving his name deep, and when Jack made no sound, he'd hooked up battery cables to shock him. And that had only been the beginning of several hours at the hands of a twisted madman. The precise, almost surgical, two-inch cuts covering nearly every inch of his body were identical to those this man had given his brother. With each slice, Jack felt his brother's pain while he could push away his own.

Jack tasted the rage in his mouth. With infinite slowness, he eased his hands to the seam of his camouflage pants, fingertip seeking the minute end of the thin wire sewn there. He began to draw it out with a smooth, practiced motion, all the while his brain working with icy precision, calculating distances to weapons, planning each step to get him into the foliage of the jungle. Once there, he was certain of his ability to elude his captors, but he had to first cover bare ground and get through a dozen trained soldiers. The one and only thing he knew, without a shadow of a doubt, was that Major Keon Biyoya was a walking dead man.

Two soldiers tramped through the camp toward him. Jack felt the coil inside of him winding tighter and tighter. It was now or never. His hands were tied in front of him, but his captors had been careless, leaving his feet free after the last torture session, believing him incapacitated. Biyoya had smashed the butt of a rifle into the wound on his leg several times, angry that Jack had given no response. Jack had learned at a very young age never to make a sound, to go somewhere far away in his head and separate mind from body, but men like Biyoya couldn't conceive of that possibility. Some men didn't, *couldn't* break, even with drugs in their system and pain wracking their bodies.

A hand bunched in Jack's hair and yanked hard to bring

his head up. Ice-cold water splashed in his face, ran down his chest into the wounds. The second soldier rubbed a paste of salt and burning leaves into the wounds on his chest as both laughed.

"Major wants his name to show up nice and pretty," one taunted in his native tongue. He leaned down to peer into Jack's eyes.

He must have seen death there—the cold rage and icy determination. He gasped, but was a heartbeat too slow in trying to jerk away. Jack moved fast, his hands a speeding blur as he looped the thin wire around the rebel's neck, dragging him backward off balance, using him as a shield as the other soldier jerked up his gun and fired. The bullet slammed into the first rebel and drove Jack back.

Chaos erupted in the camp, men scattering for cover and firing toward the jungle, confused as to where the shooting was coming from. Jack had only seconds to make his way to cover. Pulling a knife from the waistband of the rebel, he stabbed the dying soldier in the lung and turned the blade to the ropes binding him, still holding the soldier as a shield. Jack threw the knife with deadly accuracy, drilling the rebel with the gun through the throat. Dropping the dead body, Jack ran.

He zigzagged his way across the open ground, kicking logs out of the fire-pit, sending them scattering in all directions, deliberately running through the soldiers so that anyone firing at him would chance hitting one of their own. He ran at one soldier, slamming his fist into the man's throat with one hand, relieving him of his weapon with the other. He leapt over the body and kept running, ducking into a group of five men scrambling to their feet. Jack kicked one in the knee, dropping him hard, wrenching the machete from his hand and delivering a killing blow before whirling through the other four, slicing with an expertise born of long experience and sheer desperation.

Shouts and bullets rang through the jungle so that birds rose from the treetops, screeching into the air. Screams of the wounded mingled with the desperate sounds of angry leaders shouting to establish order. A soldier rose up in front of Jack, sweeping the area with an assault rifle. Jack hit the ground and somersaulted, lashing out with his foot, taking the man to the ground, ripping the rifle out of his hands and, using his enhanced strength, delivered a killing blow with the butt of the gun. He slung the weapons around his neck to leave his hands free and snagged a long knife and another rifle as he raced toward the cover of the jungle. The soldier had inadvertently provided him with covering fire, shooting several of his fellow rebels.

Jack dove for the thick foliage nearest him, somersaulting into the leafy ferns, and ran at a low crouch along the narrow trail made by some small animal. Bullets rained around him, one or two coming too close for comfort. He kept moving fast into deeper jungle where the light barely penetrated the thick canopy. He was a GhostWalker and the shadows welcomed him.

The rainforest was made up of several layers. At the emergent level, trees grew as high as 270 feet. The canopy was about sixty to ninety feet above him, where most of the birds and wildlife resided. Mosses, lichen, and orchids covered the trunks and branches. Snakelike vines dropped like tentacles. Palms, philodendrons, and ferns reached out with large leaves to provide even more cover. The understory saw very little sunlight and was dark and humid—perfect for what he needed.

Once into the darker areas, he blended into the foliage, the stripes and patterns of the jungle covering his skin from his face down his neck to his chest and arms. His specially designed camouflage pants picked up the colors surrounding him and reflected them back so he virtually disappeared into the vegetation as if the jungle had eaten him.

Jack leapt into the trees, using low-lying branches to climb swiftly up to the crotch of a tall evergreen tree that was particularly heavy with foliage. From this view, he could easily see the forest floor. It looked bare, but he knew it was teeming with insects, like a living carpet over the poor soil. He waited, knowing the rebels would come swarming through the jungle. Major Biyoya would be furious that Jack had escaped. Biyoya would have to answer to the general, and General Ekabela wasn't known to treat anyone failing him kindly.

Shouted curses and orders, anger and fear in the voices drifted with the smoke through the trees. Jack hoped one of the burning logs he'd kicked out of the fire pit had lit on fire the small leaf-covered hut the major liked to use.

Jack took stock of his weapons. He had two assault rifles with limited ammunition, a machete, two knives, and sewn into his pants were several garrotes. More than guns and knives, Jack had his psychic and physical enhancements, products of experimentation enabling him to become a member of the covert GhostWalker team.

Around him, the heavy foliage kept him hidden and the vines enabled fast travel up and down the trees should he need it. The sound of the rain was a steady companion, but the heavy drops barely penetrated the thick canopy above him. The moisture that did touch him helped to ease the oppressive heat.

The soldiers entered the jungle in a standard search pattern, each man spaced no more than four feet apart, but spread out to cover a wide area. That told him the major was on scene and directing his men, establishing order in the midst of chaos. Jack hunkered down, rifle in his arms, and watched the rebels emerging through the broad leafy plants and giant ferns. They thought they were quiet, but he heard the steady gasp of breath as air moved through their lungs. Even without that he would still have spotted them easily. To his GhostWalker-enhanced vision, the yellow and red heat waves of their bodies glowed neon bright against the cooler jungle foliage. He smelled the excitement oozing from their pores. It should have been fear. They knew they were going into the jungle after a wounded predator, and he would be hunting them, but they had no way of knowing what kind of man he was.

Jack had moved fast across the bare ground of the camp, but once under cover of the shadows, he was certain he'd hidden his tracks. He'd been careful not to disturb the plants on the trees as he'd gone up, leaping most of the way, landing lightly on the balls of his feet so as not to smear moss or lichen to give away his presence. They expected him to run toward Kinshasa, to get away as quickly as possible. None of them looked up, certainly not into the high canopy, and he sat quietly while the first-wave of about thirty soldiers passed him by.

He examined the weapons thoroughly, familiarizing himself with the feel of each one. He took his time weaving a sheath for the machete, using a vine for the sling. All the while he watched and listened, hunting in his mind, picking his trails from his vantage point, listening to the whispers of the men as they passed directly under his tree. Thirst was a problem, and as soon as the last of the stragglers had passed, he stashed one of the rifles in the crotch of the tree branch and made his way back toward the edge of the camp in silence. Using the vines to spider across the treetops, he cut a succulent vine containing replenishing liquid and held it to his mouth, careful to keep from spilling a drop.

A howler monkey screamed a warning a few hundred yards to his left and he froze, gradually allowing the hollow vine to slide back into the tangle with the rest. Inverting his body with slow precision, he moved like a wraith, head first, down the vine toward the forest floor. Dangling a few feet above ground, he made a graceful turn to set his feet carefully in the damp surface, landing in a crouching position, weapon up and ready. He froze when the two perimeter guards looked directly at him, his body blending in with the trees and foliage around him. The two lone soldiers looked around them warily and then exchanged heated comments, culminating in one handing the other a joint.

Smoke billowed from one of the huts, and he caught glimpses of small flames still flickering in the remains. Two soldiers worked to stack the bodies of the dead while a third and fourth helped the injured. Jack skirted around the clearing, keeping to the heavier foliage as he closed in on the armory. He knew the weapons cache was enormous. The supplies had belonged to the former government and had come from the United States. When the general and soldiers abandoned their jobs in the military and scattered, they raided a number of the government armories. As an army they were well stocked, well trained, and completely mobile, a good five thousand troops strong. The general ruled the area with a ruthless and bloody hand, keeping people in line with swift violence whenever he deemed lessons necessary. The main encampment was at least a hundred miles into the interior and the smaller, satellite camps spread out from there like a spider's web.

Near the armory, Jack dropped to his knees and elbows, crawling through the layers of rotting vegetation. Ants, beetles, and termites poured through the leaves and branches, over and around him. He ignored them as he kept moving forward at a snail's pace, staying to the shadows as much as possible. One guard walked over to another and gestured toward the wounded, talking animatedly.

Jack moved forward inch by inch until he was out in plain sight, his skin and clothing now reflecting the deeper colors of the ground. Night had fallen and the sounds emerging from the interior of the forest had changed subtly. A jaguar coughed in the distance. Birds called to one another as they settled in the higher canopy. The monkeys quieted as the larger predators emerged. The insects grew louder, a sound that never ceased. Fog rolled in over the mountains and drifted into the forest and along the floor.

Jack kept moving steadily across the ground, heading for the area where the guards were heaviest, his goal the circle of vehicles with the cargo inside. The main armory would be a bunker at the central camp, but all the outlying camps had to carry supplies with them—and they would keep those supplies under heavy guard and as mobile as possible. That meant in the vehicles. The Jeeps and trucks were parked a short distance away from the camp for safety.

The guards were set six feet apart. Most were smoking or talking or watching the surrounding jungle. The two closest were taking bets on what the major would do to the prisoner when they got him back. Jack slithered through the grass to the first Jeep parked in the tight circle. He rolled beneath it and examined the area with a cautious lift of his head. The arms were in crates in the truck to the center of the circle, right where he'd guessed they would be. He made his way to the back of the covered truck and once again waited in the grass while the beetles crawled over his body. When the closest guard looked away, Jack went up the bumper and in like a human spider.

They were well supplied with guns. He helped himself to several clips for the M16s as well as for a nine-millimeter handgun he took. The boxes contained assault rifles, belts, and cans of ammunition as well as crates of clips. Boxes of grenades were toward the front and claymore mines with detonators and wire were at the back.

Jack shifted back toward the tailgate, needing to stash his supplies, when a bloody barrel caught his eye. His heart jumped in his chest as he reached down to clear debris from the weapon. The sniper rifle was carelessly thrown in with a crate of AK-47s. It was a Remington, covered in his brother's blood, even bearing a few smudged prints. He recognized it immediately and knew it had never before been treated with other than the utmost respect. He picked it up and cradled it to him, running his hand over the barrel as if he could wipe away what had been done.

Jack's fingers tightened on the rifle as memories poured over him. Sweat broke out on his body and he shook his head, driving away the sound of childish screams and the feeling of pain and humiliation, the sight of his brother staring at him, tears streaming down his face. That face changed to that of a man's, and Ken was looking at him with that same despair, same pain and humiliation. When Jack lifted him, he had been horrified to see that the skin had been peeled from Ken's back, leaving a raw mass of muscle and tissue covered in flies and insects. He heard the screaming in his own head and looked down at his hands and saw blood. There was no washing it away and there never would be. He breathed deeply, forcing his mind away from the madness of his perpetual and all-too-real nightmares.

Major Biyoya had a lot to answer for, and torturing Ken

was first on the list. Jack wasn't walking away quietly. He'd never just walked away in his life. It wasn't in him and never would be. Biyoya was going to be brought to justice—his justice—one way or another, because that was what Jack did.

He slung the rifle around his neck, tucking the scope and shells into an ammo belt. As fast and efficiently as possible, he gathered his weapons, using a pack from the back of the truck. The nine-millimeter handgun was a must. He took as many grenades, blocks of C4, and claymore mines as he could carry. Loaded down, he crept to the tailgate of the truck and peered out. The guards were watching the clean-up of the mess he'd made of the camp. Jack went out of the truck headfirst, going down to the ground and sliding beneath the truck for added cover.

It was a much more difficult challenge moving his supplies from the circle of vehicles back to the jungle. He inched his way, feeling the numerous bites from insects, the oppressive heat, the ground and grasses tearing up his body, and the mind-numbing fatigue. He could no longer block the fiery pain of his various wounds. In spite of the darkness, it took longer than he'd anticipated crossing the open circle and making his way through the guards.

He was nearly to the vehicles when one of the guards turned abruptly and walked straight toward him. Jack froze, sliding his cache of weapons under the broad-leaf plant closest to his hand. He had no choice but to lie prone in the darkness, relying on the camouflage of his body. The guard called to a second one and the man ambled over, shifting his rifle across his body. They spoke in Congolese, a language Jack was somewhat familiar with, but they were speaking rapidly, making it difficult to make out everything they were saying.

The Fespam Music Festival in Kinshasa was supposed to be larger and even better this time, with the performances that had been brought over from Europe. The guard desperately wanted to go because The Flying Five were performing. The general had promised them they could go, and unless they found the prisoner, no one would be going anywhere. The other guard agreed and dropped a cigarette almost on

Jack's head, crushing it with the toe of his boot before adding his own complaints.

Jack's breath stilled. The Flying Five. What kind of a coincidence could that be? Or was it sheer luck. Jebediah Jenkins was a member of The Flying Five and he had served with Jack in the SEALs. If Jack could make his way to Kinshasa and find Jebediah, he could get the hell out of Dodge—or would he be walking into another trap?

The moment the guards moved on, he began to inch toward the forest again. Once into the heavier foliage, he went up into the trees, stashing his supplies and taking the time for another satisfying drink. He repeated the trip into the circle of vehicles, making his way back through the guards to the supply truck. This time, he went for more claymore mines, wires, and detonators. Patience and discipline went hand in hand with his profession and he had both in abundance. He took his time, thorough in his set-up, never once allowing his mind to freeze under the pressure, not even when soldiers nearly stepped on him.

He wired the beaten path leading into the jungle, tents, the outhouse, and every remaining vehicle. Minutes turned into hours. It was a long time to be in the enemy camp, and he felt the strain. Sweat dripped into his eyes and stung. His chest and especially his back were on fire, and his leg throbbed with pain. Infection in the jungle was dangerous, and he'd been stripped of his gear and all medical supplies.

Somewhere in the distance, Jack caught the cry of the monkeys and immediately sorted through the sounds in the rainforest until he caught the one he was waiting for—the sound of movement through brush. Biyoya was bringing his soldiers home, wanting to wait until they could examine the damp ground for tracks. Jack knew Biyoya would have confidence in regaining his prisoner. Rebel camps were spread throughout the region and villagers would not risk retribution and death by hiding a foreigner. Major Biyoya believed in torturing as well as ethnic cleansing. His reputation for brutality was widespread, and few would be willing to oppose him.

Jack finished his last task without haste before beginning to crawl backward toward the jungle. He angled his entry away from the well-used trail and into the thicker foliage. The smell of the returning soldiers hit him hard. They were sweating from the suffocating heat in the interior. He forced himself to maintain his slow pace, making certain not to draw the eyes of a sentry to him as he slipped under the creeper vines and broad-leaf plants surrounding the camp.

He lay for a moment, his face in the muck, and let himself breathe before pushing to his feet and running in a crouch back toward the taller trees. He could hear the soldiers' breath blasting out of their lungs as they hurried back to their camp, their angry leader berating them every step of the way.

Jack stood for a moment under the chosen tree, breathing his way through the pain, gathering his strength before crouching and leaping up to the nearest broad branch. He worked his way from branch to branch until he was in the thickest of the branches, sitting comfortably, his brother's rifle cradled in his arms while he waited. The night was comforting, the familiar shadows home.

The first group of rebels came into sight in a semi-loose formation, eyes wary as they tried to pierce the veil of darkness for any enemies. Two Jeeps had gone out with the group, taking the muddy torn-up road that curved away from the forest and then looped back in for miles into the interior. The Jeeps were coming toward camp, motors whining and mud splattering around them. The main body of soldiers came through the trees, still spread out, guns at ready, nervous as hell.

Jack fitted the scope to his brother's rifle and calmly loaded the shells in.

The blast was loud in the quiet of the night, sending a fireball into the sky. It rained metal and shrapnel, sending debris slamming into the camp and embedding metal into trees. The screams of dying men mingled with the cries of birds and monkeys as the world around them exploded into orange-red flames. The lead Jeep hit the wire right at the entrance to the camp, tripping the claymore and blowing everything around it into pieces. The soldiers hit the ground, covering their heads as fragments rained from the sky.

Jack kept his eye to the scope. Biyoya was in the second Jeep, and the driver instantly veered away from the fireball, nearly spilling the passengers as the vehicle careened wildly through the trees. Biyoya leapt out, ducking into the foliage and screaming at the soldiers to fan out and look for Jack.

Using the chaos of explosions and screaming men as cover, Jack squeezed the trigger, taking out one of the soldiers on the edge of the forest. Switching targets, he rapidly fired three more times. Four shots, four kills. Not wanting the soldiers to spot where he was firing from, Jack immediately caught hold of the vine and went down head first on the opposite side of the tree from the soldiers, crawling hand over hand until he could flip to the ground. He landed softly on the balls of his feet, fading into the overgrown ferns and dropping to his belly, where he could slither along the almost-invisible game trail through the brush that brought him up behind Biyoya's personal guard.

Jack rose up, a silent phantom, blade in hand. He went in fast and hard, making certain the guard couldn't give away his presence with a single sound. Jack slipped back into the foliage, his skin and clothes blending with his surroundings.

Biyoya turned to say something to his guard and let out a shocked yell, leaping back away from the dead man, ducking around his Jeep. He shouted to his soldiers and they sprayed the jungle with bullets, lighting up the night with the flashing muzzles. Leaves and branches fell like hail raining from above, and several soldiers went down, caught in the crossfire. Biyoya had to shout several times to reestablish control. He ordered another sweep through the surrounding forest.

The soldiers looked at one another, obviously not happy with the command, but they obeyed with reluctance, once again shoulder to shoulder, walking through the trees. Jack was already back in his tree, leaning his weary body against the thick trunk.

He slumped down, but kept his eye to the scope in hopes of getting a clear shot at Biyoya. He tried to keep any thought of home and his brother from his mind, but it was impossible. Ken's body—so bloody, so raw. There hadn't been a place on him that wasn't bleeding. Had he been too late? No way. He'd know if his brother was dead, and if it was at all possible, Ken would come for him. Even now, he might be close. Intellectually he knew better—knew Ken's wounds were too severe and he was safe in a hospital thousands of miles away—but he couldn't stop himself. Jack reached out along their telepathic path, the way he'd been doing since they were toddlers and called his brother. *Ken. I'm in a fucking mess. You there, bro?*

Silence greeted his call. For one terrible moment, his resolve wavered. His gut churned and fear swamped him—fear for his own situation and something nearly amounting to terror for his brother. He held out his hand, saw it shake, and shook his head, forcing his mind away from destructive thoughts. That way lay his own destruction. His job was to escape, to survive, to make his way to Kinshasa.

The soldiers tramped through the forest, using bayonets to thrust into the thick shrubs and ferns. They stabbed the vegetation on the floor and walked along the banks of the stream feeding into the river, blades pounding the damp embankment. The Jeep slowly began to move, only the driver and soldiers surrounding it vulnerable as they made their way past the wreckage of the first vehicle and into camp.

Jack lowered the rifle. It was going to be a long night for the soldiers. In the meantime, he had to plan his way to freedom. He was west of Kinshasa. Once in the city he could find Jebediah and hide until they found a way to call for extraction. It sounded simple enough, but he had to work his way through the rebel encampments between Kinshasa and his present position. He wasn't going to kid himself, he was in bad shape. With so many open wounds, infection was a certainty rather than a possibility.

Weariness stole over him. Loneliness. He had chosen this life many years ago, the only choice he had at the time. Most of the time he didn't regret it. But sometimes, when he sat thirty feet up in a tree with a rifle in his hands and death surrounding him, he wondered what it would be like to have a home and family. A woman. Laughter. He couldn't remember laughter, not even with Ken, and Ken could be amusing even at the most inopportune times.

It was too late for him. He was rough and cold and any gentleness he may have been born with had been beaten out of him long before he was a teenager. He looked at the people and the world around him, stripped of beauty, seeing only the ugliness. It was kill or be killed in his world, and he was a survivor. He settled back and closed his eyes, needing to sleep for a few minutes.

He woke to the sounds of screams. The sound often haunted him in his nightmares, screams and gunfire and blood running in dark pools. His hands curled around the rifle, finger stroking the trigger even before his eyes snapped open. Jack took a long deep breath and looked around him. Flash fires came from the direction of the camp. Several of his traps had been sprung, and once again chaos reigned in the rebel encampment. Bullets spat into the jungle, zipped through leaves, and tore bark from trees. The ghost in the rainforest had struck again and again, and fear had the rebels by the throats.

On and off over the next few hours, some hapless soldier would trip a trap, probably trying to get rid of it, and the camp would erupt into pandemonium, confusion and panic nearly leading to rebellion. The soldiers wanted to head for the base camp and Biyoya refused, adamant that they would recover the prisoner. It was a tribute to his leadership—or cruelty—that he was able to rally them after each attack. There was no sleep for anyone and the fog crept into the forest, blanketing the trees and mixing with the smoke from the continual fires.

Through the haze, Jack saw the camp on the move, abandoning their position. Biyoya screamed at his men and shook his fist at the camp, the first real indication that the long night had taken its toll on him. He'd lost more than half of his soldiers and they were forced to group in a tight knot around him to protect him. They didn't look very happy, but they marched stoically through the forest on the muddy, torn road.

The rain began again, a steady drizzle that added to the stirring life of the jungle. Monkeys resumed their eating and birds flitted from tree to tree. Jack caught a glimpse of a boar moving through the brush. An hour went by, soaking his clothes and his skin. He never moved, waiting with the patience born of a lifetime of survival. Biyoya would have his best trackers and sharpshooters concealed, and they would wait for him to make a move. Major Biyoya didn't want to go back to General Ekabela and admit he lost skilled soldiers to his prisoner. His *escaped* prisoner. That kind of thing would lose the major his hard-earned reputation as a ruthless interrogator.

Jack's eyes were different, had always been different, and after Whitney had genetically enhanced him, his sight had become amazing. He didn't understand the workings, but he had the vision of an eagle. He didn't care how it was done, but he could see distances few others could conceive of. Out of the corner of his eye, movement to the left of his position caught his attention, the colors in bands of yellow and red. The sniper moved cautiously, keeping to the heavier foliage, so that Jack only caught glimpses of him. His spotter kept to the left, covering every step the sniper took as he examined the ground and surrounding trees.

Jack began a slow move into a better position, but halted when he heard a feminine scream in the distance followed closely by a child's frightened cry. Jack jerked his head up, his body stiffening, sweat breaking out on his brow and trickling down into his eyes. Did Biyoya know his trigger? His one weakness? That was impossible. His mouth went dry and his heart slammed in his chest. *What did Biyoya know about him?* Ken had been brutally tortured. There wasn't a square inch on his twin's body that hadn't been cut with tiny slices or stripped of skin. Could the interrogation have broken Ken?

Jack shook his head, denying the thought, and wiped the sweat from his face, the movement slow and careful. *Ken would never betray him, tortured or not*. The knowledge was certain, as much a part of him as breathing. However he'd gotten his information, Biyoya had set the perfect trap. Jack had to respond. His past, buried deep where he never looked, wouldn't let him walk away. Trap or not, he had to react, take countermeasures. His gut knotted up and his lungs burned for air. He swore under his breath and put his eye to the scope again, determined to take out Biyoya's backup.

The woman screamed again, this time the sound painful in the early morning dawn. The knots in his belly hardened into something scary. Yeah. Biyoya knew, had information on him. He was classified and the information Biyoya possessed was in a classified file with a million red flags. *So who the hell had sold him out?* Jack rubbed his eyes again to clear the sweat from them. *Someone close to them set the brothers up*. There was no other explanation.

The screams increased in strength and duration. The child sobbed, begging for mercy. Jack cursed and jerked his head up, furious with himself, with his lack of ability to ignore it. "You're going to die here, Jack," he whispered aloud. "Because you're a damned fool." It didn't matter. He couldn't let it go. The past was bile in his throat, the door in his mind creaking open, the screams growing louder in his head.

He leapt from the safety of his tree to another one, using the canopy to travel, relying on his skin and clothing to camouflage him. He moved fast, following Biyoya's trail into the darkened interior. The ribbon of road flowed below him, hacked out of the thick vegetation, pitted, mined, and trampled. It looked more like a strip of mud than an actual road. He followed it, using the trees and vines, moving fast to catch up with the main body of soldiers.

He slipped into a tall tree right above the heads of the soldiers, settling in the foliage, lying flat along a branch. Somewhere behind him the sniper was coming, but he hadn't left a trail on the ground, and he would be difficult to spot, blending in as he did with the leaves and bark. A woman lay on the ground, clothes torn, a soldier bending over her, kicking at her as she cried helplessly. A small boy of about ten struggled against the men shoving him back and forth between them. There was terror in the child's eyes.

There was no doubt in Jack's mind that Biyoya had constructed a trap, but the woman and the child were innocent victims. No one could fake that kind of terror. He swore over and over in his mind, trying to force himself to walk away. His first duty was to escape, but this—he couldn't leave the woman and child in the hands of a master torturer. He forced his mind to slow down to block out the cries and pleas.

Biyoya was the target and he had to find his place of concealment. Jack inhaled sharply, relying on his enhanced sense of smell. If his nose was right—and it nearly always was—the major crouched behind the Jeep just to the left of the woman and boy, behind a wall of soldiers. Jack circled around and lifted his rifle, taking the bead on Biyoya, knowing the soldiers would be able to pinpoint his trajectory.

The bullet took Biyoya behind the neck. Even as he fell, Jack switched his target to the man kicking the woman and fired a second round. Calmly, he let go of the sniper rifle and took up the assault weapon, laying down a covering fire to give the woman and child a chance to escape. The soldiers fired back, bullets smacking into the trees around him. Jack knew they couldn't see him, but the muzzle flash and smoke were a dead giveaway. The woman caught her child to her and took off into the rainforest. Jack gave them as long a lead as he dared before moving, sliding back into heavier foliage and leaping up through the branches to use the canopy as a highway.

Ekabela was not going to let this go. Jack would have every rebel in the Congo chasing him all the way to Kinshasa.

From *New York Times* bestselling author

CHRISTINE FEEHAN

don't miss...

DARK CELEBRATION

After centuries as the Prince of the Carpathians, Mikhail Dubrinsky fears he can't protect them for long from their greatest threat: the extinction of their species. To fight this ultimate threat, he has asked all the Carpathians to return to their home in the Carpathian mountains, for a once-in-a-lifetime reunion to remember...

Available this September in hardcover from Berkley.

penguin.com

New York Times **bestselling author**

Christine Feehan

Oceans of Fire

A Drake Sisters Novel

The third daughter of seven in a magical bloodline, Abigail Drake was born with an affinity for water and a strong bond with dolphins. After she witnesses a murder, she flees right into the arms of Alexsandr Volstov.

On the trail of stolen Russian antiques, he's a relentless Interpol agent—and the man who had once broken Abby's heart. But he isn't going to let the only woman he's ever loved slip away again.

0-515-13953-X